Christmas Wishes

on
Main Street

Christmas Wishes

on

Main Street

The Authors of Main Street

Christmas Wishes on Main Street
An anthology by The Authors of Main Street
First Paperback Edition
copyright © 2018
All rights reserved.
ISBN-13: 978-1-62522-138-4
December 2018

PUBLISHER INFORMATION
Indie Artist Press
P. O. Box 131
Brackettville, TX 78832
www.indieartistpress.com

Table of Contents

Small Town Christmas Wish

Small Town Romance Series

Stephanie Queen

One

Betsy Carter locked the back door of the restaurant at four thirty in the afternoon and looked up at the stars already in the midnight-blue sky. She watched her breath disappear in a cloud. That was how quickly her entire future and all her dreams had vanished a year and a half ago.

With a quick, solid knock on her door by a man in uniform who didn't need to open his mouth to deliver the devastating news that her Jimmy was gone, her future had vanished. The haze that followed was lifted by necessity because her mother could no longer work at the diner with her debilitating arthritis, and so the rhythm and hard work it took to run Betsy's Grill had saved her.

The family business her parents had named after her became her new life. She'd quit her job in the city and moved back home and taken control of the diner with a vengeance.

Betsy was proud of the restaurant and knew that Jimmy would have been too. They'd dreamed of having a restaurant together and she'd done it. Alone. Betsy's Diner had transformed into her baby, Betsy's Grill. She served lunch and dinner with entertainment on the weekends and her place was on its way to becoming the hub of the community.

She walked to her car, which she'd parked in a far corner of the back lot out of habit to give her patrons all the best parking spots. Even though it was a Monday, and the Grill was closed for the day, she felt a twinge about leaving early. But tonight was the memorial service for Jimmy.

At long last, his remains had been sent home and they would lay him to rest as he'd requested. The deep yawning hole in her chest that had been patched over in the past year was now opened dark and wide again, as if it were yesterday when she'd gotten the news. Her mother had told her this would be painful and worried whether it was wise to have this service, to revisit the recent scar to her heart. But there was no way Betsy would not honor Jimmy's wishes.

He had wanted this service, and he had wanted his ashes strewn over the fields of his family farm. And he'd wanted his best buddy, Elijah Walker, and his best lady, Betsy Carter, to do it. She had a frisson of anxiety thinking about meeting Eli for the first time. He'd been injured badly when Jimmy got killed, and he hadn't been able to make it to the original memorial service eighteen months ago. She'd never met him, but she felt like she knew him, the way Jimmy always talked about him. He used to say you couldn't find two more opposite people in all the army to be paired up, but they were the best pair of buddies ever to cook their way through the Middle East.

She started her Ford Bronco, the one Jimmy had bought for her the last Christmas he was alive — two years ago now — the last time she'd seen him. She smiled at the mental picture she had of him and Eli — Jimmy a short doughy white boy and Eli a tall muscled man black as the night. Jimmy had been a farmer, from a farming family, and loved food enough to want to be a cook. He'd worked with Betsy and Mama at the diner and then joined the army to get what he thought of as real culinary training since he couldn't afford school for himself.

Eli, on the other hand, was a city boy with classic culinary training. He'd joined the army to do something different, to get away from his background and the strings and ties of his family. Jimmy had confided in Betsy that he thought Eli had a small chip on his shoulder and a few issues to work out, and the Army had been a great place to do it. Betsy knew that a pairing with Jimmy would soothe anyone's soul because he'd been the most lighthearted, cheery man she'd ever met.

And the polar opposite of his serious friend Eli, according to Jimmy.

She shivered again as she pulled into the driveway of the modest old farmhouse that had been in her family for three generations. Her mother was at the front door waving her inside. Betsy felt exhausted, sad and drained. She sat behind the wheel of her car for several beats, mustering energy and resolve and swiping tears from her eyes. A Jeep she didn't recognize pulled up in front of the house.

But once the man got out and slammed the door, there was no doubt who it was. Eli Walker strode, holding a bag in his hand, toward her car. Betsy watched him in her rearview mirror and her heart raced ahead, beating against a tightening chest. When he stepped around to the driver's side she panicked, realizing he was coming to her window, no doubt to see what was wrong with her. Taking a deep breath, making one last swipe of her cheeks and giving a quick glance at herself in the mirror, she opened the door to get out and meet the man who'd been Jimmy's best friend in the world.

Before she could speak, he did.

"Are you all right?" He reached out a hand and touched her arm. Even through the sleeve of her wool coat, she felt his warmth. Or maybe it was staring into his dark eyes, deep with real concern, that warmed her.

"Oh, sure." She waved a hand and looked away. "Don't mind me. I'm being silly."

"No you're not. This is a traumatic time. It's natural you should be affected by the return of Jimmy's remains." He paused a beat and took his hand away, then added, "Hell, I am."

She looked back up at him, to stare into the deep-brown mesmerizing pools of his eyes, so strangely comforting. He wasn't smiling, serious as an undertaker. That's how Jimmy used to describe him, his friend who was always serious as an undertaker, the one Jimmy had made it his life's mission to make smile, to make laugh. The thought of Jimmy's affection for his friend made her smile too.

"Thank you. You're right."

She stared until he looked away, then remembered he was a guest. She supposed that made her the worst hostess in the entire hospitality industry.

"I'm sorry. How terrible of me. Please come on inside out of the cold." She turned to lead the way, but she couldn't make herself stop chattering. "Even I'm cold and imagine you being from down south where it's warm, how you must feel. More frozen than a devil in Alaska I bet." She hurried along the walk without looking at him, but when she heard him laugh, she stopped and turned.

He was right there, with a brilliant, perfect smile lighting his exceedingly handsome face, his skin looking like black porcelain partially lit by the light at her front door. Had her heart just stopped beating? She gulped in air then because she *knew* she'd stopped breathing.

The sound of his deep chuckle, the pleased and pleasing sonorous vibration she could hear and feel coming from his chest, hit her, surrounded her, and made her feel viscerally all the things Jimmy had said about this man.

"Well, come on in you two," her mother said from inside the open door. She leaned on her cane with one hand and held the door with the other.

Eli strode past Betsy, so graceful and smooth that he barely brushed her as he went by on the narrow path. He took over holding the door from her mother and stood waiting for Betsy to pass through before him. *The perfect gentleman*, she remembered Jimmy saying. And it seemed he was as advertised.

After a beat and realizing she'd been staring, again, she

stumbled forward and up the three steps, watching her feet so she didn't trip, and so she didn't have to meet his eyes. Could he see through her? Could he tell that she found him... intriguing? If she was honest, she found him a heck of a lot more than intriguing. He was a drop-dead gorgeous hunk of a man and that was an objective assessment. Although she'd never heard Jimmy use those words, he had hinted that ladies found him attractive.

I'll say.

On occasion her Jimmy had been given to understatement, but it was so rare and unusual it would easily go unnoticed amidst his avalanche of enthusiasm. Betsy could only guess that Jimmy's comments about Eli's attractiveness qualified as his occasional understatement in practice.

Once inside, thank heaven, her mother took over playing hostess and Betsy was left to surreptitious glances and head-nodding, agreeing with whatever her mother said and keeping her thoughts about Eli's perfect gentlemanliness to herself.

"What do you have in the bag?" her mother asked after they'd finally taken off their coats and were seated in the small, cozy living room.

She noticed Eli studying the fireplace as if it was a museum piece. Betsy and her mother had decorated it—or perhaps she should say *over*decorated it—and her mother had lit a fire. It looked like her mother had been having a good day, a break from the usually immobilizing arthritis that plagued her.

Eli took his eyes from the crackling fire and smiled at her mother.

"If you won't find it too presumptuous of me, I brought food. The ingredients for the special dish Jimmy and I used to cook, Pasta Bella. We'd always said it would be a featured meal at our restaurant." He flashed a glance in her direction. He must be aware that she and Jimmy had the same dream, the same plan to open a five-star restaurant together.

They'd talked of it a lot before he went away. After that, not as much. She knew why. She knew he'd talked of partnering with Eli, opening someplace new, maybe in the city. He'd let it slip on occasion and she never stopped him, never discouraged him. She'd been indulgent of him then because he was away at war, living in unimaginably horrible circumstances and she wouldn't do or say anything to make him upset.

But now neither of them would get their wish. She and Eli were each left with the same empty dream, a partnership with a ghost.

"A home-cooked meal made by someone else sounds wonderful. Come on into the kitchen. We don't have to be at the church for another hour," Betsy said.

Her mother rose and, with her cane and some effort, led Eli into the kitchen. He turned to Betsy and gave her that look again. A question, a hope, a request for permission to use the kitchen? She wasn't sure, but she nodded.

"I'm going upstairs to get ready, if you two don't mind." Betsy fled up the stairs and into the familiar surroundings of her bedroom, where she could pretend that things were normal, that she was the same person with the same contented life she'd had a few days ago before she found out about Jimmy's remains.

And before she met Elijah Walker.

Two

As he followed Mrs. Carter slowly into the kitchen, Eli allowed himself a small glance after Betsy. She ran up the stairs as if a demon were chasing her and he was afraid he knew who the demon was. Jimmy's ghost. He snapped his attention back to Mrs. Carter and her surprisingly large and well-appointed kitchen.

"I can tell a serious cook lives here," He said.

He ran a finger along the Wolfgang Puck stainless steel six-burner stove and made a turn around to see the double oven on the opposite wall, which included a convection chamber and warming tray. But then his eyes were drawn to the multi-paned windows overlooking the back yard as snow sprinkled from the sky, and he had the disquieting feeling that he was inside one of those make-believe worlds inside a snow globe.

It was a world he didn't feel exactly made for, didn't feel he belonged in, yet he felt comfortable and comforted in his surroundings at that moment. It was Jimmy's ghost at it again. That guy had made him feel welcome and joyous and comfortable in the middle of gunfire. It was no wonder his ghost could make him feel at home in a small town in New Hampshire while it snowed. He'd never laid foot in this place before and he could count on his fingers the number of times he'd seen snow since his early childhood.

The past year in his hospital bed in Walter E. Reed he hadn't bothered looking out the window. Maybe he should have tried harder at his recovery, gotten here sooner. His spirits were lifting higher by the minute.

"My Betsy is a fine cook and we improved the kitchen just for her. She has big ambitions, that girl. She'll go far." Betsy's mother nodded and glowed with pride in spite of her hunched back and the gnarled fingers held over the knob of her cane.

Eli knew when a person was in pain, knew when they tried to put it aside. It had been his way of life for the past year and a half. But he was alive and Jimmy was not, so he had nothing in the world to complain about.

Nothing except the question that dogged his soul — and would forever. Why had Jimmy been taken and not him? He had no heartbroken fiancée waiting for him to return home. He wasn't the one those villagers had bestowed with a precious gift because he'd saved one of their revered elders. He could go on and on with the reasons Jimmy should have lived and not him, but he reminded himself he was here for a purpose.

One that didn't include him getting bogged down in his personal guilt.

"Please make yourself at home and find whatever you need." Mrs. Clark pushed herself onto the high stool at the counter opposite him, as if she were accustomed to watching someone cook in her kitchen.

He smiled at the kind-eyed old woman because he couldn't help it. Then he got down to cooking.

Before he was finished, Betsy came into the kitchen. He didn't see her as he flipped the contents of his sauté pan, but he felt her. He turned.

She was an unexpected vision. Nothing like the skinny young girl of Jimmy's favorite picture. Without her bulky coat and shapeless cook's uniform jacket from earlier, without her hair in a net, she was another person. He felt the flip of interest in his chest, the taboo quickening in his gut as he looked her over.

She's your best friend's grieving widow. He shook his head, as a competing thought entered it. *But your best friend is dead.* It didn't matter. The stirrings he felt were still wrong.

With his internal war battling but his better, self-disciplined self winning out, as always, he refused to smile at the young woman, refused to feel the warmth of her smile. He refused to acknowledge that she was anything but his best friend's girl and he was here on a mission for Jimmy. Not for her.

No matter that Jimmy had insisted that Eli take care of her. Eli squeezed the memory out, the pain shooting through his chest like a stab of regret, a reminder from a ghost.

"Whatever you're cooking smells like a gift from the gods," she said reverently as she approached to have a look.

Eli took a step back without thinking, as if to keep a proper distance between them at all times.

"Don't get too close to the spatter. You're all dressed up and don't want to ruin your pretty dress."

The woman blushed and no amount of self-discipline could catch the lightning reaction sizzling through him. She was adorable in every way. Her deep-brown eyes were endlessly inviting, her shape round and lush and cushiony. He could imagine laying his head on her lap.

That's not the kind of thing you're here to imagine. That's not what Jimmy meant by taking care of his girl, Eli.

She smoothed her hands over the skirt and looked down as if she were a virginal maiden and he were the big bad wolf. *Which maybe I am.*

"It's almost ready to try. Jimmy and I concocted the recipe and he knew you'd like it." He kept his eyes on his pans now.

"He told me about it in general terms, but not the actual recipe. I've been tinkering with possible variations, but I've had no idea what I'm aiming for."

The smile was automatic, the subject was irresistible, and the company was gorgeous and kind. The heady combination in one person should be impossible. Eli had that sense of being inside that glass snow bubble world again.

"It's the truffle oil. That's the secret ingredient. The recipe is yours now. He wanted you to have it, but I wanted to make it for you so you'd know how special it was."

"Oh, I couldn't possibly take it from you—let's share the recipe. I'm sure that's the way Jimmy would have wanted it."

Eli nodded, seeing the glistening in her eyes and feeling the misting begin in his own.

"You're right. Jimmy was the most generous person I ever knew, ma'am."

"Please call me Betsy, Eli."

Something about her saying his name made his insides tumble around, like she held the incarnation of Jimmy's spirit inside her and was treating him to a piece of Jimmy, giving him the gift of his dead friend's presence in some more real way than the mere memory of him.

Eli reminded himself she was a cook at a small-town restaurant, a grieving woman with an ailing mother. That she should be nothing special. He thought these thoughts but from the moment he'd seen her he'd known that her soul *was* special and that no amount of adding up facts or taboos would make that any less true.

Eli was in trouble. From this moment on, he needed to keep up his guard and clamp down on his self-discipline like he never had before. And still deliver on his promise to his best friend to take care of his girl Betsy. *Betsy.* What a name.

"Were you always called Betsy?" he finally said, pulling himself from his thoughts.

"No. Mom started calling me Betsy, but my dad had always called me by my given name, Elizabeth."

"Bless his soul," Mrs. Carter said, making the sign of the cross.

"Jimmy always called you Betsy?"

"Yes," she laughed. "He thought Elizabeth was too formal, 'highfalutin,' he called it."

Eli noticed a shadow pass over her face, a pain refreshed thinking about Jimmy.

"You won't mind if I call you Elizabeth, would you? After all, I'm Jimmy's formal, highfalutin friend, or so he called me."

They both laughed.

"That would be nice. You should have your own name for me." She blushed and looked down, playing with the watch on her wrist. "As Jimmy's best friend," she added.

Did she feel the spark between them too? The special connection?

Of course they had a connection. Jimmy was their connection. *Don't be a fool, Eli.*

Concentrating on his cooking, he beat back the hyper-awareness of her presence as he finished the dish.

"It's ready for tasting now."

"Let me help you plate it."

"Nonsense. You're all dressed up."

"So are you." She smiled up at him as she approached and took the pan from him, brushing her fingers on his, closing the distance between them to nothing.

The large kitchen felt too small at that moment and he fought with himself between jumping back like a coward and withstanding the onslaught of her essence on his senses. The smell of her, the warmth of her, the kindness radiating from her. Like Jimmy, she had a gift.

Or maybe he was imagining it, projecting the memory of his friend on her to compensate for his sense of loss. That was likely it. She took three plates out of the nearby cupboard and dished out the food. He busied himself finding silverware and napkins and bringing them to the table.

"How about if we eat here at the counter?" she said.

He stopped in his tracks. He'd never been in the habit of eating at a counter. Not in anyone's kitchen, and especially not at any diner or restaurant. It went against his rules. It was one of those leftover hang-ups from his upbringing combined with his snobbishness about cooking, food, and showing proper appreciation. But as he stood halfway to the pristine glass-top kitchen table with its vase of fresh flowers at the center, he realized they probably never used it for eating.

In the end, there was no way he could justify forcing the infirm Mrs. Carter from her spot at the counter to sit at a table so he could feel proper. He turned and brought the utensils and napkins and laid them out.

"I'm sorry — did you prefer the table? It's just that Mom —"

"Don't fret another second. This is fine." He looked at her. Her face held genuine concern, probably in equal parts for her mother and for him. He could see in that moment that she was a giving person. Like her Jimmy. His Jimmy. It was no illusion, not him projecting anything. It was who Elizabeth was.

He sat on his stool with Mrs. Carter between him and Elizabeth and over the older woman's head, he smiled fully at her, watching as she took her first bite.

"Tell me what you think, Elizabeth?" He had to try her name out, feel it on his tongue. Saying it felt foreign, a tiny bit traitorous, and far too exciting. His heart raced as he waited for her reaction.

"It's refreshing with a bite, the sauce smooth and deliciously full-bodied, like a party on my tongue. The truffle oil gives it a decadent richness and defines the taste without taking over the dish. If pasta wasn't so darned bad for my waistline, I'd sit here and eat it all night." She had her eyes closed and a small smile formed as she finished, licking her lips.

Eli held onto his reserve, donned his professional mask, and tensed every muscle in an effort to stay in control, to steady the uneven pounding in his chest, to keep calm. His stoic persona had gone on hiatus since he'd arrived on her doorstep, and he needed to get it back.

But all the wishing in the world wouldn't let him chalk up his loss of control to the emotional overload over Jim's long overdue memorial service. No, the reason was sitting two seats away from him, with a crippled woman in between.

She opened her eyes, those dark bottomless eyes and he took a bone-deep breath that vibrated down to his toes.

"Well said. I can tell you're a pro. Jimmy was proud of you. Proud of how ambitious and smart and hardworking you were—you are."

"Yeah." She laughed. And then she blushed and his pulse raced as he clenched down, stopping himself from smiling back. But that felt all wrong.

"This is delish, Eli. We could use a cook like you at the diner—I mean the *Grill*." Mrs. Clark rolled her eyes and smiled at him. He nodded, not committing, still thinking.

"Mom don't—"

"It's true. You've been holding down the sous chef spot and the management for too long—weeks too long." Mrs. Clark admonished her daughter and then turned to him, studying him like only a wizened old woman could. Reminded him of his grandmother and the way she'd looked at him when he was a boy, as if she were taking his measure. He wondered if her illness had aged her, or if she'd had Elizabeth late in life.

"We need you at Betsy's Grill, Eli. Need the help. Our sous chef retired a month ago and went to Florida. We haven't found a replacement yet. It's tough out there. I need someone professional and reliable who's willing to work in a small New Hampshire town. You know anyone like that?"

"No ma'am, but I will help out. I'd be honored." He turned to Betsy. "Jimmy would want me to help you." Her smile turned big until her dimple showed, and warmth emanated from her in waves of gratitude. "It would be a real pleasure," he added.

It would be pleasurable in a purely innocent way and there was nothing wrong with admitting it.

"I'm sure the pleasure will be all mine. I mean—" She looked away, hiding another of those intoxicating blushes. "I mean I really could use the help and you're obviously an exceptional cook and I would love working with you. Especially since we can talk about Jimmy and catch up and share stories and all and—"

"Quit your babbling, Betsy. Let's finish up here and get to that service before we're late." Mrs. Clark slipped off her stool, gripping the counter with one hand like she'd done it too many times, grabbing her cane as she put one foot on the floor then the other, then straightening deliberately, steadying herself.

"You're right," Betsy rose and began gathering dishes, bustling around in a whirlwind, like a person who was well practiced and in familiar surroundings. Her home kitchen. There was no place more familiar, more dear, than a cook's own kitchen.

Eli looked around, picking up what he could, and soaked in the surroundings again, as if he were taking an intimate look into Elizabeth's diary, seeing the soul of her in practice.

The bright bold colors spoke volumes about her bright outlook, the practical and exquisite appliances told of another side of her — she clearly wasn't afraid to spend her money on the most important things.

The oil painting of a brightly colored rooster surrounded by hens outside a picturesque farmhouse told him something else, something about her. Eli placed a few dishes in the Bosch dishwasher, carefully keeping his distance from her and keeping his breathing regular.

"You love this small town, don't you?"

"Is it that obvious?"

He looked around the room.

"It suits you." He smiled to let her know he wasn't judging.

"I really love it here." She stopped speaking as if she wanted to say more and didn't know how or where to begin.

"What is it?"

"I know you and Jimmy wanted to go into business together, open a new, chic restaurant in the city."

"We talked. We had a few ideas of a place that was both comfortable and cutting edge. We wanted a big market, a large city like Boston."

"Or Washington, DC?"

Eli didn't answer. "That's my neck of the woods. That's where I'll end up now that Jimmy's gone, but that's not where we planned to start out."

She looked away.

He couldn't help himself. She wore her pain in her expression and slumped shoulders. He reached out and touched a shoulder, felt the cushiony warmth of her upper arm. A part of him wanted to hold back, to keep his distance, but the better part of him needed to console her.

"Elizabeth, he wanted to work with you most of all, to spend his life with you. Here. All the plans we had would have never interfered with that. No matter what. I promise you."

When she looked up, eyes glistening, he felt her warmth and kindness and gratitude reaching inside his impossibly tight chest and grabbing onto his heart. He was a goner.

He cleared his throat.

"I… thank you. I know. I was always worried that I'd be holding him back," Elizabeth said.

"You two were classic. He was afraid of the same thing for you, that he'd be dragging you into something you didn't want. You were an amazing, inspiring couple, Elizabeth."

"It means a lot to me that you think so."

They stood like that for a few awkward beats, with him holding her shoulder, until he finally let her go and nodded. "It's time we got our coats and got to the church, I think."

They ended up rushing from the house. Elizabeth insisted they take the four-wheel drive, and Eli insisted on driving. It wasn't far, but it was far too cold to walk. When they arrived, there were dozens of people already there and the priest was ready. Jimmy's parents had arranged it all.

As a fiancée, Betsy had no official standing. She and Jimmy had never married, so she wasn't a widow. She sat in the first row—her mother, then her, then Eli at the end of the pew. At some point, either while they were walking in or sitting down, she found her hand in Eli's. He held it for the remainder of the short service and during the words spoken by Jimmy's family. His father said they were going to scatter Jimmy's ashes over the family farm the next day, but that they were keeping it private, just for the family. Eli tensed next to her. She smiled at him, hoping her sadness didn't show, didn't overwhelm her attempt at reassurance.

She hadn't been invited to speak, but that was okay with her. She'd said all she needed to say to Jimmy at night, silently, before she fell asleep. Every night for months after he was gone. Now she felt numb everywhere except for the hand Eli held, which was warm and comforting.

Three

The snow fell in waves of white, obscuring their vision. Betsy wasn't surprised to see her car covered when they got close enough to see it. She glanced at Eli and also wasn't surprised to see the dismay on his face. She imagined he wasn't used to too much snow down in Virginia. Or maybe he just didn't like it. The notion bothered her.

"Don't worry. This will sweep off the windshield in a few seconds." She gave him a reassuring wave and reached inside the back seat to get her windshield brush.

But before she took one swipe at the snow, Eli came up beside her and gently removed the brush from her hand.

"I'll do this. You get inside the car with your mother and keep warm."

Her thoughts were a jumble and her nerve endings tingled with the nearness of him. Even through their overcoats she could feel his warmth. She wanted to say that she was perfectly capable, but she didn't. Something about him told her he *knew* she was capable, but he wanted to do this for her nevertheless. It was a kindness, so she accepted it.

Inside the car with her mother, her mother leaned in close.

"I'm so glad no one made any comments about Eli being a black man and accompanying you to the service."

Shock nearly stopped Betsy's heart.

"Why should they say anything, Mom? Why would you think such a thing?"

"There are some old conservatives in this town—you know that. Jimmy's parents are among them. If they thought there was any hint of a romance between you and Eli, you better believe you'd hear about it."

"You know there's no romance." She felt the heat suffuse her face, felt the little tingle of excitement at the possibility, the suggestion of it, and then swept it aside as nonsense. "Let them say something. I'll give them—"

The driver's door opened and Eli slid inside the car.

"Did someone say something to you—about me?" He looked prepared, at the ready, not surprised and simmering.

It shocked her to see the self-righteous determination, fierce and barely short of defiant, under the calm façade, unmistakable in the set of his jaw.

"No. No one said anything. I'm not sure what you mean." Betsy tried to gloss over her words, wondering what meaning he had implied, what meaning she could pretend.

"You know. Did someone say something about you attending the service with a black man?"

She shook her head violently.

"No one said a thing, Eli," her mother said. "I was just telling Betsy that I was surprised and glad. We have some dense, set-in-their ways people in this town."

"I know. Jimmy used those exact words, told me his parents were *set in their ways*."

"You heard that? From Jimmy?"

He nodded.

"You were best friends. Surely his parents didn't—"

"No. But Jimmy asked me to take care of you. When he was dying." He let out a long sigh. "I should have told you before. He told me he wanted me to see to you, look out for you. He told me to never mind if tongues wagged and especially to ignore his parents if they gave me a hard time. After all, there's nothing they can do to me. Nothing that hasn't been done before, anyway."

Betsy had no idea what to say. She felt a mixture of emotions about Jimmy asking Eli to take care of her. Disappointed to find that Eli was only here because Jimmy had asked him to be, admiration at Eli's stalwartness, and appalled at the notion that he'd have to put up with people's attitudes and rudeness.

He looked at her. She had to say something.

"I'm sorry. You don't need to stay here another minute on my behalf. I'm perfectly fine on my own. I've been taking care of myself for the past year and a half." The words felt stiff and defensive, but she couldn't stop them, couldn't add that she wished he'd come because he wanted to and not out of obligation. She wished that his offer to help at the restaurant hadn't been out of duty for Jimmy, but because he wanted to help *her*.

He looked away and started the car. While he watched the road, he spoke.

"If there's one thing I realized since I arrived — even before then, based on what Jimmy told me — it's that you are an extremely capable and talented woman, Elizabeth. I know you don't need taking care of. But I promised I would. At least for a while."

He didn't say that he *wanted* to. She so desperately wanted to hear him say those words.

"Don't bother. I wouldn't want to impose. I don't feel right about being someone's obligation."

"You're not." He snapped the words and then gave her a hard stare that said there was no argument or room for interpretation. But that was all he said. Enough to silence the resentment in her, but not enough to feed her desire to be more to him, to be more than his late friend's fiancée, to be his friend on her own.

They arrived back home and Betsy wanted desperately to return to a friendlier, less tense mood. She helped her mother remove her coat and said good night as the older woman went to her bedroom on the first floor at the back of the small house.

"I'll see you in the morning, Eli," her mother had said.

Busying herself taking off her coat, hat and gloves and putting them all in the closet, it took a minute for Betsy to realize that Eli stood there, still somber, watching her.

"Take off your coat. I'm making some hot cocoa — special recipe." She didn't add that it was Jimmy's favorite, couldn't form the words. She cleared her mind, tired of mourning for him. And after tonight, finally ready to put him in the past and move forward. She stopped in her tracks when she realized Eli wasn't moving, still hadn't removed his coat, and wasn't following her to the kitchen.

He was proud and she'd offended him. That must be why he looked at her that way, like he wanted to be somewhere else. She walked back into the small living room toward the front foyer where he stood on the threshold. If he was planning to leave town now, she wouldn't let him go without apologizing.

"I'd best be going now while I can. My hotel is thirty minutes away."

"Hotel? You're not planning on staying at a hotel? We have the guest room all set up for you. Mom insisted. She would be so upset with me in the morning if she finds you gone. I'm sorry if I offended you —"

"Slow down, Elizabeth." A small smile lifted the right corner of his mouth. She'd seen that before, a heart-melting expression, with that very small dimple and understated mirth peeking out from his serious demeanor. She could stare at it all day — but staring was rude, wasn't it?

"I'll be back tomorrow, but I don't think —"

She reached out and tugged his arm, not hard, and led him inside the warm living room.

"Please stay. It's awful driving and you promised to help me at the restaurant in the morning. And I could use your help shoveling out, if you want to know the god's honest truth of the matter."

"Elizabeth." The one word admonished her. He knew she

was fibbing. Of course he knew she was used to the snow and shoveling and that she would be able to deal with this little storm. Heck, she had a snow-blower she was an expert with, even if he didn't know it. She looked down, the heat in her cheeks probably a telltale pink. She hated blushing. It was the only time she truly felt like a helpless girl.

"I know you don't need my help, but I would be happy to do it if it means that much to you and your mother for me to stay. Under one condition."

She looked up and knew she wore a silly grin, knew it was uncalled for and he would wonder what had gotten into her. Heck, *she* wondered what had gotten into her. Why did she want him to stay? Why did she not want him to leave?

"What condition?" Was he teasing or serious? Of course he was serious. This was Eli, not Jimmy.

"I'll stay here tonight. But after tonight I'm going to take a room at the inn I saw down the street. The hotel is too far for a regular early morning commute to the restaurant. I will stay and work with you until you hire a new sous chef." His face was implacable as if he expected no opposition, as if the notion was foreign, as if he were the king and it was decreed.

And darned if she didn't think it was a great plan.

"Okay. Sounds good. We can check tomorrow to see if Nora and Billy have a room for you at the Stillwater."

"Check if they have a room? Are you conning me? We're in a small town in New Hampshire in the winter. Surely the place must be empty."

"No. The Stillwater Inn gets busy around the holidays between families with guests coming in from out of town and people who want a snowy New England Christmas."

"Is that right?"

She laughed because he truly looked astonished by the possibility.

"You're really not a small-town kind of guy, are you?"

"Born and raised in the city."

"A city boy."

"A city man."

A flame filled her face and crawled down her neck and chest. She'd just said an awful thing. "I'm sorry—I didn't mean—"

"No, no. Look, I'm the one who should be sorry. I know you didn't mean anything. It's my own stupid knee-jerk reaction. That chip I carry around has no place in this house or with you. I promise to do a better job of stifling that"—he waved a hand around—"chippiness."

Then he laughed. It was a low vibration that rumbled through her leaving tingles of excitement behind. His laugh was rare and something else, something undefined. She wished she could make him laugh more, see the burden of whatever made him so serious and somber lifted.

"I'll send for my bags tomorrow."

"How about that hot cocoa?" she asked.

"Sounds like a good way to end this long day. On a delicious high note with a wonderful woman."

"And sitting in a gorgeous state-of-the-art kitchen, don't forget." She spread her arms as they headed that way, accompanied by his deep, resonating laugh—not big, not loud, but soulful. She was thrilled. She could have said any one of many inanities but she wanted to make him laugh and would make it her business to do so every chance she got.

She wanted to hug him right now, just wrap her arms around him and soak him in, all his strong solid beautiful strength and goodness and give him some of herself, cheer him, soften his serious edge. She sensed that he needed it.

"I can't wait to cook with you tomorrow." She grinned while she got the cream from the fridge and assembled the ingredients for the cocoa.

"Be careful what you wish for. I'm a serious cook. No fun and games."

"What makes you think I'm about fun and games?"

"You were with Jimmy, weren't you?" He grinned back at her.

His statement troubled her on some level, but she swept that aside. The rush of seeing him smile was surprising and crazy. But it was a gorgeous smile in one of the most handsome faces she'd ever laid eyes on—Hollywood handsome. Like a younger, stronger, darker Denzel. She caught herself before she sighed like a swooning fangirl, as if he was some superstar leading man.

"True. Aren't you worried I'll wear you down and make you silly, laugh like a naive little girl?"

He studied her a moment, back to his serious dimple-free face, and she studied him back without shame.

"You're no lightweight. You're lighthearted. And you most certainly are not a little girl."

"Glad you noticed." She flushed immediately, instantly aware that she'd said the wrong thing, that he might think she was flirting.

"I... mean you're right. I am lighthearted. Not a lightweight." Now, as he regarded her with an entirely different expression, her blush disappeared and she felt herself pale. She willed him to say something, to give her a hint what was behind that unreadable expression, almost as if he didn't trust her and had shut down, shut her out.

"I know," he finally said. "I figured. As far as I'm concerned you're a lady, not a girl." He turned his attention to the hot cocoa and though his look wasn't unfriendly, he hadn't returned to his previous unguarded self. She felt abandoned.

Whatever it was about him, she had the most insane need to get to know him, to be his friend, to have him as a friend. Because she somehow knew it would be a privilege that he didn't bestow on many. Why she wanted it so much, she didn't know.

Sure, she could blame it on his being Jimmy's friend, but she couldn't be dishonest with herself. That wasn't the reason.

They finished their hot cocoa listening to the strains of the *Nutcracker Suite* coming from her mother's room. Mom played Christmas music night and day this time of year. Betsy didn't mind since it made her mother happy and added a festive air to their home.

"I should be getting to bed. I don't know about you, but I need to sleep. I rise early, before the usual breakfast hour, to meditate." He rose.

"Oh, of course." She popped up from her seat and took the mugs to the dishwasher.

He followed her, leaving more than an arm's length between them. When he cleared his throat she turned and looked at him.

"I don't have my overnight bag."

"That's right—I'm so sorry. I don't know what I was thinking. Guess I'm not much of a hostess, am I?"

"The arrangement snuck up on both of us."

She couldn't help smiling at the way he put it so delicately.

"I have some pajamas and… things you can wear. They were my father's, if you don't mind. Fresh and clean, of course."

He nodded and they both laughed.

"I have a new toothbrush and toothpaste and soap and anything else you might need too. I'll leave it all in the upstairs bathroom."

She took him by the arm and walked him from the kitchen to the front hall where the stairway was. "Let me show you your room." She let go of his arm and he followed her upstairs.

Trying not to feel self-conscious with him behind her didn't work too well. She was hyperaware of his large warm body two steps below as she attempted to climb the stairs without swaying her hips. Why she even thought about that was beyond her and that flush warmed her cheeks again, this time at the notion that he was watching her swaying rear.

Maybe it was because they'd never had a man stay in

their home before who wasn't a relative. Not even Jimmy.

That must be what made her so sensitive—she'd never had Jimmy stay over and here she was showing his best friend to their spare room. It was impossible for her face to get any hotter with shame or embarrassment or awareness or whatever it was that made her flame up. Resisting the urge to duck into the bathroom and splash cold water on her face—or dump a bucket over her head—she turned to the right and pushed the door open to the spare bedroom.

Spare was the right word. There was a double bed, a small three-drawer dresser, and an old wooden chair. She caught his reflection in the mirror above the dresser. He wore the impersonal mask from earlier.

"Here's the guest room all ready for you. I'll put a towel and things in the bathroom, but you let me know if you need anything else. My room is right down the other end of the hall on the other side of the bathroom—"

She was rambling and he stopped her with raised hands and a soft smile.

"It looks very comfortable. I'm sure I'll be fine. Don't worry about a thing."

And just like that, he put her at ease and the hot nerves of a moment before vanished. She took a deep breath and felt tension escape.

"You have to be the most gracious man I ever met." Apparently, she'd become a little too at ease. The pendulum swing of her emotions and nerves must be making her seem like a crazy person.

"You make it easy for a man to be gracious, Elizabeth." He studied her for another moment while she backed out of the small room.

"Goodnight." He gently closed the door behind her while she stood mutely, overwhelmed with his effect on her and clueless as to why or how or what on earth to do about it.

A good night's sleep would be a good start. She went to

her room and collapsed onto her bed and, while she wondered if her mind would ever stop spinning with thoughts and feelings about Eli and Jimmy and where she fit in, she fell asleep.

Four

aking was a confusing process. From the window opposite his bed, the first thing he saw was the bright snow shining under the early morning moonlight in the dark starry sky. That and the slow emergence from his dream state, muddled him until he finally remembered whose house he was in, whose company he'd spent the evening before in, and most shocking of all, how much he'd enjoyed it.

But Eli was familiar with the tantalizing nature of forbidden fruit and there was no way he had any right to feel and think about Jimmy's Elizabeth the way he had. But she wasn't Jimmy's Elizabeth. She was Jimmy's Betsy. She was Eli's Elizabeth. He'd claim that facet of her identity, her essence, for himself.

He snapped the covers off and checked his watch on the dresser. It was six a.m. Full wakefulness brought a frisson of dismay at the reason he had risen early. He'd promised to help at the Grill until they hired a new sous chef. There was never a question that he'd help. He'd made the promise a year and a half ago as he'd watched his best friend in the world, his most unlikely friend, slip away from him.

The stab to his heart that he felt as sharply as if the knife were real was as much for guilt as it was for loss. He had no right to appreciate Elizabeth the way he did. He was to watch over her, help her, make sure she was all right and on the road to a new life.

"Make sure she's happy, Eli. Can you do that for me?" Those were Jimmy's last words. At some point in this visit he promised himself he'd tell her that. He'd meant to tell her last night. He'd thought about it on the trip here. Of telling her and having her cry in his arms.

That was when Elizabeth had still been Betsy to him, a theoretical person. Jimmy's girl.

Now she wasn't. Who was she, then? Who should she be? *Who could she be to you, Eli?*

How can you even think these things one day after Jimmy's memorial service when the poor woman was still grieving? You're better than that. Jimmy expected better of you, deserves better of you.

Slipping his pants on, he opened his door and left his room. Even in the dark hall, he could see her standing there silhouetted in her white fluffy robe, watching him, stock-still as if he'd turned her to a statue with his gaze.

"You're up early." His voice, rusty from the night's sleep, was gruffer than he meant it to be.

But Elizabeth wasn't intimidated. She walked forward and smiled, undaunted.

"I could say the same thing to you." She pushed past him, went into the bathroom, and closed the door.

"Ladies first," he said, too late. He suppressed his grin out of habit in the empty hall, then went downstairs to use the first-floor bathroom. It pleased him to learn that Elizabeth was a practical woman, weighing her need to use the facilities as more important than being a star hostess. She would need that baseline in life on her own without Jimmy.

Briefly he wondered if her practical streak would lead her to quickly move past her first love and partner up with someone else instead of waiting to find someone she truly loved again. The thought annoyed him and he scolded himself that it was well beyond the scope of his promise to Jimmy to see that she was okay. *Wasn't it?*

Truth was, he really had no idea what Jimmy had had

in mind, no idea of what his friend's exact expectations of him were, only that he wanted his Betsy to be happy without him. As much as he wanted to do what was right, Eli knew he couldn't expect to make her *happy*.

That thought troubled him. Not because he couldn't make her happy, but because he realized he actually *wanted* to make her happy. *That cannot be a good thing*.

He put it out of his mind and, avoiding her, dressed and readied himself for the day. He called his hotel to arrange for his things to be sent to the inn. His clothes wouldn't arrive until later in the day, so he'd have to make do at the restaurant in his dress clothes. The smell of fresh coffee welcomed him as he entered the kitchen.

"Good morning. I hope you slept well." Mrs. Carter beamed.

Elizabeth stood behind the enormous granite island, sipping from a cup, and avoided his eyes after her first glance. He shouldn't be surprised at the awkwardness. He wasn't sure how to relate to her — was she an acquaintance and potential friend, or was she a too-attractive woman and potential lover?

The answer was easy — she had to be a friend. But tell that to his hormones. She probably sensed his attraction and it more than likely made her uncomfortable, confused her. And why shouldn't it confuse her? It was confusing the heck out of him.

"I slept very well. That coffee smells heavenly."

Elizabeth poured and handed him a cup, finally looking at him fully and offering a tentative smile. "There's cream and sugar."

"I take it black. Thank you."

"Of course you do," she said. Then she blushed pink and hot and pretty as she had a habit of doing. But she grinned like she meant it.

"I know. I've been accused of being a no-nonsense man. But I take care of myself and don't bother with extra calories or frivolities."

She dimpled. They had that in common. Dimples. Hers was only on one side and therefore all the more charming. He looked away before he showed his dimples back at her. *They would become friends and nothing more. So what if she had a dimple?*

"What time do you usually start at the grill?"

"Normally I wouldn't go in until ten but I want to show you around, so I thought we could go in at eight today and have breakfast there." She turned to her mother. "You don't mind, do you, this once?"

"Not at all. I'm very pleased that Eli is helping out—and very grateful." Mrs. Carter sat on her stool with her cane hooked on the counter and a permanent angel-smile lighting her face. He didn't think he'd seen her without that smile since he'd arrived. It inspired warmth.

He liked it. Very much.

Then he wondered if Elizabeth took after her mother and was prone to the same constant cheeriness—except that his arrival had interrupted it. *Bullcrap. Don't borrow trouble. She smiles often enough, probably more than most women in her shoes, mourning and sad.*

At the restaurant, she let them in the back door while he held back from opening it for her and preceding her inside. It was something he always did, naturally taking care of ladies as a well-trained gentleman should. He did it because he felt the value and grace in it.

Once inside, she flipped on the lights to the kitchen, which turned out to be much larger than had seemed possible when they'd driven by the front.

"This is a good size," he said taking a turn around the room, inspecting the equipment, the storage, the pans. "And it sparkles."

"Yes. I mean thank you. When we expanded, we made sure we got premium equipment and had the kitchen designed with the best, most efficient layout."

Eli whistled, enjoying her pride.

"You certainly went all-out." He wondered, but wouldn't ask, how she could have possibly afforded the spanking-new kitchen. It couldn't have been more than a year old.

Then it dawned on him. She must have used Jimmy's money that he'd saved. Jimmy told him he'd left it to her, told him he had made a will since they weren't married.

"I built it after Jimmy — after I learned that he'd passed away. He had a small life insurance policy and he'd named me as the beneficiary."

"*Small* insurance policy? You mean the one the armed services offers? That couldn't have been more than ten thousand dollars." He shouldn't have said it. "I'm sorry — it's none of my business."

She was clearly uncomfortable. She turned away and ran a hand along a gleaming stainless steel table. He wanted to go to her, put a hand on her shoulder, reassure her, comfort her, but she spoke then.

"It's okay. Most of the money was what we'd saved for our wedding. He'd send me a chunk of his pay each month to put toward a big fat farmer's wedding — that's how we referred to it." She looked up. He must have looked confused.

She waved a hand. "It's where you dress up the barn, invite everyone in town, serve more food than an army could eat and most importantly, there's free-flowing liquor all day and night."

He drew nearer. The smile she gave was the saddest thing Eli had ever seen.

"I'm so sorry. I didn't mean for you to have to explain, to relive —"

"No, it's okay. It's better than having you wonder if I'd robbed a bank to build a new kitchen." The smile went crooked and his heart contracted and the sharp pain was real enough.

She had to be the bravest lady he'd ever met—and he'd met a few. He came from a family of brave, proud, no-nonsense women. Elizabeth was all of that and sweet and generous-hearted too. He couldn't say that about all his female relatives, possibly not about any one of them. Sweetness didn't seem to run in his family.

He sighed without thinking and then clenched down on the maudlin attitude—and whatever else was running through his veins on account of this beautiful woman.

"You forgot to laugh. At my joke," she deadpanned.

That earned her a smile. "You must know from Jimmy I'm a hard nut to crack."

"Makes it all the sweeter when you crack your big beautiful smile. Now that I've seen it, I want more. Call me greedy." Her dimple bloomed fully, her color heightened, and all sadness was gone from her face, from her words, from her demeanor.

He cleared his throat, fully aware that she was up to the challenge of winning him over if he didn't watch himself. The only thing that would save him is a quick hire of a good sous chef.

"Give me the guided tour, all the bells and whistles of this baby. I want to see under the hood and kick the tires while I'm here."

She laughed at him.

"I think you may have mixed a couple of metaphors—you're talking about my kitchen, right?" The smile she wore now had to be stolen from the very devil. It did things to make his heart take a fast trip and his gut float unsteadily.

She took his arm and set about showing him every corner of the kitchen. They got to the walk-in freezer and blew out a whistle. It was large—*everything* was large, as if she was planning to expand the restaurant someday too.

"Do you want to take a look inside the freezer?"

"Of course. Besides, I'm no guest, I'm your sous chef." For

the moment. God help him if he didn't want to be her sous chef forever — and at the same time he felt a need to get out of town the first chance he got. It was ten days to Christmas and he swore to himself then and there he'd be out of there before then.

Christmas Eve would be his D-Day. Replacement cook or not, there was no way he could spend the holidays with this woman and stay sane. She'd drive him crazy with her softness and her smiles and her kindness and silly sense of humor. Above all, her giving nature would undo his best intentions if he didn't escape sooner than later.

She opened the freezer door and then engaged a latch to prevent the door from closing.

"We don't want to get trapped in here alone — I mean with no one around to let us out." As she spoke he watched that pretty blush of color rise, and he clamped down on his physical reactions to her. He backed up a step.

"That would be terribly cliché wouldn't it? Like something from a mystery novel."

He stepped inside to look around.

"I see you have a couple of empty meat hooks back here." He resisted rubbing his arms from the cold and wondered if she was also chilled.

"Yes. I don't know why I bothered with them. Maybe for future use. I get my meat already butchered."

"You don't butcher your own?" The surprise was automatic. This was a grill after all, and they specialized in grilled meat.

"No. We don't have a butcher on staff. I mean I'm not very proficient at butchering meat... That was something Jimmy would have taken care of."

Feeling like a first-class cad, he reminded himself to be more sensitive. "I can remedy that while I'm here. I can train you, or at least get you started with basics and watch out so you don't butcher yourself."

The promise was worth seeing the brightening up of her face.

"That's so generous of you—I'd love that." Rubbing her arms, she added, "Let's get out of here and have some breakfast. Another cup of coffee?"

Eli followed her back out of the freezer, realizing she'd been relying on Jimmy's return more than she'd like to admit. He also wondered what had happened to the money he'd put aside for her—the money Jimmy had told him about. There was more than the wedding money. He'd had a special account set up for her and had made a will to make sure she got it. The documents must have been part of his personal effects. But they wouldn't have gone to Elizabeth.

They would have gone to Jimmy's parents, the less than progressive Mr. and Mrs. Bell.

This was another item he put on his list—at the top—of things to do while he was here. It fell squarely under the heading of looking out for Elizabeth's best interests. If there was money she had coming to her and she hadn't received it, then Eli would find out about it and take care of it.

Even if it meant going up against Jimmy's uncooperative parents. Maybe he shouldn't assume the worst, that the Bells wouldn't be cooperative, but if that was the case then why hadn't Elizabeth heard about Jimmy's will and the additional money he wanted her to have?

He shouldn't, but Eli felt buoyed by having a real and specific mission to accomplish for Jimmy, something he knew Jimmy wanted him to do. *As opposed to hanging around his girl and helping her out at the Grill and thinking all kinds of inappropriate thoughts about her.* He could feel more at ease spending some extra time here.

And less guilty.

"I'll cook the eggs if you cook the bacon," she said and got out the pans, showing him where they were stored in the process.

"You have a deal. What do you have on the menu for lunch and dinner?"

She cracked the eggs. "I forgot you've never been here. We can look over the menus while we eat breakfast. Before the rest of the staff arrives. Then I'll introduce you."

He internally balked at the notion of meeting the staff. It made his stay seem more committed, more permanent. *And what would be so bad about that?* A part of him wanted to know.

The other, more sensible, rational, and honorable part of him knew it would lead to nothing but trouble and heartache and a giant guilty conscience. Besides, he had dreams and ambitions of his own. A financial backer for a new restaurant in DC was waiting to hear about his proposal when he returned. It was pretty much a done deal because the backer was a family friend, but Eli had insisted he treat it like any other business deal and that he should evaluate Eli's proposal first before committing the money. He'd postponed it until the new year, after the holidays. Then he'd be off and running.

He'd be long gone from this sleepy and cold New Hampshire town and the warm, inviting Elizabeth Carter.

He tried not to think about leaving already since he'd just begun his first day with her. But as she sat beside him talking animatedly about the menu, and they exchanged ideas about what his role here would be, he felt himself sinking in.

And he didn't mind. In fact, it felt right. She made it far too comfortable for him.

When the staff arrived, he was introduced around like a museum exhibit, but Eli couldn't fault them for their politeness and curiosity. Mostly they were happy to have the extra help.

Once they started prepping for lunch and the day got busy, he settled in, and the tension of being a newcomer, and an oddity at that, disappeared. His mixed feelings about being there, alongside the temptation of Elizabeth, eased. He lived in the moment, relishing the fast pace and demonstrating the skill required. Enjoyed every moment and every exchange with the ever cheery and highly competent Elizabeth.

During the lull between lunch and dinner the day server, Audrey, came into the kitchen to flirt while they were prepping as was the norm given her personality. Betsy watched Eli and noticed that he tolerated it well. But as soon as Eli went to get supplies from the refrigerator one of the cooks in salad and dessert prep cornered Audrey and Betsy to gossip.

"You're so obvious," the cook said under her breath to Audrey. "Did you ever think maybe Betsy wants dibs on him? Heck, maybe *I'm* interested. He's one of the dreamiest men to land in this kitchen ever."

"Is that true, Betsy? You have eyes for Mr. Hot and Hunky? It might be good for you to make your move now." The two women looked at her.

"He's a wonderful man, and has the kind of looks to make a woman's heart flutter, I have to admit, but it's not that way between us. I want us to be friends. I'd be really happy with that."

Audrey laughed. "You're so full of fertilizer. Who are you kidding? Why isn't it *that way* between you? He seems to think highly enough of you to take time out of his life and help out here—don't tell me that isn't just a little special."

Betsy felt a slight pink crawling up her arms, but she clenched down on it. She had nothing to be embarrassed about, did she?

"It's a little awkward is all. It feels like it's Jimmy between us. He was Eli's best friend and he promised to watch out for me. That's why he's here now. No other reason." She shrugged, wishing it didn't ring so true, wishing there was much more, or even a little more.

Oh, Eli had said he wanted to be there, but she still fought with her pride about whether she should have accepted his help. No doubt his obligation to Jimmy was a big part of the reason he was here. But darned if she didn't want to spend some time with him and get to know him better.

"You never know, though," Betsy added, feeling a little bold.

"Now that's more like it," Audrey said, elbowing Callie in the ribs.

"Sure, we'll see. But don't blame me for flirting while you're waiting."

Betsy laughed automatically, but a squinch of worry laced through her. Callie elbowed Audrey and whispered. "Speak of the devil. The man's back and look at those muscles carrying that load of meat."

All three of them turned to watch him set up. After a beat, he looked up and met Betsy's eyes. There wasn't a thing she could do but send him an appreciative look. To her great surprise, he sent her a two-dimpled smile back.

That sent a trill of sparks running through her like a string of firecrackers. Before Audrey could elbow her again, Betsy stepped aside, then made her rounds to check the kitchen.

"Cassie, it's time we started working on that pastry for the samoas."

"On it, boss." She winked and Audrey snickered and both women were far too merry for meal prep, even in Betsy's kitchen. Frank, the all-around helper, shook his head as he walked by.

"I hope you know what you're doing with that young stud in the kitchen, boss," he half whispered.

"What do you mean?" She pulled him to the other side of the grill. They'd opened the enormous metal garage bay door to the dining area for the evening. The gleaming steel exhaust hoods decorated in copper added the perfect ambience to the restaurant side. Having an audience while they cooked kept the staff on their toes. Betsy took Frank to the restaurant side now.

Alarm at whatever he might be thinking pierced a hole in her precarious bubble of joy at having Eli there.

"I'm just sayin' the man's a player—must be with those movie-star-looks and that… edge. He ain't the easy-going type like Jimmy was, that's for sure."

"He's doing me a favor, Frank. You know I needed someone. We haven't been able to open up this grill," she waved her hand at the copper trim, "since Beau retired." She didn't say how frazzled she'd been every night, like they'd won another battle with logistics and the clock, making all the dinners without having to cut down the menu. That would have been her next step if Eli hadn't shown up.

"I know it's been tough on you without a sous chef." Frank rubbed his chin and watched Eli work as if he was alone on a quiet mountaintop instead of a bustling kitchen. If he noticed their scrutiny, she couldn't tell.

"He does look like a heck of a pro. He did lunch as if he'd been working here for months." Frank turned to her. "But don't you get used to him. You know he has bigger fish to fry and won't spend his time in this place for long."

"Don't worry, Frank, I have an interview later after dinner shuts down. Maybe we'll get lucky." At this point, Betsy wasn't sure what lucky would mean. Would it be lucky to hire someone quickly so Eli could leave?

Or not to hire anyone at all and have Eli stay?

"Good." Frank went back into the kitchen area, but she took her time, gazing long and hard at Eli as he sliced meat with admirable efficiency.

Eventually, he looked up, then motioned with his head for her to get back in the kitchen. As if he was in charge. She supposed he was used to being in charge. He had a natural commanding presence. Returning to her station, she began preparing one of her special sauces. Standing so close, she was super aware of his energy, his size, and his concentration.

The opposite of her own distractedness. *Time to cook, Betsy. Stop wondering how it would feel to be kissed by him.*

"Did I mention that I have an interview for the sous chef

position tonight?"

She thought he would stop what he was doing, that she'd get his attention, but he kept moving while he kept his eye on his knife.

"Good. Do you mind if I sit in? It sometimes helps to have two people's impressions and observations."

The offer surprised her, but she figured he was still watching out for her, still needing to maintain control of the situation. She must have paused longer than he'd expected, because he stopped what he was doing, expecting a response. Ready to make a stand, to insist she could handle it herself, she changed her mind when she saw the expression on his face. Concern lined his forehead, and she could sense an apology coming so she jumped in.

"I'd love your help. You're right. It would be great to have someone — you — making observations. Maybe you'll have questions I won't. It's a plan, then."

"Good." He began applying some seasoning rub to the cuts of filet mignon in front of him.

Once the dinner crowd began arriving, Betsy's preoccupation with Eli was replaced by the swirl of activity of overseeing the kitchen, cooking, and doing some hostessing out front. The evening passed quicker than she'd expected. By the time she removed her apron, the clock out front chimed nine o'clock.

Glancing at the front desk, she saw a young man who she assumed must be the job applicant.

His name was Mason George and he was a stud.

Five

*W*ashing his hands, Eli spotted Betsy staring open-mouthed at someone. As he removed his white jacket, he followed her line of sight. A furrow formed along his forehead as he realized the young man — very young man — must be the interviewee for the sous chef job.

His job.

It came as a surprise to him that he thought of it as his job after only one day, but he felt comfortable with Betsy and most of her staff. And the fact that it was a ridiculously well-equipped state-of-the-art kitchen didn't hurt. He joined her where she stood gazing over the dining room, careful not to stand too close.

"Our interview?"

She started and pinked up as if she was embarrassed, caught staring at the young buck. Eli shouldn't enjoy her guilty look, or the flush coloring her cheeks and neck, but he did. Recovering, she smiled.

"Yes. How did you know?"

"A hunch. You ready?"

"I suppose, but I was hoping we could eat first. I'm starved."

He allowed himself a smile, not that he could have stopped it. After a while a man had to give into his natural instincts and show his appreciation. Besides, she was adorable. He liked a cook who liked to eat, and he was starved too.

"No problem. Let's take the interview in a booth and have

our meal served there. It will be an extra way of testing him."

"Great idea. Let me ask Audrey to serve us."

In less than a minute, after Betsy had freshened up and talked to Audrey, they met the young man at the hostess station.

Betsy introduced Eli as the temporary sous chef and the young buck—a little breathlessly, he thought—as Mason George.

"It's your lucky day, Mason. We're conducting this interview over dinner." Eli gestured to the empty booth nearest the kitchen and after Mason sat on one side and Betsy sat on the other, he realized his miscalculation.

In his preoccupation at sizing up Mason, and his annoyance at Betsy's obvious admiration for his youthful and athletic good looks, he'd failed to play the scene out in his head to its conclusion—the conclusion being where he'd be seated in very close proximity to the object of his tortured, taboo, and heretofore secret passion, Elizabeth Carter.

After a pause that spoke of reluctance, he tried to make amends by winking as he slid in next to her. Her pained expression turned quickly back to the ever-present dimpled smile that he was coming to have a love-hate relationship with. He loved her upbeat nature, the way she looked, the joy and sweetness that it represented, the genuineness of it. But he hated how it made him feel, the spark it lit in him, the longing for it to be for him, and him alone.

With haste, he turned his attention to Mason, as he arranged the napkin on his lap.

"How old are you, Mason?" He ignored Elizabeth's raised eyebrows in his peripheral vision and her squelched snort turned cough. He knew he was being blunt, but he may as well expose Mason's biggest weakness.

"I turned twenty years old last month, sir." Mason aimed an unabashed flirtatious expression at Betsy. "I graduated from The Culinary Institute of America Hyde Park at the top of my class." He took some papers from his jacket pocket then and shuffled the folded pages.

"You can save the references for later, son." He didn't acknowledge out loud that he was impressed that the kid came from the best culinary school in the U.S.

"Your resume says you live in the Boston area," Elizabeth spoke up, "What made you apply for a job up here in New Hampshire?"

While Mason launched into a lengthy explanation about why he loved New Hampshire, Eli decided he needed to get the interview back to brass tacks and the boy's — young man's culinary skills and experience — or lack thereof. He broke into the monologue the first chance he got.

"Tell me about your experience working as a sous chef, specifically at a grill," Eli said in his most no-nonsense voice.

When Elizabeth cleared her throat, he knew his overly professional tone might have been cold and unfriendly and he'd need to adjust. What was it about this kid that annoyed him?

It was his very presence and the fact that he was literally competing for Eli's job, of course. Never mind that Eli hadn't intended to keep the job. *Never mind that he was also competing for Elizabeth's admiration.*

When their meals were served, there was a short break in the interview while they talked about the food. They'd all ordered the prime rib that Eli had prepared earlier, rubbed with his special twist on the standard Betsy's Grill rub. It was warm and succulent and juicy, and the flavor of the rub added enough interest without detracting from the excellent meat. The prep chef had dressed it appropriately as Eli had showed her, adding the final touches of crispy onions and the signature overstuffed potato.

It was time for Eli try to stay objective and truly professional, instead as if they were in a competition. On a deep breath and renewed patience with himself, he joined Elizabeth in quizzing Mason on cooking techniques, recipes, and his career ambitions — typical job interview questions. Even so, at the back of his mind, Eli was annoyed with himself.

He was also annoyed with the excessive attention given to the young boy by every female employee who had a chance during their meal.

Eli tossed in some difficult questions. To his credit, the boy answered intelligently.

Elizabeth raised her brow again—and it appeared to be because she was impressed with Mason.

They shook hands when Mason finally left a couple of hours later. Though Eli tried, he couldn't read Elizabeth's expression. What did she think about hiring Mason? He had his own very definite idea about it.

After Mason left, Betsy returned with Eli to the office off the kitchen. Most of the staff were gone. She was anxious to discuss the interview with Eli because, after cooking with him all day, it felt natural. He fit into the role of her partner like a hand in a glove, just like she'd imagined it would be with Jimmy.

But Eli was nothing at all like Jimmy. He wasn't that lighthearted guy. He was serious and competent and solid and exciting to be around, formidable and a little edgy. He had an aura of power around him, the power of his own will, the force of his firm mind and habits. It wasn't stubbornness, it was more a sureness about himself.

"The young man could be a distraction," he said as he followed her inside and stood against the filing cabinet with his arms folded. He made quite a picture, towering there with the muscles in his arms prominent and his shoulders wide in his cotton sweater, that had been hidden under his white cook's coat. She cleared her throat.

She had an idea what he meant about Mason being a distraction, but she wondered if Eli had any idea about how much more of a distraction *he* was. He was a hundred times more attractive, and in a much manlier way.

"What did you think?" Eli didn't beat around the bush, didn't give her a chance to wonder if he hoped to be let off the assignment.

As she gazed into his serious, earnest eyes, she decided to be straightforward. It was who she was. But she mentally crossed her fingers that she wouldn't be disappointing him.

"I have to admit that maybe last week I would have given Mason the job to see if it worked. But with you here, I feel grateful that I don't have to take the chance." She held her breath as he watched her.

"I agree. The kid is not appropriate. He's too green to start as a sous chef at a high-end grill—even if it is in the New Hampshire outback."

He let his grin show at the same time she let her breath out.

"I hope I didn't take over your role. I know you asked me for your help, but I have a natural inclination to take charge of things, to go all in. Must be why they liked me in the army."

She wasn't sure if he was trying to kid about them liking him in the army, but she knew he'd done well there and was being overly modest.

"I didn't mind. I asked for it. It was fun having another person to bounce things off of."

She shuffled some papers on the desk and found a pen to make a note to herself. She wondered why she hadn't minded Eli asserting himself so strongly, but then decided it was perfectly obvious wasn't it. She worked at keeping her blush from spreading yet again and busied herself with writing.

He stood there watching her, unmoving. Although she concentrated on her note, she was hyperaware of his gaze on her.

When she was ready to look up, she had to add her own assertion.

"Besides, I knew at all times that it would be my final decision no matter what."

He nodded and said, "Yes, *Mam*."

Six

*T*he Culinary Arts Academy of Switzerland calendar on the Grill's kitchen wall told her today was December 21st. A flutter unfurled in her stomach, leaving her jittery at the passage of time. The push and pull of her competing interests had her considering antacids. She had only a few days left to hire a permanent sous chef. On the other hand, if she did, Eli would leave and likely never return.

But she'd made a promise to Eli and to herself that she'd try, so she'd scheduled two more interviews that evening. It would be tricky juggling the prospective cooks with the holiday crowd at the restaurant.

All the staff would be on the schedule full-time until they closed the Grill at three p.m. on Christmas Eve. That had always been her family's tradition and she was smart enough to continue it. The restaurant would stay closed until December 27th for lunch. Everyone, including and especially Betsy, would get a two-and-a-half-day mini Christmas vacation.

"What's the special today, boss?" Frank shouted.

Audrey shouted back, "It's beef stew, Frank. Read the darn menu, would ya?"

Eli looked up from his slab of beef as he toweled it dry, almost massaging it. It didn't take more than a moment for him to catch her eye. It seemed she always had him in her sights, always aware of where he was and what he was doing and how he was doing it. It was after the lunch crowd and they were prepping for dinner, everything going smoothly, and she'd been standing by the door to the dining room.

"How about a butchering lesson today, Elizabeth?"

He wasn't exactly asking, but she went and stood next to him, passing by Frank, who rolled his eyes.

"You sure you want to let her wield a knife?" he said to Eli.

"You're the only one who has to worry about that, Frank," she said.

Eli eyed Frank. His expression was civil, but she couldn't quite tell what he thought. She'd have to ask him later, after work while they had their hot cocoa before they each returned home. She looked up at him, not meaning to sigh out loud, but she did.

"It's not that bad. I promise."

"Oh it's not the butchering. I'm looking forward to your tutelage."

"Say it like you mean it."

She didn't bother repressing her laugh and got started.

"We'll make half-inch cubes, but first I'll trim the fat and grizzle."

"I watch?"

"You watch for now. And listen. There'll be an exam tonight," he deadpanned without even looking up at her, but she was certain he was joking and she laughed again.

The kitchen staff clearly took note. Audrey wiggled her brows as she walked by and Betsy tried to keep her blush from blooming. Eli went on as if they were the only two in the place, confident and concise. She concentrated and fell under his spell. When he finally gave her the knife, she was nervous as if she'd never cut meat before which was ridiculous. She had, though not often and not well. She turned to her slab and began trimming the way he'd showed her. He said nothing, so she continued under his watch until she was finished. Then she looked up at him expectantly.

He nodded. When she thought he wouldn't give her any more feedback than that, his two dimples showed up and a swirl of pleasure went through her.

"Betsy, there's someone out front who wants to talk with you. Something about a New Year's Eve reservation." The hostess had pushed open the kitchen door and called to her.

Sorry she couldn't bask in the glow of Eli's approval, she excused herself and headed for the dining room with a light heart, feeling more than optimistic, more than a general contentment, but more like contented with an edge of excitement.

Toward the end of lunch service, as the crowd waned, Betsy took off her white coat to mix with some of the crowd. She'd seen Jack and Julie Lamont come in. She slipped from the kitchen to the dining room and found them at their table.

"How would you like to meet any restaurateur's dream sous chef, Eli Walker, Jimmy's best army buddy?"

"I would consider it a great treat. I noticed you sitting with him at Jimmy's service, and we were sorry we didn't have a chance to meet him then," Jack said. Julie popped up from her chair and had a look of fevered excitement in her eyes.

"You know I'd love, love, love to meet him. Last time Jimmy was home all he did was talk about his friend Eli and what a great talent he was."

"I'm here to tell you, for once, Jimmy wasn't exaggerating." Betsy put up her right hand to swear her words were true. Jack and Julie laughed as they followed her around to the kitchen door.

Betsy spied Eli through the opening before swinging into the kitchen. He was still at his station, cleaning up and plating his last meals for the lunch crowd it looked like. A lump of pride rose in her throat as she guided Jack and Julie through the kitchen to meet him, as if he were hers to show off. She couldn't help herself.

These were two of her favorite people in town and she wanted Eli to meet them.

He looked up as she approached with Jack and Julie, waiting for their introduction.

"Who do we have here?" His tone was gracious and warm, the way he sounded when he talked to Betsy's mother. When she'd commented on it before, he'd called it his Sunday company manners. The knowledge sent a wave of warmth through her, with some surprising sparks scattering through her mind and body.

"My friends. And favorite patrons of Betsy's Grill. Jack and Julie Lamont. They live in the mansion down the street — you might have noticed it."

He put out his hand and shook theirs in turn. "I have indeed noticed your home. Beautiful place."

"Speaking of beautiful…" Julie said, making it clear she was referring to Eli with her exaggerated once-over.

Betsy found herself holding her breath, remembering too late Julie's tendency to boldness.

"You are a wonder," Julie continued. "Beautiful food too — remarkable sauce on that beef stew, and perfect flaky dumplings. I bet you look great while you're cooking too." She held onto her husband's arm, and he had that familiar look of loving tolerance for his wife.

"Do you know who you look like?" Julie continued, "That movie star — "

"I've heard," Eli rolled his eyes but flashed his dimples. "Speaking of celebrity look-alikes, do you know you're a dead ringer for Audrey Hepburn? Albeit a taller version."

Julie laughed. "So I've been told. Have you ever modeled?"

Betsy thought her racing heart would stop with the strain of anxiety, as if her world depended on Eli making a good impression on her friends and her friends making a good impression on him. She couldn't imagine what Eli would think of such a question. She didn't have to wait to find out. After only a beat of silence, he burst into robust laughter.

"I guess that's a no," Jack said. "I didn't think so. I won the bet about whether you had, by the way." He winked.

"Smart man." Eli nodded, his beautiful grin still wide.

Betsy's heart continued to beat too fast, but now for a different reason. She was excited beyond words at how charming he was to her friends. Since he'd arrived, he'd pretty much had Betsy charmed like she was a kid following the Pied Piper.

"I want to personally invite you to our annual Christmas party," Julie said. "It's on Christmas Eve. We start at three and everyone in town who's ambulatory will be there."

A beat of silence followed, and Betsy hoped no one else felt the awkwardness in Eli's lack of immediate response. She darted a look at him to see his smile hadn't slipped, but she felt his tension, saw it in his eyes.

"If I'm still in town, I'll be there."

Betsy was prepared for this and jumped in.

"How was the service tonight?"

Getting the enthusiastic response she expected, she began ushering Jack and Julie back out of the kitchen while they said goodbye. They had to get back to their babysitter, who was really the family chauffeur.

When Betsy returned, she found that he'd plated two meals for them to have lunch at the small table in the kitchen. Relief flooded her. "How about if we eat in the office?" she said.

He nodded and they each picked up their dishes and silverware and brought them into the office, then Betsy closed the door. She knew she'd get teased for it and heard some muffled, good-natured commentary before she took a seat behind the desk. She cleared a place for her plate and set it down.

"Let me get us some wine," Eli said as he stood.

Before she had a chance to object, he was out the door again. Wine at lunchtime was unprecedented for him, though others on the kitchen staff often had wine with every meal. No one would tease him or say boo to him, she knew. He wasn't the teasable type, at least not by a casual acquaintance. She knew Jimmy had teased him all the time and now she could too.

Most of the time.

When he returned, he carried a bottle of *The Kings Wrath Pinot Noir 2012.*

"I found a very nice pinot, a Blue-Gold award winner from the Sydney International competition in 2015." He presented as if he were a sommelier, and opened the bottle and poured the wine in silence, with all his attention on what he was doing.

Betsy screwed up her courage to broach the subject she'd been dreading. "You're returning home for the holiday?"

"I'd planned to. My Ma is counting on me for Christmas dinner." Then he sat and looked into her eyes. "But I could stay for your friends' party and leave afterwards. I like driving at night. I have the road to myself."

As excited as she was about him staying for the party, she selfishly would miss him Christmas day, would hate to let him go. *Hoped dearly that he would return.*

"What are they like? Your family?"

He smiled. "They're an intimidating lot. Ambitious, disciplined, formal. You'd think they wouldn't know how to have fun, but they do. Holiday dinners are one of those occasions where all heck breaks loose. Once the preparations are over, the wine and spirits come out, and all the aunts, uncles, cousins, sisters, brothers, and kids come and go and laugh and fight." He shook his head with a wry smile.

"You'll be there. You *have* to be there."

"Don't worry, Elizabeth. I'll be back after Christmas. I won't leave you in the lurch."

"We have two more interviews this week. Good prospects." She added, "With experience."

He laughed. "Either way, I'll be back."

Eli held her eyes when he said the words and put a hand over hers. She thought she'd melt from the inside out. She felt his vibrating intensity and held her breath, not knowing what to say, reveling in the heady feelings swirling and making her want the moment to last forever.

Finally, she spoke in a whisper.

"You know you're always welcome." *To stay forever.*

She was mesmerized by him and his towering strength and unbending will and fortitude. She was a fluff-ball by comparison.

"But I know you are ambitious. I know you have places to go, dreams to realize." She took a breath and when he looked like he was going to say something, she went on. "I think you're destined for big things. I can see you with a Michelin-starred restaurant in DC."

"I confess, that has been my dream — or rather goal. Jimmy told you about it, right?"

"He might have mentioned it." The tightness in her chest made her want to lighten the mood, relieve the intensity of her feelings in the small closed room. She resisted dashing to the door to open it for air.

Instead she took a deep breath while he ate, and said, "I wish that all your dreams will come true. That's my Christmas wish for you."

He looked up, warmth, worry, and confusion all on his face. That was how she felt, she realized, not knowing how to feel, how to be with him, with each other.

Who are we to each other, exactly?

When he didn't respond, and she couldn't stand his silence for another strained heartbeat, she spoke again, albeit with false cheeriness.

"Did I tell you that the town has an annual Santa parade? Lucky for you it's late this year so you won't miss it. It's tomorrow."

"I heard some talk in the kitchen. Something about providing refreshments."

"We provide hot chocolate and fresh-made cinnamon apple donuts for parade goers. I have a cart. It's our tradition."

He nodded and took a sip of his wine.

She forged on. "Are you up for rising early to make the donuts?"

"You're talking to a trained soldier, ma'am. You play reveille and I'm up and at 'em."

She laughed, glad for the break of tension and his return to friendly humor. Maybe she'd imagined his earlier tenderness, read too much into his hand on hers. *They were friends. That was all.*

They stood, though she had hardly touched her meal.

"We can leave early tonight and let Frank close up. We have an early morning."

He opened the office door, his smile so genuine and unexpected that she slipped her arm through his to walk down the short hall back into the kitchen. He allowed her familiarity, letting her lean into his warmth.

But then he stopped as if he remembered something.

"If we're going to be in early tomorrow morning, then I have an errand I need to run now before we get busy with dinner." He withdrew with no further explanation. He hadn't been asking for her permission. He was there as a favor, so she couldn't expect him to act like an employee.

But then, even if he *had* been her permanent sous chef, she couldn't imagine treating him as an employee, couldn't think of him as an employee. She supposed it was a good thing that he was there only temporarily. The way she felt about him was messed up and confusing. She wanted him to stay, but not as her sous chef.

As her what? There was nothing else for him here.

His manner hadn't invited inquiry so she didn't ask what the errand was and he didn't say. As she watched him leave through the back door and go to his rental car, she reminded herself that it was none of her business. She had no standing with him, only her startling attraction, messy feelings, and their undefined relationship.

Eli took his car and tapped in the address for Jimmy Bell's parents' house. He'd called the day before and left a message, but he hadn't heard back. No matter, it was best to talk to them about such matters in person. In his message, he mentioned Jimmy's will and he hoped that wasn't the reason for their lack of response, but he'd find out soon enough.

It was a short drive and he pulled into the driveway. They were retired, but Eli had no idea what retired people did with their time. His family hadn't been known for retirement or sitting back, not even in their old age.

He rang the doorbell of the modest, shingled Cape Cod house and stood under the cold, cloudy sky, blowing on his hands. He'd need to buy some warm gloves if he was going to stay.

But he couldn't stay much longer. He'd promised his mother he'd be home. His family would be disappointed after he'd missed the last three Christmases at home.

Ringing the doorbell again, he glanced around. No one was out and about in the small neighborhood, not even on the ice-covered lake at the end of the street that shone pristine and waited for skaters. It was far too cold, he supposed. After waiting another minute, he went back to the car and cranked up the heat. Maybe he ought to buy a coat too while he was at it, but he hadn't seen any men's clothing stores in this town and he had no idea where he'd find one.

On his way back to Betsy's Grill, he did stop at the local store to buy those gloves. Even if he only needed them for one more day, it was worth it. Besides, he knew he wouldn't be leaving her until Christmas Eve, even if she hired someone tomorrow.

For one thing, he had to get to the bottom of what had happened to the money Jimmy had set aside for Elizabeth in his will. It was very curious that she'd never heard about the will, or she must not care about it. Otherwise she would have brought it up when they spoke about her improvements to the restaurant. But Eli didn't want to think the worst until he had to.

Then there was another small matter that he couldn't deny any longer, and that he had no idea what to do about. His attraction to Elizabeth was harder and harder to ignore. The problem was, he was certain that was more reason to leave than to stay.

Seven

After their now familiar ritual of sharing morning coffee with Eli and her mother at the kitchen island, Eli drove Betsy to the Grill so they could make the donuts for the parade. He'd been picking her up each day and driving her home each evening. At the Grill, they were joined by Callie who'd volunteered to make the hot chocolate. By the time they were finished, taste-testing too many donuts in the process and laughing about it, Frank got the old cart out of the storage shed out back with Eli's help.

"You working the parade with Betsy?" Frank asked after the cart was loaded with fresh donuts and hot chocolate and ready to roll out to the sidewalk.

Eli looked at Betsy and, if she was right in her interpretation of this sometimes mysterious man, his look held regret and longing and resignation.

"No, I need to stay and cook," he said.

"Yes, I mean no. Eli, you don't need to stay," she said. "We have a special sandwich menu for lunch on parade day. The prep cooks can handle it. They always do." She beamed, waiting for his expression to change, but it remained reluctant at best. She added, "It's *tradition*."

Tradition seemed to be the magic word, because his face cleared. She should have known, maybe she *had* known and that's why she'd said it. A blip of pleasure rose and jiggled her heart. He was a challenging man to know, but she would know him. She *wanted* to know every little corner of him. Nearly blushing at her bold thought, she took hold of his arm and took hold of the cart and they took off for their place in the prime spot along the parade route about a block away from the town hall where the parade ended. Right out in front of Betsy's Grill.

"I suppose if we're going to be right here, I can always run inside to check on things," he said.

"You could if it'll make you feel better."

He tried not to smile. "You know it would."

She did know that.

"Besides, it's freezing out here."

"It is a bit colder than ideal," she agreed as she looked at how he was dressed, unfit for the weather with his open-collared wool coat, no hat, no scarf and what looked like discount-store gloves.

"You need a scarf," she said.

"I need some of this hot cocoa and I'll be fine." Pouring a cup for their first customers of the day, he then handed it to a teenage girl, who looked at him as if he were from Mount Olympus. He promptly took off his gloves, stuffing them into his pockets. "Don't need these."

"I'll be right back."

"Don't worry. I can handle this on my own," he said as several young boys lined up for donuts and hot chocolate.

"I like you when you're a wise guy."

"You must have me confused with someone else."

She laughed and went back inside the restaurant to sneak out the back door to her car. There was a scarf in her trunk, wrapped up as a gift. She'd knitted it herself a year ago. It had been meant for Jimmy, but it was fitting that Eli should have it, the least she could do for him. As she walked back into the restaurant, ripping the wrapping paper off, a barrage of guilt hit her. She threw the paper in the trash and kept going, needing to give the scarf to Eli.

It wasn't rational to feel like she was giving away a piece of Jimmy. It wasn't as if she was giving it to a stranger. Once she exited the front door and saw him standing at the cart, the subtle body language telling her he was cold, any trace of guilt disappeared. Eli not only handled the crowd, but it looked like he was attaining a cult following of kids. She supposed they knew who he was, or might have guessed since Jimmy's memorial service. Jimmy had been hailed a hero and so Eli was too, by association, even though they might not know he was every bit a hero in his own right. Maybe more so, according to some of the stories she'd heard.

"I have something for you," she said. "If I can tear you away from your fans for a minute."

"You mean these hungry, donut-loving customers?"

The kids hooted and giggled. She slipped the scarf from behind her, reached up, and wrapped it around his neck.

"You were underdressed for the occasion."

He gazed at her, disbelief, delight, and satisfaction playing across the chiseled features of his face. Touching the scarf, caressing it with reverence, the way he looked at her, the way he made her feel, dispelled any notion that he shouldn't have it.

In fact, he was the perfect person to give the scarf to. Satisfaction settled in, but the eyes of the crowd surrounding them pricked the bubble of her absorption with Eli and she turned to the cart and their audience of customers. Eli stood next to her, close, his energy surrounding her, penetrating her, lifting her so that she felt giddy.

"We still have donuts to give away and hot chocolate. Who wants some?" she said.

They were busy until they ran out of everything and it was time to bring the cart in. Before they did, she saw Jimmy's parents and waved.

"That looks like Mr. and Mrs. Bell," Eli said.

"Yes. It would be nice for you to have a chance to talk to

them." She waved again. They raised their hands, but Mr. Bell took his wife's arm, flashed a look in Eli's direction, and took her in the other direction. Betsy shivered as if she could feel the man's cold shoulder from thirty feet away. She hoped like heck that Eli hadn't noticed, but when she looked at him, his eyes were on the retreating couple, the line of his mouth grim.

She couldn't imagine what the problem was, but she had a feeling he knew.

"What's that all about?"

"Nothing. I don't think they want to talk to me."

"Why wouldn't they—"

He turned to her. "Because they know what I want to talk about. And I don't think they want to hear it."

What did he mean? He was making no sense.

"Let's pack up the cart," he said, giving her one of those devastating smiles. She was never sure if he knew what his smiles did, the line of devastation he could wreak with his dimples in the otherwise hard-angled face. But maybe he did know. Maybe that was why he issued the smile sparingly.

They went inside after getting the cart back into storage and put on their coats for the dinner prep. She had to ask, had to know even though she knew it wouldn't be pleasant. She put a hand on his arm before he went to his station and pulled him aside into the back hall.

"Tell me what it's about. The business with the Bells."

He gave her a long hard look, the contemplative she'd come to know, that had become achingly familiar to her, but this time with an edge, an uncertainty.

When she didn't think he would share, he spoke.

"I called them and went to see them. Told them I wanted to speak with them about Jimmy's will, the one he told me he'd written leaving everything to you."

"Everything?" Her voice sounded too high, like her throat was being squeezed. She didn't know what to think. Her mind refused to work through the implications of his words, saw the dark possibilities there.

"Yes." He looked up at the ceiling and took a deep breath before continuing. "Look, I'm sure there's an explanation. Wills and estates are never a simple thing, especially when it concerns a soldier's special effects brought in from the field. But I will talk to them. I will unravel the puzzle. And you will get what you're due."

"Eli, I don't need anything more." *Except you.*

He took her into a hug.

"Don't I know that, sugar. Don't I know." His whispered words ran through her in a shiver of pure pleasure and her giddiness returned, dispelling any foreboding sense she'd had before.

The giddiness lasted the rest of the day, long after they parted ways at the end of dinner that night.

"Betsy, what a nice surprise." Julie met her at the kitchen door of the Stillwater Inn and swept her inside amidst the overwhelming scents of baked goods.

Even though Betsy spent every day with him and had just seen Eli the night before, she'd wanted to see him again, couldn't wait to see him again. Maybe she shouldn't have come here for breakfast. Maybe she should have waited until *after* breakfast. Her waistline was already a challenge. But then she saw him.

Eli rose majestically from his chair at the farm table in the center of the kitchen. He looked at home and out of place at the same time in his starched white dress shirt and his dark skin gleaming in contrast. She didn't know when she'd seen anything so beautiful as his face, his smile, as all of him.

Her heart filled her throat and she smiled back.

"A very pleasant surprise." He swept a hand, inviting her to join him at the table.

"It took some doing to convince your Eli to eat breakfast in the kitchen with us," Julie said, "but we were dying for his very fascinating company and he decided not to deprive us."

"And Julie promised to share a recipe and baking tips. Baking has been my weak spot."

"Nonsense. You have no weaknesses, Eli."

He gave her a meaningful nod, and she nearly fainted with the thrill it sent through her veins.

Could he be thinking she *was his weakness? Could he be feeling as overwhelmed with feelings for her as she was with him?*

"My, my. I don't know how it's possible, but I think the temperature in this kitchen just jumped up about fifty degrees. You two are something." Julie grinned and Betsy's blush was instantaneous as Eli pushed in her chair as if he was the maître d' at a fancy restaurant and she was the queen of the world. He held his calm, dignified demeanor.

"Maybe you're burning some cupcakes," he said to Julie.

"Something's burning up alright."

He cleared his throat and resumed his seat. But when Betsy dared to meet his eyes, there was a twinkle. He reached his hand out and put it over hers. In plain sight, on the table next to her napkin, his dark hand covered hers and it was so magnificent a sight and feeling that she wanted to take a picture and capture it.

"What brings you to the inn for breakfast, Elizabeth?" he said.

"You do, Eli. I wanted to have breakfast with you this morning."

He nodded.

"Is your mother all right with you abandoning her for my company?"

"She sleeps in most days so I left her a note. She'll be fine." She felt the air around them crackle while the warmth of his hand over hers seeped into her bones, sending chills of excitement at the same time. It was the oddest and most exquisite feeling she'd ever felt about a man. Any man. Ever. *Even Jimmy.* She had no idea what to do with it, with herself.

This was the only thing she could do. Seek him out, spend her time with him, staring at him, feeling him touch her — even if it was just her hand — in hopes for a kiss. And heaven help her for her very naughty thoughts, maybe much more than a kiss one day. She wished it would be one day soon, but she knew better than that, knew him better than that.

Eli was the consummate gentleman. There would be no improprieties, never mind they were living in the twenty-first century and the notion didn't translate well these days. He had his standards, lived by his own set of rules. He'd told her that, and she believed him. She'd seen him in action.

"Watch the muffins for me. I need to go… do something," Julie said as she pushed through the kitchen's door into the dining room.

Betsy let out a breath and exchanged a grin with Eli. Then she ramped up her courage, her heart beating faster, rising to her throat in anticipation.

"Tomorrow's Christmas Eve." She paused, not sure what she would say next. "I know I don't have a sous chef yet, but the restaurant is closed for two days so you're off the hook if you want to go home for the holidays like I know you planned to. You don't even have to come back — "

"Stop it, Elizabeth. I'm not on any hook. You couldn't manipulate me into doing anything I don't want to do — even if you were inclined to manipulation, which I know you're not."

"What does that mean? Are you staying for the party?"

He chuckled, that wondrous deep reverberating chuckle that warmed and excited her and affected her down to her core.

"Yes, that's what it means."

Feeling giddy under his affectionate gaze, because that look he gave her couldn't mean any less, she ventured further.

"You mean as my date?" She nearly whispered the words, feeling daring, with her heart throbbing in her throat.

He nodded and leaned in.

"I will be your date. I may as well acknowledge what

everyone else seems to sense. I'm sweet on you, Elizabeth."

She felt a flash of heat like none other. No other experience compared to this dizzying excitement, this thrill, these feelings she had for Eli — wonderful, amazing, strong Eli. Her feelings for Jimmy had stewed for a long time, nurtured by the sunny cheer and good humor between them, but they had never been anything like this vortex of aliveness. She'd swear she could feel every one of the trillion nerve endings in her body right at that moment.

She laughed at his old-fashioned admission.

"You really are a throwback to another era, aren't you? A true gentleman."

"I like to think of that as a good thing."

She nodded, the tension in her spiraling up from her center to constrict her throat, making it impossible to speak for a moment. "I think you know I'm *sweet on you*, too," she finally said.

He leaned in closer, causing a sizzling, delicious heat to melt her, make her squirm with desire as his hot breath filled her senses. She felt nothing less than wicked and was glad he seemed under control, the gentleman to her unladylike stirrings.

After all, they were in the kitchen of the Stillwater Inn where anyone could walk in at any minute. No matter, she leaned closer, inviting him to kiss her, wishing and hoping he would in spite of his restraint.

When he moved, closing the small slice of air left between their mouths, it shocked her. Eyelids fluttering closed, her heart stopped for a beat, the whole world seemed to stop while all she could feel was the soft hot cushion of his lips on hers, pressing, caressing, and then gone as he pulled back on a deep croaking sigh.

With her heart stuttering back to life, pounding now as if she were sprinting, she took a breath, instantly wanting more.

"I—" he began to say. But she stopped him because if he was — about to apologize, she didn't want to hear it, didn't want him to be sorry.

"No. I mean, that was so… dreamy," she said.

He put a hand to her cheek, large and warm, rough calluses on the pads of his fingertips where he gripped the kitchen knives gently caressing her skin. She closed her eyes.

"I know what you mean." He sighed.

They both turned when they heard Julie making noise at the dining room door, announcing her return, with throat clearing and bumping the door open partially, then again before she came fully back inside. He dropped his hand from Betsy's cheek, although he still leaned closer than he'd been before Julie left the room.

"I'm back," Julie announced.

Betsy exchanged a glance with Eli and they both broke into laughter.

Eight

There hadn't been much time, but he'd needed to find a gift appropriate for Elizabeth and one for her mother. It wasn't his normal habit to shop on Christmas Eve morning, but this day had been an exception. It was right no matter if she expected it, no matter that he wouldn't be there when she woke up on Christmas day. He pulled his car into the Carters' driveway.

That morning he'd called to promise his mother that he'd be home for Christmas dinner. He was cutting it close, but he was used to cutting the meat close to the bone. Used to having people depend on him and not letting them down.

He would attend the Christmas party at Julie and Jack's house that evening, like he'd promised Elizabeth. He was going to take care of Jimmy's last wishes like he'd promised him, even if that meant he needed to confront Jimmy's parents. The Christmas party would be his last chance to do so before going home.

He wasn't sure he'd be coming back. He'd never made a promise about that. They'd managed to hire a sous chef the other day—not Mason George—and he'd start after the New Year. Eli had a commitment to buy a restaurant in DC, had promised his backers he'd create a Michelin-rated restaurant for them. It was all in writing, but that didn't matter. He'd given his word.

Now, as he got out of his rental car, after two short weeks, his ritual of picking up Elizabeth to take her to the Grill had become his life, had become something he cherished. Something he hated to think he'd be giving up.

But he'd given his word. People were counting on him to keep it.

When he would have pressed the doorbell, Mrs. Carter swung the door open to let him in.

"You're still ringing the doorbell like you don't belong here. Step inside, make yourself at home, young man." She grinned at him, dressed in red and looking peppy and moving with more ease than he'd seen in days.

He went into the kitchen where Elizabeth stood at the counter pouring rich-smelling hot cocoa into three mugs. This was the time to give her his gift. And Jimmy's gift too. As he sat on his stool between the two women as was his habit, he pulled the small box from his pocket.

He gave her his gift. "This is for you." He probably should have given her mother her gift first, but he couldn't wait to see the smile on her face that he saw now. Wonder and appreciation and, most of all, that adoration, undeserved as it was, that made him wish he could have more, have her in his future, see where it would take him. But all he could see was trouble in that line of thinking.

"I'm so excited." She tore open the wrapping paper and opened the box. He watched her face light up as she lifted the crystal angel ornament up to the light. "It's so beautiful and special." She twirled it around. "And you had it engraved."

In the space where the year was usually carved were the words, "Eli was here." He watched her face as she read the words, watched the sparkle of tears and the wavering smile.

"It's perfect." She put the ornament in the box on the counter and opened her arms, leaned in and hugged him, warm hands caressing his back, scorching him through his sweater. He wrapped his arms around her and drew her closer, squeezing his eyes shut and taking her in, her loving, giving soul, her strength, her beauty and the warmth that reached his bones and beyond to his manly desire. Then he let her go.

"It's a lovely gift, Eli," Mrs. Carter said. "You've certainly left your mark." She nodded and he felt like Mrs. Carter knew what was in his mind and heart and he felt her sympathy.

"I have a gift for you too." He pulled a wrapped package from a bag he had and gave it to her. She opened it to find a book.

"It's a historical novel that takes place in a small town in New Hampshire. It was written by a resident of this town about fifty years ago."

"Oh, I might know her." Mrs. Carter flipped it open to the bio of the author and her eyes widened. "I do know her! She was a teacher of mine when I went to school here. How amazing." The older woman proceeded to throw her arms around him and plant a kiss on his cheek.

"How thoughtful, Eli," she continued. "How ever did you find that book?"

"I talked to some people and found a used book store that I was told had everything, and so I went and looked around. This one was recommended to me by the owner."

He reached back into his bag and pulled out one more thing.

"This is what Jimmy wanted you to have." He handed her a leather pouch. He had no idea what was in it. He speculated it was love letters, maybe some money. But he had promised himself he wouldn't open it, and he hadn't. Jimmy had meant for Elizabeth to have it, not him.

"I have something for you, too. I made it to match the scarf."

He opened the package to find a warm woolen hat with *Hamlin, NH* knitted into it. He looked up at her as he put it on.

"So you'll remember me — us, always." She stretched out her arm to include her mother.

"Don't you bother. I got my own gift for Eli." Mrs. Carter slipped a wrapped gift from a cabinet drawer. "Had it stashed for the occasion." She handed it to him and said, "I made it myself. It's for when you're back up to this cold part of the country."

He felt his chest tighten as he took the gift. Putting form aside, he reached out and hugged the woman. She hugged him back with no hint at any weakness or that she was scrawny and fragile. Tearing open the package, he wasn't surprised to find a perfect pair of hand-knit wool mittens — that happened to match the scarf and hat — and put them on.

"It's exactly what I needed, exactly what I wanted. I'll wear them from now on. It gets cold down in Virginia too." He knew his words fell short of expressing how he felt. It must have been hard for her to knit these for him with her arthritis. He hoped the hug he gave Mrs. Carter told her everything.

"Now I'm all cheery and wound up and you two are going off to work, but I suppose you must."

"It'll be a fun day. You should come for lunch, Mom."

Mrs. Carter waved a hand. "Don't want to spoil my appetite for the big party."

"That's right. We'll be bringing some of Jimmy's special dish and dessert," he said. He hoped he could enjoy himself in spite of the fact that he would need to speak with the Bells there. It would be his last chance before he left town. His last chance for a good long while, with the schedule he had waiting for him.

"Will the Bells be at the party?" He felt the need to confirm their presence as he and Elizabeth stepped out into the bright cold morning.

She stopped and turned to him just before they reached the car.

"Yes, of course. Why? You aren't — "

"Yes, I am." He put up a hand when she began to protest. "You're right if you're going to tell me it's terrible form, impolite, even uncivil to bring up the subject of their son's will at a Christmas party. But I have no choice. They won't talk to me. It's better that I talk to them before I hire an attorney to look into things."

"An attorney? You really think—"

"Absolutely. I'm firm on this, Elizabeth. Jimmy didn't ask me for much, but he asked for this one thing, for me to see to it that you were taken care of, to see that his will leaving you his things was honored."

Eli watched the shock and dismay evaporate into an almost frown, as if she were fighting her displeasure and determined to beat it. Then the worshipful smile returned to her lips, whether he deserved it or not. He mostly didn't. Like Jimmy, she didn't ask much of him. But she gave him all the benefit of the doubt, all her confidence, all her sweet disposition had to offer. He had to make sure he didn't take more than he could afford to repay.

He was already teetering on the edge of what was right with his stolen kiss. Heaven help him, but he couldn't bring himself to wish it back. The only question was what would he do about it? Would he be able to forego kissing her ever again? And what did Elizabeth want?

He could only imagine, and he imagined he would fall far short when he left here tomorrow morning never to return. But she'd get over him. *She'd gotten over Jimmy, hadn't she?*

He didn't want to think those thoughts. They caused nauseating bile to reach his throat as he contemplated leaving this place. Leaving her. And he was made of stronger stuff than that. He'd withstood whatever the armed services had thrown at him, including the loss of his best friend, so he ought to be able to handle leaving a woman behind after such a short time knowing her.

So far, it didn't feel like something that would be easy at all, not even compared to war.

They talked about food as he drove her to the restaurant.

"Today I'll guess your favorite dessert," she said.

"You know I have a devilish sweet tooth?" he confessed.

"No, but it doesn't surprise me."

"No, I guess not. After all I'm falling for you and you are the sweetest thing I've ever met."

She snapped her head to look at him and he braced himself as she wrapped her arms around him, careful not to interfere with the steering wheel.

"I'm so glad I'm not the only one," she whispered and kissed his temple. He held the hand she'd placed over his heart and cursed himself for letting his mouth run. But he was a man, not made of granite or ice, and she'd melted his heart as sure as if it were a slab of butter on a hot grill.

She pulled back and looked at him with that giddy smile she had that made his heart race, heating him up to boiling. He held her hand and felt her warmth through their gloves the rest of the short drive.

When they arrived at the grill, as they walked in the back door, she held his arm, halting him, and said, "What are we going to do about it?"

He waited a few painful beats, aware that he looked grim, unable to give her false hope.

"I don't know. I have commitments in DC. I have to leave tomorrow, Elizabeth."

Her sweet smile wavered slightly before she cemented it in place.

"We'll work something out."

She let him go and then walked inside her kitchen.

He should have said something, shouldn't have let her go thinking they might work things out, impossible things. But he was too weak to argue. And he wanted desperately to believe she was right, that there was a glimmer of hope.

The truth was, he couldn't see a way for it to work. Their goals and dreams and wishes were at cross purposes. He had dreams for a Michelin-starred restaurant in D.C. and her whole life was filled with this small town and Betsy's Grill. He knew she loved it here, knew she'd never leave her mother alone. Knew it was hopeless and he'd been a fool to express his feelings.

He'd have to make things right tonight, stop leading her on. And leave with honor.

They'd both gone home to get ready for the Lamont's Christmas party which was more like a gala. Betsy felt excitement rise in her as she dressed. Her mother had already left for the party with their neighbors, so when Eli came to pick her up, it would be just the two of them. It would be like they were on a date and she would feel like it, but she wasn't sure if that's how he meant it when he'd insisted he wanted to pick her up and take her to the party. He'd said it was on the way, but still...

Taking special care with her make up and hair, Betsy looked older to herself in the mirror, more mature and sophisticated than she'd ever felt. Her dress was red and scooped to a daring level, but it was tasteful her mother had insisted when she bought it for the party. The A-line style was flattering and she felt pretty. She felt like she needed to get out more.

Maybe she would if Eli came back...

When the doorbell rang, she was more than ready, her heart feeling like a runaway train, and yet she hesitated, nervous. Eli was on the other side of the door, and good, bad or otherwise, she adored him, wanted a relationship with him, more than friends, more than a flirtation. She wanted a full-fledged romance.

She opened the door and satisfaction sizzled through her at his expression of lustful appreciation as he looked her over.

"Wow." It was all he said and she laughed and grabbed her coat.

They arrived at the party and went in the back door to the kitchen with Eli bringing the large containers of Pasta Bella inside and her carrying the desserts. The caterers took over and they went through the kitchen to the foyer.

"That was some kitchen," Eli said when she led him to the great-room where the party was being held.

"I know. This whole place is impressive, especially since Julie took charge. You'd think all the money would change her, but it hasn't."

"I could tell. I like the Lamonts," Eli said as Julie and Jack approached them.

"That's what we like to hear," Jack said slapping Eli on the back and shaking his hand. "Thanks for bringing in that pasta dish. It smells great."

"Wait til you taste it," Betsy said. "I think it's going to be the new star of my menu. Thanks to Jimmy and Eli." She couldn't help the wisp of melancholy mixing with her excitement and joy at the thought of Jimmy. The holidays had always been difficult. Until now.

She looked at Eli and felt like he was reading her mind, saw the wistfulness in his expression, felt comforted and yet giddy at the same time when he took her hand and squeezed it. They each took a glass of champagne from a server passing by and then Eli escorted her with his hand touching and torching the small of her back. His hand was the only thing she could feel, the sole occupant of her mind as she absorbed the heat, the proprietary nature of the pressure, leading her.

Not caring where she was going, she was surprised and pleased when he found them a spot on a love seat in an out of the way corner.

"Let's sit here so we can talk."

She nodded, not sure at all if she could talk with all the emotions clogging her throat and him sitting so near, his thigh against hers, his scent surrounding her. She felt like a school girl might feel, but like she never had back then. She'd never had this intense a feeling about a boy or a man. It struck her again that it had been so very different with Jimmy.

Allowing the momentary twinge of something, wistfulness

or guilt, to pass her by, the party faded away, and she saw and heard only Eli as he spoke.

"What's your fondest Christmas wish, Elizabeth?"

You.

She didn't dare say how she felt aloud. She had no right, no hold on him, hardly a wisp of a chance of seeing him again, let alone having the kind of relationship where she could call him her own. Instead she shrugged and turned the tables.

"What is your Christmas wish? What are your dreams and hopes, Eli?" She wanted to know, hoped she could be part of it. He gave her a long, almost hard look before answering her. Her heart banged around, her stomach felt queasy and she suddenly wanted to take the question back as if it would change anything.

"I've always wanted to own a Michelin Star restaurant in Washington, D.C., one of the most sophisticated and competitive markets in the world for restaurants."

She nodded. "I'm not surprised. That's a big wish."

When he looked away from her for a beat, the dread rose in her throat, her emotions were running wild inside her. And then he turned back, his face a mask, determined and distant.

"I have a deal in the works now. I have a meeting with financiers willing to back me." He paused another beat. "Next week."

The bottom dropped from under her and she felt like her heart and all her insides fell through a black hole. He'd known all along that he wouldn't be coming back, wouldn't be seeing her again, wouldn't have a real lasting relationship with her. A shudder took her, gave her the shake she needed for self-preservation.

"It's closer to a reality than a dream. I hadn't realized," she turned away.

"Elizabeth…" He touched her cheek. She felt the pink blush appear, felt the sparkle of tears in her eyes, but she held them back.

"I know. I knew… you were a city boy — man, after all."

"A city boy. That's me." He forced a smile. It didn't help. She felt him slipping away, but couldn't let him go, not yet.

"Tell me about your dreams, Elizabeth. What's your Christmas wish?"

She needed to let him know that she couldn't see herself as part of his future, in case he didn't already know it. In case it meant anything to him.

"I… I want to establish Betsy's Grill as the place to go. Make it the center piece of the town's social life, make it a town institution, a place people treasure and will continue to treasure." She turned to him, cleared her throat, and spoke in a strong, almost defiant voice. "I want to get married and have babies and bring them up in this town, proud to live here, steeped in our traditions. Pass Betsy's Grill on to the next generation."

"Exactly what I thought." He might have looked sad under his resignation, but there was too much steel in his eyes to know. She felt emotion welling, but she held it firmly in place when she saw Julie heading their way.

"There you are," Julie said. "Come on with me, you two. It's time for Harold to sing us some Christmas carols and we need plenty of people to join in the chorus." She took Elizabeth's hand and, just like that, their moment ended.

Elizabeth stood, separating from him, leaving him with a chill. He stood too. He needed to make the most of this night, enjoy her sweetness and do his best to leave her whole and with dignity. No tears, no regrets, only appreciation for sharing this slice of their lives with each other.

There was one other thing he had to do tonight. It was something that might spoil the evening if she witnessed it, so he needed to be discreet. It was time to confront Jimmy's parents.

Nine

Spotting the Bells on the other side of the room, near the entry to the foyer, he took a deep breath and steeled himself. He didn't relish confronting them about their dead son and his final wishes. But this was for Elizabeth. It had to be done.

They saw him when he was only a few feet away and escaped into the foyer. That worked fine for Eli. He didn't want to have this conversation in the middle of the party. He followed them with his long strides and caught up to them near the grand staircase.

"I'd like to have a word with you, Mr. and Mrs. Bell."

They stopped and turned to him. Mr. Bell looked resigned, and nodded. "Go ahead. Say what you have to say."

"It's about Jimmy's last wishes. He told me he'd made a will. He wanted me to know he'd left everything to Elizabeth."

"Betsy?" Mr. Bell said, incredulity lacing his words — and maybe a few drinks as well.

"Now, dear." Mrs. Bell put a hand on her husband's arm.

"Yes. He left a substantial sum of money to her. It was money he had put aside for purchasing a restaurant when he got out of the service." Eli didn't bother mentioning that Jimmy had planned to partner with him in a restaurant out of town. Something told him that wouldn't please Mr. Bell.

The older man scoffed.

"So you say. Let me get this straight," his voice rose. "You're saying there's a will somewhere and it says *Betsy* is supposed to get all Jimmy's money?"

"Yes." He took a deep breath. "I thought you would know about it because you received all Jimmy's personal effects. The will must have been among them."

And there it was. His cards on the table. His accusation was clear enough to make Mrs. Bell's eyes to widen while she squeezed her husband's arm tighter.

"There is no will." Bell's voice boomed now. "You don't know what you're talking about, boy."

Eli couldn't help flinching. But he didn't move, held himself still as a mountain, cool as an iceberg, even while he felt people's attention moving toward them, heard the din of the party quieting.

"You have any proof that Jimmy left a will?" Mr. Bell stepped forward as he bellowed, wrenching free from his wife's grip. She looked worried.

Eli had no proof, only a quiet, last conversation with his best friend before he'd slipped away. He had the name of a lawyer Jimmy mentioned and Eli hoped he could track the attorney down and that the attorney would have a copy of the will. He'd hoped it wouldn't come to that, hoped he wouldn't need to involve anyone else.

He said nothing. There was no point.

"Where is this will you're talking about? Do you have a copy of it? Have you ever even seen it?"

"No." Eli spoke surely, but quietly, abhorring the scene Mr. Bell's loud voice caused, drawing the attention of more and more people until Elizabeth appeared with Julie and Jack, their hosts, circling behind him.

"I didn't think so. Maybe you should leave—"

"No, he shouldn't leave." Elizabeth came to stand next to him, taking his arm and lifting her chin.

Eli had no choice then, he didn't want to be responsible for any rift between her and Jimmy's parents, any more than he'd already caused. They were all she had left of him, such as they were.

"It's all right, Elizabeth. I was just leaving. It's time I returned home." *For good.*

"That's right. Go back to wherever you came from with your vile accusations and your uppity ways. We don't need you and your kind here."

He heard Elizabeth's intake of breath and her tensing beside him. He heard the intake of a lot of breath around the room.

It was crazy, but the hurled insult calmed him, solidified his decision to leave, took all the guesswork, all the hesitation, out of it. He turned and met Elizabeth's glistening, hurt eyes with the anger brimming underneath. He couldn't say goodbye to her, not here, not with all these people. But maybe it was better that way.

He took her arms and gave them a squeeze and then he walked away. Spine ramrod straight, he walked through the entry hall and left through the front door. If the look on her face hadn't stopped him, then he wouldn't let the suffocating tightening of his chest stop him either. He got in the car and drove away on that dark starry cold night.

Betsy stayed at Julie and Jack's party with her mother and did her best to hide her disappointment that Eli had left. She felt emptier than ever, even more empty than she'd felt when Jimmy died, heaven help her. The spark she'd had with Eli made her feel more alive than she'd ever felt and now that it was gone and she feared she'd never see him again, she realized the depth of her feelings.

It looked like her unspoken Christmas wish for a lasting romance, a future with Eli, would not come true after all. But she had already made a Christmas wish. Hers had been for Eli's dreams to come true. Ironically it was he who'd told her to make a wish and that he would wish and hope and pray for it to come true.

And now he was the only one who could make it come true for real, and he was the one who kept it from happening. She'd made two wishes. One for herself and one for him and they both couldn't come true. Only one. It was in Eli's power to pick which one it was.

And he'd made his choice.

He'd left her to pursue his dream of having a restaurant in DC instead of a romance with her. She glanced out the window into the night sky. Snowflakes floated down, but she couldn't get excited about having a white Christmas now. She would have loved to share the excitement with Eli.

He'd chosen his Michelin-starred restaurant over her and it was hard for her to accept. Harder than it should have been since they'd only met a couple of weeks ago. She had no real claim to him.

But they'd had a connection. It had been deep and alive and soulful and had filled her with contentment, the kind she'd never had before, the kind that made her think she'd found the missing piece of her soul, her other half. The other side of herself. It had never been that way with Jimmy. They'd been too much alike in so many ways, more like comrades, two peas in a pod. It had been lovely, but it hadn't given her soul the kind of zap she got from seeing Eli across a room, or from touching his face.

Or from his kiss, his mind-blowing, bone-melting kiss.

The kiss she'd never forget. The kiss whose memory would have to satisfy her for the rest of her life.

Until the front door opened.

Betsy could feel the arctic breeze that floated inside with the smell of fresh snow as she stepped out into the foyer. She stopped short when she saw Eli standing on the threshold, the tall majestic black man against the glowing white snowy background and the starry night. The sight started her heart and she ran forward to him, without a thought, without a decision. She threw herself into his arms after he'd barely had a chance to close out the cold behind him.

"I couldn't go," he said into her hair, wrapping her in his strong arms, pulling her against his strong body. She pushed her arms inside his cold coat to find his body warm and thrilling to the touch.

"Elizabeth, you know we're in public. You're testing my resolve to remain a gentleman." She heard the smiling note in his voice and pulled back to look up at him.

"You know you've granted my wish."

He nodded his head.

"You know you've granted *my* wish," he said back to her.

"I think that's impossible, Eli," she whispered. Her excitement ebbed even as her heart beat fast and all kinds of things were swirling around inside her, throwing her off balance.

"No, it's not. It'll be a challenge. But I've made up my mind, and I'll move heaven and earth to make this work."

"What about your restaurant? The plans, the deal you made?"

She thought she saw a flinch, but his mouth turned up in a surprising smile instead of the grim line she'd expected.

"I'll work it out. Besides, we already have a restaurant."

"What about Jimmy's parents?" she whispered the words, glad that they'd left the party after some discreet words from Jack.

"I'll have an attorney handle it. I probably should have done that in the first place, but I thought it would be better if I spoke with them." He heaved a sigh. "I was wrong. I'm sorry I ruined the Christmas party." He looked over her head, into the large room off the foyer where someone played "Jingle Bells" on the piano and people sang along.

"You didn't ruin anything. You've made my night. But we shouldn't stay too late if you're going to leave early enough in the morning to make it home for Christmas dinner."

He nodded and looked into her eyes.

"Did I ever tell you that you're one of the most giving women I've ever known?"

She couldn't speak past the clog of emotion in her throat, but she shook her head.

"You know I'll be back as fast as I can?"

She nodded and wrapped her arms around his neck.

"Elizabeth, you're being naughty again. There are people in the next room." She kissed his jaw, then trailed kisses all the way to the corner of his mouth until their lips met.

Then Eli, the strong, stoic man she'd grown to love, gave her a taste of the passion hidden inside him.

The End — for now…

A Note from the Author

Dear Reader,

I hope you enjoyed Betsy and Eli's story and their struggle to overcome so much to get to the cusp of their romance. If you want to know when the next book in the series will be released, sign up for my newsletter at http://www.stephaniequeen.com.

If you liked the story, I would greatly appreciate if you would leave an honest review. Reviews are very helpful to me and to other readers to help them decide whether to read my book. Please feel free to drop me a note any time at stephanie@stephaniequeen.com. I love hearing from you and always respond personally to every email I get.

In the meantime, I'll be busy writing more stories from my heart for you to enjoy.

Warm Regards,

Stephanie Q

Other Books by Stephanie Queen

Small Town Series
Small Town Glamour Girl Christmas
Small Town Glamour Girl Wedding
Small Town Hot Shot Bride
Small Town Christmas Baby
A Complicated Bride

Margo & George Series
Margo & George Christmas
Margo & George Forever
A Holiday Affair (coming soon…)

Beachcomber Investigations Series
The Beachcombers - Prequel Edition
Beachcomber Investigations - Book 1
Beachcomber Santa - Novella
Beachcomber Valentine - Novella
Beachcomber Baby - Book 2
Beachcomber Trouble - Book 3
Beachcomber Heat - Book 4
Beachcomber Wedding - Book 5
Beachcomber Reckoning - Book 6
Let it Snow - Novella - Book 9
Falling for Captain Hunk - Novella Spinoff
Beachcomber Billionaire - Novella Spinoff
Beachcomber Test - Book 7
Beachcomber Love - Novella
Beachcomber Love - Book 8
Beachcomber Gone - Book 9 (coming soon...)

Playing the Game

Scotland Yard Exchange Series
Between a Rock & a Mad Woman
The Throwbacks
The Hotshots
The Romantics
The Beachcombers

The Music of You and Me

Kristy Tate

One

This is my future. Tara set her suitcase on the porch of her Uncle's craftsman style home and gazed at the front door. Her feet froze on the bottom step. Her knees locked. She tried to coax herself forward, but remained rooted, frozen in place.

"Darling," her Uncle Will called from inside the open doorway, "come on in! What'cha waiting for?"

After his urging. Tara planted a smile on her lips, picked up her suitcase, and pushed her way across the porch.

Uncle Will shuffled through the darkened foyer and opened the screen door to welcome her in. Reaching for her bag, he took it from her before giving her a one-armed hug.

Tara pulled away as soon as it was polite to do so. "Where's Auntie Darrel?" Her nose wrinkled from the cooked cabbage smell coming from the kitchen.

"Still at the dad-burned school. Since they started rehearsals for the fall play, I hardly see hide nor hair of her." He nodded sagely. "She'll be right glad to see you."

"I'm not really sure how much help I can be," Tara said, apprehension fluttering in her belly at the thought. She had been home-schooled so a private ritzy school like Canterbury Academy both fascinated and terrified her.

Uncle Will squeezed her arm reassuringly. "You'll be fine. It's more about herding cats than teaching music."

Tara nodded and tried to look buoyed up by his words. Uncle Will shared her disorder, so he should understand her concerns, but since he worked the farm for his living, his interaction with the outside world was very limited. Which was just the way he liked it.

And that was just the way Tara planned on living, too. She followed Uncle Will up the stairs that led to the guest bedroom. He climbed slowly, his breath labored, making her wonder how long he'd be able to dedicate the long hours the farm demanded. Auntie Darrel worked at the school teaching music and acting as the nurse, but Tara didn't know if that income alone could support her aunt and uncle. She felt a twinge of guilt and promised herself that she wouldn't contribute to their financial burdens. She prayed that she'd be able to help, rather than hurt. But given her condition, she didn't know if that was a prayer Heaven could answer. Especially since Heaven had ignored her prior pleas for help.

Uncle Will dropped her bag in the doorway of the guest bedroom and brushed his hands on his overalls. "Take all the time you need to settle in. I better get back to picking the apples. If I don't, the deer will do it for me."

"Thanks, Uncle Will, I'll come and help you." She looked longingly at the crazy quilt on the bed. "I don't need to settle in."

"Nope. I promised your aunt that I would get you behind the piano first thing. I'm under strict instructions that you're not to be out in the yard… with me. You're to learn the music pronto." He turned to leave. "The score is on the dresser," he said over his shoulder.

Tara picked up the music and flipped through it. Much like her aunt, the songs were predictable and bordered on boring.

Tara lugged her bag to the closet and pushed it inside. Her case wasn't very big—not because she didn't plan on staying very long—but because she didn't own a lot of clothes. It didn't take her long to hang up her four dresses, stow her three pairs of pants, five tops, and collection of underwear in the dresser. She placed a framed photo of her mom and her Bible on the nightstand. That done, she sat down on the bed, closed her eyes, and tucked her feet beneath her. As much as she wanted to, she didn't allow herself to lie down. She breathed in through her nose, pushed away homesickness, and reminded herself of her plan.

Earn enough money working at her aunt's school to buy her own laptop and then start teaching English to foreign students via the internet. She only hoped that the light from the computer wouldn't trigger episodes.

Liam Grant pulled his Ford 150 down his Gram's bumpy drive. The scent of burning brush that always reminded him of this time of year hung in the air. He parked near the barn, shut off the engine and climbed out. The tinkling from a piano escaped the windows of the neighboring farmhouse. In the distance, a man in overalls pulling a wagon plucked apples from gnarled trees. Liam tried to place the music, it sounded like a familiar tune, but—like the trees—twisted somehow, as if the pianist had chosen a familiar tune and had decided to change it.

He closed the truck's door and went to find his gram and her cat, Ragamuffin. A once white picket fence surrounded the gray-blue farmhouse and kept the daisies as well as the chickens in the yard. Ragamuffin perched on a branch of a maple tree and stared down her nose at him.

"You look fine to me," Liam said. "What's wrong with you now?"

Gram banged through the back door. "Don't you be fooled by him," she told Liam. "He might be acting all la-dee-da, but he's not eating his kibble."

Since Gram called him at least once a week to come out and check on Ragamuffin's health, the cat's lack of appetite didn't worry Liam. He suspected that the frequent house calls had more to do with his gram's loneliness than with the cat's well-being.

A warm cinnamon smell wafted through the open door. *Apple pie.* If Liam wasn't careful, Ragamuffin's lack of appetite would make him fat.

Liam nodded at the neighbor's house. "Sounds like a musician moved in."

Gram huffed. "That racket has been going on day and night ever since that scrap of a girl got here." She held the door open for Liam and he followed his gram through the mudroom to the kitchen. A pie sat on the counter. Steam escaped through the lattice crust. His stomach rumbled just from looking at it.

"Ragamuffin?" he asked in a strangled voice.

"He'll come in when he's done with his adventures," Gram said. "We might as well enjoy ourselves until then." She slid him a glance. "Do you want ice cream with your pie?"

Did she really need to ask? "Always. But here, let me get it."

She pushed him aside before selecting a knife and slicing up the pie while Liam went to the freezer and pulled out a container. His shoulders screamed a complaint while he scooped up the ice cream.

Gram must have noticed, because she asked, "What's wrong?"

"Nothing much," Liam said after he placed a scoop of ice cream in a bowl. "I helped deliver a colt this afternoon." He had spent almost an hour with his arm inserted into the back-end of the mare and this hadn't been pleasant for any of them. He flexed his hand, grateful it still worked.

"Where's Teague today?" Gram asked as she took a seat in the ladderback kitchen chair and poised her spoon above the pie.

"With his mom." Liam couldn't help it, he moaned in pleasure as soon as the pie crossed his lips.

Gram made a noise that was a cross between a grunt and snort. "What about school?"

"He's having a hard time," Liam admitted. "Eva wants to send him to a private school, but—"

"And where would that be?" Gram huffed.

"Exactly," Liam said. "I'm not willing to give up custody just so he can attend —"

The sound of drums interrupted his sentence.

"What in the tarnation?" Gram bounced to her feet and went to the window. She pulled back the lace curtain and stared through the window at the neighboring farmhouse. "I have had just about enough of this!" She rested her ample butt against the kitchen counter and pushed her hand through her gray curls. "All this noise has upset my girls."

"The chickens," Liam murmured.

"They're so distraught, they're molting! The yard looks like there's been a pillow fight and the pillows lost."

"All chickens molt in the fall. Are they still laying?"

"Yes, but... you should see that child. Pale, skinny as a broomstick with a shock of bright red-hair. She looks like a walking cherry tootsie pop!"

Liam continued eating his pie, amused by the thought of a tootsie pop playing the drums.

"Will you go and talk to her? Tell her she has to take it down a knotch or two?"

"Why me?" His gram had never been shy.

"You know Darrel hates me."

"Mrs. Poole hates everyone," Liam said.

"But she especially hates me, and if I tried to suggest that her niece stop her infernal noise, I just know the woman would be urging the chit to ramp it up."

"You're being silly." Liam licked his spoon, sad that he'd taken the last bite.

"No, I'm not. I need you to go over there and talk to her... the niece, not Darrel."

Liam set down his spoon. "My visit had nothing to do with Ragamuffin, did it?"

Gram blushed. "Just go over there and speak to the girl. I'm sure she won't be as difficult as her terrible aunt. Please ask her to close her windows when she practices."

Liam rolled his eyes, but he didn't dare say no. His endless supply of baked goods depended on his staying in his gram's good graces.

An avocado orchard and a couple of split rail fences separated Gram's property from the neighbor's. The music stopped before Liam even got halfway through the trees.

He knocked on the door and peered through the window. The piano stood in a shaft of sunlight. He couldn't see the drums. Maybe they were set up in the barn. Thinking that that was where he'd put a set of drums, he went in search of them and the girl that may or may not look like a cherry tootsie pop.

"Can I help you?" The man he'd spied earlier in the apple trees stopped him and ran his gaze over him.

"I'm Doctor Grant." Liam extended his hand and the man took it. His hands were calloused and his skin weather-beaten. His thin hair blew about in the breeze. "My grandmother sent me to ask if whoever is playing could turn down the volume, she and her chickens would really appreciate it."

The man didn't respond but stared at Liam with cold eyes, one of which wasn't looking directly at him. "Her chickens?"

"Yes. They don't like the noise. They're molting."

"All chickens molt this time of year."

"Could I speak to your niece?"

"No." The man turned on his heel and strode away.

Tara trailed after her aunt through the school's parking lot.

"This is a very prestigious academy," Aunt Darrel said over her shoulder. "These girls are all from very wealthy families."

"All of them?" Tara tried to swallow down her fears.

"Well, there are few here on scholarship," Darrel admitted. "But my point is, our productions are always top-notch!" She sucked in a deep breath. "Or at least, they always were in the past." She shook her head. "But now, we have a new English teacher."

"You don't like her?" Tara asked in a hushed tone.

"She's just not cut out for the school! I honestly don't know how she got this job!"

"If you don't think she's qualified, then what am I doing here?"

Aunt Darrel swiveled and pointed her finger at Tara's thin chest. "You're the finest pianist I know — and that's saying a lot, because I know a lot of people! You don't need a Ph.D. to accompany a children's choir! You need musical talent and you have that in abundance. But —" Aunt Darrel hesitated.

"Yes?"

Aunt Darrel wrinkled her nose. "I heard what you were doing to the songs. I think it's best to keep them simple, don't you?"

"It's Alice in Wonderland. I thought the score could use some… jazzing up?"

Aunt Darrel shook her head. "With these girls, it's best to keep things uncomplicated." She dropped her voice to a whisper. "Believe me, they don't want to think too hard."

"It doesn't necessarily need to be harder, just more fun."

"No." Aunt Darrel pushed her way through the wide double doors of the building bearing a sign that read Humanities Hall.

Hundreds of lockers lined the walls. Tara peeked in the small windows of the classroom doors at the students sitting at the desks as she trotted after her aunt. Tara had finished high school at sixteen and college, via the internet, at twenty. So, she'd be older than the girls, but she guessed she would be smaller than most of them.

She reminded herself that her brusque aunt would be issuing the orders and keeping the girls inline. If Tara kept her head down, no one need know she was hiding behind the piano.

"That went as well as can be expected," Aunt Darrel said at the end of the day.

Tara, still rooted behind the piano, felt the tension between her shoulders begin to ease as the last of the girls filed from the auditorium. She envied them their giggles and whispers. She'd had a few friends from church, her choir, neighbors — but most had left Simi Valley for college or careers.

Darrel gathered up the sheet music and placed it in a plastic crate on top of the piano. Tara added the score to the collection. She caught the whispers of the owner of the school, a stunning but middle-aged brunette, and the English teacher/play director, a tall, willowy blonde coming from the orchestra pit. Darrel had introduced her to them earlier, but Tara had already forgotten their names.

As she followed her aunt down the now deserted hallway, her head swam with the music and the potential for change, even though Darrel had asked her not to modify or embellish it in any way, she couldn't help herself. If the alterations were subtle, there was a good chance that Darrel wouldn't even notice.

To get from the Humanities Hall to the parking lot, they had to cross the quad. The fading sun hovered on the tops of the distant foothills. The giant oaks cast long shadows across their path. A man stepped out from behind a building. Even though he wore mud-caked jeans, boots, and a corduroy jacket, something about him told her he wasn't a laborer, but because of his casual, and filthy appearance, she also knew he wasn't a faculty member. He was Cary Grant-handsome and when his brown eyes met her gaze, she flushed.

He smiled as if he knew her.

Tara hurried after her aunt and slipped into the Dodge Stratus. "Who was that man?" Tara whispered as soon as Darrel got into the car. It smelled faintly of over-ripe apples despite the fact that Darrel kept her car spotless and bare.

"What man?"

"That man—" She nodded in his direction, but he had disappeared. "Never mind," she said out loud with a sigh, reminding herself of her vow.

Aunt Darrel cut her a sideways glance and put the car into gear.

"Auntie, how long after you met Uncle Will did he tell you about his epilepsy?"

Darrel pulled the car out of the school parking lot and headed for the road that led to the tiny town of Oak Hollow. "We grew up together. He didn't have to tell me. I saw it for myself."

"And it didn't frighten you?"

"Of course, it did. It's a terrifying thing."

"But you still married him."

Darrel rolled her eyes. "We're all packages, girlie. Every one of us comes with good parts and bad. If I wanted the good parts of Will, I had to be okay with the parts that frighten me."

"And you were okay with not having children?"

"I work with children all day long. It's enough."

"You're special." Tara knew that most people found her aunt difficult, but Tara's heart warmed toward her.

"Someday, you'll find someone special, too," Darrel predicted.

"No," Tara said with conviction. "I'm married to my music." She smiled and echoed her aunt. "It's enough."

Darrel pinned Tara with a hard stare. "Now girlie—"

A large brown bear wandered on to the road.

Tara screamed.

Darrel returned her attention to the road and slammed on her brakes. The car skittered to the gravel shoulder and went into a tailspin. The bear yelped as the front bumper sent him flying.

Two

The dodge shuttered to a stop. Darrel shut off the engine and leaned her head back to gaze at the roof of the car.

"Are you okay?" Tara asked, disliking the sudden pallor of her aunt's skin.

Darrel nodded. "Let me catch my breath."

Tara stared at the creature in the middle of the road. "We can't just leave him there."

"He almost killed us!" Darrel said.

"I'm sure it wasn't intentional." Tara placed her hand on the doorknob.

Darrel shot out her hand and gripped Tara's wrist. "You can't go out there!"

"We have to see if he's alive!"

"No, we don't." Darrel's voice rose and she fumbled in her bag and pulled out her phone. "We can call animal control if you'd like."

Tara shook off her aunt's grip and climbed from the car. She hesitantly approached the bear. He gazed at her with sad eyes.

"He's not a bear," Tara called to her aunt. "He's a dog, a really big one."

"Stay away from him," Darrel called through the window. "An injured creature is a dangerous one."

True, but still. "He's probably someone's pet," Tara said.

A truck pulled up behind them. The man Tara had seen earlier at the school and a young man climbed out. "What happened?" the man said.

His voice was as lovely as his face. The kid looked like a miniature version of him, but thinner. They were clearly father and son, but the father looked too young to have a pre-teen son. Maybe they were brothers?

The man knelt beside the big dog and placed his hand on the barrel of the dog's chest.

Darrel climbed from the car. The color had returned to her cheeks, but she still seemed shaky. "The creature just darted in front of me."

"Will he be okay?" the kid asked.

The dog responded by climbing to his feet and shaking himself.

The man laughed. "I think he may have done more damage to the car than to himself."

Darrel snorted as she examined her smashed front bumper.

"Does he have a tag?" Tara asked.

The man ran his fingers through the dog's thick fur. "He doesn't seem to have a collar."

"Dad, can we keep him?" the kid breathed out in a rush.

"Now Teague," his dad began.

"We have to take care of him," Teague whined.

"I'll make sure he's okay, but—"

"We're lucky it was you who came by, Dr. Grant," Darrel said.

Grant? Like Cary? Despite the tense situation, Tara smiled and wondered if Liam could be related to her movie-star idol.

"No, *Chewbacca* is lucky we came by," Teague said.

"Oh, is that his name now?" Dr. Grant asked with a smile.

Teague nodded.

Dr. Grant studied his son. "You know your mom isn't going to let you keep this monster, right?"

Teague nodded again. "Maybe Gram will let him stay at her place?"

"Not a chance." Dr. Grant ran his hands over the dog. "He'll scare the chickens to death and Ragamuffin would probably bolt."

Tara sent her aunt a sideways glance. "Can he stay with us? Just until we find his owner?"

Darrel grunted.

"He could stay in the barn, couldn't he?" Tara asked.

"And who's going to pay to feed him?" Darrel asked. "A mammoth like that will go through a bag of chow a day!"

Tara twisted her lips. She couldn't ask her aunt and uncle to feed and house the dog when they were already feeding and housing her. They already had one charity case, they didn't need another.

"If he's at your house," the boy said to Darrel. "I could visit him and take care of him. I'll walk him every day."

"Are we neighbors?" Tara asked.

Dr. Grant climbed to his feet. The giant dog leaned against him as if he'd already found his master. "We haven't been formally introduced. I'm Liam Grant, the local vet." He held out his hand.

Tara placed her hand in his and liked the strong, warm grip. "I'm Tara Allen."

"My niece," Darrel put in.

"The musician," Dr. Grant said. "I've heard you play."

"You're the one making Gram's chickens molt," Teague said.

His dad dropped a heavy hand on Teague's shoulder.

"What?" Tara asked.

"Nothing," Dr. Grant said.

"No, tell me."

"My Gram thinks your drumming is upsetting her chickens," Teague said.

"Oh, dear…" Tara began. "Tell her I'm sorry. I guess I'll have to practice with the doors and windows closed."

"The chickens will be fine," Dr. Grant said. "But this dog—he really does need someone to look after him."

"Let me do it!" Teague said.

"How are you going to do that?" his dad asked.

"I can live with Gram and take care of Chewbacca if he lives with Tara," Teague said.

"Your mom will never agree to that," Dr. Grant said. "What about school?"

"I hate school," Teague spit out.

"We don't need to have this discussion right now," Dr. Grant said. "We'll take Chewbacca to my office. Maybe his owners are looking for him as we speak." Dr. Grant slapped his leg and called to the dog. Chewbacca didn't hesitate but happily followed Dr. Grant and Teague to Dr. Grant's truck.

"It was nice to meet you, Tara," Dr. Grant said as he held open the door for the dog to climb in.

Chewbacca jumped onto the car seat and Teague clambered up beside him. Tara watched them drive away, two matched human heads and the furry lump beside them. Even though they completely filled the truck cab, Tara had the odd desire to wedge herself in there with them.

At the end of the week, Tara accompanied Darrel into town and stopped by the vet's office, a white, clapboard house that looked like it served dual purposes as an office in the front and a home in the back. While Darrel went to the grocery store, Tara climbed the front steps. She wondered if Liam and Teague lived here, and she itched with curiosity.

Inside, it was obvious the formal living areas had been converted into a surgical waiting room. Carpet had been replaced with linoleum, and stiff plastic chairs lined the walls, but a friendly fireplace remained as did a large chandelier over what had once been the dining room but was now the counter where a receptionist sat. Tara spotted a picture of Chewbacca with the inscription *lost dog* on a giant bulletin board with photos of animals and fliers for pet services pinned on it.

"Can I help you?" a gum-smacking teenager behind the reception desk asked. She stared at Tara with open curiosity. Although she was probably the same age as the girls who attended Canterbury, in her tie-dye T-shirt, skin-tight jeans, and hoop earrings, she looked like a different species from the uniform-clad girls at the private school.

"I was just dropping by to ask about this dog." Tara pointed at the flier. "Is he still here?"

"Yep. He's a sweetie," the girl said. "Do you know him?"

Tara flushed. "We, um, ran into each other last week. What will happen to him if no one claims him?"

"It's hard to say. Teague, that's the doctor's son, really wants to take him home, but Eva, that's the mom, wants nothing to do with Chewy." She grinned. "It's causing drama."

"Oh dear," Tara murmured. "If I had my own place, I'd take him. But I live with my aunt and uncle."

"Hi Tara," Dr. Grant spoke from an open doorway.

Tara perked up. "Hi, Dr. Grant. I've come to visit Chewbacca."

"He'll appreciate that." He nodded to the closed door behind him. "He's back here."

They passed through a room filled with cages and crates in all sizes. Most were empty, save a few cats. Chewbacca was so big, it was hard to imagine him in one of them. Dr. Grant pulled open a back door that led to a fenced lawn. Chewbacca lounged in the shade of a large tree but bounced to his feet as soon as he saw them.

"Chewy, you've got company!" Dr. Grant patted his thigh, calling to the dog.

Chewy lumbered over and Tara held out her hand for him to smell. He nuzzled against her and knocked her off balance.

Dr. Grant shot out his hand, steadying her. "Careful. He probably outweighs you!"

"Can I take him for a walk, or something?" Tara stroked the dog's head and gazed into his deep chocolate eyes. He batted his lashes at her.

"I'm sure he'd love that, but…" Dr. Grant hesitated.

"But what?"

"I wasn't kidding about his outweighing you. If he decided to pit his strength against yours, I'm sorry to tell you this, but I'd bet on the dog."

"I don't think we'll have a wrestling match, will we Chewbacca?" She ruffled the dog's ears and he tried to lick her.

"You might not plan to…" He glanced at his watch. "I'll come with you," he said in a rush.

"Are you sure? I'll be fine on my own."

"It's time to close the office, anyway."

"Don't you have someone waiting for you at home?" Tara asked.

Dr. Grant shook his head as he stepped back inside and pulled a leash off a rack of hooks. "Teague is at his mom's."

Tara pressed her lips closed while she watched Dr. Grant fasten the leash on Chewbacca's collar because she wanted to ask about his ex-wife, but also didn't want to pry. "May I?" she asked, holding her hand out for the leash.

"It's your poison," he said, giving her the dog's lead while he closed and locked the back door of the office.

"Where shall we go?" Tara asked.

"If we follow the alley, it will take us to the Legionnaire's Park."

"I did some internet research," Tara told him. "Chewbacca looks like he's a Newfoundland. They're supposed to be great dogs."

"I wish we could keep him, but with my hours—it just wouldn't be fair."

"Where do you think his owners are?"

"I don't know."

They followed the alley behind the shops until they reached the park. Massive oaks towered over the buttercup strewn lawn. They walked side-by-side with Chewbacca slightly ahead of them to the gazebo at the end of the edge of the arroyo. Dr. Grant sat on the bench, Chewbacca settled with a humph at his feet, and not knowing what else to do, Tara sat at the opposite end of the bench.

"Will he stay at your office this weekend?"

"I haven't figured that out, yet. Normally, I would say yes, because I have Teague on the weekends, but I'm going to a wedding on Saturday…"

"He could stay with me."

"Really? Don't you think you should check with your aunt first?" His smirk told her he remembered Aunt Darrel's first impression of the dog.

"I don't need to. My aunt and uncle are going out of town this weekend. Fortunately for Chewbacca, there's a big car show in Monterey." She winked at him. "They'll never know."

"Are you sure you don't mind?"

"You'll be doing me a favor." She glanced around at the acres of open land leading to the foothill's sharp incline. "The truth is, I find my uncle's farm a little isolated. I lived in the suburbs my entire life. Having the dog with me will make me feel safer."

"If you're sure, that would be great. Teague will be right next door at my grandmother's, so if you don't mind, I know he'd love to come by and play with Chewy."

She sucked in a deep breath. "But you'll have to deliver him."

"No problem. We'll swing by right after I drop Teague off."

"Great. What time do you think that will be?"

"Around seven? My mom and Teague plan on watching Harry Potter movies."

"Perfect. My aunt and uncle should be gone by then."

He grinned. "Sounds like a date."

And all the happiness bubbling inside Tara fizzled away, because it did sound like a date and she knew that at some point she would need to tell Dr. Grant that dating was something she simply did not do.

"You're wearing cologne," Teague said, his voice thick with suspicion.

Liam looked over Chewbacca's great big furry head at his son. "I'm surprised you can smell me over the dog."

"Chewy smells just fine," Teague said. "He's clean. It's you that stinks."

Liam started the truck and put it into gear. "Stink, huh?"

Teague stared straight ahead and the black pavement. "Yep."

Liam turned the truck toward his grandmother's place. Typically, he enjoyed the weekends with his son, but this one would be atypical in that he would be at a wedding for most of it. He decided to change the subject. "So, you and Gram have a Harry Potter fest planned?"

Teague didn't directly answer the question. "She said she'd take me to Harry Potter World once I finish reading the series."

"What does your mom think about that?"

"Mom's psycho."

"Teague!" Liam tightened his fingers around the steering wheel.

"It's true and you know it." Teague looked out the passenger side window, his face averted. "Ever since she started dating Pastor Millet, the only book she thinks worth reading is The Bible. She told me she's afraid if I read books about magic, I'll start thinking I can be a wizard. Like I'm going to find a wand or a dragon and start casting spells or something."

Liam grinned. "But it would be really cool if you did, right?"

Teague turned back to him. The shadows on his face, the spark in his eye, the wickedness of his grin all made Liam's heart ache with love. "Yeah," Liam said.

"Your mom loves you. She only wants what's best for you. You know that, right?"

"It's so weird that Mom was only two years older than I am when she had me. What were you guys thinking?"

Liam chuckled. "Clearly, we weren't thinking! But you're going to be a lot smarter than us, right?"

"Yeah. I don't want to have a kid at fifteen."

"It was rough." His thoughts cruised over that painful chapter of his life. Telling his and Eva's parents, disappointing his grandmother, dropping out of school and getting a job to pay the medical bills… "It wasn't all bad, you know, given the end result was you. And, not to get all mushy, but you are the best thing that ever happened to me."

"Is that why you're ditching me at Gram's while you're going to make googly eyes at Tara?"

"I'm not ditching you! You know that once Harry turns on, you won't even notice I'm gone."

Teague grinned and ruffled Chewbacca's ears. "I'm just teasing you. You can make googly eyes at Tara."

"Thanks for your permission."

"You're welcome."

At precisely eight o'clock, Tara's doorbell rang. Even though she'd intentionally worn a baggy sweatshirt, a pair of pajama bottoms, and tied her hair up in a messy knot, she still slid a glance at her reflection in the entryway mirror.

She opened the door and found Chewbacca sitting beside Liam's feet. Liam had a bowl and plastic baggy full of dog food in one hand, a blanket draped over his arm, and a bottle in the other hand. "This is for Chewy," he said, lifting the hand with the baggy of dog food. "And this is for us." He showed her the bottle. "It's my Gram's blackberry wine."

"Oh…" She plucked the dog food from his fingers and took the dog leash. "I'll take these, but not that." She nodded at the bottle. "I don't drink."

He rocked back on his heels. "For religious reasons?"

"Health." No matter how many times she explained her situation, it never got easier. Although, no one after witnessing her having a grand mal seizure had ever tried to weasel her into breaking her strict dietary code. She held the door open for the dog and to her surprise, Liam followed him inside.

"Where should I set up his bed?" Liam asked.

"By the fireplace?" She had lit the fire earlier. The Mary Stewart novel she'd just put down sat on the overstuffed chair near the hearth. A Scrabble game she and Uncle Will had started was laid out on the coffee table.

"Do you play?" Liam asked, nodding at the game.

"Yes." She hesitated because she knew what he was really asking. She decided that a Scrabble match wasn't as dangerous as getting a cup of coffee, and once she whooped him, he'd see that he was wasting his time with her. Besides, a game of Scrabble could be more entertaining than an evening with a book. *If* he was a worthy opponent. "But I have to warn you, I'm very good."

Unfazed, Liam grinned, rubbed his hands together, and took a seat on the sofa while Chewbacca inspected his bed.

Tara pulled the ottoman close to the coffee table and began to pluck the Scrabble tiles off the board. "You're a brave man. I have a fifty-seven-game winning streak."

He whistled. "You keep score."

"Of course, doesn't everyone?"

"Do you play Scrabble With Friends?"

"No, do you?"

He nodded. "So, I've lots of practice."

"It's nice to see a man with so much confidence." After all the tiles were face down, she shuffled them around. "Too bad I'm going to crush it."

She turned over a C and he an X.

"I'm first," Tara said.

"Who says?"

"C before X."

"Or boys before girls."

"That's not even a thing. It's girls before boys."

"That's truly a sexist remark."

She sighed. "I'm not sexist… so, go ahead, if you want to go."

"This is a trick, isn't it?" He studied his tiles. "I think you want me to go first."

"I don't mind going first."

He nodded without looking at her and rearranged the tiles on his stand.

She put her tiles out. "Q-U-I-B-B-L-E for forty."

"Forty!" He rocked back and pinned her with his gaze. "Come on, you're cheating."

"I don't see how. Now, take your turn."

He spelled out cow for five points before asking, "What brought you to Oak Hollow?"

She shrugged. "All of my friends were leaving. I wanted to go somewhere too. I was in a band, but that didn't work out. Aunt Darrel got me the gig at the school, so…"

"What happened with the band?"

She laughed. "We were good… really good. But we kept booking gigs where we were staying out later and later." She shrugged. "It messed with my sleep."

"I guess I can see that."

"And a lot of the clubs where we played had flashing lights. I can't handle flashing lights."

If he thought this was weird, he didn't say so.

"How about you? Have you always lived in Oak Hollow?"

"I was born and raised here, but I joined the military as soon as they would let me. They paid my way through veterinarian school."

"So, you weren't around much when Teague was little?"

"My biggest regret." He bit his lower lip and wouldn't meet her eye.

"I'm sorry." She placed her hand over his briefly.

He shook his head. "I was just a kid. A stupid kid. The

responsibilities of parenthood terrified me. It worked out okay. Mine and Eva's parents really stepped up. Eva had married by the time I finished school, but…"

"What happened?"

"After she and Mark divorced, I stepped in and asked for shared custody. Eva and I… it took a while, but we're friends now."

They played intently for a few turns. Chewbacca's snores and the snapping and popping flames in the fireplace broke the silence. When the score was tied, Liam put down K-I-S-S.

"You're not even trying," Tara said.

"Yes, I am."

"That's only worth seven points."

He looked at her lips. "Who said I'm trying to score points?"

She huffed and shifted uncomfortably and spelled, O-X-E-N using a triple word space.

Liam retaliated with the word *pretty.*

"That's a dumb word," Tara told him.

"It's a perfectly fine adjective."

"Adjectives are weak."

He blinked. "Some are weak, true. Some are strong. But are you really sure you want to talk about grammar right now?"

"What do you want to talk about? How badly you're losing?"

"I'm not losing."

"You're not winning."

"I'm sitting in a cozy room with a beautiful, smart woman. In my book, I'm winning." He leaned forward as if to kiss her.

Tara stopped him with a finger to his lips. "Dr. Grant, I'm sorry if I gave you the wrong impression."

"Dr. Grant?" He leaned back, his expression hurt but still hopeful.

She nodded and folded her hands in her lap. "There's something you should know about me."

"Sounds serious."

"Well, it is. To me. I don't want to lead you on."

"What? I know you're not married."

"How do you know that?"

"I asked Cole."

"The principal at the academy?"

He nodded.

"If you want a casual fling—I'm not that girl. Friendship is all I have to offer."

"Friendship, huh?" He narrowed his eyes. "Why do you say that? I'm not proposing marriage or anything, after all, we just met, but I'm curious. Is it just me? Or, do you—"

"I won't marry."

"Why not?" He looked genuinely confused.

"Because I can't take care of myself, let alone anyone else."

"I can't speak for all mankind, but I know I'm not looking for someone to take care of me. Quite the opposite."

"I can't have children."

"I'm sorry, but I still don't know why…"

"Most people want a family."

"I have Teague." He paused. "Not everyone wants children."

"They might say that, but when it comes down to it…"

Liam frowned at the Scrabble board before pulling tiles off his stand to spell the word *pursuit.* "I'm definitely going to win."

"I don't know what sort of game you think we're playing."

"I'm playing Scrabble, and, as I just told you, I'm going to win."

"No, you're not. I told you, I never lose." She spelled out the word whizz and put a Z on a double letter square.

"Mmm," he murmured. "I'm definitely going to win." And he put down the word ass for three points.

She laughed and used the rest of her tiles to spell the word equal. "Add up the score, dog doctor."

He tallied up the numbers and put the sheet down on the coffee table. "You may have won the match, but I still say I'm going to win the war."

She shook her head. "No. There's no point. Eventually, you're going to want to have children—"

He climbed to his feet and shrugged into his jacket. "We've had *one* evening together. It wasn't even a date. It's way too soon to say never."

She followed him to the entry. "But—"

He pulled the door open and let in a cold breeze that circled through the room.

She shivered and hugged herself.

Leaning forward, he kissed her softly on the cheek. "I'm going to win," he whispered in her ear. His breath sent tingles down her back, making her shiver again. But this time it had nothing to do with the cold.

Three

*B*arking woke Tara. She rolled over, put a pillow over her head, and then remembered that the dog might have a legitimate reason for waking her. Sitting up, she rolled her shoulders and glanced at the clock near her bed. Eight a.m. After slipping into her robe, she padded through the house.

Chewbacca quivered with excitement. With his nose pressed against the front door, he whimpered.

"Okay, I get it," Tara muttered. She pulled the door open, expecting Chewbacca to bolt, but he reared up on his hind legs and placed his enormous paws on Teague's shoulders.

"Hey, boy!" Teague ran his hands over the dog's sides. "I'm glad to see you, too."

Tara pushed her hands through her messy curls. "Good morning, Teague."

"Morning." He gave her a speculative look and held out the leash as if it were evidence. "I've come to walk Chewy."

"Great. I'm sure he'll love that."

Teague pushed Chewbacca back to all fours and secured the leash. "We'll be back in a bit."

"Okay," Tara said, picking up on Teague's frosty tone and wondering what she'd done—if anything—to make the boy dislike her. She watched him lead the dog down the front drive, noticing how much he resembled Liam, not just in appearance, but also in the way he carried himself. She tried to imagine Liam at that age, or a few years older, learning that he'd just fathered a child.

Then her thoughts skittered into the dangerous imaginings of having a child of her own. She shut them down, as she always did, and wandered into the kitchen in search of breakfast. But nothing interested her.

After taking a quick shower and throwing on some clothes, Tara settled in front of the piano to tinker with the score for *Alice in Wonderland*. Hours passed and Teague and Chewbacca hadn't returned.

Tara glanced out the window at the dark ominous clouds hovering over the foothills. Where was Teague? Maybe he took the dog back to his Gram's. But that didn't make sense. Hadn't Liam said that the dog couldn't go there because of a cat? Maybe something had happened to him?

After another glance at the gathering storm, Tara slipped on her boots and grabbed a jacket. Outside, the wind toyed with her curls and pierced through her clothes. Lowering her head, she braced through the weather and cut through the pasture that separated her uncle's property from Mrs. Grant's.

She climbed up the steps, crossed the porch and knocked on the door. Mrs. Grant lifted the curtains and peeked out at her. A frown flashed across her face, but she pulled open the door.

"Good morning, Mrs. Grant. Is Teague here?" Tara asked.

"No, I thought he was at your house," Mrs. Grant replied.

Tara shook her head. "They've been gone awhile."

Mrs. Grant rolled her eyes. "That boy! I told him we were going to help clean the church this morning. I guess this is his way of dodging his Christian duty!" She clucked her tongue but didn't look put out. "I wouldn't worry about him. No harm will come to him as long as he has the brute with him."

"You're probably right, but it looks like it might rain."

Mrs. Grant chuckled. "I hope it does. It will serve him right! Well, if you see him, tell him I've gone to the church on my own!"

"Will do. Have a good day." Tara headed back home, but midway across the pasture, she detoured through the orchard and called for Teague. She followed a path through the woods and called a few more times. Squirrels chattered and birds sang out, but Teague didn't answer. Not knowing what else to do, she started for the house as soon as scattered raindrops fell.

Back inside, she shed off her jacket and peeled off her boots in the mudroom. Then she did what she always did when worried.

She made cookies.

Liam had been pleasantly surprised when his best friend's wedding had been moved at the last minute from Orange County to a nearby ranch. Blaine, a horror flick screenwriter, had always been unorthodox, so when Liam had learned that the wedding was to be held in an abandoned cemetery, he wasn't as thrown as others who didn't know Blaine as well.

Liam took a seat on the groom's side. Having been raised in the area, he knew Chad, the grandson of the ranch owner who was hosting the wedding, very well. Not only had they grown up together, but they still occasionally saw each other at Canterbury Academy where Chad taught P.E., and now Tara, worked. Liam also sporadically visited the school to check on the 4-H club animals. He hoped he'd get a chance to talk to Chad about Tara.

Liam glanced around at the grounds. He had played here often as a kid and he was surprised that other than the folding white chairs and wedding bower, very little had changed. It was as if time had stood still on the ranch.

A cold wind tugged at the bridesmaid's dresses, but the clouds gathering over the foothills had yet to rain. Blaine stood before the priest, his face full of love as he watched Sloane follow a little girl tossing rose petals down the aisle. A band began to play Wagner's "Here Comes the Bride."

Sloane stopped beside Blaine. He took her hand. Liam's thoughts skittered back to high school and from there to Eva and finally to Teague. The ever-present guilt threatened to swamp him, but he tried to dial into the priest's sermon.

"From the Song of Solomon, Set a seal upon your heart, as a seal upon your arm, for love is strong as death, jealousy is fierce as the grave. Its flashes are flashes of fire, a very flame from the Lord. Many waters cannot quench love, neither can floods drown. And now, I believe that Sloane and Blaine would like to share their thoughts," Father Dolan said.

Blaine gazed into Sloane's face. "Sloane, I pledge my life, heart, and body to you."

"And I to you," Sloane replied.

Tears gathered in Liam's eyes, but he blinked them away. Unlike Blaine, he would never have a traditional family. Sloane came from a large family and hoped to have a lot of children as well. Liam tried to imagine Blaine writing his horror stories surrounded by screaming babies. It was as plausible as a wedding in a cemetery.

As the ceremony ended the band crashed into a twisted version of Mendelssohn's "Wedding March" and the sound of popping corks and fizzing champagne filled the air. Sloane and Blaine dashed down the aisle while the photographers followed. As arranged, they would have a quick photo shoot while the wedding party assembled on the back lawn. Men loosened their ties and pulled off their jackets. Women tiptoed through the grass so as not to damage their high heels. Children ran for the catering tent, hoping to be the first in line for the food.

Chad wound through the crowd, his expression tight with concern.

"Do any of you know where Floyd is?" Chad asked.

A bridesmaid wrinkled her nose. "Isn't he with the other Rabbits?"

This sparked Liam's interested and he glanced around for

actual Rabbits, but then he followed Chad's gaze to the stage and realized that Rabbits had to be the name of the band. Some were toying with their instruments, but no one was anywhere near the center microphone.

"Maybe he's still in his room," a groomsman suggested.

Another bridesmaid touched Chad's arm. "I'll go and look."

Chad threw her a glance that said thank you, while two other bridesmaids headed for the makeshift stage.

A guitarist shook his head and made his shock of white hair dance around his face as he tuned up his guitar. "This is not like him, man."

"He's never been late," the softspoken guy behind the electric keyboard said.

"I know he looks like a flake," said the lead guitarist, "and that none of you like him. But when it comes to shows and performances, he's a solid guy."

Just then, a young Hispanic girl ran up, grabbed Chad's arm, and whispered in his ear. He paled and muttered a word that made the priest give him a stern look.

Chad strode off but Liam caught up to him. "Yeah, man. What's going on?"

"It looks like the band's lead singer has run off with Jess."

Liam's eyebrows shot up. "Your Jess?"

Chad threw him a glance. "We broke up weeks ago."

"Yeah, okay. Is there anything I can do to help?"

Chad smirked. "Do you sing?"

"That's a big fat no."

"I thought as much." Chad slapped his arm. "Go back to the party. I'm sure things will work out."

When Liam got back to the reception, the bridesmaids were still buzzing about the missing bandmember.

"Well, I sure hope someone else can sing." Sloane's grandmother lifted her greying eyebrows suggestively at a bridesmaid. "It's either you or me, baby," the grandma said.

"Grandma, you wouldn't," a bridesmaid said.

Grandma's eyes twinkled. "Just watch me!"

The bridesmaid climbed to her feet, grabbed the hem of her dress and headed for the stage. She passed a sniffling Sloane.

"How could this happen?" Sloane cried to Blaine. "Why would Floyd do this?"

"Don't worry, love," Sloane's mom said to as she patted her shoulder. "Doug can lead the band, can't you sweetie?" She addressed a large-boned man. All of the Rabbits wore vintage tuxedos, but Doug's looked especially ill-fitting, as if he'd recently lost a lot of weight.

"Floyd's the singer," Doug said.

"Yeah, none of us can sing," another bandmember said. "Except Floyd."

The bridesmaid climbed onto the stage and conferred with Doug. The drummer nodded and started with a slow and steady beat. The guitarist plucked out a few notes. But just as she spun around, mouth open, ready to burst into song, she spotted a man striding across the grass.

She dropped the microphone. The amplifier let out an electronic wail and wedding guests cringed and covered their ears. Somewhere in the woods, coyotes began to howl. Scrambling, the bridesmaid picked up the mic, flipped it off, and when she stood to place it on the stand, she came face to face with a woman that had to be another sister.

"Isn't that Benjamin?" this bridesmaid asked.

"Didn't someone tell him that only family was invited?" Sloane's mom asked.

Behind her, the band started playing again. Liam watched the grandmother sashaying up across the stage, thinking that this had to be the most entertaining wedding he'd ever been to.

"Oh no," Sloane's mom wailed. "Mother, no!"

The guitarist strummed a few notes.

"You broke up with him, right?" the bridesmaid asked her sister.

"Yes, of course," the other sister said.

"You told him how you felt?"

"Well, sort of," the bridesmaid hedged. "I thought… what was the point? I mean, he wasn't returning my calls, so—"

"You have to tell him. You have to be honest. You can't just dodge—"

"Darby?" Benjamin began, just as Grandma Betty launched into, "All You Need is Love."

Darby tripped off the stage. "Benjamin! What are you doing here?"

"Henley invited me." He waved at Darby's sister.

"Why would you do that?" Darby faced Henley and demanded.

"It's easy!" Grandma wailed.

Henley folded her arms across her chest, making the bridesmaid dress bunch up into ugly little points. "I knew from what you said that you hadn't truly broken up with him. And he'd come all the way from England! He was devastated by the way you treated him."

"The way I treated him?" Darby pressed her hand against her chest. "This is totally unbelievable! You have no clue."

"We didn't really break up," Benjamin broke in. "You just disappeared."

"You disappeared first," Darby shot back.

"I had auditions and people to meet at parties." He scratched his forehead. "But sadly, nothing's panned out the way I thought it would." He bit his lip. "See, the thing is…" He paused. "Can we go and talk somewhere alone?"

"Why? Are you too embarrassed to ask me for money in front of my family?"

He flushed an ugly shade of pink. "If we could go and talk things out…"

Henley folded her arms and hitched an eyebrow as if to say I told you so.

"I have nothing to say to you!" Darby said.

"So not right, Darby," Meg said. "You have to be courageous.

You have to be strong enough to be vulnerable."

"I don't even know what that means!"

"So, all those emails, all those late-night chats — they were just lies?" Benjamin asked.

"I don't know, Benji," Darby said. "Were they? They seemed real to me, but then you —"

Benjamin spun like a top on a string. Chad pulled back his fist and slammed it into Benjamin's face.

Benjamin grabbed his nose and howled. Blood spurt between his fingers. "My face! My face! My face is my currency! It's my ticket to fame and now you've broken it!"

Chad leaped back, shaking his hand as if it stung. Which it probably did. Liam, who had been amused up until now, sprung to his feet. He couldn't let his best friend's wedding be ruined by a brawl. He quickly intercepted Chad, pulled him away, before turning to Benjamin. "Let me see, I'm a doctor." He looked up at one of the bridesmaids. "Where can we get some ice?"

Grandma stopped singing. "Oh, stop your caterwauling!" she said to Benjamin. "Geesh, don't be such a baby."

"A baby? I'm an actor! Most actors insure their faces, but I can't afford that! That's why I need to talk to you, Darby," Benjamin persisted.

Behind him, Sloane's grandma keened into the microphone about love and all that anyone really needs. But Liam wondered if maybe the animals had the right idea. They didn't need a formal ceremony to create a family. But then, who was he to criticize?

Just as Tara pulled the first batch of cookies from the oven, she heard a knock on the door. As soon as she opened it, Chewbacca stuck his snout inside. Tara jumped back so that the dog wouldn't run her over.

Teague and Chewbacca both shook themselves, sending rain water spraying across the room.

"Can you drive us back to Gram's house?" Teague asked.

"I'm sorry," Tara said, frowning at the puddles of water on the floor. She'd have to mop before her aunt returned. "I don't drive."

"You don't drive?" Teague pushed his fingers through his hair, making it stand on end. "Don't all adults drive?"

"Not all of them. Not me, at least."

He cocked his head, studying her as if she was a strange and rare insect. "Why not?"

She shrugged, not wanting to get into it. "It's a medical thing."

"What? You're allergic to transportation? How do you get around?"

"I ride a bike."

"Everywhere?"

"Mostly. But sometimes I take an Uber."

"Huh. Well, I guess you save money on gas." He glanced at the rain sliding down the windows.

"You can stay here until your grandmother gets back."

"And do what?"

"Do you like music?"

He looked skeptical.

"I made cookies."

His expression brightened marginally.

"Do you want to learn how to play the drums?"

Nerves roiled in Liam's belly, but he didn't know why. Tara was just a girl — not especially pretty, but clever. Different. Why did he find her so compelling? Could it be because she said she wasn't interested and therefore was even more of a challenge than her Scrabble game? Hesitation crawled down his back. It didn't help that he had five Rapid

Rabbits watching him as he crossed the yard of Tara's aunt and uncle's home.

The sound of drumming came from the garage and Liam's lips twitched as he thought about his aunt's chickens. He followed the racket, his nerves mounting. The noise really was awful—inconsistent, spasmodic, full of fits and starts. Maybe she lacked musical talent. The expressions on the Rabbits' faces told him they had the same impression.

But when they got to the garage, he spotted Teague on the drums. Tara, looking adorable in a Mickie Mouse T-shirt and black leggings, stood behind Teague with her arms folded. Chewy lounged at her feet.

"What's going on?" Liam asked.

Tara and Teague looked up at him in guilty surprise—as if they had been caught in a compromising position.

"An impromptu lesson," Tara said. "Who's your posse?" She nodded at the Rabbits.

"Tara, these are the Rapid Rabbits," Liam introduced them. "They just lost their lead singer."

"I'm sure he'll be back," one of the Rabbits said, and the members of the gang all nodded.

"We have a contract with Atlantic Records," one of the guys carrying a guitar said.

"And a gig on the Tonight show," another said.

"Goodness," Tara breathed out. "That's impressive, but why are you here?"

"I thought you should meet," Liam said, but now that he caught several of the Rabbits looking at Tara as if she was a lollipop they wanted to lick, he was beginning to rethink his rash decision. "You're without a band and this band is without a lead singer…"

"We need someone to practice with… just until Floyd turns up," the guitarist said.

"Tara, let me introduce you to the Rabbits," Liam said. He pointed to the closest who also happened to be the tallest.

He had that soft, deflated appearance of someone who had recently lost a lot of weight. "This is Doug, he plays the guitar. And this is Skip." He motioned to a guy who looked like Bob Denver from Gilligan's Island. "He's magical on the electric keyboard. Hal plays the drums." Hal, a potato-shaped dude in a Van Halen t-shirt pointed his drum stick at her and grunted a greeting. "And this is Cooper." Cooper flipped his shock of white hair out of his beady-eyes and smiled at Tara. He had pointy white teeth and reminded Liam of a Pomeranian.

"I'm happy to help," Tara said. "But there's only one problem—I don't drive."

"We could practice here," Doug suggested.

"Here?" Tara's voice squeaked as she glanced around the empty garage.

"Sure. Why not?" Skip put in.

"Works for me," Cooper said.

Hal grunted and all the Rabbits nodded in agreement.

"You don't even know if I'm any good," Tara said.

"You're just a filler for Floyd—if you can come in and shut up at the right times, you're good."

"What can I do?" Teague asked.

Liam lifted his eyebrow, questioning his son. It had been a long time since he'd seen Teague excited in anything.

"Can you play an instrument?" Cooper asked. "Other than the drums, of course," he added with a smirk.

"Why don't you sing with me?" Tara asked. "I can cue you in."

Liam's heart warmed toward her when Teague expression lit with excitement.

"Want to try it out?" Tara asked.

"You mean right now?" Doug asked, he threw a questioning glance at his mates. "It'll take us a while to set up."

"I can help," Teague offered with that heart-breaking eager puppy look on his face that Liam had been missing for months—if not years.

"I've got some cookies in the kitchen," Tara offered, "in case anyone's hungry."

Liam smiled, watching her, wondering if she had the natural ability to turn every day into a party.

Teague fell into a pattern of coming over to Tara's as often as he could after school so he could practice the drums and learn the Rabid Rabbit's musical numbers. Of course, Chewy always came with him, and on most days, Tara would have cookies waiting for him. Liam would pick his son up every night and return him to Eva's house, but before he did that, he'd often stay for a Scrabble rematch.

He'd yet to win.

Darrel and Will mostly hung out in their bedroom, watching TV and neither seemed to have a problem with the band practicing in their garage or Teague, Liam, and Chewy hanging around.

Liam couldn't remember a time where he'd seen Teague so excited. In fact, everyone seemed happy.

Everyone but Eva.

She sent Liam a text. I NEED TO SPEAK TO YOU

The six little words sent a warning chill down Liam's spine. He'd learned long ago that any conversation with Eva that had been preceded by I NEED TO SPEAK TO YOU was a conversation he didn't want to have.

Still, she was the mother of his only child and since he couldn't avoid her, he always did his best to appease her.

That evening when he dropped Teague off at Eva's place, he reluctantly followed his son up the steps of the front porch. A nasty-tempered calico cat gave him the stink-eye when Teague pushed open the front door.

"Your mom wants to talk to me." Liam dropped his hand on his son's shoulder. "Can you tell her I'm here?"

"Mom!" Teague called out.

"Not like that—" Liam started to chastise his son, but cut his words short when Eva emerged from the door leading to the kitchen. Her frown told him they weren't about to have a friendly conversation. What had he ever seen in her?

She still wore her hair long and straight, but instead of the cut-off jeans and t-shirts she'd worn in high school, she now wore power suits and heels. He usually saw her at the end of the day when she could have let her hair down, but he knew that her working days at Steele and Anderson were long. He also knew that he should be proud of her for being able to attend law school as a single mom, but he credited that to Eva's supportive and yet ambitious parents. And, of course, Teague, always an easy child, who had to grow up with two teenage parents who both had something to prove.

Of course, they'd only been fourteen when they'd started dating. That had been a mistake. But Teague? No one could ever call him a mistake.

Eva stepped forward, dropped a kiss on her son's cheek. "Did you have dinner?"

"At Gram's," Teague answered with a nod.

"And your homework?"

"It's done."

"Good job," Eva said. "Now beat it so I can talk to your dad."

Teague bounded up the stairs.

"How's Chewy?" Eva asked as Teague's door closed with a click.

"Huh, good. Teague loves him."

"That's not all he loves." She sucked in a deep breath before continuing. "Tell me about the Rancid Rabbits."

"Rabid Rabbits," Liam corrected with a grin.

"Tell me about them."

"Huh, what do you want to know? They have a band. They're actually pretty good. They have a contract with Atlantic Records and a spot on the Tonight show."

Eva paled. "Teague doesn't have anything to do with that though, right?"

"Of course not. He's just singing back up with Tara."

"Tell me about her. Teague talks about her nonstop."

"Again, what do you want to know?" When had Eva's kitchen transformed into an interrogation room? He glanced around at the slick empty counters, the stainless-steel appliances, the sterile surfaces, and compared it to the messy chaos in Tara's aunt's kitchen that usually carried a heavy but heavenly scent of something fresh from the heavens. Eva's kitchen smelled like cleanser.

"Who is she? Do you think it's weird that she's spending so much time with a teenage boy?"

"No. She's giving him drum lessons."

"But why?"

"Why not?"

"Are you paying her?"

"Yes," he lied, but he promised himself that he'd start paying her immediately. He should have thought of this, but he'd been so caught up in the planning of the upcoming Pet Adoption Day…

His answer eased the worried look in Eva's eye, but she responded with, "What's her story? She can't be all that Teague says she is."

Ha, that was it. Eva was jealous. "She's great. Teague loves her. Her aunt is the music teacher at Canterbury and she's helping out with the school play."

"Why doesn't she have a fulltime job?"

"I don't know," Liam said slowly.

Eva wrinkled her nose. "I'm not comfortable with Teague spending so much time with this person. She doesn't seem like a very good role model."

The back of Liam's neck prickled. "Why would you say that? You don't even know her."

"She's in a *band*. A rock band."

Actually, she wasn't, but Liam didn't feel the need to explain anything to Eva. "So?"

"I just don't think this is the best environment for a teenage kid."

"Environment? It's a garage. On a farm!" He turned to leave. "You really should come and listen to them practice before you make any judgment calls."

"Okay, I'll do that," Eva said, her words a challenge.

He grinned. "Yeah? When?" It would have to be a Saturday or Sunday — and those were his days with Teague — because Eva rarely left the office before eight and Tara insisted on ending practices before it got too late. She had an obsession about not over-tiring herself that he found odd but also adorable.

"I'll be there on Saturday."

Her tone told Liam that he'd need to warn Tara and the Rabbits.

Aunt Darrel stormed into the kitchen and plopped a bushel of apples onto the table so hard that a few bounced out of the basket and rolled to the floor with a series of kerplops.

Tara, who had been cracking eggs into a souffle dish, paused to stare at her aunt. It wasn't as if Aunt Darrel didn't frequently lose her temper about something — she had a fuse about has long as a Schnauzer's tail and almost as smelly — but five minutes ago Aunt Darrel had been gushing about this year's bumper crop of apples. What had happened to make her willing to bruise them?

"That woman! She really fries my fish!"

Tara glanced out the window at the lone house across the pasture. Was Aunt Darrel talking about Liam's Gram?

"She says your band practices are disturbing her chickens." Aunt Darrel's face had turned a scary shade of red and a vein throbbed in her neck. "What makes it worse is her grand-nephew is a part of the band! Doesn't that woman understand the power of music?"

"Sure, she does." Uncle Will shuffled into the room. "She's worried about the power the music has over her chickens."

"Double drat the chickens!" Aunt Darrel slammed her hands on the counter. "Children and music are much more important than chickens! Who cares if her chickens happen to lose a few feathers? Music not only improves creativity, it's also a known fact that it increases concentration, coordination, and boosts self-confidence!" Aunt Darrel launched into a rant lauding the merits of musical training.

Uncle Will and Tara shared a secret smile while Tara whipped her eggs.

A knock on the door interrupted Aunt Darrel's tirade. Bristling, she stomped across the room, squaring her shoulders and looking ready for a fight.

She flung open the back door, but visibly wilted when she saw Teague standing on the porch looking unsure of himself. Chewy stuck his nose in the door.

"What do you want?" Aunt Darrel asked.

"I, uh, my dad has offered to let us practice at his house," Teague told Tara. "He said it would keep the peace and preserve the feathers."

"That's nice of him," Tara said.

"And totally unnecessary!" Aunt Darrel huffed. "The Rotting Rabbits are not running away from the likes of her."

"They're the Rabid Rabbits," Teague corrected her.

"And this is my property!" Aunt Darrel said. "You tell your grandma that I can do whatever I like on my land! This is America!"

Tara wasn't sure what the state of the country had to do with anything, but she would rather keep practicing at her aunt's since it relieved her no-transportation dilemma.

"Now see here, Darrel," Uncle Will began. "The boy and his dad are offering a compromise—"

"Why should we compromise?" Aunt Darrel asked.

"There's no reason why the rodents can't practice in my garage!"

Uncle Will sighed and rubbed the top of his bald head, something he often did when he had to crosshairs with his wife.

"I told my dad you don't drive," Teague said to Tara. "You don't mind, do you? He said that if we're practicing when he's not working he'd pick you up."

"Um, that's nice, thanks," Tara said, although she agreed with Aunt Darrel and that was something that didn't happen too often.

Four

These are adorable," Liam told her when she handed him the new and improved fliers she'd created for Pet Adoption Day.

"I'm glad you like them." Tara flushed with pleasure. She'd had fun making them, and if she said so herself, they were way better than the antiseptic one Liam had made. "It was easy, because the animals were all so cute."

"Like you," Liam said.

"You probably will be singing a different song after I whomp you." She led him to the Scrabble board she'd set up on the dining room table.

He settled across from her, but they hadn't played for very long when she began to suspect that something was off.

"What's wrong?" she asked.

"Why?" He looked up from his tiles and met her gaze.

"Well, for one thing, you just passed up a triple word score to spell FOX over here when you could have just spelled OX and gotten three times as many points."

He blew out a sigh. "Just because I passed up a…" He swallowed and looked away from her. "I got some bad news."

She covered his hand with her own.

He blinked, refused to meet her gaze, making her wonder if he was tearing up. She squeezed his hand. "What is it?"

"Eva's moving to Redding and she wants to take Teague with her."

"Oh!" The small sound escaped Tara. Because she felt

as if she'd been punched in the gut, she could only imagine Liam's pain.

"He'll visit on school holidays," he said in a strangled voice. "And I can drive up there on the weekends."

"It's like ten-hours!"

"I know."

"Can she do that?"

"Technically, yes, especially since it's not out of state. Neither one of us want to go to court." His voice wobbled. "But I don't want to lose him."

"What does he have to say about it?"

"He doesn't know yet. She's telling him tonight." He glanced at his watch. "Maybe even right now."

"Well, doesn't he have a say?"

He shook his head. "When he's fourteen he can legally have a choice. But that's a crap decision to force a child to make."

"What's in Redding?"

"Pastor Millet. He's going to start a program for troubled youth." He shrugged. "It's a noble cause."

"And Eva's just going to go with him?"

"She's going to marry him."

"Ah. I wonder what Teague thinks about that."

"You can ask him tomorrow." He grinned as he put down the word equalize. But he didn't look happy, even though he just scored seventy-six points.

The next day, Tara was surprised to find Teague and Chewy on her doorstep.

"Hey, Teague, how are you?"

Teague gazed at her with a fierce intensity. "I have something I want to ask you."

"Sure." Tara ruffled the fur between Chewy's ears. "What is it?"

Teague looked past her to where her aunt and uncle sat

in the living room watching TV. "Can we go for a walk, or something?"

"Hmm, sounds serious."

"It is," Teague assured her.

"Okay, let me get my coat." Tara left the door open while she went to the closet and pulled out a jacket. She put it on and buttoned up against the sharp autumn chill. Away from the house, Tara matched her pace to Teague's. They wandered into the apple orchard. The trees were barren now and their craggy branches pointed at the graying November sky.

"You heard about my mom marrying Pastor Millet?" He slid her a glance.

"Yes."

"And that she's moving to Redding?"

Tara nodded. "It's pretty up there. I'm sure you'll like it. You can probably have a big yard. There'll be lots of squirrels for Chewy to chase."

"Chewy can't come. And neither can the drums."

"What?"

Teague kicked at rocks as he walked. "She thinks my music is *distracting* me."

"Distracting you? From what?"

"My *real potential*." He used air quotes to emphasize his words.

Tara couldn't help herself, she harrumphed and sounded a lot like Aunt Darrel.

"She doesn't get me like you do." Teague slid her a sideways glance before stepping in front of her, squaring his shoulders, and pronouncing, "I want you to marry my dad."

"What?" Tara froze as the world around her went still. The breeze that had been rustling through the trees hushed. The birds flitting through the air disappeared. Even squirrels chattering in the trees fell silent.

"Don't you see?" Teague gazed at her with sad but intense eyes. "If you married my dad, then I could stay with him."

"What?" She wanted to help him, but she couldn't follow

his logic. "I don't see —"

"It's perfect! I like you and I know he likes you. If I asked him to marry you, I'm sure he would."

Tara scrambled for the right words. "Your mom loves you. She'd be devastated if she could hear this conversation."

Teague started walking again. "But Bob hates me."

"That can't be true." Tara caught up to him in two long strides.

"Well, I hate him."

Tara tucked her hands in her pockets. She felt frozen on the inside as well as on the outside. "Why? I'm sure he's a nice man or else your mom wouldn't like him."

"He's a poser. He pretends he's all goody-goody, but he's really just about the money. He didn't want me to keep Chewy because he eats too much. He suggested I get a chihuahua. A chihuahua! Like the Taco Bell dog!"

"Well, that's bad, but —"

"He has no soul! Who would trade Chewy for a dog in a sombrero?"

"You know chihuahuas don't really wear sombreros, right?"

"I don't care what they wear, they're not Chewy!"

Tears rained down Teague's cheeks and he brushed them away with the back of his hand. "Can I tell my dad that you'll marry him?"

"Teague, your dad and I —"

He interrupted her. "Are perfect for each other! Besides, if he marries you then you won't have to work at that Academy for stuck-ups. You can stay at home and be there when I get home from school. Or, if you don't want to do that, I can still stay with Gram!"

Tara felt her heart breaking for him. "I'm so sorry, Teague."

"No!" He battled tears and his lips quivered. "Don't be sorry! You can fix this!"

"Teague, this is something for your parents to discuss."

"Why? Why don't I get a say? Why can't I decide where I want to live?"

"You can. Next year when —"

"A whole year! Do you know how long that is? It's not like summer camp!"

"I know."

Teague opened his mouth to say something but fell silent. Tara followed his gaze to a car cresting the hill. She guessed the Mercedes belonged to someone he knew.

"Is that your mom?" she asked gently.

He pressed his lips together and nodded.

The Mercedes pulled to a stop beside them and the window rolled down. A stunning brunette with severe eyebrows, prominent cheekbones, and thin red lips flashed Tara a quick glance before directing her attention to Teague. "I have been worried sick! Your great-grandmother didn't know where you were. She said you just disappeared."

"Why are you here?" Teague asked.

She searched for traces of Eva in Teague's face, but only saw Liam.

"I thought we could go and do something fun," Eva said, her voice unnaturally cheery.

"Aren't you like, supposed to be at work?" Teague asked.

Eva brightened. "I'm going to be working from home from now on." She tacked on, "Except for when I have dispositions or court."

Tara wanted to know how that would work but decided it wasn't her place to ask.

"You'll go to court in Redding?" Teague asked.

"No, I'll have to come to L.A., but," she waved her hand as if all those future court procedures didn't matter, "you and I need to chat. Now."

Teague's gaze met Tara's for a heartbreaking moment before he handed Tara Chewy's leash. "Can you take him to my Gram's house for me?"

"Sure." Tara wanted to hug him, but she held herself back, took possession of Chewy's leash, and waved goodbye as Teague and Eva drove away.

The Pet Adoption Day was mainly sponsored by the Oak Hollow chapter of the Humane Society, but many of the local merchants like the Pet Parlor, Pattie's Poodle Up-dos, and the Hay, Feed, and Farm Supply store also participated.

Liam didn't have a booth, per se, but since it was a large gathering of animals as well as people, he had agreed to spend the day in the park in case of an emergency. Santa Ana winds blew off the desert, making the day unseasonably warm for early November. If he was uncomfortable, he knew the animals had to be not only hot but also keyed up and nervous.

Tables, booths, and makeshift cages had been set up across the park. Mr. Frank had brought three of his horses and was offering ten-minute rides for ten dollars. Mrs. Jorgensen who owned the bakery was sponsoring a pie-eating contest that cost ten dollars to enter — all of the proceeds would go to the Humane Society. The Canterbury School, where Tara was temporarily working, ran the Pet Parade.

He spotted Barry Sprog, Canterbury's science teacher, leading Capra, the school's goat, by a leash. Barry hailed him. "How's it going, Doc?"

"Good, Barry. They let you spring Capra from his pen?" Liam patted the goat while Capra sniffed his sweat-shirt pocket looking for the strips of beef jerky Liam had tucked away.

"Crazy, right?" Barry gave the animal an affectionate grin. "This varmint is a handful when he's locked up. Let loose, there's no telling what sort of mischief he'll get into."

"Well, keep him on his leash and we'll all be safe."

But Barry wasn't looking at Capra. Liam followed Barry's gaze and spotted Tara across the green. Wearing a flowy floral skirt and peasant blouse with her vibrant hair tied back in a ribbon, she looked lovely. She held a giant, fluffy white rabbit in her arms while chatting with Doug and Skip.

"She's a pretty little filly, isn't she?" Barry asked.

Liam guessed he wasn't talking about any of Mr. Frank's horses.

"You're talking about Tara?" Liam asked in a tight voice.

"She's working at the school as the accompanist for the choir. Really gifted. I wonder what she's doing with those losers."

"You mean the Rabid Rabbits?"

Barry snorted. "Well, that would explain why she's holding the bunny."

"The Rabbits are actually pretty good. She's been filling in for them while their lead singer is away."

"They're not much to look at, though, are they?"

Liam had to admit the Rabbits were a motley bunch. "They're more about how they sound than how they look."

"Most of the animals here are better groomed." Barry straightened his shoulders and headed her way. "I think I need to introduce her to Capra."

Liam followed, but Capra had other ideas — especially when he caught a whiff of Mrs. Jorgensen's pies. While Barry tried to steer Capra away from the bakery booth, Liam caught up with Tara.

"Hi." Other than that, he wasn't sure what to say. He wanted to ask her if Teague had mentioned his crazy idea to her, and if so, he needed to apologize for his son. But if Teague hadn't said anything, then Liam didn't want to tell her about it. Feeling awkward, he scratched his chin while scrambling for something to say.

"Hi," she returned. "Do you have a booth here?"

"No, I'm on call in case there's an animal medical emergency."

"That's nice." She stroked the bunny in her arms without meeting his gaze. "I mean — it won't be nice if there's an emergency, but it's nice of you to be here... just in case."

"Are you guys performing?" Liam asked, nodding hello to the Rabbits.

"We were going to," Doug said, "but there's some sort of problem with the sound system."

"Ah good." He caught himself. "I didn't mean I don't want to hear you perform—although I do get to hear you almost every day." Feeling increasingly uncomfortable, he ran a finger under his collar and said to Tara, "What I meant was, now you're free to take a walk… if you'd like."

"Sure." She smiled at him and placed the bunny back in his pen. "But are you sure you can leave?"

"Most people here have my number. Someone will call me if things get out of hand." He felt Teague's conversation hanging between them, making things difficult and awkward. They walked in silence to the river's edge. Once he knew that no one could overhear them, he blurted out, "Did my son suggest—"

Tara laughed and took his arm. "I won't hold you responsible for your son's ideas. It was his idea, right?" She bumped him with her hip.

"Of course!" He slid her a glance. "What idea exactly are we talking about?"

She gazed out over the river, not meeting his gaze. "That we should get married so you could get full custody and he wouldn't have to move to Redding."

"Right. That's what I thought we were talking about." He slid his hand down to hers and laced their fingers together. "Crazy, right?" He laughed, but it sounded forced, even in his own ears.

"That could never work."

Why would she think that? Was it him? Or Teague? He couldn't look her in the face. Instead, he gazed out over the river and watched a pair of Mallard ducks—male and female—floating on the water. "It sounds barbaric and marriage is, or at least it should be, sacred."

"I'm glad you feel that way."

"And I know you said you'd never marry, although—"

She laughed and turned so that she stood directly in front of him. "Just stop, okay? We're not getting married."

He wanted to argue with her, but she continued, "What I don't understand is why you can't have custody of Teague? If he doesn't want to go…"

"Eva has full custody."

"But why?"

"Well, in the beginning, it made sense. I was going to school…" Not wanting to admit that he'd been young and dumb, he let his words drift away. He still felt guilty that he'd been so irresponsible when Teague was a baby. He doubted he could ever forgive himself, and he knew that Eva — and her parents — never would.

"But if he doesn't want to go, if he'd rather stay here, shouldn't he be able to?"

Liam swallowed. "If you think Eva would just hand him over, you don't know Eva."

"You make him sound like he's a toy, but he's not. He's a kid. He should get a vote."

"And he will. Next year." He swallowed. "But one year is a long time, especially to someone his age. If he goes up there now, he'll make friends, start high school. He won't want to come back."

"He has friends here." She squeezed his hand. "Not to mention, you."

"And you." He leaned down so he could rest his forehead against hers and inhale her warm, flowery scent. "He loves hanging with you and the Rabbits."

"But we're temporary."

Another point Liam wanted to argue.

She broke away from him and a chill passed through him. He wanted to press against her, but she moved to the railing that lined the river walk.

"Floyd, that's the elusive leader-singer, called," Tara told him. "He'll be back by next week."

"That's good," Liam said. "For the Rabbits, but it won't change Teague's new-found passion for music and the drums."

"Eva's going to try and squelch that, isn't she?"

Liam bit his lip and didn't answer.

"Can't you take her to court, or something?"

"She's an attorney! You can't argue with an attorney and expect to win. She's a professional! Arguing is how she makes her living. I deliver calves and stitch up wounds. What chance do I have against her?"

"I just think—" She stopped herself and squeezed his hand. "I'm sorry. It's none of my business. But I'll miss him, too."

"Let's talk about something else," Liam said in a strangled voice.

She dipped her head and after a moment launched into a funny story about something that had happened at school. "There's this girl who has a wild crush on Principal Rowling. I mean, there are lots of girls who are probably secretly in love with Principal Rowling."

Liam's heart twisted with a flash of jealousy, but he chose to ignore it.

"But only one who's really overt about it," Tara continued.

But Liam just half-listened. He desperately wanted to drop to his knee and beg Tara to marry him. When Teague had first introduced the idea, he, like Tara, had thought it crazy, but the more he thought about it, the more he wanted it. Even though he barely knew her.

But being with Tara only made him want it more.

On the next Monday afternoon, Eva surprised Tara by showing up at Canterbury Academy. The choir had just been dismissed and Tara had about a twenty-minute break until play rehearsal started. Eva stood in the hall while the girls swarmed past. She wore a black suit and with her dark hair, she looked like a raven surrounded by the girls in their bright school uniforms.

Tara didn't know whether to be terrified or flattered that Eva had come to visit her. But wait—maybe she hadn't. Maybe she had some other reason for coming to the all-girls' school. Tara racked her brain, trying to find some logical excuse that had nothing to do with her, for Eva's sudden appearance.

Sighing, she tucked her sheet music into her bag and headed for the door and the inevitable but unavoidable confrontation. Her thoughts went back to what Liam had said: Eva specialized in arguments, while Tara did her best to avoid them.

"This is where you work?" Eva said with a sniff.

"Yes," Tara countered, refusing to be embarrassed for Canterbury. It had an excellent reputation as an outstanding school.

"And what do you do here?" Eva asked although Tara thought it pretty obvious given she'd just been sitting behind the piano and was now toting sheet music.

Tara willed herself not to be intimidated by Eva. "I think a better question might be what are you doing here?"

"I've come to talk about my son."

Tara looked at her wrist, even though she didn't own a watch, and marched past Eva. "He's a great kid. You must be really proud of him."

Eva matched her pace. "I am." Her voice softened. "But I'm also worried. I want to make this transition as easy on him as possible."

"But why force him to make a transition at all?"

Eva blinked at her and placed her hand on her chest. The diamond ring on her finger sparkled in the fading afternoon light. "I'm getting married! Bob and I will be a family, and we want Teague to be a part of that."

"Well, of course he will be."

"I'm glad you see it that way."

"But I just don't see why your getting married means that Teague has to move away from his dad and his friends."

"His *dad* basically wasn't around for the first five years of Teague's life," Eva's voice dripped with scorn.

"So, that means he doesn't get to be around for the next five? Is that what Teague wants? Revenge?"

"Revenge?" Eva scoffed. "Nobody said anything about *revenge.* I just think that Liam doesn't get to have a say—"

"But I didn't say anything about Liam. I asked about Teague... and what he wants."

Eva snorted. "He's a child!"

"He's a great kid with ideas of his own. Have you asked him how he feels about moving?" She stopped and studied Eva.

The woman flinched beneath her gaze.

"You have. That's why you're here." Tara laughed. "Don't worry. I'm not going to marry Liam."

"Marry Liam?" Eva's voice squeaked with surprise.

"Oh, so Teague didn't tell you his scheme." Tara scratched her head, now puzzled more than ever. "Why are you here, Eva?"

"To ask you, as a fellow mom—"

"But I'm not a mom."

"Whatever." Eva waved away Tara's non-existent motherhood, making Tara hate her. "I want to terminate Teague's music lessons."

Aunt Darrel passed by and must have overheard the conversation because she stopped to put in her two cents. "Why would you, as a *mom*, do that?"

Eva swallowed, clearly surprised that Tara now had a backup conspirator.

Darrel stepped in front of Eva, balled her fists and planted them on her beefy hips. Standing almost nose to nose, she spat out, "Music not only improves creativity, it's also a known fact that it increases concentration, coordination, and boosts self-confidence!" Darrel's face turned a scary shade of red. "Plus, students who study music statistically perform better at math and language skills!"

"That's a skewed statistic," Eva sneered without backing away.

"Why would you say that?" Darrel leaned in with squinty

eyes and lowered eyebrows.

"Well, *obviously*," Eva spoke with a know-it-all arch in her voice, "parents who can afford to pay for music lessons are also more likely to also be better educated."

"Music transcends socioeconomics barriers," Darrel pronounced and she jabbed her finger in the air and pointed at the ceiling.

"It's not that I disapprove of music education," Eva said, folding her arms and looking bored. "I just don't think that a rock band is a good influence on him."

"You got a problem with the Rocking Rabbits?" Darrel braced her legs shoulder-width apart as if bracing against a storm surge.

"It's Rapid Rabbits," Tara muttered.

"Well, yes," Eva said. "Why would they want a kid hanging around?"

"There are plenty of child proteges that have gone on to have tremendous success," Darrel pronounced.

"Success at what?" Eva asked, her tone dripping with sarcasm.

"In the music industry, of course!" Darrel exclaimed.

A few of the girls who still lingered in the hall, hushed their conversations and paused at their lockers. One of the girls, a senior with long blonde hair, watched with a smirk on her face. Tara tried to remember the girl's name… it had something to do with the sky.

"Teague doesn't have a future in the music industry," Eva said.

"Have you asked him?" Darrel asked. "Maybe that's what he wants."

Eva's mouth dropped open, but she quickly regrouped and turned back to Tara. "Obviously, my visit here was a waste of time. I had hoped you would see reason and willingly terminate Teague's music lessons, but I guess I'll have to do it myself."

Tara suddenly understood and her compassion level for Eva skipped up a beat. "Ah, you don't want to be the bad guy. Again."

"Yes! Damn it!" Eva exploded, sending Tara's compassion-level into a tailspin.

Tara opened her mouth to tell Eva that swearing in front of the girls wouldn't be tolerated, but Eva's rant continued.

"I'm sick of being the villain!" Eva pushed her hair off her face. "Liam gets to be all fun and games! You want a giant, furball of a dog? Sure! You want ice cream for dinner? Why not? Meanwhile, I have to enforce things like homework, vegetables, and bathing!"

Being a single mom had to be a lot of work and a constant balancing act. And although Eva looked like she had it all together, maybe she didn't want to do it by herself any longer. Tara couldn't blame her for wanting to get married and create a new home that included Teague. "I'll talk to the Rabbits," Tara said. "But they're probably not going to be around much longer, anyway. Floyd, their lead singer, is back, and he has plans."

"What?" Aunt Darrel grabbed Tara's arm and spun her to face her. "You're giving into this woman's demands? Is she the one paying for the music lessons?"

Tara lifted a questioning eyebrow at Eva.

"No," Eva conceded.

"So, you can't cancel them, can you?" Darrel asked.

"I can discourage Teague," Eva said.

Tara guessed that wouldn't make her very popular. "I wouldn't try to do that," she said gently.

Eva pressed her lips together and gave Tara a dirty look.

"Well, it seems we're at an impasse." Darrel looked at her wristwatch. "Come on, Tara. Play rehearsal will start any minute and we can't be late."

Darrel marched down the hall. Tara trailed after her, but her heart hurt for Teague, Liam, *and* Eva.

The first thing Tara noticed when she walked into the room where she and the Rabbits practiced was a large bouquet of red roses in a cut crystal vase.

"What are these?"

Teague flushed. "There for you! From my dad!"

"Your dad?" Tara questioned, disliking the guilty look on Teague's face.

The Rabbits shuffled around, looking uncomfortable. No one would meet her eye.

"Where is he?" Tara asked.

Teague perked up. "You want to see him, right? To thank him?" He stood a little straighter. "I'll go and see if I can find him." He bolted from the room.

As soon as he'd disappeared down the hall, Tara faced the Rabbits. "Those are from Teague, right?"

Hal shuffled his feet while Doug fiddled with his guitar.

"You guys are worthless," Tara said, her voice thick with laughter.

Teague burst back into the room. "My dad's not here, but he said to give you this." He shoved a coupon for See's Candy at her. "He said he was going to buy you a box, but he…" Teague struggled to find the right words. "He, huh… didn't know what kind of chocolates you like." He cocked his head. "What's your favorite?"

"That's really hard to say," she said. "I guess I like them all."

Relief swept over Teague's face. "Maybe you and my dad can pick out your chocolate's together. There's a See's Candy shop at the mall. He can probably go tonight."

"We should probably just practice." Tara flashed a glance at the Rabbits. They didn't seem put out that the chocolate discussion was eating into their jam session. "That's why we're here." She took her place behind the microphone while

Teague, looking really pleased with his match-making scheme, fixed himself in front of the standing microphone beside her.

Anger pulsed through Tara as she thought about Eva trying to take Teague away from his dad, his home, his friends, and his love of music. Already, she'd grown to care for the boy. Not just because he reminded her of a young Liam, but because he was earnest, so intense, and eager to learn.

Cooper strummed a few chords, Doug chimed in, and after a few beats, Tara joined them. When Teague came in, she had to admire his ability — his feel for the music. As her aunt would say, he had a gifted interpretation. It was a shame his mom couldn't hear it.

Her thoughts skittered to a quote by Friedrich Nietzsche, *and those who were seen dancing were thought to be insane by those who couldn't hear the music.* Some people heard the music and others couldn't. How many could if they would only stop to listen? But how many just lacked the ear? What role did choice play in the matter?

There's a reason they say you *play* an instrument. If you play because it brings you joy, that joy resonates in your performance. If you perform for another reason — that's also evident. *It's really hard to hide your true feelings,* Tara thought. And if she wasn't careful, her own would soon be too tangled around Liam and Teague to pull away without getting hurt.

The band practiced non-stop for a couple of hours. When Skip demanded a break, Tara touched her forehead, worried. Why did she let music do this to her? It carried her away, made her forget. Was it this way for everyone? Or was her total immersion in music unique? She stumbled out of the room, down the hall, and past the Rabbits lining up in front of the bathroom door.

"Let me get you water," Teague said, coming behind her

and touching her elbow. "Or do you want something else? I think we have some juice. If we were at my mom's house, she'd have cranberry juice. I don't know why." He made a face. "Nasty stuff, but she drinks it like it's Coke."

Tara didn't listen but hurried for the door. Once outside, she took a deep breath and let the cool air fill her lungs. The distant hills with their bright fall colors swam before her eyes. Reaching out, she steadied herself against the house. The wood clapboard beneath her hand stabilized her. She stepped closer, eased around a large hydrangea bush and leaned against the wall. Her knees softened. She closed her eyes and watched fireworks exploding inside her head.

Five

Dad! You have to find her!" Teague cried, obviously distressed. "She just disappeared!"

Liam's gaze went from his son's distressed face to the vase of flowers. "You told her the flowers were from me?"

"What does that have to do with anything?" Teague asked.

"Well, maybe she left because she felt pressured." Liam dropped a heavy hand on his son's shoulder. "You and I need to have a talk about honesty."

"Dad! Right now is not the time to talk!" Teague pushed past Liam, grabbed his jacket from the hook on the wall and strode for the door. "We need to find her!"

Liam trailed after Teague, refusing to let his concern escalate.

"She doesn't even drive!" Teague said. "You were supposed to drive her home!" He banged out the front door.

Liam followed, neglecting to get his own jacket.

Teague threw over his shoulder, "I promised her you would take her to the mall to pick out a box of candy."

"What?" Liam caught up to his son in two large strides, but he was losing ground on the conversation. "Son," he placed his hand on Teague's arm and spun him around, "you have to accept that Tara isn't going to marry me so that you can stay in Oak Hollow."

"Dad, you aren't even trying!" Teague blinked back tears and jerked his arm out of Liam's grip.

Liam knew if he didn't do something, he'd lose his son—again. But he couldn't marry Tara just to win his son's custody—and good graces. Teague needed to see that.

"Marriage isn't something to take lightly," he said. "It's a covenant two people make before God."

Teague crossed his arms and braced his feet shoulder width apart. "Then why are there all those chapels of love in Las Vegas?"

Liam knew Teague was referring to the Elvis Presley movie they had watched with Gram last Sunday where Elvis had married Ann Margaret. "Do you really want me to take Tara to a chapel of love in Las Vegas? She's not that kind of girl."

Teague sniffed and Liam watched his son's anger softening. "She doesn't take things lightly," Liam continued. "She's not brash or impetuous. She's cautious. She thinks things through. She feels deeply." She was everything he was not. Everything he wanted to be.

Besides, she'd told him from the beginning that she had no intention of marrying.

Which just didn't make sense.

If anyone should marry, it should be her. He warmed thinking of her in his home… in his bed. He shook himself and concentrated on his son.

"We have to find her," Teague repeated, sounding like a broken record. "Do you think she tried to walk home?"

"Seven miles? I wouldn't think so," Liam said. And it hurt his pride to think she'd go to such lengths just to get away from him.

Tara sat on a bench flicking the dirt off her jeans. Somewhere, she'd lost her phone. She hoped it was at Liam's house in the room where she'd been practicing, but she worried that she'd dropped it behind the hydrangea bush when she'd fallen… when she'd had an episode.

Her doctors had told her that she'd outgrow the seizures as she matured, but that hadn't been the case for Uncle Will and she didn't want to get her hopes up and believe that she would be any different. In her experience, the disorder, like lightning without rain, struck without much warning. Sure, it helped if she avoided the obvious triggers like sleeplessness, stress, and flashing lights, but even if she carefully monitored her lifestyle and environment, a seizure could take her by surprise and destroy her.

That's why Uncle Will remained on the farm—away from peering people. That's why she needed to build her own solitary life.

She sucked in a deep breath and watched the sun fade behind the hills. Her attention drifted to an elderly couple playing chess. They were arguing over some play that the man was claiming legal. Tara smiled, thinking of her last Scramble game with Liam. He liked to use obscure medical terms—words that no one without a science background would be likely to know. It didn't help him. He'd yet to win.

Her smile faded and she bit her lip. She had to give him—and Teague—up. They were not a part of her plan.

"Tara, isn't it?"

She swiveled when she heard her name and spotted Chad, the P.E. teacher from Canterbury, heading her way. She stood. Her legs still felt wobbly, so she gripped the back of the bench. How had she managed to walk the two blocks into town?

The elderly couple stopped arguing as he approached. The woman grinned and moved her pawn so it trapped the man's queen.

"Darn, you black-haired buzzard!" the man exploded once he returned his attention to the game.

Chad smiled and called out, "Looks like you're ready to head home, hey gramps?"

The man shuffled to his feet, grumbling.

The woman also stood, gathered her purse, and gave Chad a winning smile. "Nothing like a good game to get the juices flowing!"

Chad chuckled, but his expression turned serious when he gazed back at Tara. He reached out and plucked a leaf from her hair. He studied it as if he expected it to tell him how it had gotten lodged in her curls. "You weren't tree climbing, were you?"

"No, of course not." Her voice sounded as shaky as her knees. She cleared her throat.

"Everything okay?" he asked.

She nodded. "But I've lost my phone... and I need a ride home."

Chad flipped his keys in his hand. "We can give you a ride, can't we Gramps?"

"No!" Tara's voice came out too sharply. "I mean, that's not necessary. I live with my aunt and uncle and it's quite a way out of town."

"I know where your aunt lives," Chad said. "And it's not out of our way. Actually, we're neighbors. Come on."

"If I call my aunt—"

"But why?" Chad flipped his keys and looked impatient. "Unless, she's expecting you?"

"No." He was probably wanting an explanation but she didn't feel she had one to offer—even if he was driving her home. She decided to change the subject. "Will we need to wait for your wife?" she asked the elderly gentleman.

"My what?" Chad's grandfather sputtered.

Tara's hand flew to her mouth. "Oh! My mistake. I thought that—"

"You thought that buzzard was my wife?" Chad's grandfather pretended to be outraged, but Tara caught his hidden smile.

"If we wanted to wait for his wife, we'd have to wait for a long time," Chad said.

"'Til resurrection day," the man huffed. He held out his hand and Tara shook it.

"My name's Bern. This here is my grandson, Chad."

"We've met," Chad said. "Tara accompanies our school choir."

"And I'm playing for the school play," she added.

"Ah, you must be talented," Bern said.

They headed for the parking lot and Tara and Chad both slowed their pace to match Bern's.

"Everyone is at something," Tara told him.

Bern made a harrumphing sound.

Tara looked over her shoulder and watched Bern's chess opponent shuffle into the bakery. She would have sworn the elderly couple was married. "Do you play chess often?"

"Not often enough," Bern said at the same time Chad said, "Every day."

Bern shot his grandson a look. "Not when it rains!"

Chad stopped in front of a truck with a crew cab and held open the door for Bern.

"So, you come and play with the buzzard every day… unless it's raining?" Tara asked.

Chad waited for his grandfather to climb in before closing the passenger side door. "And we're in a drought," he told Tara. "So, he plays a lot."

Tara climbed into the backseat, wondering about the elderly couple's relationship. Obviously, they must enjoy each other's company, so why not marry?

She closed her eyes and leaned back against the seat. Liam's face swam into her memory.

"How long have you and Liam been dating?" Chad asked.

"Oh! We're not dating!"

"You're not?" he chuckled and glanced at her through the rearview mirror.

"What made you think we are?"

"The Canterbury rumor-mill. Let me put it this way, quite a few of the girls make sure they're in the barn when Liam checks in on the 4-H animals." He turned the ignition and the truck roared to life.

"Oh." Tara had noticed that not all of the girls were particularly friendly. Was that why? She had just thought they were snotty, but could it be they saw her as competition? She didn't know what to say. Should she tell Chad that there was nothing between her and Liam?

"We're kind of like Bern and…" Tara began.

"The buzzard?" Bern quipped.

Tara finished, "But we play Scrable, not chess."

"I've known Liam since grade-school," Chad said. "He's a good guy."

She didn't need Chad to tell her this.

"What happened to you?" Liam asked her the next day when she came to practice.

"What do you mean?" she asked.

"According to Teague, you disappeared during a practice."

"I didn't disappear, I just went home because I wasn't feeling well."

"How did you get there?"

"I got a ride from a friend."

He reached into his pocket and pulled out her phone.

"Thank you!" She plucked it from his hand.

"The gardener found it under a bush in my front yard." His voice dripped with suspicion.

"Weird," she said.

"That's what I thought, too."

Tara glanced around at the nearly empty house. "Where's Teague?"

"His mom is holding him captive."

"Oh." Tara didn't know how to respond to this. Everything that her aunt would say about the situation floated to her mind, but she didn't want to undermine Eva's parenting or interfere with Liam's so she bit back her opinion. "And the guys?"

"They've gone to argue with Eva." Liam's lips quirked in a smile.

"I'd like to see that," Tara said.

"Me, too, but I thought it best if I stayed out of it. Eva has enough reasons to hate me."

"I'm sure she doesn't *hate* you."

Liam bit his lip and looked unsure. "I gave her a lot of reasons why she should."

"You were a kid." She put her hand on his arm. "Besides, it looks to me like you've been doing an awesome job of making it up to her *and* Teague."

"Thanks, but I'm not the good guy you think I am." His buzzing phone interrupted their argument. After scrounging it out of his pocket and glancing at the screen, he said, "Sorry, I have to take this."

She only half-listened to his conversation and her gaze flitted around his home. The formal living room and dining room had been converted into his veterinarian office. On the ground floor, only the kitchen and family room served their original purpose. The securely fenced backyard and enclosed back-porch housed visiting animals, although, there didn't seem to be any of those at the moment, save Chewy, who lounged at Liam's feet.

Liam pocketed his phone. "That was Cole Rowlings. Something is wrong with Capra."

"The goat?"

Liam nodded, looking hopeful. "You want to come with me?"

"Of course," Tara said. "Who would want to miss out on a goat emergency." She hesitated, unsure. "But what if Teague and the Rabbits come back to practice?"

"They can call us. The other option is you can stay here and wait."

"I'll come," she said.

"Sorry to bother you on a Saturday." Cole Rawlings sent Tara a smile and clapped his hand on Liam's shoulder. "But Capra didn't give me a choice."

Liam and Tara followed Cole across the quad and through the pasture that led to the stables.

Capra stood trembling in the center of her pen. He gulped, hacked out a series of retching coughs and sent saliva flying through the air.

Tara eased away from the spittle, but Liam didn't. He strode across the strewn-hay floor and motioned for Cole to follow. "Hold him against the wall so I can look in this mouth." After pulling on a pair of plastic gloves, he tried to pry the goat's jaws apart.

"MAWEE!" Capra bleated, sounding almost human-like while Liam pinned him against the wall.

"There's something back there," Liam said. "I can touch it, but—"

Capra jerked her head around and Liam stepped back, frowning.

"There's something in the back of her throat, but it's soft," Liam said. "Goats will eat almost anything, but I can't understand why if it's a piece of cloth she hasn't swallowed it."

Cole ran his hand over the goat's quivering hide. "Maybe he can just get rid of it himself?"

"No, I think whatever it is, is somehow lodged in his throat. I've got to get it out because he's beginning to fill with gas." He pointed at the goat's bloated belly. Capra responded with another succession of heaving coughs.

Liam shot Tara a quick glance. "Tara, could you go and get my flashlight from the truck? It's in a kit behind the seat." He tossed her the keys.

Tara hurried to the truck, retrieved the flashlight, and came through the pen. She didn't want to get in the way, but she liked feeling useful—rather like a nurse assisting a surgeon.

"Turn it on and hold it so I can look down his throat," Liam told her.

Capra wailed his child-like cry as Liam once again inserted his hand.

"I can see it!" Liam exclaimed. "It's hooked around the tongue with some sort of string."

He pulled and very slowly extracted a sodden, raggedy bra.

Cole, Tara, and Liam laughed while Liam held it in the air.

"I'm going to have to tell the girls to be more careful where they hang their laundry." Cole laughed and leaned against the side of the stable.

Capra responded with a giant burp.

Tara jumped away.

"He'll be doing that all day," Liam said.

"If she had swallowed it, could it have killed her?" Tara asked.

"Probably not," Liam answered as he pulled off his gloves. "It's crazy what ruminants can carry around in their bellies."

"Thanks again, Liam," Cole said. "See you on Monday, Tara."

She nodded and followed Liam to the truck. "Is your whole life like this?" Tara asked.

"Pretty much, although I do spend a lot of time in the office," he said. "But I love being outside with the animals. It's an incredibly rewarding job."

"Hi, Dr. Grant!" A girl with long blonde hair jogged up to them. Tara recognized Skylar from her aunt's first period choir class. She was one of those girls who took a lot of pride in being a first soprano, as if having a voice in a high register was something she'd worked hard for rather than a trait she'd been blessed with. Skylar, in Tara's opinion, seemed to have been abundantly blessed, and she lorded over the other girls in the choir.

"Hi, Skylar," Liam said before depositing his bag in the truck's crew cab.

Skylar tossed her mane over her shoulder and flashed

Liam a dazzling smile without acknowledging Tara. "I saw you at the movies last night with Teague. I wanted to say hi, but couldn't catch up with you. Did you like the show?"

"I had to leave half-way through." His gaze shifted to Tara as if he had something to explain to her, rather than Skylar. "Cat emergency."

"Oh! That's why I couldn't find you!" Skylar laughed, and sounded relieved. "Want me to tell you how it ended? We could grab some coffee, or something."

"Teague already filled me in," Liam said as he held the door open for Tara.

Skylar flashed Tara a quick, venomous glance. "Okay. See you around."

Liam climbed in the driver's side, started the truck, and eased it out of the Canterbury parking lot.

"Do you know Skylar from school?" Tara asked, hoping that she didn't sound jealous.

"I've known her for most of her life. Her parents raise Arabians. Horses," he clarified when she looked confused. "They have a ranch just outside of town. I've been attending their horses ever since Skylar was young."

Tara didn't want to talk about Skylar and she cast around for a change of subject. "It's cool that you found something that you love that you're also good at."

He sent her questioning glance. "But so have you."

"No, not really."

"What do you mean?"

"My position at the school isn't full-time. It can't support me."

"Have you talked to Irena? She may be willing to increase your hours and responsibilities."

"I can't do that." She could only work at the school as long as she was in close proximity to her aunt, but of course she couldn't admit that to Liam.

"Why not? You're a gifted musician, you like kids—I'm assuming because you're so great with Teague—"

She cut him off, hoping to stem the conversation. "Teague's a great kid. He's easy to teach… and love."

He grinned. "You love my kid?"

"Who doesn't?"

His expression clouded. "Not to speak ill of my ex, but this whole situation is killing me." He gripped the steering wheel. "Don't worry. I don't think Teague's solution is viable."

She wrinkled her nose, once again disliking the sudden turn in the conversation.

"It would be silly just to get married, so I could fight for full custody," he said.

"Of course," she agreed.

"But sometimes I feel like Eva uses Teague as a weapon. He's the sword she uses to flay me."

"You look unscathed to me," Tara said gently. "And she's probably not intentionally trying to hurt you."

"Yeah, but she still is… and what's she's doing to Teague is even worse."

"What would you have her do?"

"Leave Teague with me," he said without missing a beat.

"Would you ever take her away from him? If the situation was reversed, would you ask him to leave her so that you could marry someone who lived five-hundred miles away?"

He thought for a moment. "No." With his gaze straight ahead and his arms rigid, he held very still. "In the beginning, I wasn't a great dad."

"But you are now."

"I'm sure that's debatable. Eva has a different opinion."

"So what? Teague's opinion on that is the only one that matters, and he loves you."

Liam blew out a breath. "I really don't want to go to court. What chance would I have? She's a lawyer!"

"So, don't go."

"But I don't want to lose him!"

She put her hand on his thigh. "He has a year until he can decide for himself, right?"

Liam nodded. "But what if after a year, he decides he wants to stay in Redding?"

"That's a risk you'll have to take. In the meantime, he can come and visit on weekends and holidays. And three months of the year will be summer break!"

"What if he doesn't want to come?"

"We'll just have to make sure that he loves it so much, he'll be dying to come." Tara caught herself, aware that she'd accidentally clumped herself into Liam's camp. The smile on his face told her he'd noticed her slip as well.

Six

Two juniors, Maddie and Chloe, banged out a boisterous rendition of "Chop Sticks" on the piano. Since they monopolized the bench where Tara typically sat, she wasn't one hundred percent sure of what to do with herself. Where was Aunt Darrel and why hadn't practice started yet? Tara glanced at the clock and tried to avoid eye-contact with the girls milling around the music room.

Voices coming from the nearby auditorium told her that Nora, the English teacher/play director, had already started the rehearsal of lines.

Aunt Darrel, who was a stickler for order and lived to the beat of a clock as rigidly as a well-tuned metronome, typically had the girls lined up on the bleachers and warming up their voices by now. Was this something Tara should do in her absence? Would Aunt Darrel appreciate her interference?

Tara hovered near the piano, unsure how to get the girls' attention. Tara, who had been homeschooled, found the atmosphere at Canterbury fascinating and she tried to picture herself being friends with anyone in this jostling, exuberant crowd. But then she'd remember her episodes and the fantasies would fade…

Marcy, the girl who starred as Alice, marched to the front of the room. Using a ruler, she banged on a music stand. "Attention! Attention!"

A few of the girls stopped chattering but most carried on,

ignoring Marcy. Tara, who felt a wave of embarrassment for Marcy wash over her, was surprised when Marcy didn't seem to mind this insubordination at all. She simply rapped her ruler harder and raised her voice. "Guys! We need to learn this music!" Marcy shot Tara a glance. "Ms. Allen is going to play it through once."

Thankfully, the girls at the piano were obviously a couple of the few listening to Marcy. They vacated the bench and slunk away to find seats.

Without the tinkling piano the room fell unnaturally still. Tara hurried to fill it. She'd only played a few bars when Darrel bustled in the room.

"Thanks, dear, for getting the beasts in line," Aunt Darrel whispered to Tara over the top of the piano.

Tara opened her mouth to say that the person she should be thanking was Marcy, but Aunt Darrel had already positioned herself in front of the choir. When she raised her baton, the girls hurried into their positions on the bleachers.

How did she do that? Tara wondered. How did she make the girls line up and shut up by just picking up a baton?

"We missed our entrance, dear," Aunt Darrel said. "Pick up on measure six, please."

Tara circled back to the measure right before the girls joined in. Her spine relaxed as the choir voices lifted.

Aunt Darrel led the music with her entire body. She didn't just wave her arms. She swayed, rocked on her feet, gestured wildly with crescendos, and hunched her shoulders and pinched her fingers when she wanted the girls to drop their volume. Aunt Darrel lived and breathed the music whole-heartedly.

Tara tried to match her piano performance to Aunt Darrel's conducting. The first two numbers were easy, but midway through the third piece, Darrel faltered. She stepped to the side.

At first, Tara thought this new movement must be somehow music related, but then Darrel clutched her heart. Her knees buckled. She stumbled before she fell.

Several of the girls screamed. A few bounced off the bleachers.

"She's dead!" a freshman named Jilly announced.

Tara sprung away from the piano bench to go to her aunt's side. She picked up Darrel's limp wrist. A steady thrum of a pulse reassured her. "She's alive," she announced to the girls, "but she needs help. Someone go and get Dr. Rowling."

A crowd of girls surged for the door while Tara held her aunt's hand and willed her to live.

"This changes everything," Tara told her mom over the phone. "I can't work at the school without Auntie Darrel!" She stood over her suitcase with her phone wedged between her shoulder and her ear.

"Darling," Mom murmured, "of course, you can."

"No, I can't. When I was at the school, I never left Auntie's side. If I were to have an episode, she'd be there and she could recognize the warning signs and triggers."

"Uncle Will said that Darrel should be back in business in a few weeks," Mom said. "She's planning on going back to school after Christmas break."

"But don't you see? That's too late!" Tara's voice squeaked in fear. "The school play is the first week of December. I can't do this without Aunt Darrel!"

Without listening to her mom's arguments, Tara threw her clothes into the suitcase. She hesitated when she picked up the Scramble game. For an odd reason, the memory of Bern and black-haired woman he'd called the buzzard flashed in her mind. Liam's image quickly followed. Then she saw Teague's excitement over the drums... what if she taught music in her own home?

She'd have to live closer to town. Maybe somewhere where kids could walk after school. Liam's house would be perfect.

No. Impossible.

She had a plan and Liam and Teague weren't part of it. Why deviate?

When she had tucked everything into her bag, she bumped it into the hall and down the stairs. She paused when she passed her aunt and uncle's room and spotted the unmade bed.

Of course, Darrel had always made the bed. Uncle Will would be lost without her. Like so many men of his generation, he didn't even know how to make a sandwich. He only ate what Darrel put in front of him. Even when she taught at the school, she made his lunch as well as her own every morning. Tara needed to stay — for his sake.

But that didn't mean she could work at the school.

Slowly, she wheeled her suitcase back into her room and tucked it into her closet. Then she went to make her uncle his favorite lasagna.

That night while her uncle was at the hospital with Auntie Darrel, the doorbell rang.

Tara set down her book and padded across the floor to peer out the window at the shadowy figure on the porch. Irena Rawlings stood in the lamplight's glow with a bouquet of flowers in her arms.

Slowly, Tara pulled open the door. She still hadn't decided how — or if — she was going to school the next day. Maybe Irena had an idea? The time had come where she needed to confess her disorder to Irena, but then, maybe Irena had already figured it out. And now that she knew, she had come to let Tara go.

"I brought these for your aunt." Irena held up the bouquet of yellow roses.

"That's so sweet, she'll love them." Tara took the bouquet from Irena. "But she's still at the hospital."

"I know, but I wanted to speak to you."

Tara nodded and held the door open. "Would you like to sit down? Or will this be quick?"

"Do you mind if we sit and chat? We have some things to discuss."

A dismissal would be easy-peasy. In fact, Irena could have dismissed her over the phone. Tara led Irena into the living room and motioned at the sofa. Ignoring her beckoning book and the afghan she'd been curled into just moments ago, Tara sat in the club chair directly opposite of Irena.

"With your aunt out of commission for the next few weeks," Irena began, "changes will need to be made."

"I'm aware of that," Tara said.

"Of course, finding another music director is requisite," Irena said. "But I don't want to add finding an accompanist to my to-do list."

"You know I don't drive."

Irena nodded. "I hope you don't mind, but I've taken the liberty of speaking to Chad, our P.E. teacher. He has agreed to drive you to and from the school."

Tara shook her head. "You must know, or have guessed, that transportation isn't my only problem." Irena waited while Tara twisted her hands in her lap. "I have epilepsy. There's no way I can teach without my aunt."

Irena lifted an eyebrow, waiting for further information. When Tara didn't provide any, she prompted, "And why do you think that is?"

"Well, for one thing, Auntie Darrel is not only a nurse, but she's lived with my uncle who shares my disorder. She can recognize the symptoms and warning signs, steer me clear of triggers." She sucked in a deep breath. "I'm sorry, but I just can't imagine being at the school without her."

"What if we found someone else who, like your aunt, can recognize the warning signs?" Irena leaned forward and placed her hands on her knees.

"Someone who would just babysit me all day?" Tara couldn't see where this conversation was headed. "That would make me a very expensive music teacher."

"Not necessarily. I wouldn't pay him."

Tara shook her head, disbelieving. "Who would do that?"

"A dog."

"You would let me bring a dog to school?"

"Of course. The girls would love it."

"But getting a dog and training it would cost thousands of dollars!"

"Probably, but I know someone who could lend you the money. She'd be happy to. In fact, I've already asked her."

"Who?"

"Nora."

"The English teacher?"

Irena nodded.

"Why would she do that?"

"Because she wants the play to be a success and she knows you'll do an amazing job." Irena leaned forward and put her hand over Tara's. "You're an incredible musician with a generous spirit. I can't let you hide away from the world because of your condition."

Tara blinked back tears. "You don't understand…"

"No, I'm sure I don't. But can we at least try?"

"But the performance is in just a few weeks. We can't train a dog in so little time."

Irena stood. "There's someone I'd like you to meet. He's waiting in the car."

Tara followed Irena to her car where a beautiful golden retriever sat in the passenger seat. His tail thumped against the seat, welcoming her.

"He's a seizure response dog. Of course, he can't prevent seizures, but he can alert you to the warning signs and find help in case you need it. He comes with an instruction notebook!"

"He's beautiful," Tara breathed. "But I can't even…"

"Why not?"

"I'm already a charity case," Tara said. "My aunt and uncle aren't rich and they've already taken me in. This amazingly beautiful gift is another mouth to feed."

"If you'll accept a position as a music teacher at our school, I'll pay you the same salary as all the other teachers."

When Tara opened her mouth to argue, Irena continued, "And, if you wish, I can also arrange for you to teach private after school lessons and believe me, the parents are much more generous than even me."

"I find that really hard to believe," Tara said.

Irena pulled open the door and the massive dog jumped out. He wiggled a welcome and pushed himself against Tara's legs.

"Goodness, he probably outweighs you!" Irena exclaimed.

"What's his name?" Tara asked as she ruffled his ears and gazed into his warm brown eyes.

"That's up to you," Irena told her.

"Amadeus? No, Wolfgang!"

He plopped down at her feet and gazed up at her with adoring eyes.

"As a matter of fact," Irena said, "I have a gig lined up for you for next Saturday."

"Anything," Tara answered, battling tears as she stared at the creature in front of her.

Liam flipped through the morning mail, pulling out Christmas cards. He paused to read the postcard his parents had sent from Mali where they were serving as missionaries. This would be the first Christmas in years where they hadn't been together. He had spent several Christmas's without Teague, but none without his parents since he was discharged from the military. He wondered if they missed him as much as he missed them.

He collected the bills and rounded up the advertisements

for the trash, but noticed an expensive-looking envelope addressed to Dr. Trent Grant. The gold-embossed invitation felt heavy in his hand.

"What's that?" Teague strode into the room, his voice making Liam jump.

"Geeze! What are you doing here?" Liam said. "I thought you left with your mom!"

"I don't want to go." Teague grabbed an apple off the counter and took a bite.

Liam's thoughts sputtered. "Well, I don't want you to go."

"Then what's the problem?" Teague asked.

"Your mom will answer that. Does she know you're here?"

Teague shook his head. "She's too wrapped up in Barking Bob to notice I'm not in the moving van."

"Barking Bob?"

"It fits him."

"Don't tell your mom."

"She gets it and you would, too, if you ever listened to one of his sermons."

Liam glanced at his watch. "Aren't you supposed to be leaving about now?"

"I'm not going." Teague nodded at the card in Liam's hand. "What's that?"

"An invitation to a gala."

"Gal-who?"

"It's a fancy party."

"Yeah? Who's?"

"Mitzi."

Teague wrinkled his nose. "Do I know Mitzi?"

"I don't think so; she's a patient."

"Of yours?"

"Yes."

"You mean, she's a pet-owner."

"No. She's a pet." Liam handed Teague the invitation. "A Pekinese, to be exact."

"She calls you Uncle Liam?"

"Well, she mostly just yaps, but Mrs. Havers refers to me as Uncle Liam."

"Are you going to go?"

"Do I have a suit?"

"Will you need one?"

"And a tie," Liam said with a sigh. "Mrs. Havers throws really lavish parties." Liam set down the invitation and looked out the window. He had to go because he couldn't afford to offend Mrs. Havers.

The sound of crunching gravel made Teague dash to the window. "It's my mom!"

"You knew this was going to happen," Liam said.

"Why can't you fight for me?" Teague shook his apple in Liam's face.

"It's not that simple. Besides, I'd lose."

"How do you know that?" Teague asked. "You're not even trying." He bolted from the room, stomped down the hall and slammed his bedroom door.

Liam stood in the middle of his kitchen, feeling torn. His heart ached for his son, but he also knew he needed to confront Eva. If he didn't say or do something, she or Teague could cause irreparable harm to their tenuous relationship.

For the second time that morning, Liam wished for his mom or dad. His mom always knew how to calm a hostile situation while his dad always knew how to win an argument.

Eva blew into the room, her eyes darted about, searching for a sign of Teague. "This is kidnapping!" she said through clenched teeth.

"Hardly," Liam replied.

"You can't keep him!"

"And neither can you." Liam strolled across the room and parked his butt against the counter. "You might be able to get him to go with you to Redding, but for how long?"

Eva narrowed her eyes. "I knew you'd try something like this!"

"Calm down, Eva. I didn't even know he was here until five minutes ago." Liam knew immediately that those were the wrong words to say.

She pointed her finger at his chest. "And that's why you're an unfit parent!"

"Did you know he was here?"

She stared at him, but didn't answer. After glancing at her watch, she said, "We were supposed to leave thirty minutes ago. The traffic on the Five is going to be hell."

"Why don't you let him stay through the holidays?"

"But it's my turn for Christmas!"

"He can come up for New Year's." He tacked on, "If he wants."

"He's not old enough to know what he wants!"

Liam snorted.

Eva folded her arms across her chest and upped the wattage in her glare. "What is that supposed to mean?"

"Whatever you want it to, Eva." Liam pulled himself away from the counter and went to stand in front of her. Almost daily, he faced frightened, hurting, and sometimes dangerous animals. For his son, he could stand up against Eva. "But when you're thinking of everything that *you* want, please take a moment to consider *our* son."

Eva began to hurl insults at him as he headed for Teague's room, but he didn't listen. Her words were almost as futile as a Pekinese's bark.

"I've been driving your girlfriend to and from school," Chad told Liam.

"What?" Liam had one hand wrapped around a horse's tongue and the other clenched the balling gun. He shot the horse pill into the stallion's mouth before releasing the tongue and pulling away so he could look at Chad. Why had he chosen that particular moment to tell him this? He thought about asking who, but settled on, "Why?"

Chad ran his hand over the horse's back, calming him. "Darrel Poole had a heart attack. Didn't you know?"

"No. There's been so much drama going on with Teague and his mom, I haven't spoken to her in a few days…" Liam gathered up his equipment, stowed it in his bag, and tried to sound casual when he asked, "Do you know why she doesn't drive?"

Chad nodded. "She's epileptic. She and her aunt tried to keep it a secret, but it all came out when Darrel had to go to the hospital."

Liam breathed out a sigh and pulled off his gloves. "Why didn't she tell me?"

"She's probably ashamed."

He dropped the gloves in a plastic bag and wadded it up. "It's a medical condition, not a felony." Is that why she said she'd never marry or have children? He glanced out over the foothills at the fading sun, thinking that so much he hadn't understood about Tara now made sense. He knew that this news should be devastating, but it had the opposite effect. Rather than repulse him, it drew her to him.

"Irena got her a seizure response dog and he goes to school with her," Chad told him. "The girls are crazy about him."

"I have to meet him," Liam said. "You know, in a strictly professional sense."

Chad grinned at him. "You should now. She's worried that you know but are avoiding her."

Liam swore.

"What's the matter?"

"I have a party tonight!"

"Mrs. Haver's Twelfth Night?"

"Yes! How did you know?"

Chad nodded. "I'll be there and so will Tara."

Liam scrunched his eyebrows together. "Did Mitzi invite her, too?"

"Who's Mitzi?"

"The Pekinese."

"What?"

"Never mind, tell me about Tara."

"Mrs. Havers is paying her to play the piano."

"You're driving her?"

Chad nodded.

"I'll be there," Liam said. "She can go with you, but she's leaving with me."

Chad answered with a grin.

Liam steered his truck through the wrought-iron gates of Mrs. Haver's sizeable property. After parking, he climbed out and glanced at the Christmas lights streaming from the mansion across the wide lawn. Holly wreaths and boughs of pine tied with jaunty red ribbons decorated the front doors and porch. At some point, there had to have been a Mr. Havers, but Mrs. Havers had never mentioned him and Liam hadn't known how to ask.

He climbed the steps and a maid opened the door and led him inside. Above the clamor of dozens of conversations, he heard the tinkling piano. The music drew him like a magnet.

Mrs. Havers, a rail-thin, silver-haired beauty in a shimmery silky blue dress, had been chatting with her guests, but as soon as she spotted Liam, her expression lit up. "Why Dr. Grant! I'm so glad you could come! Mitzi will be so happy to see you! She's been fretting all day, but now that you're here I know she'll be pleased." She took Liam's arm. "You will pop in and say hi, won't you?"

Liam cast Tara a glance. With her porcelain skin and thin arms, she looked radiant. He longed to sit beside her and tell her that her disorder only bothered him to the extent it bothered her.

Mrs. Havers guided him down the hall, away from the piano and Tara. He told himself that visiting Mitzi would only take a moment and Tara would be easy to find.

Inside the study, a wood-paneled room decorated to look like a hunting lodge, Mitzi was curled up in an armchair before the fireplace. She jumped up and began barking a happy welcome when she saw him. As he drew closer, the little dog launched herself into his arms. He easily caught her, but stumbled when his shoe hit something. He glanced down at the dog bowl filled with a giant slice of chocolate cake.

"Mrs. Havers! You can't give a dog cake! She'll get sick!"

Mrs. Havers looked guilty, but didn't make a move to retrieve the bowl. "It's just a little something. She hates my shindigs and I thought this would cheer her up."

Liam set the dog back into the chair and bent to get the bowl. Holding it in front of him, he strode into the adjacent washroom and flushed the cake down the toilet.

"You understand why I did that?" he asked when he returned.

Mrs. Havers nodded, her lower lip stuck out in a pout. "I only hope that Mitzi will forgive you."

Liam opened his mouth, but words failed him.

"Come." Mrs. Havers took his arm. "Let me introduce you to my friends." She propelled him from the room and out into the party.

To his horror, Tara was gone. The piano bench had been deserted. He squirmed with embarrassment and impatience as Mrs. Havers repeatedly introduced him to her friends as Mitzi's favorite uncle. And then he spotted Chad across the room, laughing in a group of men.

He felt like a fish swimming upstream through a crowd of well-dressed and beautiful people, but he finally reached Chad's side. His friend nodded as if reading his mind, and motioned out the French doors.

Liam didn't even say a word, but hurried outside. The cold almost-winter air took his breath. But then he saw her leaning against the railing and looking out over the distant twinkling lights of the small town of Oak Hallow. Her dress swirled around her calves. She wore a shimmering wrap over her bare shoulders and diamond studs twinkled in her ears. There was something old-fashioned and lovely about her. She looked like she'd stepped out of a black and white movie and the moonlight made everything appear monochromatic.

Before he could reach her, his phone buzzed. His heart sank when he got the call.

Seven

$\mathcal{T}$ara glanced over her shoulder and spotted Liam staring at her. He held his phone in his open palm and looked stricken.

"Liam?"

"I have to go," he said, his shoulders slumping against his reality. "Mr. Duggan's dog Suzie…" His voice trailed away and he crossed the patio in three steps. "Come with me?"

"There's something I need to tell you," she began.

"I don't care that you have epilepsy," he said in a rush. "That doesn't matter to me at all. Well, it does, because I care about you and I know that it must matter to you a great deal. But—"

She squeezed his hand but didn't pull away. "You don't know what you're saying."

"I know I want to be around you all of the time."

"No, you don't," she began.

He leaned in and kissed her hard. In that instant, the party's noise fell away. Hopeless longing swept through her. She fought against it, against him, but he pulled her closer, kissed her deeper, and she melted. Her knees softened and she held onto him as if she'd drown if left on her own.

After pulling away, he leaned his forehead against hers. "I want to do that again and again, but right now—"

"I know." The normality of her voice surprised her. She inhaled deeply, loving his warm scent. "You have to go—for Suzie."

He bent low and nuzzled her neck. "Please say you'll

come." His breath jittered across the nape of her neck and she trembled from his nearness.

She wanted to argue—to tell him all the reasons why going with him didn't make sense—to help him see what a life with an epileptic would mean. She stopped herself. He wasn't asking her to share his life—not really—he was asking her to go with him to rescue a dog. Who could say no?

He had to go back to the office to get his bag and change his clothes, but he kissed her as he stood on the back porch beneath the moon. Then he kissed her again in the kitchen. He wanted to take her into his bedroom, but decided against it. He hurriedly changed into jeans and an old sweatshirt and left his suit crumpled on the floor. He promised himself that someday Tara would share this room with him and that thought made him kiss her again as they passed through the mudroom to the garage.

"What's this?" Teague stumbled from his bedroom, wiped the sleep from his eyes and grinned when his gazed focused on Tara. "Ah," he said. "Don't mind me!"

Grinning, Liam pulled Tara through to the garage and held open the truck door for her. He kissed her again before closing the door and jogging around to the driver's side.

His truck roared to life and they didn't speak for the two miles to Mr. Duggan's farmhouse. Tara rested her head on his shoulder and placed her hand on his thigh and he thought he'd die from his overwhelming sense of happiness and peace.

The Duggan's had a small collection of farm animals that Liam saw fairly regularly, but their little motley terrier Suzie had never been a patient before. Mike was a truck driver by trade and his wife Geraldine ran the farm. Because Suzie's appearance seemed to coincide with Mike's, Liam guessed that the little dog kept Big Mike company on his long hauls.

Mike Duggan, a bear of a man, met them at the door. "Sorry to bother you so late," he said before stepping outside and joining them on the porch. "But Suzie is scaring us. Her pups should be here and she's been rutting around all day, but about an hour ago she started panting…" He motioned for them to follow him inside, through the living room and to a warm kitchen where Suzie lay on her bed. Her ribs heaved as she glanced at Liam with scared and anxious eyes.

Geraldine appeared nearly as anxious. She sat on the floor beside the little dog and stroked her head.

Liam ran his hand over her abdomen. "She's ready to pop," he said.

"What can you do?" Mike asked.

"A cesarean?" Geraldine's voice quivered.

"You'd cut her open?" Mike sounded frantic.

"As a last resort." Liam dropped to one knee beside Suzie. "Can you bring me some hot water?" He slipped on some plastic gloves and carefully explored inside Suzie with one finger. "There's a big pup that's holding everyone else up." He tried to make his voice light, despite the knowledge that the leading pup would most likely be dead. "If we can get him out of the way, I bet the others will come easily." Not that he would want to bet on it.

He glanced at Tara and she sent him a smile that said, *I trust you. I know you can do this.*

"I don't like using forceps, but I'll give it one gentle try," Liam said. "If that doesn't work…"

"It'll work," Geraldine said with complete confidence.

"We should never have had her mated," Mike groaned. "I knew this was a bad idea."

"Just wait," Tara said softly. She put her hand on Mike's arm.

Mike turned pale when Liam poised the forceps above the dog and Liam worried that the big man might faint. Mike tore away from Tara, put his fist in his mouth and bolted from the room.

Suzie began to strain and within moments, Liam drew out a tiny, lifeless pup. It lay in the palm of Liam's hand. He pinched the chest and felt a weak heartbeat. After opening the pup's mouth, Liam softly blew into the creature's lungs a few times. When nothing happened, he laid the puppy on the bed to focus on the other arriving puppies.

After a few moments, Tara clapped her hands. "Look! He's alive!"

A teary-eyed Mike came back into the room to watch the miracle of life.

It was nearly two a.m. by the time Suzie finished delivering her brood. Liam examined each of them and Suzie didn't seem to mind in the least. She gazed up at him with tired, but happy, eyes.

Tara sagged against the kitchen chair, looking equally as drained. Liam thought back to her comments about the importance of her sleep and his heart twisted with remorse. He shouldn't have kept her out so late. After washing his hands and saying goodnight to Mike and Geraldine, he wrapped his hand around Tara's arm and pulled her to her feet.

"Let's get you home," he whispered in her ear.

She leaned heavily against him as they made their way to the truck. The moon smiled down on them and the stars glistened on the dew-soaked lawn.

"Thank you for coming with me," Liam.

"I wouldn't have missed it for the world," Tara said.

"Tomorrow's the town's tree-lighting ceremony." He slid her a glance. "Will you come with me?"

"Of course."

Of course, of course. Two little words had never carried so much meaning.

☜☞

Tara thought her jittery tingling were due to excitement. With Liam, she allowed herself a glimpse of a future she had never thought possible. He knew about her epilepsy, but he didn't care. Of course, he'd never actually witnessed a seizure. But her doctor had said she'd outgrow them. Maybe the one she'd had just a few days ago had been her last. She could always hope.

She smiled at her reflection in the entryway hall mirror and slipped in a pair of earrings.

"You can't take the dog, you know." Auntie Darrel stood behind her, looking stern. Ever since Darrel's release from the hospital, she'd been even crankier than usual. Tara chalked that up to pain and probably a heaping dose of frustration at her unaccustomed sense of helplessness. Not to mention, her aunt didn't like losing at Scrable and Tara didn't know how not to win. "There'll be fireworks and dogs don't like the noise."

"Fireworks at a tree-lighting ceremony?" Tara pulled her red pea-coat out of the hall closet and wrapped a tartan scarf around her neck.

"Every year. It's a waste of money, I say, but no one ever listens to me." Auntie Darrel harrumphed and ambled back into the kitchen. "Come, Wolfgang!"

The dog, who sat at Tara's feet, cast her mournful, pleading eyes.

"Are you sure you want him with you?" she called after her aunt.

"Well, he can't very well hide out in your room all night, now can he?" Auntie Darrel shot back

Tara didn't know why he couldn't, but decided everyone, including the dog, would always be happier if Darrel got her way. The sooner Wolfgang learned that, the better. "You better do as she says, sweetie," Tara told her dog.

After the doorbell rang, Tara stopped thinking about her aunt and dog and all her focus zoomed in on Liam. He stood under the porch light and the reflection bounced off his warm-brown hair and glinted in his eyes. Heat traveled from the top of her head to her toes. How could someone like him be interested in her?

"Hey, beautiful." He reached for her hand and pulled her close. After sending a quick glance over her shoulder to make sure no one was watching, he kissed her lightly on the lips—like a promise of good things to come.

On the drive into town, he told her about an angry, but giant, Clydesdale horse that had gone on a rampage on a neighboring farm. Then she told him about that day's play rehearsal.

"Will you attend our play?" she asked.

"I would love to," he said. "Only—"

"I know. Sometimes you get called away."

He shrugged. "Yeah."

"I know," she said.

He parked in his garage and climbed from the truck. They would walk the two blocks into town. A wave of weariness swept through Tara and she realized she should have expected this because finding a parking place any closer to Legionnaire's Park would be impossible. Maybe Liam could have dropped her closer, but then she'd have to wait for him. It was nicer being together. She tucked her hand around his arm.

"Where's Teague?" she asked.

He smiled down at her as if he loved that she cared about his son. "He'll be playing with the marching band. I dropped him off at the high school right before I picked you up."

"Ah, that's sweet. Do they play Christmas carols?"

He nodded. "I wish his mom could show a little interest in his music."

"Do you play an instrument?"

He grinned. "I played the trumpet until..." His voice trailed away.

"Until Teague?" she finished gently.

He tightened his lips.

"You can't regret him, you know."

"I know."

They crossed Elm and came to the corner of Main. Strings of Christmas lights crisscrossed the street and boughs of pine and holly tied with giant red ribbons adorned every lamppost. A giant Douglas Fir had been erected in the center of Legionnaire Park.

Liam glanced around at the crowd. "I should have brought us chairs or a blanket."

"I'm okay," Tara said with a smile, but the truth was, she was getting tired. Last night, because of the puppies, she hadn't gotten to bed until nearly three a.m. And then this morning, because she was dependent on Chad for a ride to the school and he needed to be there early for volleyball practice, she'd been at the school since six a.m. Couple the nearly sleepless night with the long school day plus play rehearsal, she was exhausted. But it felt so good to lean against Liam, to feel his arm around her and the length of him pressing against her, his breath in her hair — she couldn't imagine ever wanting to be anywhere else.

"Dr. Grant!" A breathless woman called to him, waving her arm above the crowd. She looked to be in her early thirties, so much closer to Liam's age than her own. She had long brown hair and wore a chic leather coat and tight jeans. "Could you come and check on Harry? He's trying to hack up something."

"Is he here?" Liam asked.

"No, he's at my grandma's nursing home." She nodded at the complex at the end of the street. "You don't mind, do you? Grandma is beside herself."

"No, of course not." He glanced at Tara. "You don't mind, do you?"

"No," Tara said, because what else could she say?

"You don't want to miss the tree lighting," the woman said to Tara, making it clear she didn't want Tara to join them. "I mean, there's no point in both of you missing it."

"I'll be right back," Liam said. As if as an afterthought, he dropped a quick kiss on her lips—sealing her as his.

She flushed from the attention the crowd gave her. Everyone knew and loved Liam, so of course, they'd be curious about her... and her relationship with the local vet. What was their relationship? She didn't know. But whatever it was, she liked it. And she could see herself growing to love it.

But without Liam, she felt cold. And tired. The crowd pressed around her. She needed to find a place to sit. But what if Liam came back and didn't know where to find her? He could call. Her fingers closed around the phone in her pocket as she went in search of a park bench.

But, of course, they were all full. Even the swings were occupied. She decided she could sit on the teeter-totter or on the edge of the merry-go-round, but then she found children playing on them.

She spotted a booth where hot cocoa was being sold. If she had something warm to hold and to drink, maybe she'd feel better. The line snaked around the city block. Parents tried to entertain their impatient children. Tara wobbled on her tired feet. She couldn't wait in this long line. Maybe if she leaned up against a lamppost...

Tara woke to find a crowd gathered around her. She tried to sit up, but a wave of nausea swept through her. She rolled onto her hands and knees and vomited.

"Ah, gross!" a familiar voice said.

Tara wiped her mouth and looked around and spotted Skylar standing amongst a group of other Canterbury students.

"Can I help you?" a woman with fly-away hair and kind eyes asked, extending her hand. "I'm a nurse."

The woman, despite her small size, had a warm and strong grip.

"I called 911," the woman told her.

"You didn't have to do that," Tara said. "I'll be okay."

"You didn't look okay," Skylar said. "That was the sickest thing I've ever seen."

The woman and Tara shared a glance.

"I know it's not pretty," Tara said.

"Yeah, it's *pretty* disgusting," Skylar said.

The nurse in the red parka took Tara's arm. "Is there someone I can call for you?"

She nodded. "Liam. He'll—"

"Dr. Grant?" Skylar asked. "He was here. He saw this."

"He did?" Tara's thoughts sputtered. "He was here and he left?"

"Yeah, he was probably so sicked-out, he couldn't watch."

"He's a doctor," the woman said.

"He was here and then he disappeared," Skylar pronounced. "You tell me what happened."

Tara weaved on her feet. Could this be true? But she knew it could. It had been happening to her all her life. People that she'd thought were her friends disappeared after witnessing a seizure. Even her own dad hadn't been able to handle it.

The woman rubbed her arm. "Here comes the paramedics."

Tara shook her head. "I can't afford an ambulance." An idea struck her. "Can you walk with me to the train station?"

By the time Harry, a Persian in desperate need of a grooming, had coughed up his furball, the Christmas tree had been lit and the crowd dispersed. Liam strode across the park while worry churned in his belly. What had happened to Tara? Maybe she had gone to his house. He hoped so.

"Dad!" Teague, still in his band uniform, caught up to him. "Where's Tara?"

"I'm not sure," Liam said, scratching his head. He pulled

his phone from his pocket and sent it a curious glance. Why wasn't she returning his calls?

"Well, is she okay?"

"Why wouldn't she be?" Liam asked.

"Some of the guys said she had some sort of fit. Frothing at the mouth. Rolling around on the ground…"

Feeling ill, Liam dropped his hand on his son's shoulder. "She's an epileptic."

"What's that? It's like a disease?"

"A disorder," he clarified. "It's like if you had an electric wire and one of them shorted out. It would spark and the wire might bounce around, but it only lasts a minute or two." He bit his lips. "But it would be a really scary couple of minutes."

"And she can't help it? Like puking? You just have to do it?"

"But when you're vomiting you know what you're doing. An epileptic won't remember anything that happens during a seizure."

"That's so weird."

"Not really. Every night, you go to sleep and, in the morning, you really can't remember what happened during your last eight or so hours." A wave of remorse hit him. Of course, he'd kept her out until the early morning the night before and then she'd had a long day at the school… this was his fault.

He elbowed Teague. "I have to go!" He sprinted across the now deserted park.

"Where?" Teague jogged beside him.

"I have to find her!"

"Yeah, but… where?" Teague repeated.

"Let's see if she's at the house," Liam said.

Teague shook his head. "I was just there."

"Then she went home to her uncle's."

"But how?"

Liam stopped and glanced around as if he could find her hiding somewhere. Liam started running.

It wasn't until Tara was on her way to Simi Valley that she realized she'd lost her phone. It had to have fallen out of her pocket during her seizure.

It was just one more casualty of her condition. She leaned back against her seat, grateful that she hadn't had to wait too long for the train. Of course, it would be nice if she could warn her mom of her arrival, but since her mom's house was within walking distance of the station and she knew where to find the hidden key, she knew she had a place to stay.

Home.

She closed her eyes and tried to sleep while the train click-clacked along the tracks. Her mom would be glad to see her.

But memories of her dad swam before her eyes. "Men aren't as strong as us women," her mom had told her with a wink. "They like to think they are, but they're not. Your dad — he'll be back."

But he never returned and Tara knew why. She'd been thirteen when she'd had the first seizure. That night, she'd heard her parents fighting. This wasn't something new. They fought a lot. But this had been the first time they'd fought about her.

"I can't live with a spaz," her dad had said.

Tara didn't even know what that word meant, so she'd looked it up. *Noun: short for spastic. Verb: to lose physical or emotional control.*

He'd been yelling about her. He couldn't live with her. At first, she thought if she could control her seizures, maybe her dad would come back.

"We don't need him," her mom had said.

And then, years later, her mom had said, "Who wants him?"

Tara leaned her forehead against the window and watched the world slide by, sad because she knew that her mom both needed and wanted Tara's dad — one of the people who should have loved her best.

And had left.

"She's not here, boy," Will Poole told him. "I thought she was with you."

Liam considered filling him in on Harry's furball but decided against it. He shoved his hands into his pockets because he wanted to hit something. "Do you know where she could be?"

"What happened?" Will demanded.

After Liam recounted what little he knew, Will waved him inside and motioned for him to take a chair near the fire. "You and me, boy, are going to have a heart to heart."

"But Tara—" Liam felt frantic.

"She's a smart one, but if it makes you feel better, I'll call the hospital and police station and see if they've seen her. You best sit and cool your engine."

Liam couldn't sit, but began to pace across the room, crossing in front of the Scrabble board set up on the coffee table. He ran his fingers through his hair, remembering the many nights he had tried to beat Tara at her game.

He couldn't lose her now.

Will pocketed his phone. "I just talked to a nice woman named Shelly—she's a nurse at Community Memorial Hospital. She said she took Tara to the train station. She's probably on her way home. Let me call Sharon—that's my sister, Tara's mom, and see what she knows."

Liam only half-listened to Will's telephone conversation.

"Call me as soon as she gets there," Will said, "so's we don't worry." Will pocketed the phone took a seat across from Liam and pinned him with his gaze. "Do you love her?"

"I… I guess I do."

"Do you have an idea what it's like to live with epilepsy?"

"No. How could I?"

"Good answer." He pointed a finger at Liam's chest. "You think your life is bouncing along right as rain and then it hits you. It's like a lightning bolt and it shakes you to the core—reminds you that you're not like other people."

"But, sir, begging your pardon, we all have our weaknesses —things that we have to deal with."

"True." Will pressed his lips together. "But this girl's not only had to deal with her own weaknesses, but also those around her. If you love her, you'll have to convince her that you won't be like her scumbag dad and ditch her."

"Gladly, but how? She's not even returning my phone calls."

Darrel spoke from the kitchen door. Obviously, she'd been listening to the entire conversation. "I have an idea."

Eight

Tara rubbed the sleep from her eyes when the announcer called out, *next stop. Simi Valley*. She didn't have any bags, of course. Maybe her mom could drive her to Oak Hollow on the day of the play and they could pick up her things then.

She couldn't go back to the school. Skylar and the other girls — how could she face them?

But how would she pay off her debt to Irena? Would she be able to keep Wolfgang? Knowing she'd acted impulsively — and stupidly — she pushed her curls away from her face and promised herself that she'd think things through over the weekend and come up with a plan… and a way to tell Irena that she couldn't return to the school.

Too many of the girls had seen her seizure. They must have been, to use Skylar's words, *sicked-out*. As the train slid to a stop, Tara swallowed her disappointment, climbed to her feet, and made her way down the aisle.

She'd expected the tiny depot to be empty, but a cluster of men with their backs turned to her stood near the back gate. And then as if on the count of three, they twirled around.

Tara froze when she recognized Liam, Teague, Doug, Hal, Skip, and Cooper. They all held guitars except for Liam who held a large bouquet of red roses and a hand-held microphone. The Rabbits and Teague began to strum and Liam sang, "*All I want for Christmas is you*

Wrapped in ribbon, tied in string,

You're the only carol I'll ever want to sing."

Tara stood as if mute and dumb and bit her fist as she battled tears. The few fellow passengers stopped to clap while Tara struggled to know what to say.

Liam dropped to one knee. "Tara Allen, will you marry me?" He gazed up at her with pleading eyes. When she didn't respond right away, Teague also dropped to his knees, clasped his hands and assumed a beggar's position. The Rabbits followed.

"Guys, get up!" Tara said laughing and crying at the same time.

"Not until you say yes," Liam said.

"Right," Teague said. "You have to say yes."

Liam looked over his shoulder at his son. "And this has nothing to do with him."

"What?" Teague squeaked.

"He still has to go and live with his mom," Liam said.

"No way!" Teague exclaimed.

"But he can come and visit and stay for as long as he wants," Tara said.

"No, because I want you to myself," Liam said.

"He doesn't mean that," Tara told Teague.

"No, I do," Liam said.

"It's okay," Teague said. "Mom said she'll wait to marry Barking Bob. It's actually Bob's idea. He said he doesn't want to cause problems."

"Well, good for Bob," Tara said.

"What do you say?" Liam asked. "Not to pressure you or anything, but my knee is getting sore."

"Yeah," Teague put in.

All the Rabbits nodded in agreement. "What's your answer?" Doug asked.

"What's your answer, lady?" someone called through the train's open window.

"I say yes!" Tara said.

Liam jumped to his feet and Tara launched into his arms. His lips found hers, he pushed his hand through her hair, and she held him as tightly as she could.

She was home.

He was her future.

Epilogue

Five years later

Liam's belly clutched with nerves as he scanned the stage, searching for a sign that the show would soon start.

"I think I might be the oldest person in this room," Gram said with a huff as she settled into her chair.

"Make that the second oldest," Darrel said as she sat beside her.

"You two would rather fight over a banana peel than enjoy a sundae," Will groused.

"But you're older than Verla." Darrel elbowed Will. "Show her your driver's license!"

"I will not!" Will said.

A wave of gratitude for Will swept through Liam. The older gentleman always provided a buffer between Gram and Darrel. He was like Switzerland, but with a sense of humor.

Eva, Bob, and Chloe, their three-year-old daughter hurried down the aisle.

"Uncle Liam! Hi!" Chloe bounced into Liam's arms.

Liam kissed her cheek, marveling that Teague's half-sister could look almost nothing like her brother or her mother but had her father's fair skin and golden curls.

The lights dimmed.

Where was Tara? Liam was just about to go and look for her when he spotted her at the base of the stage.

She smiled and waved. In her jeans and t-shirt, she looked like a child, but she'd proven to him over and over again that she was all woman. All he ever needed or wanted.

She scooted down the aisle, hugging Eva and Bob as she passed them, and waving to Gram and her aunt and uncle.

"How's Teague?" Liam whispered as Tara took Chloe from his arms and settled into the seat beside him.

"You'll see for yourself in just a second."

The Rapid Rabbits — including their newest member, Teague — crashed onto the stage.

All around them, the crowd cheered and lights flashed while Teague took his place behind a microphone and began to sing. *"All I want for Christmas is you. Wrapped in ribbon, tied in string, You're the only carol I'll ever want to sing."* The girls in the audience screamed and Liam wanted to join them.

"He's singing our song," Liam said in surprise.

Tara nodded.

"Did you know?" Liam asked.

"No, but I know I love you," she said, her eyes shining with love, pride, and glistening excitement.

Liam dropped a kiss on the top of her head and wondered if life could be any sweeter than this moment.

Greener Pastures Calling

Once Upon a Vet School, Part 10

Lizzi Tremayne

One

After one look inside the cowshed at 25 Wharewhero Road, I didn't think I'd ever be able to touch even my favorite Tip Top Chocolate Ice Cream again... not ever.

And that was before the putrid odor hit me.

"Eh, where's the vet?" someone called from the pit between the cows and I peered down into the darkness. Sure enough, there was a little man in there, barely visible. His overalls were so crusted with unmentionables that he was hard to distinguish from the oily, black muck covering every surface of the shed—rails, floor, and halfway up the walls.

I swallowed hard and forced my gorge to stay down.

"I'm here," I called from the doorway. I wanted to leave and never come back, but after glancing at the miserable-looking cows standing in the row, I picked my way through the morass covering the floor and stepped down into the pit. I stopped a meter away from the man, my eyes watering. He smelled, if possible, worse than his shed.

My God, didn't the dairy factory monitor these places?

As he hadn't said anything more, I gazed past him to the far end of the shed where the six cows stood with their heads down, eyes lackluster, and coats staring. From each of the cows' backsides hung the rotting remnants of their calf fetal membranes. I guess something *could* smell worse than this man.

"So why'd they send a girl?" The man's brows narrowed over a pursed mouth.

"They sent a veterinarian. I'm Dr. Scott. Nice to meet you, Mr. Somerfield," I said, dryly, then turned to the cows. "How long ago did these girls calve?"

"Ah" — his scowl remained undiminished, but he seemed at a loss — "some a week, some more, maybe two weeks."

I scanned the row of dejected, probably septic, cows and held back a shudder of revulsion. "That long?" I gritted my teeth to keep from screaming at him.

"I didn't want to waste my money, what with having the vets come out too many times." He scowled.

"It costs less to —" I stopped and shut my trap before it got me into trouble again and spun back toward the ute. "Please put them into the vet race so I can treat them properly," I called over my shoulder, not trusting myself to say more. I rather liked my job.

Tossing gloves, disinfectant, antibiotics, needles and syringes, a fluid pump, and an old stomach tube into several buckets, I prepared for the ordeal ahead. By the clanging of pipe gates and shouting behind me, at least I knew he was moving the cows.

When I returned to the shed, Somerfield's eyes bugged at the buckets weighing me down. I could see him ticking off the fees in his head. "You don't need all that, just some foaming pessaries and you'll be away."

I locked my jaw as I stared at him. Setting down the buckets, I pulled a thermometer from my pocket. With a deep breath, I tried for patience while I lubed the thing and inserted it gently into the cow's rectum. "Mr. Somerfield," I finally said, "if you'd rung a week or two ago, that might have been all we needed. As it is" — I removed the thermometer and glanced at it, shook it down, and replaced it to double check the ridiculously high temperature — "it appears these cows are far past simple antibiotic pessaries."

He jerked his head toward me for a moment then scowled. "They're just soft," he muttered, and stalked away. The cows, to a one, cringed away as he passed them. Never a good sign.

I consulted the thermometer again. *41 degrees C...* over 105 degrees F. I let my breath out and checked the next. Her temperature wasn't far below that, nor the next.

When he came back, I turned to him, my face as impassive as I could make it. "Mr. Somerfield, your cows are septic. They have very bad infections. I'm going to try to remove what's left of their placentas, flush out their uteri, and put antibiotics in, plus give them intravenous antibiotics. I'll return tomorrow. I'll not lie to you, you may lose some of them. They are *that* sick."

By the look on his face — the stunned mullet look, as they call it in New Zealand — I could see he finally understood the gravity of the situation.

I was finally all dressed up for the party in my calving gown and doubled rectal sleeves, with another glove over the top. A bit pathetic, of course; they all leaked within minutes. I cleaned the first cow's backside as best I could with a running hose before lubing up and starting. With the time that'd elapsed since she calved, it was a struggle to get my hand through the mostly-closed cervix of that first cow. My goal was to somehow remove whatever tissues hadn't yet liquified, then to flush whatever remained. Tricky business.

There's nothing quite like the scent of two-week-old rotting tissue.

While a calving or a prolapsed uterus on a cow probably took more sheer strength, "cleaning" a cow of its retained fetal membranes was probably the most truly unpleasant job I knew. For both the vet *and* the cow. And this farm didn't have the usual one or two, but six.

It took hours.

Needless to say, by the end of it, I was covered. Wisps of my long hair, once clipped back and braided to within an inch of their lives, had escaped their fetters and straggled down around my face. And I'm sure I smeared the back of my none-too-clean gloves across my cheek more than once.

I couldn't wait to get back to the clinic for a much-needed shower.

Even Somerville bordered on chartreuse beneath his grime by the time we were done. He, of course, got the job of holding the cows' tails and pumping fluid through the tube when I needed it. He was drowned by the upset cows' excrement more than once. I'm sure I didn't fully escape that, either, but at least it wasn't on my head.

"I'll see you tomorrow," I said lightly to Mr. Somerville, after the last cow had been injected with antibiotics and he'd opened the gate to let her out.

He only nodded and kept his head down.

Heaving a great sigh, I picked up my grotty buckets and headed for the vat room to give my gear a perfunctory wash — nothing was going into my vehicle in its current state, including me. A few moments later, as it steamed into my buckets, the water from the ever-present, blessed boiler looked almost warm enough to do the job.

I picked up a scrubbing brush from beside the tank, then dropped it back to the floor — I'd get my own. This one was as disgusting as everything else on the place.

Still too filthy to even touch my door handles, I ducked down to rinse my hands and arms from the cold hose.

Somewhere out on the tanker track loop, a vehicle door slammed.

"Somerfield?" A loud male voice rang out only moments later in the doorway beside me.

I glanced up to see a young man stride in. His face red and angry, he stared through the open doors of the vat room toward the cowshed from his considerable height and nearly tripped over me. He looked down in horror and our eyes locked as he stopped in his tracks. I'd like to think it was my beauty, but I suspect it was mostly the smell.

"I wouldn't get too close if I were you," I said faintly, unable to look away. "You might smell like this forever."

"Oh, I'm sorry," he said, and glanced away, then back, and offered me a strained smile. "I was looking for Somerfield."

"I gathered that." I raised a brow at him, wishing I didn't look like a veterinary ghoul. "He's in there. Looking rather green, I might add." I flicked my head back toward the shed and some bedraggled tendrils of what used to be hair slapped against my face. I shuddered and closed my eyes, wishing I were anywhere else.

"You okay there?" His voice, when it wasn't at full noise, was smooth as old port.

"I will be after I'm gone" — I gulped and tried not to look into his extraordinary eyes again — "and I've soaked in a bubble bath for a week."

"I'll leave you to it, then." He grinned as he passed me. "Good luck."

He didn't return before I managed to scrub the worst off my gear and roll it up inside my calving gown. I shoved the packet into one of the buckets and glanced over my shoulder to see the man gesticulating wildly at the cringing Somerfield.

Good on him. Somebody needed to do that.

As I drove around the roundabout heading for the gate, he stepped out the door and waved.

Just my luck the only guy I'd met in New Zealand who looked like he could've graced the covers of GQ had to meet me when I looked like I'd just been dragged through a cesspool.

"Come on, Lena, it'll be fun," Moira said, reaching high above her head to shove the last box of dry-cow therapy into its place. "You haven't gone out with a guy since you went rock-and-rolling with that wet noodle in Hamilton. That was ages ago."

I winced. My toes still hurt, even three months later. "He talked a good line. I thought he could dance."

"Yeah, well, you should've listened to me, but you were so desperate to hit a dance floor, you went anyway."

"What can I say, I've missed it terribly since I left the States — that and missing out on the veterinary acupuncture course I'd booked before I left."

"The one you've nearly completed now in Australia?" she said, with a twist of her lips.

I laughed at her. "Okay, so things are looking up. Now it's just the dancing I miss."

"That, and a good Kiwi Bloke to go along with it."

"Mmm…" I'd picked up the wonderful Kiwi term that can mean anything from agreement to disagreement, from *absolutely!* to f-off — and only the speaker knows what he or she meant. Handy. We don't have anything like it in America.

Granted, I was generally either working or sleeping these days, but the Kiwi men I'd met so far seemed to be either married farmers or usually-drunk rugby boys — neither of which appealed.

"I know a guy — "

" — been there, Moira, not going there again. Your blind dates… lack… something. I daren't elaborate. I'm meant to have a clean mouth here." I looked around us at the front room of the big veterinary clinic.

The equine section comprised a one by two-meter area of shelf space. The rest of the massive showroom was dedicated to cattle–specifically, dairy cattle–medicines and supplements, but I was working on that. I'd been hired to service the equine side of the practice, taking over for a man who'd been the sole equine practitioner in this area for the past thirty-three years. It would take some doing to convince some of the racing guys that the first female vet this practice had ever hired — and one the age of their granddaughters to boot — was worth her salt.

" — Lena?"

I blinked. Moira looked at me, one brow raised. "Yes?" I mumbled.

"Really?" Her eyes widened and her mouth dropped open.

"Pardon?"

She laughed. "You said yes to double dating with Mark and me."

"Sorry." I frowned. "I hadn't heard you."

"It'll be fun. He's nice. You'll like him."

"Who?"

"Marcus. He's a stock agent — with a gorgeous Holden."

"Stock agent." I close my eyes and took a deep breath.

"They're okay," she assured me, with a laugh.

"Bit like a used car salesman, if you ask me."

"Well… maybe, but it'll be fun."

I shook my head and rubbed my forehead. "So, what have you cooked up?"

"Fawlty Towers dinner and show."

"Where? I haven't seen it advertised."

"Well" — she squirmed a little — "it's down the line a little ways."

"I see." I stared her down. "Like how far down the line?"

"Ahhh… Taumarunui. But it'll be fun."

"Taumarunui? That's hours away." I dragged in another deep breath. "Okay, I'll go, but we'll drive together, right?"

"Sure, it's on Saturday night."

I didn't like the thought of the nearly two hours of questionable roads, each way. That show'd better be good.

Two

The show was good, hysterical even, but my date, Marcus, got progressively more drunk as the evening went on. Obnoxiously drunk, to boot. I was trying to figure out how to get the keys for his shiny black Holden out of his hand and into mine, because as luck would have it, Moira had to cancel to care for her injured sister's children. How could I complain about that?

So here I was, wondering what to do next, wondering at my brilliance, and feeling trapped. The concept of a bus way out here was a joke, and a taxi? I didn't make enough money for that, if one even existed in this little backwater town.

"Arm-wrestle for the key?" Marcus laughed playfully.

Asking nicely hadn't worked. It seems Marcus thought it all a bit of fun.

Drinking and driving just wasn't done where I'd come from. Unfortunately, it was treated lightly here. New Zealand's rugby culture, with its associated "drinkies" in the clubroom before going—*driving*—home, was strong. It wasn't confined to the rugby boys, though. The culture spread across many sports—and it didn't bear thinking about.

And it appeared I was about to go home with *this* drunk. Not bloody likely, if I had anything to say about it.

"Arm-wrestle *you*, you big galumph?" I finally answered, trying to keep the knife edge from my voice. I don't think I succeeded, but he didn't seem to notice.

I gave it my best, but then, rubbing my sore arm, I tried cajoling, also to no avail.

By this time, only the servers remained.

No, none of us live up north.

Very sorry, they said, wincing, as they took in the condition of my erstwhile "date".

In the end, I trusted to Providence, but still cursed Moira, him, myself, and anyone else I could think of.

An hour on, as we drove through Otorohranga, Marcus turned north toward Te Awamutu. The narrow road wound on past Te Kawa and on toward Pokuru. I tried not to stare out into the dark, tried to forget about the ditches and sheer banks I knew dropped away just past the sides of the road.

Marcus nattered on as we drove north. From the sideways glances he kept sending in my direction, I suspected he might be sobering up. "I'm so tired," he said, finally, as we clattered over a railway bridge. "What say we stop by my place for a nightcap?"

I blinked. He certainly didn't need one and damned if I was about to share one with him.

He swung the black beast into a driveway beside a cowshed and revved the engine as he pulled up before a darkened worker's house.

"Home Sweet Home." He smiled at me and reached a hand across the car toward me. I shrank away, one hand tight on the door handle.

"No, thanks. Can you please take me home now?"

The space between his brows narrowed. "You can at least come in for a drink."

"No, thank you. I don't want one."

"Well, then, just come in, and let me get a warmer jacket."

I frowned at him, then bit my lip. "I'll wait in the car."

"Come on, I won't hurt you. You're being silly."

Somehow, call me thick, he persuaded me to get out of the car and climb the three concrete steps to his porch. I'd barely stepped over the threshold when he wrapped his arms around me and started nuzzling my neck.

"Back off," I growled. He didn't listen, so I drove my heel into his instep and spun out of his grasp before he could respond, then reached for a handy fireplace poker. Seems he wasn't game to try again, at the sight of his own poker in my hand. Suddenly Marcus seemed acutely sober and his Adams apple jumped as he swallowed hard.

"Let me give you a ride home," he tried, his eyes not quite meeting mine.

"I'd rather walk," I said, and stepped unchallenged past him and out the door. I held onto the poker until I was well out of his driveway, then threw it back toward his house.

Wondering why I'd been stupid enough to wear heels, I kicked them off and started walking north. It should only be about three kilometers to home—nearly long enough to cool off. For now, I let the expletives fly at full volume. There was no one out here but the roadside cows, and they didn't seem bothered—in fact, they came to the fence to stare. Few people coming along the road could be worse than the idiot I'd just left, soI walked on, stomping my bare feet as much as the tar-sealed road would allow.

Unfortunately, my mood hadn't improved by the time I reached Moira on the phone early the next morning. I suspect she won't try to set me up again.

By Monday morning, my attitude had improved, thanks to Sunday's half-tub of Tip Top chocolate ice cream (even that cowshed didn't rate next to Marcus, it seemed), and I showed up at the clinic bright and early.

Karen lifted a hand to me and returned to her telephone call. No one else was in yet, so I picked up my call list for the day. No farm visits until ten. *Good*. The call sheets and records yet to be completed piled on my desk took up an ominous amount of space. Almost as much space as my dead monitor–the one I brought from the States. Its 110 or 240 volt switch on the back worked, but it seems the input still had to be only 110 volts, not 230. One glorious burst of light and the screen squealed to its black death, never to light up again. I really did need to get rid of it.

Line two rang and a glance over to Karen's desk showed she was still tied up.

I bit my lip for a moment, then decided I had to answer it.

"Hello, Te Awamutu Animal Medical Center," I said, as cheerily as possible, given my terror of what was to come.

"Hi, this is *mumble, mumble, mumble* from out *mumble mumble*. I have three cows with *mumble mumble*."

I took a deep breath. I hadn't been in New Zealand very long and some of the local farmers spoke a strain of Kiwi that passed for English, but completely eluded me over the telephone. I could decipher some of these men's meaning by watching their mouths and hands in person. On the phone, however, I was lost. "Ahh… could you please repeat that? I didn't get it all." Or any of it, actually, but he didn't need to know that.

Same answer. Couldn't even get the name after I asked him to speak more slowly. Twice more.

After his final attempt, I was ready to smack my forehead on the desk and he sounded more than a little annoyed.

A flood of relief washed over me when I realized Karen was hovering beside me.

"One moment please, sir," I managed with a strangled cry and thrust the phone at the ever-efficient office manager.

She smiled, but a twitch had started up at the corner of her eye as she grabbed for the phone. All professionalism, she took the call. "Hello, Karen here, may I help you?"

I took a deep breath to attempt to regain some equanimity while I listened.

"Ahh, Mr. Peabody-James, you have three cows to be cleaned? Out at your Paterangi runoff? Excellent," she muttered moving sideways to the daybook she ruled with an iron fist. "And no, we won't send her. Jarrod Woodsley will be there at 10 a.m. if it suits? Wonderful. Thank you for your call." She ran off and winced. "He does speak rather fast," she said, and chuckled.

"With a mouthful of marbles, I suspect," I mumbled to myself, as my face heated.

"You'll get used to it."

I wondered how long it would be, as I gave thanks most of my horse clients spoke the good Kings English. The fact of the matter was that I was the only horse vet to the eight dairy vets in the practice. I'd been hard-pressed to learn about cows during my first "calving season", the week I'd arrived.

I wondered why my new boss had told me, upon hiring me earlier in the year, to "go on home to California and sell up. Just make sure you're here by the first of July."

I must have had some image in my mind of waltzing through fields of spring flowers as the days gave way to balmy summer temperatures. I knew the seasons were reversed, but it had somehow slipped my mind.

I flew into Auckland on the first of July to torrential rain—rain that barely let up for the next three months–and a cloud cover that only lifted for a few hours each afternoon, if you were lucky.

Cows in the mud, anyone?

"So what would you like for Christmas? " Karen smiled as she handed me the on-call schedule for the next three months, including the Christmas holidays. "Surprise! Early bird gets the worm. You're off from Christmas to New Year's!"

"Thanks, that's a pretty nice Christmas present," I said, with a smile, but I felt a little empty inside. It wasn't what I *really* wanted for the holiday, but it seemed it would have to do. With no family in New Zealand, I wasn't even sure what I was going to do for the holiday, but I'd find something. Having survived a Waikato winter and springtime, I was sure I'd earned my summertime Christmas, pictured so vividly on the pages of my *New Zealand the Beautiful Cookbook*: sunny-looking kids on the beach against a backdrop of sailboats, the glittering sea, and red-flowering Pohutakawa trees, with luscious Kiwi summertime holiday fare spread out before them.

It sounded a lot more fun than shoveling snow. And I'd done plenty of that.

After a hellish day a week later — defined by this horse vet as a full day of pregnancy testing cows — I'd finally gotten blessedly clean, though I'd probably be green-stained and smell like cow manure forever. Luckily, Moira wouldn't care. Tomorrow, she and I were going out to the movies–said she owed me, and I didn't disagree. I needed a good night out — without drunken louts.

I was snuggled warm under my goosedown duvet when the jangle of the phone in my ear jerked me from my pleasant stupor. I wasn't on call, but my body didn't know that… the effect was identical. One deep breath to still my brain, and I picked up.

"Hello, Marcus Madsen here. Look, I wondered if you'd like to — umm — well. I just wanted to apologize. Sorry about last week. I don't know what came over me."

It must be getting close to date night.

"It was probably all the booze you drank." Tersely.

"Yes, that was it," he said, with palpable relief in his voice. "So, would you like to try again? Saturday, there's a party — "

" — you're blaming your behavior on the alcohol? Now I've heard everything." I snorted, then laughed outright.

"Ahh…" Silence. "I'm not usually — "

"Look, Marcus, you may not go to church, but does the phrase 'a cold day in Hell' mean anything to you?"

"Ahh…"

"Forget it. You've melted your brains. First off, you don't ring people at this hour. Second, the answer is no, and it always will be. I don't do drunks. I certainly don't do drunk drivers. Good *night*," I growled, and slammed the phone down onto the receiver with relish.

Despite my late-night wind up, I was somewhere past exhaustion, so sleep pulled me under the minute my head hit the pillow. With a smile on my face.

Three

I'd injected the final cow in John Munro's cowshed when I saw an old girl standing in the paddock next to the vet race.

"What's with her, Mr. Munro?"

"She's been dragging her toes… she's been barely moving around since she calved and she's off her tucker," he said, glancing away.

"She hasn't been eating much while I've been here," I murmured. The Jersey stood in deep grass, but none of it near her appeared to have been touched.

"Nope, she hasn't really eaten in two days," he said, "and I filled that water bucket last night. She hasn't had a drop."

I swallowed hard. Not a good look, but I'd seen worse.

"She's been a good 'un." He shook his head and blinked a few times, then drew his sleeve across his eyes and shook his head, staring away from me out across the paddocks.

The ancient Jersey raised her head and gave him a long look, then dropped it again, still not eating despite the knee-high grass surrounding her.

"How old is she?" She seemed to hold the knowledge of the world in her big, soft eyes.

"Last count, nineteen." He swallowed hard. "She's calved every year, usually a heifer."

"So why is she up here?" I said, a sick feeling growing in the pit of my stomach.

The farmer winced and glanced at the shiny black car

sitting in the cowshed roundabout. "Madsen. He'll be back up here at the shed soon."

I flinched at Marcus' name. I'd seen the car on my way in, but in my hurry, it hadn't clicked.

I frowned. "We might be able to help that cow, if you're not ready to let her go yet."

His eyes shot to my face. Hope leapt in them for a moment before the shutters slammed closed and he looked at the ground again. "Nobody's been able to fix 'em before. You just spend more money before they have to go on the truck," he muttered.

I hesitated before answering. Some of these older farmers were tough nuts to crack with unusual therapies. "As long as her pelvis isn't fractured, acupuncture should help her" — I looked away myself now, from the crusty old cow cocky's glistening eyes — "and that paresis, the weakness, in her hind end should go away soon."

He jerked his eyes up from their study of his gumboots. "Really?" He straightened up and took a deep breath. "Nobody's done that before on this place."

"Most vets around here haven't had the opportunity to learn acupuncture yet, but I have. It's the best thing for these cows."

"Hey, John!" came Madsen's voice from around the front of the shed.

"We're in here," he said and gritted his teeth.

The agent's slicked-back hair shined around the corner and he nodded at me. "Mornin, miss, um" — his voice trailed off as he recognised me — "Doc."

I raised a brow and nodded back. "Mr. Madsen," I said through tight lips. The steely gaze I shot at him was safer than the words trying to scream their way out of my mouth.

Marcus gulped and turned back to John. "We're takin' that old screw too, right?" He waved his biro at the doe-eyed cow.

John looked at me and I shook my head, trying to keep the triumph from showing on my face.

"Nope," he said.

The stock agent's brows narrowed for a moment. "Well, I'll be off then," he said, to no one in particular, and soon the glistening jet SRV raced away, enveloped in a cloud of dust. Hopefully, covered with it.

John and I turned back to the cow.

"Please, Doc, if you can do anything for her, I'd sure appreciate it," he said, his face hidden from me. He snuffled a little as I went back to the vat room to wash up and get my needles.

The lovely old Jersey stood like a rock in the middle of the paddock while I placed her acupuncture needles. The only restraint we needed was the farmer's hand scratching her ears and behind her horn nubs as she softly breathed, eyes closed, rubbing against his hand, until she fell asleep with the needles in her.

"Can you keep her out of the herd?" I said when I'd finished, as I snapped my bag closed.

"She can stay in here."

I smiled.

In the vat room, he handed me a clean, white scrubbing brush and the near-boiling water hose to wash my boots. "You coming in? The missus has new feijoa jam and a leg of hogget for lunch."

"Don't mind if I do." I grinned up at him. "Thank you, John. I hear your wife makes the best hogget in the district."

"Who says that?" He peered sideways as he led the way to the house.

"My boss."

"Ah, of course… the fine Mr. Harrington. Yes, I imagine he does. Funny how his visits are always right on lunchtime." His eyes danced. "Thanks to you, we've got something to celebrate today."

I winced. "She looks better, but let's not count our chickens yet."

He motioned me to precede him up the back steps to the washroom. "Sara," he called out to his wife through the open back door as he kicked off his gumboots, "I've brought the new lady vet up for lunch."

Mrs. Munro came to the back door and welcomed me. She was a tall, buxom brunette who managed to look a lady, even in her farm attire. I followed her up the back steps through the washroom and into the big farmhouse kitchen.

"Mrs. Munro, thanks for having me to lunch," I said, then froze in my tracks.

A veritable feast was laid out on the massive kitchen table. The old totara table took up half of the oversized room, crowned by its enamelled Aga built into the far wall. The gorgeous old stove was big enough to roast the whole leg of hogget taking pride of place in the middle of the spread. "Ah, I don't mean to intrude if you're having a party today."

"Party? Oh no," she laughed, "this is just regular, everyday lunch. The boys get hungry. They'll be up in a few minutes — they're taking their sweet time scrubbing up today." She chuckled at her husband, then stifled her mirth as she turned to me. "Would you like to use my bathroom to tidy up? It's a lot cleaner. Third door on the left." She gestured down the hallway. "And please, call me Sara."

"Thank you," I said, and turned in time to see him walk in the door.

He had to be Sara's son: same eyes, hair and height. As he glanced my way, molten chocolate eyes melted into mine and I was caught. I found my mouth was open and hurriedly slapped it shut. He looked vaguely familiar, but I couldn't remember where I'd seen him before. Maybe in some dream.

As if from far away, Sara's voice came to me. "Nigel, this is Lena. She's the new vet at Harrington's practice."

"Ah, so finally we meet, officially," he murmured. "I've heard so much about you." He, at least, could speak — and smoothly at that. Nigel reached for my hand and I remembered to offer it and shake in return. "I guess, this is what you do with lady vets? You warned me against getting too close the last time," he said, and chuckled.

I must've been smiling like an idiot, my face hot, but then I remembered where I'd seen him before.

Oh no… it wasn't possible… but yes, it was.

Somerfield's cowshed.

With the realization, I wanted to crawl into a hole, but I somehow managed to extricate my hand and drop my gaze to the floor.

"You scrub up okay," he said, his voice warm. "You'd clearly had a rough day when I met you. And you smell so much better today."

I looked up into his face again and saw nothing but approval and kindness.

His face and muscular arms were tanned, as was the rest of him, or whatever skin showed around the edges of his tight, black wool shearing singlet and rugger shorts. Plenty. I swallowed and averted my eyes before I embarrassed myself any further.

"I was just going to wash up," I murmured at my socks and escaped down the hall. Locating the promised bathroom, I slid the bolt across and leaned back against the door, breathing more quickly than a walk down the hall should've engendered. When I finally opened my eyes, I stared straight at my flushed reflection in the mirror.

Get a grip, girl, it's just a man.

But what a man.

And he still likes you, even after your first… meeting.

I washed carefully and just as carefully schooled my thoughts on the way back to the table. I loved New Zealand. Loved everything about it, so different from the country where I'd grown up and learned my veterinary profession, but this was the side I'd yearned for, the real farming side. And the sight of the last farmer I'd seen didn't hurt.

Not one bit.

In all, three "boys" had come in.

"Lena" — Nigel nodded at the other two men — "this is my brother Jake, and Sam, our worker."

"Nice to meet you both," I said, my wits returned.

Sam looked at me and grinned as I sat in the chair Sara indicated. "Always wondered what a girl cow vet looked like."

"Well, actually a horse vet, but cows come with the job."

Nigel laughed. "You're the first female vet that practice's ever had." He picked up the tray of hogget from the top of the Aga and held it before me. My face positively glowed as I gritted my teeth and forked some of the perfectly-roasted meat.

I'm twenty-eight, for goodness sake, and acting like a bloody virgin.

"Ladies can do anything now, gentlemen." Sara smiled and shook her head. "So Lena, John says you've acupunctured our Georgette."

"Georgette?" I glanced at John, who ducked his head and gulped his tea.

Nigel's mother continued in a soft voice. "She's a very special cow to us. Thank you for helping her."

An unexplained shiver ran up my spine. Something about her tone, but I could find no reason for it. "There's no evidence of a pelvic fracture," I said. "Hopefully the needles will quiet down her inflamed pelvic nerves and relieve the pain that's put her off her feed and slowed her down."

Sara looked out the window toward the cowshed yard, and a smile spread across her face. "She looks to be eating now. She hasn't really done much of that for the past few days."

"She started ripping up grass halfway through her treatment" — John puffed out his chest — "and she scoffed the whole bucket of water that's been sitting there untouched for the past day."

Two pairs of cocoa eyes turned my way, one brimming with tears.

"She was our boy's 'calf club' calf. He loved her to bits," Sara murmured, and stared at her plate.

I looked at Nigel and smiled. "Your heifer, or your brother's?" I looked from him to Jake.

Jake pressed his lips together and looked away.

"His brother's." John mumbled.

"Oh," I said, and promptly bit my lips together, as everyone silently busied themselves with lunch or their fingernails. There didn't seem to be anything else to say, but I wondered what I could've possibly said.

"Try some feijoa jam," Sara said with forced brightness. Sunlight shone through the jar's golden-gem-coloured goodness as she handed it over.

Maybe I'd imagined it.

The talk picked up again gradually — the incident forgotten or buried — prices at stock saleyards, girl vets, and talk of the job Nigel had recently left, managing a big station in Taumarunui.

"So my boys have both come back to run the farm and we can retire," Sara said with a sigh.

"Don't think you'll get rid of me yet, boys," John nodded in their direction and laughed.

"I'll leave that up to Mum," Nigel said, and squeezed his mother's hand on the table beside him.

They didn't seem to have even made a dent in the food by the time everyone had tucked into the not one, but two desserts — no, puddings, Kiwis called them — gracing the table. I wondered how Sara kept her figure. Probably by catching and cooking her own sheep for dinner and running after all these men.

I finally stood up, not sure if I'd be able to eat for the next week. "Mrs. Munro — Sara — thank you so much for having me to lunch. It was fantastic, but I need to get going to my next call. It's way out in Ngaroto."

"It's been lovely to meet you," she said, and the rest called their goodbyes as I left the room. I didn't dare meet Nigel's eyes. As I slipped into my gumboots at the bottom of the stairs and turned to wave, my hand met flesh with a resounding slap and I froze. It was Nigel's cheek. I'd caught him as he leaned forward to pull on his paddock boots.

"Oh, I'm so sorry!" I closed my eyes and straightened up, wishing the ground would just go on and swallow me. My face, hot before, positively steamed now.

His eyes danced. "Forfeit," he said, and walked away toward the cowshed, and my ute.

"Forfeit?"

"Yep, forfeit. You owe me now."

I stared after him, struggling to match his long stride.

"You slapped me, so I choose the forfeit," he said, with that lazy grin.

Biting my cheek, I frowned up at him. "And you choose?"

"A date, Saturday night. That is, if you're not going out with anyone." His eyes searched my face as he bit his lip, with a slight narrowing of his brows.

"Oh, no, definitely not," I said with vehemence, and glanced at his left hand.

No ring.

His sunny smile returned, but was there a shadow of something behind his eyes? I took a deep breath, unsure if I was ready to try again.

Why the heck not?

"Okay," I finally said. Not all guys could be as bad as the last jerk. But then, I always said that…

We walked on and he gazed down at me, then frowned. "You have a question."

"Two, actually. First, the easy one. Do you drink and drive?"

He looked at me in horror. "My mum would have my guts for garters, no matter my age. Absolutely not."

"Good. Thanks for that. And not so simple" — I hesitated, then went on carefully — "what did I stick my foot into back there, with Georgette?"

He was silent, then he stopped and leaned against a fencepost. "My other brother" — His chest rose and fell a few times before he straightened up and looked straight at me— "was nine… when he had Georgette for his 'calf club' calf. He spent every waking moment with her, but when she fell into the Waikato River, over there" —he pointed— "he couldn't pull her out. Determined to save her, he knotted her rope around his hand and leapt in—"

"Oh my God, Nigel," I said, as he went all blurry thorough my tears.

" —but the current was so strong, Dad and I couldn't get to them. Georgette eventually reached a place along the mostly-sheer riverbank where she could climb out, a kilometre or so down, but Adam had been sucked under and drowned by the time she dragged him out." He drew in a ragged breath. "But she… she brought him back to us. She's pretty special, and I thank you for giving her another chance."

He led me to my ute and opened the door, then handed me in. I was still stunned by his revelation and could only stare up at him.

"Until Saturday, then?" he said, his voice soft as he pulled a folded piece of paper from the pocket of his jeans. "Here's my number. Let me know where to find you."

"Yes," I said, then took a deep breath, squeezed the hand he offered, and drove away.

The weekend seemed a long way off, but for him, I think I could wait.

Four

"How's Georgette?" I asked Nigel, as he opened the passenger door of his restored '68 SS Camaro and handed me in.

"She's looking okay," he said lightly, after he'd seated himself and the engine roared into life. He pulled away from the curb and turned the car away from town.

"I thought we were going to Hamilton," I murmured, then swallowed hard, my heart beginning to beat faster. Shadows of my last date flooded my mind as my hand squeezed tighter on the door handle.

Nigel flicked a smile at me. "We are, but I've something to show you first."

We headed south on State Highway 1 out of town, and turned left at Kihikihi.

His eyes met mine as we continued on toward Arapuni, then turned right. "Don't worry, we'll be back in time for the movie."

When he turned into his own driveway, I finally figured out what he was up to.

In the paddock beside the driveway with her head turned toward us stood Georgette, her fawn and black coat shining in the sun. We clambered out and I nearly hopped the fence, skirt or no skirt, but with a shake of his head, Nigel opened a nearby gate and motioned me through. Georgette's languid eyes perused us as she slowly chewed, while two calves cavorted about her in grass up to their bellies.

"Thank you," he murmured, and leaned down to kiss me. "Was that worth the drive out here?"

"Thank you for showing her to me. She looks wonderful." And she did. She'd gained weight and her bag swung full as she strode toward us. She nosed us both, then sidled closer, so we could scratch her withers.

The rest of the evening, despite our Jersey-hair-dusted clothing, was pure fairytale. We drove up to Hamilton and started looking for dinner. California food snob I might be, but it still made me shudder to think the fourth largest city in New Zealand still sported Copp and Co. as their "finest" dining establishment. I was grateful there was a Mexican restaurant in town, no matter how anglicized its menu.

Halfway through ordering dinner, Nigel ask for a beer and I froze. He flicked a glance at me and raised a questioning brow.

I gulped, my heart pounding in my chest.

"What is it, Lena, are you okay?" He looked at me oddly.

I took a deep breath. "I'm still a little gun-shy from my last date."

"Why, what happened?" he asked, and I told him about my trip to Taumarunui.

He shook his head. "You don't need to worry about that with me. I don't do things like that, any of them," he said, as he reached for my hand and squeezed it. "I thought I'd seen you before."

I flicked my gaze from his hand holding mine up to his face. "Pardon? Where?" I closed my eyes and squirmed. "Other than in that disgusting cowshed."

He laughed. "Like I said before, you scrub up well. I was in that pub in Taumarunui, the one with the dinner show. Glanced through the door from the public bar into the dining room and saw the prettiest girl I'd ever seen, dressed to the nines. Sitting at a table with a loser drunk."

"You were there?" A chill began in the pit of my stomach.

"Yes. Now I wish I'd stayed a little bit longer. I wasn't keen to get in the middle of a domestic when you looked like you were handling the situation, so I didn't worry too much."

"Well, I didn't handle it very well."

"Sounds like it. So, you ended up letting him drive?"

"I couldn't get the keys off him."

Nigel shook his head. "I'd have dealt to him if I knew. You looked in full control of the situation—cool and calm."

"Yeah, well, vets *have* to look like that. All the time. I should've taken the keys from him or refused to drive home with him, but shoulda, coulda, woulda. It's over now, but it hasn't endeared me to drunks. Hence my concern about a beer."

"Like I said"—Nigel's gaze locked with mine—"it's not a problem with me. Ever. I promise you that."

Chiles Rellenos filling my stomach and the sight of Nigel filling my head, we danced the night away to the live band at the RSA. We taught each other a few new moves and had a blast. Yes, he could even dance.

No better combination, bar none.

Especially after my last train wreck of a date.

Later that night, he handed me out of his car and kept my hand in his as he led me to the door.

His lips warm against mine, our first real kiss was all I could've asked for as we held to each other for long minutes.

"Next weekend, would you like to head out to Kiritehere? I could take you out to my uncle's farm and maybe go for a swim."

"Sounds wonderful," I breathed, and took his lips again.

It'd been a long time.

"Well, good night," he said finally, drawing away with reluctance. I bit my lips together. It would be so easy to invite him… but no, not yet. Much as I'd like to, it never worked.

"Until Sunday, then," he whispered, and kissed me fleetingly once again before he turned to go.

I was still smiling as the tail lights of his Camaro flicked on, then disappeared into the night.

"Hello, Nigel here." His voice warmed me more than even my fireplace on this cold evening.

"Good to hear from you," I murmured lazily. The man sounded as keen as I felt. And it was only Wednesday.

"I said I'd see you Sunday," he said, "but I didn't want to wait that long to talk with you."

I didn't think I could get any warmer, but I was wrong.

"Nice." *Good one, Lena.* My brain clearly wasn't working, although he was twenty kilometers away. "Me, either," I managed.

"I had an actual excuse to ring, anyway. Two, actually. First, Georgette is looking well, and Dad wants you to come out and treat her again. 'Just so she doesn't slip backwards,' he says."

"No problem. What else?"

"Thought if you don't mind cold water, we could go whitebaiting while we're out at the coast on Sunday."

"Ohhh, I'd love to. I've always wanted to try it, and water's no problem—I'm a fish."

He chuckled, and my stomach clenched at the rumble of his deep voice. "Sounds good. It's a date, then. Pick you up at seven a.m.? We want to make the tide."

"I'll be ready. Have a lovely week," I said wistfully.

"Ta da. See you soon," he said, and rang off.

As it turned out, Georgette *was* looking better when I visited them a few days later. Much better. Only the slightest limp remained, and she continued to pick up weight. I kept catching knowing smiles between Nigel's mom and dad, but they said nothing about the blossoming relationship between their son and me.

I acupunctured Georgette again and afterward had to attend the requisite lunchtime feast. My boss was right.

Sara was amazing.

Seven a.m. Sunday couldn't come early enough for me. My togs and towel packed, I leapt up at the sound of his ute in the drive.

This time, kisses came first. It seemed we were on our way to starting something real.

On the long drive out to the coast, he kept taking my hand. I couldn't keep the idiot-grin from my face.

"Biscuits?" I waggled a brow at him.

"Before breakfast?" He glanced at me, brows narrowed in mock horror.

"These are healthy ones, well, maybe other than the chocolate," I said, as we exited Otorohanga, heading south.

"So, that's why you wanted some milk fresh from the vat."

"Mmmm…" I said, grinning. "Jersey milk, no better."

By the time we reached the deathtrap of a Waitomo turnoff, we'd each had several bikkies, washed down with the fresh milk. "I was taking you to the hotel here for breakfast," he said.

"I'll never say no to breakfast, but won't we miss the tide?"

"There is that." He looked sideways at me.

"Let's go. I've brought lunch, too."

He positively beamed. "Woman after my own heart. I'd best watch out," he said, then his jaw tightened, and he swallowed hard.

I looked out the windshield to see what he'd seen, but there was nothing amiss. By the time my eyes returned to his face, the shadow was gone.

Must've imagined it.

The 19th century Waitomo Caves Hotel on top of a bluff beside the road flashed past, its woodwork reminiscent of days long past.

He saw me staring up the hill. "We'll go there sometime, if you like. Nice place. Have you been to the caves?"

"I have, but only to walk through, which is pretty awe-inspiring anyway. I'd love to take one of their adventure tours with the underwater rafting, rapelling, and caving."

"Me too. We can go rapelling out in our valley." He looked away from the road briefly to give me a warm smile.

"That'd be great. I've seen people rapelling on those bluffs from the road."

"Yes, that's the place. Our neighbors let me use them whenever I want."

"How did I find another adventurer?" I couldn't help beaming at him.

Again. Or was it *still*?

Therapeutic chocolate and Nigel's tour-guide chatter notwithstanding, by the time we'd driven the sixty-odd kilometers of roads out to the coast—roads that would make you cry if you were in a hurry and got behind one of the ever-present tourist motorhomes: tortuous, narrow, bush covered, partly tar-sealed—albeit beautiful—I was sick as a dog. I'd firmly planted my gaze on the winding goat track before us and didn't look away, but I was still ill. I'm sure it was despite, not because of, the chocolate.

My stomach settled when I hit the water at Marokopa, a big, fine net in my hands. Nigel had placed me in the waist-deep tidal river. Several other whitebaiters fished beside us. Their leathery, bronzed skin bespoke their enthusiasm for fishing in general and whitebaiting in particular.

"What are they, the whitebait? Are they full grown?" I asked.

"They're juvenile forms of several kinds of galaxiids. We're catching them as they migrate upriver to grow. Some of them spawn up there and others come back down to estuaries to lay their eggs."

I caught one up in my hand and inspected it. "They're so tiny… doesn't seem right to eat them." Their translucent little bodies, only a few inches long by an eighth of an inch thick, wouldn't make much of a meal.

He winced. "Not individually no, but cooked into an omelette—well they have to be tasted to be believed."

Poor little beggars. I'd be sure to give plenty of thanks.

"Ready to go in?" Nigel called from his position upriver after we'd been at it for three hours.

"Yes. It's wonderful being out here in the water, but I'm getting pretty stiff."

His eyes twinkled. "Most newbies don't last half as long as you did."

"So now, we make a fire and cook them?" I threw over my shoulder as I scrambled up the crumbling sandbank.

"Nothing so primitive as that." He gave me a mock frown as he took the heavy net from my aching hands. "We go up to my uncle's and use *his* stove. I'm sure he and old Ben will appreciate fresh fish for lunch."

"Does he know we're coming?"

"No, but we'll have hot food waiting when he gets in for lunch," Nigel said, as he put the container of little fish into his chilly bin.

"All prepared, aren't you?" I peered into the ice chest, complete with ice, on the back of his ute.

His eyes glittered as he snapped the lid shut and took my hand. "Come here, I've missed you," he said, as he pulled me into his arms and kissed my lips.

"But we've only been a few feet apart," I protested, when we finally came up for air.

"Yeah, well, I didn't want to give those old boys out there fishing with us a heart attack."

I shook my head at him and laughed.

"Let's load these nets and get up the hill. I'm starving." He flashed me one of his molten glances. "But I want food, too," he whispered.

My knees had already melted *before* that comment. I could only take a deep breath to steady myself as I stepped back. More winding roads, straight up the hill towering high above the ocean cliffs, and we were there.

Five

Kiritehere.

I suspect it was once more populated than the handful of houses there now. It was somewhere almost off the map but had the distinction of being on the sole coastal backroad from Raglan to Awakino. Two hundred kilometers of narrow, tightly-winding road. Ideal if you had several days to enjoy the gorgeous, bush-clad journey — and a stomach of iron.

Before us stood a farm gate with a small house that'd probably been there at the turn of the century. The garden had clearly seen better days; only the remnants of dried-up greens from spring bulbs remained amidst the weeds and the little lawn before the house was mowed, but still, the dwelling looked forlorn.

"My Uncle Don's place. Land of Angus cattle, Romney sheep, and steep hills." Nigel cut the engine and hopped out. Before I could untangle myself from the seatbelt, he was already there, holding the door open for me.

"I could get used to this, you'd better watch out," I said, lifting my chin for another kiss.

"That seems to be my aim." His eyes smoked. A day in cold water hadn't dampened his enthusiasm, or mine.

I hoped I knew what I was doing, because I was falling fast.

Straightening up, I shook my head. "I can see I won't get much done around you," I said, looking past his shoulder at the sad little house. "Does your uncle live out here all alone?"

"Yes. His wife died of cancer a few years back."

"Oh, no," I whispered.

He nodded. "She only told him about it when she was on death's door. There was nothing that could be done."

"Didn't they have any children?"

"Their two sons are long escaped to the city. The block is steep on the hills, boggy on the flats and sandy everywhere else. It's lovely, but it's a hard place to survive on, much less make a living. I'm not sure what he's going to do with the place—neither of his kids wants to farm, especially not," he broke off and surveyed the precipitous, sheep-covered hill country as far as the eye could see, "way out here. It seems to be the way of it in New Zealand these days."

"So he truly *is* alone."

"Well, no. He's got Ben."

I looked askance at him.

"Ben, his working dog. Uncle Don is my mother's eldest brother—and he's getting on a bit. Problem is, Ben's not young, either." Nigel frowned and bit his lip, then seemed to remember I was there and squeezed my hand, tugging me toward the front door.

It opened to his touch. He stepped inside and looked around. "Uncle Don?" No one answered, so he turned and motioned me in.

"He doesn't mind us walking in like this?"

He turned to me, his brow furrowed. "He's my uncle."

"And he doesn't lock it?"

Nigel laughed and gave me a hug as he gazed down into my eyes. "There's only one road out here. We know everyone living along it and no one takes kindly to things like that. You'd be pretty stupid to steal out here." His eyes hardened. "Someone was doing the rounds during a community event when everyone was at the local hall. They later found the guys' van, but nothing else. Hasn't happened since."

I swallowed hard. It was tough to eke out a living on these hills—tough men and women. Not good people to mess with.

I gulped. "I'll remember that."

"You'll do fine," he said, his gaze lightning. "I'll protect you."

"Who needs protecting?" said a gruff voice from the doorway, as a wet nose edged between us.

Nigel stepped back and turned to face the grizzled man at the entrance. "Uncle Don!" He went to him and threw his arms around him. "It's been a long time. I'd like you to meet Lena."

He nodded, then thrust out his hand. "Pleased to meet you," he murmured, then turned back to Nigel. "So, who needs protecting?" he repeated.

"No one, Uncle. It's all good," Nigel said, bending down to greet the even grayer black and white eye dog. "How are you going, old man?"

Ben glanced back and forth between Nigel and Don while he submitted to the pats handed out by Nigel, then stepped lightly toward me.

"This is Lena, Ben, prettiest girl horse vet in Te Awamutu."

I quirked my lips. "I'm not so sure that's much of a complement. I'm the *only* girl horse vet in Te Awamutu."

"Trust me, it'll always be a complement for you," Nigel murmured.

Ben nosed at my hand and I ducked down beside him and stroked his fine-boned face.

One last look up at his master to confirm I was okay, then Ben glued himself to my side.

"Good to see you, Nigel. It has been a while... too long. Sorry you thought you had to go so far down the line to get over—"

"—it's okay, Don," Nigel cut in sharply and flicked a glance over his shoulder at me.

What was that about?

His uncle turned to me for a moment, too, then cleared his throat and continued. "Anyway, glad you're back. What brings you out here?"

"Came to see you and take Lena out for a fish."

Don's eyes lit up. "Whitebait?"

"You came home too early. We just got here. I thought it'd go easier on us if I trashed *your* kitchen making whitebait fritters instead of mums." Nigel's glowing eyes met mine, then he headed for a cupboard and started pulling out ingredients.

Don smiled at me. "The boy knows how to make friends, eh? So you're a vet, are you? Dogs and cats?"

"Horses. The rest just go with the job."

His brows shot up. "Maybe," he looked up at me hopefully for a moment, then dropped his eyes, "but no. It's Sunday."

"Can I help you with something? I'm happy to."

"Well, it's just that…"

"What is it, Don?" Nigel frowned, peering into the fridge. "Where are the eggs?"

"Where they've always been—in the butter safe," Don said, then turned back to me. "It's the young horse. I think he's done a tendon."

"Oh, no," I said, glancing out at the steep hill farm. Not a good outlook for a horse with a bowed tendon on those steep sidelings. "Why do you think it's a tendon?"

"It's all swollen and he's nearly three-legged lame."

"When did it start?"

"He was a little off yesterday, but today he's quite bad."

"Let's look at him now. Is there time, Nigel?"

"Sure. I'll put the whitebait in the fridge."

"With my old horse full of arthritis, I need this young one for the farm."

"What about your motorbike, Uncle?"

Don snorted. "The tracks don't go everywhere on this farm. Way too steep. No wonder my sons ran for the city." He sobered, then took a deep breath. "I'm safer on a young horse than on a four-wheeler."

I shuddered. That said a lot about the farm. And this old man was out here all alone? "I thought four-wheelers were pretty stable."

Both men chuckled. "More stable than three-wheelers, but all four wheels really do is make them roll straighter down the hills."

"Oh." I winced, as they laughed. Another glance out the open door showed me it really wasn't a laughing matter. "No wonder you'd rather ride a horse. Let's go see him."

Don led me to the barn behind his house. "Got him over Gisborne way," he said, beaming, as he grabbed a halter and lead from a hook on the wall.

"Gisborne-bred, eh? Nice horses," I said.

And he was. The big strapping bay Clydesdale-cross stood a good sixteen and a half hands, with a chest nearly that wide. A veritable tractor. The hill-country bred stock from the Hawkes Bay region, including Gisborne, were the most surefooted and unflappable horses I'd ever met. This one was no exception.

He stood with his right front toe barely touching the ground. Don haltered the gelding and I reached out to greet him. He pricked his ears and snuffled my hand, then licked it. Satisfied, he let his ears flop again and lifted his sore hoof, then reached down to nose at it.

"You poor darlin'," I murmured, as I moved to his right side and slid my hand down his leg. Sure enough, he had plenty of filling around the flexor tendons, from his suspensory ligament all the way to his hoof. He let out a big sigh when I lifted his foot, flexing the leg and holding it clear of the ground. He never moved while I palpated his tendons. None of them were painful or thickened, but the digital pulses at the back of his fetlock were pounding.

I smiled up into Don's and Nigel's worried eyes. I could do something about this, anyway.

"Don, his tendons feel fine. I think it's in his foot. Do you have a hoof knife?"

He nodded. "Do you want an apron, too?"

"Yes, please." Thank God for that—the insides of my knees had enough bruises, without adding more.

I buckled on the old apron and lifted the hoof again. A light pare over the surface of the sole and sulci revealed a black crack near his inside heel. I followed it with my knife until with one final flick of its sharp tip, the horse jerked as a stream of thick, dark gray, stinky material oozed from the small hole.

"Ah, there it is," Don said, with a satisfied grin. "Better than a tendon."

"Infinitely so," I agreed. "Have you any povidone-iodine?"

He nodded. "I set the Zip to boil when I went for the knife. I can hot-soak it while you two play in the kitchen."

"You took the words out of my mouth, Don. Do you have a boot?"

"Sure do. I'll save some clean soaking liquid for it."

"Excellent. Is he current on his tetanus?" I asked.

"Yes, luckily he was done three months ago."

"Perfect." As the pus drained out onto the concrete floor of the shed, the horse lowered his head again and closed his eyes, then stood his whole weight on the bad hoof.

"If you can keep soaking it twice a day for twenty minutes in the hottest iodine water you can get your hand into, keeping it covered in a boot in-between, that should be all he needs," I said, as I unbuckled the apron and rolled it up and wiped the worst of the gunk off the knife with some straw.

"Sure can. I'll put a shoe and a pad on it after it's healed up, and pop a shoe on his other front," Don said.

"Looks like he'll be a new horse soon." Nigel smiled as he reached out to take the shoeing gear.

"Thanks again," Don said. He swiped at his eyes with his sleeve, then turned back to his horse. "Thank you, Lena," he said, with feeling, then turned back to the great horse. "You don't know how much this means to me," he mumbled into his mane. "I'll see you both up at the house."

I patted his shoulder and turned to go.

Outside the barn, Nigel smiled down at me and wrapped an arm around my shoulders as we walked back to the house. "You didn't need to do that, you know."

"I didn't do much."

"Tell that to the horse, or Don. You should send him an invoice, anyway."

"Can't," I said lightly. "Not meant to be working outside the practice."

He shook his head with a bemused smile and pulled me hard against his side. "You're a tough nut, you know?"

"I've heard it said. So, tell me about whitebait fritters…" I said, and his attention turned.

Six

The fritters were a success. Eggy batter, its edges fried crispy brown in butter, enveloped the little fish. The hundred or so tiny eyes were a bit disconcerting, but their crunchy, salty taste was exquisite.

Don couldn't be happier. His precious horse was on the mend and he loved whitebait fritters. Ben, however, was in ecstasy with a new friend to latch on to on top of the fish. Once I sat down, his grizzled chin never lifted from my thigh until Nigel mentioned the word "bike".

His head shot up, floppy-tipped ears pointed at Nigel. He stared at him with an expectancy only a heading dog could hope to match—every muscle tensed, ready for action.

"Okay," Nigel said quickly, and Ben was out the door, gone in a flash of black, white, and grey.

"He's gettin' pretty stiff, but he can still move," Don's mouth worked and he looked away for a moment. When he turned back to us, his eyes were watering. "He's coming home so sore lately, I'm tempted to leave him home, but he hates bein' left behind. Howls the place down the whole time. I haven't the heart to do it to him."

"The old boy's onto a pretty good thing here—getting to stay in at night," Nigel said, as he got to his feet. "We'd best get out there or he might move all the sheep by himself."

"Let you in on a secret, you two," Don said with a twist

of his lips, "as long as you don't tell anyone. I'm already the laughing stock of the district, lettin' that dog stay in the house." Don's eyes were merry. "He even sleeps on my bed. He's partial to your Auntie's pillow, not that she'd have shared" — he winced — "but I'm sure she'd be pleased we both have the comfort of another soul at night."

"I didn't know your wife, Don, but I'm sure she'd be glad of it. And that's probably why Ben can still get around like he does, even at his age."

"Let's go for a ride," Nigel said, taking my hand. "You can ride 'Big Red', the Honda. Have you ever ridden a bike?"

"I rode a dirt bike in my teens and loved it."

"It shouldn't take you long to figure this one out, then. Similar gears, only easier."

Big Red was a bit of a monster, and it'd been years. I was slightly terrified, but it was still fun. "I like motorcycles — two-wheelers — more, much easier to turn," I shouted to Don, who stood beside Nigel, mounted on a Yamaha in the center of the small, flat paddock behind Don's house.

Nigel was laughing as I hauled on the handlebars to get it around the last corner and rode back to them. "It'll turn just fine when you're going fast."

I smiled, then sobered. I couldn't get up much speed in this paddock… And this was the only level ground in sight. I shivered as my stomach got that funny feeling. He couldn't possibly think I'd be riding it on the steep tracks leading down into the valley below?

"Ready to go?" Nigel said, as Don started walking back to the house.

"*Go?*"

"Down the back of the farm. Don has to wait for a truck, but we can take the bikes."

I blinked. "Ahh —" I took in the sheer cliffs making up most of the farm. "Is-is there a track?" I swallowed hard.

"Of sorts." His eyes sparkled at me. "You'll do fine. Let's go."

My mouth dried at the sight of Nigel's "track". A narrow strip of steepness, akin to a goat track, had been cut away from the side of a steep sideling — with what, I have no idea — leaving a sheer bank to the left and… a nearly vertical drop to the rocky stream bed at the bottom of the hill. I finally found my voice. "Nigel, I can't… I've never…"

"You'll be fine," he said, the corners of his mouth lifting as he reached out a hand to squeeze mine on the handlebar. "Just follow. Toot the horn if you need me to stop."

Any other objections I may've had were drowned by the sound of his Yamaha revving off and down the path before me.

Certainly I can do this.

I turned the engine on again and flicked the brake off. With a deep breath, I hit the throttle and buzzed off with my heart somewhere near my tonsils.

Couldn't I just shut my eyes?

Nigel was already far ahead as I snail-crawled down the sorry excuse for a track. Sure it was plenty wide — for sheep, maybe two abreast and crowding each other toward the bank. At a stretch, a horse. A steady, well behaved one.

I swallowed hard.

As I began to take control of my four or five horsepower, bouncing down the trail, I started noticing the mountains in the distance and the sheep scuttling off the trail. The ewes bleated at their lambs, who ignored them and scattered, bucking around on the nearly vertical face before me. I daren't look behind.

Soon, the bike began to listen to even my slightest whim and I began to smile.

"It really wasn't as narrow as I thought." I said, quirking my lips, when Nigel stopped to wait for me at a wide spot on an open ridge. "It just looks like such a long drop on the downhill side."

"It does, doesn't it?" He chuckled. "You've done just fine. The sea air suits you." He leaned across and kissed me.

"We'll have to borrow some horses next time. You'd like that better, eh?"

"I don't mind the bike now. This bike and I—we have an understanding," I said as I tore my eyes from his and surveyed the farm spread out before us. To my right, a wooden bar topped the fence wires between two fenceposts and the top two high-tensile wires were tacked down level with the third one from the top. "Is that a spar? For hunting?"

"Sure is, the Kingson Hunt rides up here from time to time."

"On this steep land?"

"Yep." He caught my eye and held it. "Where do you think our Olympians come from? This is the sort of place they begin."

"What a way to start!" One couldn't help but be impressed.

"I love it out here." Nigel's voice was husky as he stared off into the distance across the valleys below. "My mother was born out here."

"But you've got your home farm in Te Awamutu?"

"Yes, but this place seems to call to me."

I nodded. "Its immensity and wildness"—I slowly filled my lungs—"it gets me, too." Our gazes locked for a long moment, then I followed as he led off again.

We detoured from the main track to check troughs on the way across the farm, but finally, Nigel stopped his bike and cut the engine. I rode up beside him and stopped.

"Care for some afternoon tea, milady?" He half-bowed and gestured toward a narrow gully ahead.

"Afternoon tea? Here?"

He laughed and tugged a wicker basket from its bungees on the front rack of his bike.

"I never even saw that." I chuckled.

"You were too busy gulping air to see much. What'd I tell you? You needn't have worried about the bike, you did fine. Uphill's easier, but forget about that now. Come on."

"Where now, Casanova?" I asked, as I slid from the saddle of my bike.

"You'll see," he said, mystery in his voice. A soft roaring sound in the distance became ever louder as we walked beside the tinkling stream running through the little valley .

"Wait here," he said, seating me on a moss-covered log, "and close your eyes.

I played along and waited, my heart beating faster as I waited. The roaring sound was seemed louder since he'd sat me down, and the tiny cheep-cheeps of native Fantails, *piwakawaka*, sounded all around me. I sucked air in between my pursed lips in a fair imitation and they flew so close I felt the breeze of their passing. I always swore they wanted to play with me, though most Kiwis always told me the birds just wanted to eat the insects I scared up for them.

With my eyes closed, my senses were heightened, and my skin tingled at the soft crunching of trail beneath Nigel's boots. He didn't say a word, but soon his lips were soft on the back of my neck, then on my own lips.

"You can open your eyes now."

His glowed into mine as he took my hand and led me around the next bend.

I froze at the sight.

The ocean spread out before me, its surface a sea of glittering diamonds — a beautiful backdrop for the veritable feast spread out on a tartan picnic blanket.

I shook my head and turned to Nigel. "You did… all this?"

He smiled and led me to my place. Crystal glasses, sparkling cider, and the inevitable thermos of tea.

"Biscuits?" He opened a tin to show the ANZAC biscuits inside.

"You *made* these?"

"Well, no." He had the grace to look sheepish. "Mum's contribution, though I did the mutton."

"Good job, Nigel." I gazed over the spread again and stood on my tiptoes to kiss him. "Thank you. After my near-death experience up there, it's a wonderful reward."

He stared, and his hand stopped stock-still on its way to the buttered rolls. "Were you genuinely scared?"

"Actually, yes, until I got my hand in, but then it was fun."

"Oh, good," he said, and resumed his creation of a filled roll. "Roll?"

"Yes, please. It smells heavenly. I didn't think I could possibly eat after our huge lunch. Must be the sea air."

He grinned and started on his own sandwich.

We ate until we could eat no more, then I lay down on the blanket beside him.

"You know," Nigel's fingers entwined with mine, "I could get used to this," he murmured.

"Me too. I haven't felt so sated—"

As I spoke, Nigel shot up to a sitting position facing away from me, every muscle taut, poised to bolt. I climbed up to my knees, eyeing our surroundings for any sign of danger, but other than a few Fantails, nothing moved.

"What's the matter?"

"Nothing," he said, as he stared off into the distance.

I watched him for a few moments, then turned away and made myself as comfortable as I could with my thoughts screaming around in my head.

Another commit-o-phobe, eh? I'd had enough of those to last me a lifetime. *Please, not again.*

When I glanced back at him, he looked up and smiled.

"Ready to go?" he asked, his voice overly bright.

I glanced at him from the corners of my eyes, but he didn't respond. We packed it all up, loaded the basket, and set off— without one touch.

Disappointing, at best.

I wouldn't think about devastation. I'd leave it for now. Surely he'd show his cards sometime soon. Then I'd know what was really up.

Seven

"Enjoy that?" Don roared over the bikes when we arrived back at his yard.

"Sure did," I said, after I stopped my engine.

"You should've seen her — like she'd ridden a bike every day of her life," Nigel said, and pecked me on the cheek.

I slapped my mouth shut from where it was hanging while I stared after him.

The man was a yo-yo.

Maybe I was reading too much into it. Probably. I'd been known to do it before.

"Oh, Lena," Don piped up, "Ngaire stopped by. She's with the Kingson Hunt and they're having a hunt out on their farm next weekend. They have extra horses fitted up, and she wondered if you two would like to ride with them?"

Sounds like a bit of me.

"I've heard of them," I said. "I hear they're pretty wild and ride any country under any conditions — at speed."

Nigel's eyes lit up and he grinned. "Yep."

"I'll check my on-call schedule and let you guys know," I said, heart racing. "I haven't had the chance to ride since I left the States and I sure miss it."

"We'll ride before then, if you'd like," Nigel said. "I'm sure Mum won't mind if we take a few of ours out around the farm. They're not very fit, but at least you can get on a horse before you go out hunting."

Then I remembered. I'd only been thinking of the galloping. "Hunting over wire?" I winced.

"Yes, 'full-wire', but there are always gates if you don't want to jump, and some fences are sparred, as you saw up the top."

I shuddered. "All the fences we hunted over on the East Coast of the U.S. were either wooden or sparred." It made my heart stop to even think of jumping wire fences.

"Our horses are used to it."

"As a vet, it still terrifies me."

Nigel's eyes sparkled. "You'll be amazed at our mounts, then."

"I'm sure I will. For a country the size of New Zealand, its Olympic teams certainly exceed expectation."

Don grinned at Nigel. "George has offered Lena their stallion to ride."

"A stallion, on the hunt field?" My jaw dropped.

"He's the coolest of the lot. Full Clyde, but the New Zealand type. Much lighter than the beer-dray horses you're used to from the States."

I laughed. "The ones I'm used to could step over the fences."

"Well, this one jumps like a stag."

This I couldn't *wait* to see.

Ben nosed his way under my hand, looking for a pat. I sat on a handy anvil mounted on a big stump and ensconced his grizzled muzzle between my fingers. He gazed up with adoration, his slim body swaying with the slowly waving tail. Every few moments he peered at Don. Checking up.

I was glad the old man had someone looking after him, even if the dog was as aged as he was.

Don stood up and with a quick slip of Ben's tongue on my hand, he bolted to his master's side, ready for anything.

Nigel stood, too. "We'd best be going, Don, but it's been wonderful to see you. Thank you."

"Any time, you two. See you next weekend?"

The week flew by. I'd made a few hunting acquaintances and could ask them about New Zealand hunting etiquette, which thankfully differed little from the hunts I'd attended in the States.

Nigel rang to invite me riding, and on Wednesday I met him at the farm after work. Mounted on Sara's sensible Welsh Cob, with Nigel beside me on his big East Coast horse, we rode over their farm. It was a lovely afternoon to ride over the hundreds of rolling acres filled with sheep, Angus, and their small Jersey herd. On the way home, we popped over a few fences and to my relief, my six-month hiatus from riding was as if it'd never been.

"Do you need any clothes for the hunt?" Nigel asked.

"I brought my riding clothes from the states, so I'm good, thanks, other than being totally unfit for riding."

He laughed. "I am, too. You'll be fine on Saturday, by the way. I wouldn't put you up on Jake if he wasn't completely trustworthy."

"Jake?"

"George's stallion."

"Oh." I frowned. "The weather's looking bad for the rest of the week." I gazed up at the darkening skies.

"Should stop by Saturday."

"Won't it be slippery?" I said, my voice sounding small to my ears. Racing around anywhere, under any conditions, sounded great last weekend, but the reality was beginning to hit me.

He sighed. "It'll be fine. My advice? If things get scary, shut your eyes, give him his head, and stay balanced. Let Jake manage it. He's grown up on these hills and the horses do pretty well out there, despite our interference."

Somehow that wasn't a huge comfort.

Thankfully, back in the home paddock, Georgette waited. And she *was* a comfort. The cow looked wonderful and her two calves cavorted about her while she placidly gazed at me over the sea of grass in her private palace paddock.

"She fell on her feet, didn't she?" Nigel caught my eye.

I nodded as he nudged his horse closer, closing the distance between us, then took my hand and didn't let go until it was time to dismount.

Later, he opened my ute door and handed me in, then kissed me before closing the door. "I'll pick you up at six on Saturday morning, then?"

"I'll be ready." I'm sure I was glowing.

The man was definitely confusing, but he seemed to be over whatever it was. It seemed we were back on…

Whatever that meant.

"Sorry, couldn't wait 'till the weekend to see you again." Nigel's voice flowed smooth as silk across the phone line just after I arrived home from work on Thursday.

"Six a.m. Saturday not soon enough, eh?"

"Nope."

"I'd have to agree with you." I chuckled. "What are we to do about it, then?"

"They do a nice flame-grilled steak over at Lake Karapiro."

"Karapiro?" I snorted. "There's nothing out there but farms."

"Oh ye of little faith. Pick you up in an hour?"

"Want me to bring anything?"

"Nope, just yourself."

I shook my head as I hung up the phone.

By the time he arrived, I still had no idea how we were to get steak in the middle of nowhere. And he wouldn't tell me, as we drove out the half hour to Karapiro.

"There are faster ways, but I like this one," he said, as he took my hand. His eyes sparkled at me briefly, then returned to the road. We crossed over the old one-way bridge over the hydro dam, then took the main road south. After another two kilometers, we turned off toward the lake.

"Where the heck are we going?" I couldn't help asking. We were getting further and further from civilization.

He drove off the narrow road into a wide turnout on the edge of the lake and cut the engine.

I shook my head and smiled as he hopped out, slammed his door and scooted around to open mine.

"Your dinner awaits, madame."

I looked all around me before placing my hand in his and getting to my feet.

Nigel opened the tailgate and flicked open the bungees holding the tarp down over the back of his ute, revealing a big red esky.

"Here, you take a side?" he said, sliding it off the back.

I finally got it.

"Cool, a picnic! Perfect." I beamed at him.

"I figured we might as well take advantage of the good weather."

We carried the ice chest around the edge of the lake to a secluded area under a shady tree.

"What can I do?" I asked, as he pumped up a little folding backpacking stove.

"There's a picnic blanket in there, you'll probably recognize it." He grinned. "You could set up our fine dining establishment, if you would, please."

I shook out the blanket and laid the tableware he'd expertly packed while he chopped garlic and crushed peppercorns.

The man could cook.

In no time at all, he flash-steamed some veggies and handed me the pot. I'd just finished plating them up when our garlicky pepper steak hissed into the pan.

"Madame?" He cocked a brow at me.

I couldn't help shaking my head. "Medium rare, please. Charred."

"Excellent. Just the way I like it. Leaves some respect for the meat. Never could stand killing meat twice."

And excellent, it was.

"That was exquisite, Nigel," I said as he moved toward me and took my lips with his.

"You like that?" He waved around our impromptu campsite.

"Absolutely. What a perfect night."

"Mmm... I'm glad." His eyes glowed as he leaned over me again in the deepening twilight and bent his head to kiss me again.

"Wherever did you learn to cook like that?"

He stiffened and sat up, not looking at me. "It doesn't matter," he said gruffly.

"No, it doesn't," I whispered, and he turned back to face me with the ghost of a smile, then took me in his arms and kissed me until I forgot my question — and his lack of an answer.

As darkness fell, so did the temperature. Soon even our ardent kisses weren't enough to keep us warm.

"Shall we go?" Nigel sounded disappointed.

"Since there's only one blanket and I suspect you start work even earlier than I do, it's probably a good idea." I kissed him once more for good measure and sat up.

It was warm in his ute — my legs from the incredible heater in his diesel wagon, and my heart from his kisses and his warm grip on my hand.

Friday's rainstorms boded no good for the Saturday hunt, but when I queried Nigel on the phone on Friday night, he only laughed.

"They'll hunt in a downpour. On vertical sidelings."

I gulped. *On a horse I'd never seen before.* A stallion, for Pete's sake.

"You'll be fine. Just remember what I told you. Shut your eyes, give the beast his head, and stay balanced."

Eight

I tried to remember Nigel's words of wisdom as the massive bay Clydesdale half-slid, half-bounded down the steep face of a hill, just behind the master, who rode just behind the pack of hounds and the whip.

The fact this horse was often ridden by the whip didn't help much. He was used to being in front of the master, and I had all I could do to keep him behind the red coat before me.

As the hounds ran baying at full cry, Jake got away from me, his reins slipping through my slithering gloves. I cursed myself for wearing leather—not string—gloves. String gloves wouldn't have slipped. With 17 hands of bolting light draught horse beneath me, I was trying to climb up my reins, eyes tearing from the strands of mane blowing back in my face, when I saw the fence. We were ten strides out, then five, then three.

I gave up trying to rate him and just balanced myself.

Thankfully, because two full strides out, he left the ground. As we flew from a good twenty feet back, the slow motion effect let me take in the stunned, frozen faces of the riders around us as they pulled up their mounts to watch the carnage about to unfold before them. Sure I was about to die when we hit the full-wire fence, I held my breath and kept my eyes up between his perky little — much too little for a Clydesdale, I remember thinking, ridiculously — ears.

Somehow, against all odds, we cleared it, but—not surprisingly—I was unbalanced when his platter feet hit the ground again, and I landed on the pommel of the saddle. Painful, but worlds better than what could have happened — or if I'd been male.

Jake threw in a few bucks, just because he could, and slowed in response to my tugging on one rein.

"You bloody beast," I murmured into his mane, as I hugged his neck, when we'd finally stopped, "but what a bloody jump you've got."

He snorted and dropped his head to graze, and I nearly fell off over his neck.

"Oh God, Lena, I thought you were dead," Nigel said, as he slid from his Thoroughbred's saddle and ran to my side.

Jake eyed him, but never lifted his head from the grass.

"What a jump," I said, my voice — and the rest of me — quivering as I looked up to see Nigel's white face.

"Let's not see it again, okay?" Nigel reached one hand to take mine after he took Jake's reins in the other.

"What a good idea." I took a deep breath and held it, as we moved aside, so the field could pass us.

"I'll ride him if you want," Nigel said.

"No, it'll be fine. He's had his blat, and I'll hold on better next time."

"Sure footed or no," Nigel growled, "that's the last time I put you on the whip's horse. Didn't know George was a whip now."

"Amen to that," I said, shaking my head.

Jake was a perfect gentleman the rest of the day.

"Guess he needed to let me know what he could do," I said to a contrite George.

"I'm so sorry," he said, for the hundredth time. "He never does that with me."

I laughed outright and laid my arm along his on the table

of the wee Te Anga Pub. "George, see any difference?" I fluttered my lashes at him.

"Ah, a bit more muscle, aye?" He laughed as he picked up his beer and stood up to leave. "I'll see you two soon, eh?"

"Yes, thanks again for the loan of the horses," Nigel said, and I echoed him, watching as he moved away to speak with someone else.

"I'm just glad you're okay," Nigel gripped my hand tighter under the table. "Plus, my mum would kill me if I'd gotten you hurt. She rather likes the new girl vet."

We'd taken George's horses home and set them up for the night, but the horses of the non-local hunt members still stood in their massive horse trucks outside the tavern, a long line of them stretching down the road.

"They're all going home tonight?" I murmured to my partner.

He nodded and followed my eyes to a particularly loud and noisy man getting seriously drunk.

"He's driving his horses? Like that?"

Nigel winced. "He does it all the time."

"Over sixty km of winding, almost one-way road, with a twenty tonne truck and four horses' lives at stake?" My mouth dropped open. "Surely he has a sober driver."

Nigel shook his head.

Then I took a better look around the room. He wasn't the only one. And many had already started drinking from their silver hip flasks when they were still out on the hunting field.

Suddenly it wasn't so much fun anymore.

"Can we go, please? I don't think I can watch this."

He squeezed my fingers and stood, then led me to the door. A wave to the chattering crowd and we were on our way. I shuddered for the horses in the trucks, standing and getting stiffer by the hour until it was time for their owners to finish getting drunk, then wobbling home. If they were lucky.

"I enjoyed the hunting," I answered Nigel, as he opened the ute door, "but next time, let's skip the pub?"

"You got it. Excellent idea," he said, and kissed me again.

"Dinner?" Nigel queried, as he pulled up before my flat.

"I'd love it," I said, after a cursory thought of my empty fridge. I glanced down my grubby shirt and then shifted my gaze to the smear of dried mud coating one side of Nigel's cheek and the tiny spatters all over his neck "But we'll both need a shower first. If you have clean clothes, you could shower here."

His grin at that idea warmed me to the tips of my toes and made my insides quiver. It must have done the same for him, by the blush suffusing his grubby face and neck.

"I-I have a change of clothes with me," he said, recovering his — shaky — aplomb.

I'm not quite sure how it happened, but we ended up in the shower — together.

Let's just say we both got squeaky clean by the time the water started going cold — and he leapt out to give me room to wash my hair in my tiny cubicle.

A kiss against the glass and his towel-dried, tanned body exited the steaming bathroom. The ring of the telephone sounded over the noise of the water.

"Want me to get that?" Nigel called.

"Please," I said. I finished rinsing my hair and opened the door a crack to grab my towel. Nigel's voice, raised, came from the other room.

Who could that be?

I hurried to dry myself and wrap a towel around me. I entered the kitchen at a trot to see a red-faced, scowling Nigel holding the phone receiver out toward me.

Whoever could it be?

"Hello?" I said, but the phone was dead. "Who was it?"

"Said he was your boyfriend." Nigel's voice was cold. "Rather nasty about it, too. Told me to piss off."

I jerked toward him. "Who? I don't have a boyfriend — other than you, maybe. I'm certainly not going out with anyone else." My face steamed in the cool evening air coming through the open window.

"Madsen?"

"Oh," I barely stopped before I growled. "*Him*. I went out with him once, and what a mistake that was. But I've already told you about that."

Nigel eyed me sideways then took a deep breath and let it out slowly. He hesitated, then accepted the hand I offered.

"Now, about that dinner," he said lightly, "why don't you get dressed before I get other ideas?" He wrapped his arms around my towel-clad body for a moment, but his embrace felt… hesitant? Wooden, even?

Maybe I was just imagining it.

I sure hoped so.

"Mum and Dad invited you to come out to our bach at Kiritehere for Christmas." Nigel's deep voice warmed even my frozen hands as I stood on the linoleum of the bathroom floor, water still dripping from the ends of my hair after my last vet call in the pouring rain.

"Yes, please," I managed. A flood of nostalgia engulfed me and my heart gave a jerk. "I'd love that." I missed my family and hadn't been invited anywhere by the family of a boyfriend… well, probably since high school.

I couldn't ask for more. My Christmas wish… if I didn't mess it up somehow… might just come true.

And I couldn't wipe the idiot smile from my face.

"Can you get any time off?" Nigel asked

"I've actually been given Christmas off, right through New Year's Day. Not sure how I got so lucky, but it's rostered."

"That's fine," he murmured. "And it's not long away."

"What do I need?"

"Just your togs and clothes, really. Everything else is there."

I'd ring Sara to find out what I could contribute.

Nigel's voice dragged my wandering thoughts back. "…wondered if you'd like to meet me at the sale yard tomorrow, if you're free. In your lunchtime, maybe?"

"If I can get a lunch break, I'll be there."

"Good. I'll arrive for noon. We can get some tucker."

"I'll do my level best." My smile probably went all the way through the wires.

" 'Till tomorrow, then. I'm looking forward to spending Christmas with you. Kisses," he murmured, and rang off.

I stripped off and stood under the hot shower, as warm inside from our conversation as I soon became on the outside. The glow stayed with me until I closed my eyes and knew no more.

❧

Jersey cows have always been my favorites, with their doe eyes and tiny cloven hooves. It always got me in trouble though, because I'd let my guard down… and the little beggars were the only cows who tended to damage me. Those wee hooves were like knives—at ninja-speed. Their bigger, slower Friesian cousins had nothin' on them.

And so I stood, leaning on the saleyard fence, wishing I had a farm so I could buy the little ones in the pen below me and take them home. Maybe someday… maybe even soon. My heart skipped a beat, thinking of Nigel, and I checked my watch.

He should be here any minute.

Somehow, I'd managed to take a lunchtime, rather than wolfing down my food in the ute on the way to my next call.

I shivered at a sudden chill on my back and turned to see Marcus Madsen, nearly close enough to touch me. Behind him, Nigel was turning away, his dark brows almost touching. His face a storm waiting to break.

Marcus reached an arm around me. Not his wisest move, but then he hadn't shown himself to be terribly bright. I twisted around and broke his hold, the slammed my elbow toward his face. I caught him in the nose, with a sickening crunch, and raced after the retreating Nigel.

"Nigel, wait!" I called, but he never turned. Plenty of other farmers did, though, their brows lifted as they watched me run toward the parking lot. I finally caught him, just as he reached his ute.

"Nigel, what's the matter?"

The look on his face froze me to the core.

"Leaving you to your boyfriend," he snarled.

"He's *not* my boyfriend. I told you before."

"Sure looked like it, with his hand on your arse."

"He never touched my arse, though I probably just broke his nose when I saw what he was up to."

"I'm meant to believe that?" he growled low, then added, "I won't be responsible for—" He froze, then spun away, jumped into his ute and peeled out of the parking lot with a spray of metal and a cloud of dust.

The few farmers still watching the show turned away. I gazed back toward the sound of the auctioneer starting up his chant, then got into my practice ute and headed back to work.

Lunch no longer appealed. I don't think I could eat a bite.

Nine

*I*t was a long night, followed by an even longer workday. The rain never let up and I had three farms for herd pregnancy tests on my list. I tried to keep my mind on the job, but it kept wandering. By the end of the day, I was seriously wondering about my choice of careers.

No matter how many scenarios I dreamed up, I couldn't imagine how merely standing beside Madsen could have caused such a disaster. I wanted to ring Nigel and talk, but whether it was cowardice or a desire to give him time to think, I'll never know. So, I left it… and cried myself to sleep.

It'd felt so right – but now?

My blood chilled at the message on my answering machine when I returned home from work. It was Sara.

"Could you please ring me?" she said, "Nigel hasn't been home since yesterday morning and I wondered if you'd seen him?"

I flicked the machine off and rang her straight back.

"I haven't seen him today, but—" I began, then broke down in tears and told her about our meeting at the saleyard. "I have no idea why he was so upset," I finished on a whisper.

Sara gave a heavy sigh. "Would you please come out for supper?" she asked. "Maybe I can help explain."

The scenery, usually slipping by with such grandeur — the rolling Te Awamutu farmland with its hedges, the raw gray buttes of Wharepapa South — went unnoticed as I drove like an automaton toward the lovely old homestead.

"I'm glad you could join me tonight," Sara murmured.

I turned my face up to her, eyes spilling over once again... or was it *still*?

She took me in her arms and held me, rocking me as she must've once rocked Nigel. "The men are off at a meeting."

"Nigel?" I jerked my eyes up to meet hers.

She shook her head, her own eyes filled with tears. "I fear he's left again."

"But... why?" I couldn't keep the plea from escaping my lips.

"Come and sit down. Let's eat and then we can talk."

She pulled me to her big table, set for two. I didn't think I'd be able to eat, but it seemed to help. Afterwards, we moved to soft seats in her gracious living room before a flickering fire.

"I don't know what to do about him, myself," Sara whispered to the hands folded in her lap, then gazed up at me. "He was married to a very pretty young thing, Jamie. She was a bit flighty, but seemed to love him. Nigel was different from the man he's become — less thoughtful, more of your 'good old Kiwi rugby boy'. They were sharemilking, but he liked to go drinking with the guys and, I suspect, left her alone on the farm too often."

I swallowed hard. This couldn't end well.

"One night, he came home earlier than usual and found her just coming home — in a g-string and little else. They got to fighting and he accused her of messing around on him. She left in a huff... and never came back." Sara choked on her words and sat for a moment to regain enough composure to continue. "He found her in her wrecked car, upside down in a water-filled ditch on a straight piece of road — both her and my unborn grandchild, dead."

My world spun as I gripped Sara's hand. We cried together for their loss. I cried for their loss... and my own. This was more than I could've forseen, or even imagined.

"Nigel left that day," Sara continued, "and we didn't hear from him for six months. Then he left a phone message to say he was alive and 'well', though he sounded far from it. We were just thankful he was alive. He said he was staying away from women and sporting clubs, but he only came home a short time before we met you over Georgette. Quite changed, he was… we thought… but it appears the old scars remain."

"I truly only saw that creep Madsen once—and walked two kilometers home in heels to get away from him," I said, in a small voice. "I adore Nigel."

Sara laughed wetly through her tears. "I know, but things are black and white for that boy. Always have been. Let's hope he sees reason. For now, I'll try to go on with my life and suggest you do the same. You're always welcome out here, remember that."

"Thank you, Sara, I appreciate you telling me all this. It makes a big difference. Please let me know if you hear anything?"

"Of course, sweetie. As soon as I hear. For now, we might not be going out to Kiritehere for Christmas—with Nigel back, we thought we'd be ahead on the farm jobs and could take the time, but with him gone, probably not."

"Let me know if I can help with anything."

Now she did laugh. "You've already got a full time vet job on your hands—that's plenty."

I smiled ruefully. "True."

"We'll see how we go. If we *do* go out there, we'd love to have you. I wouldn't want you to be alone in the holidays."

I smiled as she hugged me and led me to the door.

It was only a week until Christmas, and then suddenly it was already the weekend before. While I'd been working, I managed my grief, but then my Christmas days off began, and things, namely me, started getting a bit touchy.

I wandered the aisles of the grocery store to restock my empty cupboards, but Christmas displays bombarded me from all sides. I nearly bolted out the front door, but I truly had nothing in the house, so I buckled down and shopped. I picked out meat and veggies, plus oats, flour and sugar—I was truly out of food—and headed for the checkout.

A voice from right behind me sent shivers down my spine.

"Payback's a bitch," it whispered.

Madsen.

I didn't give him the pleasure of a response. The man was evil. The worst thing was, he probably didn't even know how evil he was.

Straightening, I pushed my cart forward, willing the tears to stay back. I paid and carried the bags up the block to my flat.

I had to do something. I wasn't used to being sedentary—my constitution couldn't handle it, but where could I go? I couldn't bother Sara all the time and my own family was unreachable over the holiday period.

I steadied myself and focused. Then I saw my neglected rollerblades beside the door and hugged them to my chest like an old friend.

They were a good outlet for what ailed me. For the next days, I spent most of my waking hours skating around the Te Awamutu College grounds.

The deep stillness and peace in the deserted school grounds helped fill the hole in my heart. Warbling birds and the occasional sleeping neighborhood cat shared with me their pristine acres of smooth pavement and gentle ramps. The graceful curves of the netball courts let me perfect my figure skating. Most importantly, though, the skating let me think of something besides Nigel—even if only for an hour or two—and how I may have just wrecked his life, no matter how unintentionally.

Ten

Christmas Eve finally came, more slowly than it ever had before. Suffice it to say I finally made it to sleep, rubbing my sore, tear-filled eyes, wondering what I was going to do to celebrate the big day.

I didn't have long to wonder how I'd spend my Christmas morning. The phone jangled me awake at five-something a.m. and I smiled at the first happy thought I'd had in days. My mother must have found a telephone in that jungle she was traipsing through and forgotten about time differences.

"Hello? Mom?" I answered eagerly.

"Lena? Sorry, no, this is Jarrod. Look, sorry to bother you at this hour, and on Christmas Day, too, but Barkley's top colt just tried to geld himself. I know you're not on call, but can you please come help me? I need you to do the anesthesia."

I let out my breath with a whoosh and swallowed the disappointment. The horse needed help and Jarrod was one of the practice partners.

No time for wobblies.

"Is he stable?" I heard myself ask.

"Seems to be."

"What's his color like, and is he bleeding?"

"His color is okay and he's only cut the scrotum, so there's not much blood, but I need you."

Barkley is our top racing trainer and his horses were no slouches. "No" simply wasn't an option. Besides, if I couldn't spend Christmas with the people I loved, it might as well be with a horse.

They were always good for a cuddle.

Equally as important, unflappable Jarrod sounded shook. "Of course, Boss, I'll be there. He's at the stable?"

"Yep. Thanks mate, I owe you." The relief in his voice was palpable.

"Not at all. Be right there."

I flew into my clothes and roared out the driveway only minutes later. Jarrod rarely asked for help and was generally bullet proof, certainly not a man to panic needlessly. I'd jumped into pens of rutting stags beside him to clip and TB test them—him because he was fearless and me because I had no idea how stupid it was, and blindly followed him—wearing shorts, for Pete's sake, but today, for the first time in my experience, Jarrod was pale beneath his tan.

Ten minutes later, I hopped out of my ute at the barn and trotted, stethoscope in hand, toward the barn, slowing my pace as I neared the crowd at the other end of the aisle. The stablemen opened a path as I arrived to reveal the massive colt, in all his shining splendor, before me.

I blinked. And blinked again, but nothing changed as I stared in horror at the right testicle of the top-selling colt at last year's Manukau Magic Billions sale, hanging free of the shredded remains of his scrotum, between the fidgeting bay's knees.

I'd watched him at the track, and I'd had to agree he was unparalleled in this district, maybe even in New Zealand. The colt had been purchased for an exorbitant sum and was truly the prize of Barkleys' stable—not to mention the top breeding prospect of his syndicated owners.

I'm sure everyone heard my gulp. This wasn't a surgery we wanted to mess up. The big, lanky bay kicked with annoyance at the naked nut. I took one look at Jarrod and headed back to my ute with the other vet in hot pursuit. I began pulling out trays and filling them with catheters, flush, IV lines, anesthetic drugs, and fluid bags.

"I put a weight tape on him, 575 kilograms," Jarrod said, "and his lungs, trachea, heart rate and rhythm are fine."

"Great, thanks. No problem with anesthetics before?"

"None that Barkley knows about. And he was vaccinated for tetanus a few months ago. Otherwise healthy."

"Great, thanks. How'd he do it?"

"Went over the divider in the horse truck on the way home from the track."

"They're keen, working out on Christmas Day."

"I gather the horses get Boxing Day off, instead."

"Frank," I called to one of the hovering stablemen, "could you please get me a couple buckets of hot water for these fluids?"

"No problem, be right there." He scuttled off.

"There's no way the colt can keep that dropped testicle," Jarrod said, "the remnants of the cremaster muscle has rubber-banded up inside him. Let's just castrate him."

I nearly dropped my tray of already-filled syringes and I had trouble drawing a breath. "Are you out of your ever-loving' mind?" I hissed from between gritted teeth and glanced at the faces of the assembled crowd in the barn looking curiously at us.

"He could get orchitis from having the scrotum ripped up and castrating the other side."

"That's a chance I'm willing to take." I could breathe again, but my heart was still pounding. "Anti-inflammatories and antibiotics will help with that. We can always take the other testicle out later if it becomes a problem. The exposed one's been out for awhile and it's probably got to go, but he needs to keep that other one."

"I'm not so sure." Jarrod frowned.

"Look, do you want to keep your license to practice? That horse is worth more as a breeding prospect than the two of us put together." I stopped, staring and breathing hard. "Do you want to be the one to tell the syndicate bosses you removed his only remaining testicle on the possibility it could cause a problem? Do you know who they are? I do, and I have no desire to come to their attention in any sort of negative way. Horse heads in beds and all that. *No.*" I shook my head. "*Just no.*"

"I'll get my gear out," he whispered, and fled.

Mr. Barkley walked up, probably more pale than Jarrod, if that were possible.

"Sir," I said, and returned to my bottles, averting my eyes. He hadn't been keen on having me, a girl vet, on his farm before, but he wasn't prepared to argue right about now.

"Thank you for coming," he said softly, and met my gaze for a moment. I figured this was as close to an apology as I'd ever get.

"No problem," I said, and attempted a smile, but I fear it was more of a grimace.

"You know who this colt is?"

I nodded. "We'll do our best for him."

And we did.

He went down like a baby with my hands on both sides of his halter and lay still while I tied up his leg. Jarrod removed the loose testicle and cleaned up the area, then we left it open to drain.

"The other testicle is still fully enclosed," Jared murmured to me, "so I'm done here."

"Good job," I said, as I reached forward to tug the slip bowline from the rope holding his near hind up to his shoulder, then checked the padding between his head and halter rings. I left the towel draped loosely over his top eye while he slept off the anesthetic drugs so he'd awaken gradually. He sat up woozily ten minutes later, then climbed to his feet with my hands on his halter to stabilize his head.

Mr. Barkley stared. "I've never seen such a smooth recovery," he said, with a shake of his head.

"New drugs from the young girl vet," I couldn't help saying. My mother always told me it wasn't nice to smirk, so I bit my lips together instead, and turned to watch the colt, who dropped his head to nose at the grass. He only ineffectively lipped at it in his woozy state, but that would be gone soon.

I removed his catheter when he was more awake, and with a pat for the colt, returned to my ute.

"Regular post-castration exercise?" Mr. Barkley called after me.

"Yes, give him 24 hours, then trot him ten minutes each way on the lunge twice a day. And for goodness sake, do *not* run water on it. Below the wound is fine." I'd seen people hose castration incisions too many times for my liking — it introduced bacteria that just didn't need to be in a clean wound.

He frowned, but nodded. "Thanks for coming, Lena. Sorry to interrupt your Christmas."

"It's fine. Not much on, anyway." Tears brimmed at his mention of the holiday. I turned away before they spilled out.

"Luckily we got you this morning," Jarrod said, then looked sideways at me. "Weren't you going away with your—"

"—was," I interrupted, swallowing hard, and swiped at the tears surreptitiously.

"Why don't you come around this afternoon? The family'd love to have you with us."

I gulped. "I'd like that, thanks." I packed up and even managed a smile as I waved and drove away.

Mr. Barkley flagged me down as I passed his house.

"Thank you, and Merry Christmas," he said. "There's something on your passenger seat. Don't drink it all at once."

I glanced across my cab to see a bottle of Courvoisier VSOP, complete with a glittering gold bow.

Merry Christmas, indeed.

It seemed I was on my way to acceptance.

A Christmas afternoon chocker-full of Jarrod and Janet's three young children and the rest of their relatives distracted me from my cares. They were all kind and impressed with Jarrod's and my exciting morning.

Janet was amazing. I'd marveled before at her skill of somehow remaining clean while working in her garden for hours at a time in white, classy clothing with three small helpers upon my last visit. She did the same with a full Christmas dinner today. I have no idea how. I can't stay clean on a good day, even without children.

With a cheery wave I headed for home, my heart lighter than it'd been in days. As I stepped in the door, the piney scent of Christmas made my heart twinge. The only things missing were cinnamon and cloves—and my loved ones. I dropped to my knees before the little pine tree and was still for a moment, just remembering. One after the other, I touched the few precious ornaments I'd brought to New Zealand from California—one for every year, each encircled with its own memories. I held myself in check and tried to enjoy the memories, but as I turned on the string of lights at the wall, the tiny fairy lights blazed and I promptly had a meltdown.

I spent the next two hours trying to stop crying and draw myself out of this funk, while staring longingly at the glittering Courvoisier. I daren't start on it in this state.

A roll of wrapping paper, red on one side and white on the other, caught my eye and reminded me of the Danish Christmas tree baskets I made with my mum so many years ago. I pulled some sharp-sharp scissors from the nonsterile spares kit in my vet truck and proceeded to make snowflakes. Many, many snowflakes. Big ones, little ones, and everything in-between. I scattered some under the tree and taped others to the windows and gazed at them in the deepening twilight.

At an inspiration, I untaped the biggest ones and stood at the window, pencil in hand.

What did the holiday mean to me?

Christmas isn't about the presents or the getting.

I sat at the table and wrote in tiny letters—all around the edges of one snowflake, and then another.

It's about the giving of love, of caring to the people who love you and those you love… and sharing time with those most special to you.

I stopped and cried some more.

Giving of my time, my caring, to animals, people, and the earth. And more.

The names of people who love me, those I love.

Eventually, I ran out of room to write. The snowflakes were full, their writing in full circles—and gone full circle.

I sat gazing at the delicate snowflakes with their intricate cuts bordered by tiny lettering around their perimeters… and slowly pivoted them, reading around and around, thoughts repeated like a mantra. Repeated in hope the expressions of plenty would overpower my overwhelming sense of loss. It worked until I collapsed into a heap of tears.

Again.

But was it all really that bad? I had everything I could want, the fantastic new career for which I'd studied nearly a decade, a job in a great practice, and a wonderful new country of my own choosing. I should be satisfied—but I wasn't.

The snowflake blurred before my eyes. Bed was probably the best place for me, though it wasn't full dark.

With one more glance at the little tree, I locked up. I thought the tree might cry as well—bereft of anything but the few presents I'd bought for others and not yet delivered—and a scattering of my snowflakes.

I picked up a handful of snowflakes from beneath a pine bough and took them to bed with me, focusing on the messages of love and care. My family seemed very far away tonight. If only—Nigel—but no, no use wishing for things I couldn't have. Christmas wasn't just about wishes. It just wasn't.

I tried to forget the joy of the past two months, but the days rolled over and over through my head as I lay awake, wet snowflakes clutched to my chest.

I must have slept, if fitfully, images of Nigel's stricken face, an upside down car, death, and destruction swirling through my dreams until a shrieking beside the bed ripped me from my nightmares.

Eleven

I leapt up in a panic until I realized it was the phone. In my haste to stop the demonic shriek, I knocked it off the table and had to dive down beside the bed to find it—and nearly fell off in the process.

"Hello?" I asked, as civilly as possible through gritted teeth.

"Lena, can ye come?" The strain in the elderly gentleman's voice cooled my temper in a way ice could never do. A familiar voice… but whose?

"Lena? It's D—" the man's voice cut out.

"Don, is that you?"

"Yes, lass, it's m—"

The phone line was terrible, but I'd never heard him sound this worried.

Oh my God, no. I broke out into a cold sweat. *Ben.* It could only be Ben—*or Nigel.* My eyes snapped fully open and my head cleared.

"Of course," I said, as I swung my legs out of bed and rubbed my streaming eyes. "Just a mo."

"Sorry to bother—this early-out mov—stock…" The line crackled, then was silent.

I gulped and glanced at the clock. 9:30 p.m.

"Is it Ben?"

"How's that?"

"Is it Ben?" I shouted into the phone.

"—not so good today."

After fifteen years chasing sheep and cattle on Don's steep cliffs, tongue lolling, his lips pulled back into a grin, I thought he'd done pretty well, myself. Most working sheep dogs here didn't live half that long.

"Down the back—farm—reception—left the old boy in—house. Howling the place—he was, had to—him home, he hates…" his voice trailed off.

I shuddered. *Down the back of the farm.* I didn't think there was any cell phone coverage out there at all. I quivered, guts tensing at the thought of the special afternoon I'd spent with Nigel out there, and dragged my thoughts back to where they belonged.

"On my way."

"See you—house," he said.

Other than an incredible blanket of stars covering the dark sky, only a few lights showed across the countryside at this hour. The tiny sparks of farm bikes bounced their way across paddocks to finish putting the dairy cows away after a late Christmas milking and clumps of dazzling brilliance marked the remote milking sheds. I always thought they reminded me of something out of *Dune*—the sudden blaze looking like a factory in the middle of the sands of nowhere.

My mind drifted into that half alert state in which country veterinarians seem to survive.

Farm bikes drew my memories back to Nigel and Don's farm. Though it was only a few weeks it felt like forever ago—and my heart wrenched.

Leave it, said the little voice on my shoulder. *You have other things to worry about tonight.*

I flew past the faded once-were-townships of Pokuru and Te Kawa, and somehow the ute stuck to the winding roads. The lights of Otorohanga blazed for a few minutes, before they, too, were gone from my rearview mirror. Right at the deathtrap of a Waitomo turnoff, then past the signs for the limestone caves and Waitomo Caves Hotel.

The two-lane country road narrowed even further as the vet truck and I negotiated the tortuous bends between Waitomo and the coast. As I rounded a corner in a dense stand of bush, my headlights picked out a flash of white fur in the middle of the one lane road before me.

Hell.

I slammed on the brakes. Somehow, the ute juddered to a halt on the hairpin turn just before I hit it.

Heart in my mouth, praying someone hadn't smacked it with a car already, I leapt from the cab. The tiny black and white pup cowered just in front of my wheel.

He was shaking, heck, *I* was shaking. When he saw me in the headlights, he started to whine and came to me. I carefully scooped him up and gave him a once-over in the patch of bright moonlight beside the door. I could finally let out the breath I'd been holding. He was alive and well. Something was right in the world tonight—this pup was needed.

I slipped the little guy into the copious pocket of my outback jacket and slid back into the cab, grateful to my mechanic and the universe for the little life warming my hip.

With half an hour more travelling to go, I settled back down to drive.

Nigel.

I had time to think now, and my mind was finally clear. What could I do to get over this? The man would clearly never believe me, probably would never believe anyone. Who was I to think I could make a difference?

When—if—he returned to town, perhaps we could speak. Perhaps he'd more likely see me in the street and turn the other way. My guts turned over.

Maybe thinking about this wasn't such a good idea. Instead, I cupped the little sleeping life in my pocket between downshifts for tight bends in the road.

I shot through Te Anga then left at the Marokopa turnoff, flying along the long straight stretches until I reached

Marokopa, then hard left up the hill towards my final destination, doing everything in my power to think of *anything* other than Nigel.

I shook myself at the sight of Don's gateway and skidded to a halt. Grabbing my emergency bag, I hurried out of the car, barely noticing the other ute parked beside Don's Land Cruiser.

I forgot all about Nigel until he appeared in front of me like a wraith. I shock my head to clear it of the apparition, but it still stood there, blocking the gateway.

"Leave me alone," I said, with a shudder, and made to walk through the vision, but Nigel was very real. His chest where I rammed into him was solid hard, warm flesh. I leapt back, wringing my hands where I'd touched him.

"What the hell are you doing here?" he growled.

"I might ask you the same thing," I said. "Don rang—"

"Lena," Don called, as he trotted down the steps toward me. "Oh, Nigel, there you are. Lena, come on in." Don grabbed my hand and tugged me up the stairs and through the house, tears streaming from his reddened eyes.

"Thank you for coming. Ben wasn't good when I left him this afternoon to head down to the farm, that's why I called you. Sorry to disturb your Christmas." He closed his eyes and bit his lips together for a moment. "I just got home. Ben waited for me, Lena… he licked my hand, closed his eyes, then was… *gone*." The last at a whisper.

The dog's grizzled head lay on Don's pillow, eyes closed.

"Poor old man," I said, stroking his soft fur. "But how many working dogs get to end their days on their favorite people's pillow?"

"Thank you so much for coming, Lena," Don said, then broke down beside Ben, sobbing as if his heart would break. I put an arm around him, but I don't think he even knew I was there.

I glanced up to see Nigel holding up the doorway, his face unreadable and his body rigid.

Don slowly quieted and I reached into my pocket. The little beggar had gone to sleep. I lifted him out carefully and slid him beneath Don's armpit. The pup awakened, whined, and squirmed until he came up for air beside the old man's face.

"What the?" Don slowly straightened up, staring at the tiny sheepdog pup. He looked up at me curiously, shivered, then curled himself around both the wee dog and his old friend, crooning softly to them both.

"He was nearly road pizza," I whispered, "but I guess Ben knew you needed help, so here he is." I straightened and backed slowly from the room.

I only remembered about Nigel when I backed straight into him.

Twelve

$\mathcal{O}$of—" I jumped when my body contacted Nigel's in the doorway and lost my balance, but his arms around me kept me from landing on the floor. "What are you do—"

"—ssh," Nigel cut off my furious whisper with one of his own, and he nodded at Don on the bed.

We both stepped backward and out the door, and I glanced back at Don in time to see him look at us with the first smile I'd seen since I arrived.

Out in the hallway, Nigel dropped his arms away from me and closed the door as I turned to leave.

"Where do you think you're going, and why are you here?"

"Isn't that fairly obvious?" I growled. "Your uncle rang and asked me to come."

"Why?"

"He was worried about Ben. What the hell are you doing out here? Your mother's worried sick."

"Hiding out."

"Really. Isn't it time you grew up and got over yourself?"

"What do you know about it?" he hissed.

"Enough to see what's in front of my eyes."

"And what's that?" he said, barely audible, but I heard him because he was only a breath away from me, his arms on either side of me against the wall.

"That you're afraid to try again. That you want love and are capable of giving love, but you're not willing to try."

He closed his eyes for a moment, his jaw tensed. "So tell me the truth about Madsen."

"What truth about Madsen? That we had one disastrous date and I walked two miles home in high heels rather than get in the car with him again? You've got it *so* wrong. I have no idea why I've been pining for you since you ran away from the sale yards."

His eyes jerked up to mine. "You've been… ran away?" He didn't seem to know which part of our conversation to focus on.

"Yes, ran away. You wouldn't even talk with me."

"But you were—"

"—*waiting for you*. I was *waiting for you*."

"But Madsen—"

"He appeared out of nowhere, just as you showed up. So help me God."

He froze and his arms dropped to his sides.

"I couldn't… I couldn't be responsible for—"

"And you wouldn't. You weren't responsible for your wife's death, not directly."

He stiffened and I thought he was going to bolt again, so I grabbed his shirt front and held on for dear life.

"You know?"

I nodded and leaned my forehead on his chest. Wishing, begging, inside my head. Afraid to speak. Afraid I'd never see him again.

He didn't say a word for long minutes, then, "Did you mean that?"

"What?" I breathed, afraid to trust my voice.

"About missing me."

I lifted my head and our eyes locked. "Of course, you great lug. I've missed you every minute of every day. Christmas has been a nightmare. In more ways than one."

"Not half as much as I've missed you." He wrapped his arms around me and held me. Held me as I'd dreamed he would, for these long weeks, and then his mouth was on mine. The minutes stretched out to infinity as our hunger for each other overtook us.

I don't know how long we'd have stood in the hallway in each other's arms if Don hadn't come out of his room with the pup, tears still in his eyes, but purpose in his gait.

"About time you two figured this out. Nigel, meet Lena. Lena, Nigel. I see you've kissed and made up, now get on the phone and ring your poor mother, young man, and wish her a happy holiday. Then take yourselves off home. Merry Christmas to you both, thank you for coming out, Lena, and I hope you both got your Christmas wishes," he said, as he headed into the kitchen.

"Guess we've been told," Nigel said, and kissed me on the forehead. "Merry Christmas. Now I've got my wish."

My smile probably lit up the night.

"So have I, and with only" — I glanced at my watch — "two minutes to spare. But seriously, Nigel, do you finally believe me?"

He took a deep breath and looked me in the eyes, his own finally clear, and I could see all the way into his soul for the very first time.

"Yes, I do. Are you willing to let me try again… to love you properly this time, no shadows?"

"Lead the way, Nigel, lead the way," I said, as our lips met once again.

Epilogue

The sun glistened off the sea as the whole Munro family, plus one, relaxed in the warm black sand beside the river mouth at Marokopa Beach.

I reached out for Nigel's hand and he turned his head to gaze up at me with a lazy smile.

"We didn't make it out here for Christmas, but we couldn't miss New Year's," Sara said, her gaze locking with mine.

"So glad we could come out. I wouldn't have missed this for the world."

"Oh," John said, "I nearly forgot. Lena, you're safe to eat ice cream again."

"Pardon?"

"Well, remember that cowshed next door to us where the two of you met?"

I shuddered as I met Nigel's eyes. "I'm afraid I can't forget that one."

"Well," John continued, "the dairy company's been visiting. I don't think they'll be putting a cow through that shed for quite some time, if ever. I believe he's buying the shed next door to him for the time being. And improving sanitation."

"Well, that's a relief," I said, finally letting my breath out.

"And now we can eat our dessert," Sara said, reaching for the chilly bin. "Homemade chocolate ice cream!"

Dedicated to
John and Janet Harrison

John,

Thank you for taking a risk on the first girl horse vet in your practice – a Yank, no less – so very long ago and taking me under your wing. You taught me cows are so much more than a black and white box I couldn't previously see inside. And all about road user charges – sorry to take ten years off your life.

Your 'non-existent' (read: hidden) skills in small animal surgery which I was blessed to see (read: caught you at) that day in the clinic astounded me. I figure by now it's safe to 'let the cat out of the bag' that this cow vet is a brilliant small animal surgeon. To this day, I've never seen such delicate tissue handling.

That little cat probably never even knew she'd been spayed.

Janet,

Thank you for welcoming me into your home and your family when John took this waif from California into the practice, shocking as I might have been. Your dry humor warmed me on many otherwise very chilly days.

The twins (who have children of their own by now) were gorgeous and your beautiful daughter, sharp girl that she was even at eleven, taught me more about global affairs than I'd ever learned in the States in my entire lifetime.

It certainly explained why so many Kiwis thought Yanks didn't give a hoot about other countries. Unless they had highly educated parents and watch BBC or such, they were only presented with domestic affairs... and they didn't know about the rest of the world.

Thank you all for making a huge difference in my life.

Acknowledgements

A huge appreciation for my wonderful friends and beta readers, who, incidentally, did this on ridiculously short notice. Thank you to Elizabeth Ellen Carter, Kirsten Davidson, Matthew Tremayne, Rue Allyn, and Jude Knight. Your consideration and wonderful ideas improved this story.

Thank you to Meredith Reece for helping me choose the title for this story. You suggested *Greener Pastures*. I can't seem to manage short titles, and there were far too many books with that title, so I added *Calling*. As a fellow author, you'll understand why!

Thank you to all the dairy great veterinarians with whom I worked with when I first came to New Zealand — John Harrison, Mike Woods, Brian McKay, Steve Murray, Noel Powers, Richard Jerram, and Neil Houston… and our indomitable office manager, Kathy, who kept us all on our toes.

And last, but not least, my gratitude also goes to the veterinarians who either collaborated with me, encouraged me to speak and publish on complimentary therapies, or referred their valued clients and patients for Postural Rehabilitation back in the early days when there were exceedingly few people doing bodywork on New Zealand horses. Thank you for helping so many horses — David Sim, Corin Murfitt, Mark Ethell, Ian Robertson, Nigel Perkins, and many others.

Thank you all!
xx
Lizzi

Glossary of Kiwi Terms

Bach~~summer beach house

Deal to~~Sort out. E.g.: to "deal to him" is to sort him out, probably physically

Esky ~~ an ice cooler

Good on ya~~Well done

Ute~~"utility vehicle", or mini pickup truck

Wobbly~~hysterics Eg: to "chuck a wobbly" or to "pack a wobbly" is to throw a tantrum or fit. Think of a 2 1/2 year old who wants a toy. Badly. They wobble, don't they?

Dummy~~pacifier for a baby. E.g. to "spit the dummy" is to have hysterics, like a baby spitting out their dummy or pacifier. C.f.: "to pack/chuck a wobbly"

Also by Lizzi Tremayne

The Long Trail Series
A Long Trail Rolling - Book 1
The Hills of Gold Unchanging - Book 2
A Sea of Green Unfolding - Book 3

Get Lizzi Tremayne's FREE GIFT book, exclusively for VIPs!
https://www.lizzitremayne.com/vip

The Once Upon a Vet School Series
Fifty Miles at a Breath - Book 6
Lena Takes a Foal - Book 7

Boxed Sets!
The Authors of Main Street
Christmas Babies on Main Street
Summer Romance on Main Street

The Bluestocking Belles
Follow Your Star Home

A Long Trail Rolling

"... vivid, light and fast-paced... it will appeal in particular to anyone interested in American... history, and in general to those looking for a ripping good read. I'm looking forward to reading *The Hills of Gold Unchanging*, the next volume in the Aleksandra and Xavier saga."
–*Deborah Challinor, #1 bestselling author and historian*

"The mystery, adventure, and danger of life in Utah in the 1860s is beautifully described... an authentic, emotional story of one woman's fight for survival in an unforgiving landscape. I couldn't put Lizzi Tremayne's book down."
–*Leeanna Morgan, USA Today bestselling author*

"An impressive debut from a New Zealand (ex-American) author... a romance, a western, and an adventure story, all rolled up into a compelling read... I devoured this one and am hungry for more."
–*Booksellers NZ*

Awards and Recognition for A Long Trail Rolling
With this, her debut novel, Lizzi was:
Finalist 2013 RWNZ Great Beginnings
Winner 2014 RWNZ Pacific Hearts Award
Winner 2015 RWNZ Koru Award for Best First Novel
Third 2015 RWNZ Koru Long Novel
Finalist 2015 Best Indie Book Award

The Hills of Gold Unchanging
"The pace is fast, there's plenty of action and adventure and a few twists I didn't see coming. Lizzi Tremayne writes good characters, and that definitely includes the horses. For me, though, it's the history that's the star in this story. Good characters plus excellent history equals a great read, which is what this is."
–*Deborah Challinor, #1 bestselling author and historian*

"… superb storytelling. As Aleksandra and Xavier faced and survived human malevolence, natural disaster and accidents, and their own doubts and insecurities, I kept turning pages to find out what happened next. I love books in which adversity sculptures character and where challenges to relationships bend them to breakpoint and rebuild them stronger. This is one of those books. I can't wait to read the sequel."

–Judy Knighton, editor

"Aleks has a stubborn streak and a determination to survive, no matter what. Both inspired me to cheer them on as they faced one problem after another along the way from Utah to California. The plot is well developed, and I particularly liked the attention to historical detail… This is an author who does her homework, and it shows… this story… is a cracking good yarn."

–Shelagh Merlin, NetGalley Reviewer

A Sea of Green Unfolding

"As usual in this series, the historical research is excellent…well-integrated into the narrative. The description of the environs through which Lizzi Tremayne's characters travel are particularly good—lush and vibrant. In the New Zealand section of the novel she makes our country sound like paradise. Which it is. There is one more volume to come after this, Tatiana, and I'm looking forward to it."

–Deborah Challinor, #1 bestselling author and historian

"A lovely combination of historical accuracy and adventure… beautifully researched and engrossing story… kept me on the edge of my seat throughout… [it was] interwoven with New Zealand's turbulent mid-19th century history as European settlers and Maori tribes battled. Most of all, though, I loved travelling… through the Waikato countryside in her bid to be reunited with Xavier. Lizzi Tremayne has stamped her mark as an excellent story teller who does her homework well and puts her knowledge to good use in her writing. I look forward to seeing what she comes up with next."

–Shelagh Merlin, NetGalley reviewer

"Loved this book. The characters draw you in on a story filled with interest and suspense. A great read and I love how I always learn some thing from reading Lizzi Tremayne books."

-Kate Le Petit, reader

Once Upon a Vet School #6: Fifty Miles at a Breath

"This is wonderful series about the path to becoming a veterinarian, the love of horses and sweet romance. The characters in this book, Lena and Blake will grab your heart. Long distance romances are difficult. Determined to find a way to a happiness, they experience life's bumps along the way.
The story develops at a nice pace and was very enjoyable. I would love to see this and the other books made into a Hallmark series. It would be perfect."

-Teri Donaldson, reader

"Lizzi Tremayne is a born storyteller. After reading her amazing Long Trail historical series, to switch to her contemporary Once Upon a Vet School series has been so much fun… The author is able to make the characters almost three dimensional and you can feel Lena and Blake's emotions. I enjoyed this story just as much as the first one and can only hope the next book in this series comes out soon to continue Lena's journey!"

-Lori Dykes, reader

Once Upon a Vet School #7: Lena Takes a Foal

"Perfect for horse lovers and a nice love story too. This story is well told and displays Lizzi Tremayne's ability to develop strong characters. Lena is clearly passionate and dedicated to her chosen career path while Kit is torn between his professional ethics, his attraction to Lena and the impact of his past experiences… the story is concluded well, with a nice strong black moment to challenge our heroine and prove her worth."

-Shelagh Merlin, NetGalley reviewer

"I did not know what to expect when started this story but as I turned the last page I cannot stop smiling! If you love horses or any animals, you will get a behind the scenes look at what goes on with a vet… Two souls who had similar goals and past hurts that were hard to resolve. But through many ups and downs they triumph. I look forward to more in this series and from this author!!!"

Abbie's Wish

Jude Knight

One

"No, Mumma," Abbie insisted. "Jus' me." She pointed to the sign.

"Christmas Wishing Tree," it proclaimed. "One gold coin. No adults." And, in much smaller letters, "All proceeds to Pukanui High School Cycle Team uniform fund."

The school had barricaded one corner of the large exhibition hall at the show grounds, close to the short hallway to the cafeteria, where the enormous Christmas tree would attract passers-by. It had certainly caught Abbie, who begged for a dollar entry fee, forgetting the hunger that had driven them inside.

An improbably large Santa's elf gave the child paper and a crayon in return for her coin, and Abbie tolerated Claudia opening the safety gate that led into the enclosure. In moments, Abbie was lying on her tummy on the rug by the enormous Christmas tree, bare feet waving in the air, face screwed up in concentration.

"It's two months till Christmas," Claudia muttered. Her father never permitted discussion of the festival before December, and wouldn't tolerate any decorating until a few days before the twenty-fifth. "Stupid commercial feast," he would say. "It's Little Lent, or that's what it used to be. Prayer, fasting, and penitence. Besides, we don't have time for all that nonsense, Princess." And he would send her back to repeat whatever exercise she had just finished.

"It's never too early to have fun," her grandmother retorted the first year she'd come to the A&P Show, held every year in late October, and found references to Christmas among the stalls and exhibits. Raised in the United States since she was eight, she'd needed a translation — A&P: Agriculture and Pastoral — and many of the exhibits were true to those origins. But not all.

Abbie folded her paper, and then concentrated on making it to her feet without incident. The hardest part of the child's increasing agility was leaving her to manage on her own.

"Excuse me." The speaker was a tall, thin woman with square spectacles, bright purple hair, and an anxious smile. "I'm Maggie. From Maggie's Martonvale? We met at RDA?"

Oh yes. The journalist. She worked for the local news site; once a newspaper but now a local website and a small spot on the local television station.

"I took some photos of Abigail," the woman said. "She looked so cute, concentrating so hard on her wish. I won't… That is, would you sign the consent form for me to use them? It'll be good advertising for the A&P Show, and might help the cycle team get their uniforms."

Claudia was silent, considering different angles, wondering if she was imagining the danger, and Maggie hurried on with more persuasion. "I could mention RDA in the caption, if you liked. I know they always need more volunteers and more money."

The Riding for the Disabled Association provided hippotherapy for children and adults. "The movements of the horse's muscles teach Abbie's muscles how to move again and balancing on the horse improves her sense of where her body is in relation to the ground," the doctor had said when he wrote the prescription that gave her child access. Claudia owed RDA a great deal, but no. Agreeing to publicity in order to help them might be a step too far.

Abbie was struggling with the peg, the tip of her tongue shoved out between her teeth as she concentrated.

"Do you need to go help?" The reporter asked.

"She wants to do it herself," Claudia explained, and Maggie laughed. "I have one just like that. It can be hard to watch, can't it?"

The shared mother moment tipped the scale. "Yes, I'll sign the consent," Claudia agreed. "But no names, Maggie. And just make it about the A&P Show and the cycle team. No details about Abbie."

In the end, the woman took two more photos, one with Abbie showing Claudia the sticker the elf had put on her tee shirt. "I made a Christmas wish," with a border of red, green, and yellow bicycles.

After all, what harm could it do?

He followed the seller into the garage, which was as filthy, cluttered, and disorganized as he'd feared. But the man owned a twin to the Triumph carburetor he had come to see, and the pair together were worth four times the asking price. Not that he'd let on. Far from it. He had every intention of beating the price down, if only because he was inside this disgusting hole risking septicemia or worse.

He cast a disgusted look at the sink bench, where car parts, tools, greasy rags, and other bits and pieces lay scattered among plates with congealed food scraps, dirty cups half-filled with cold liquid substances, and a tottering stack of fast-food boxes. He curled his lip at the pinups above the bench — little girls, none of them over ten, the pictures home printed and ornamented with hearts and comments.

Where was the man? He craned to see over a pile of boxes of parts, some labelled, most anonymous, but as he did something about the disturbing montage registered in his mind, and in two short strides he was next to the bench, peering at the little girl with the dark curly hair and the delighted smile.

The same girl was on the next clipping, which had been pinned up first, and half covered so he could see there was someone else in the picture, but not who it was. He checked again to make sure the owner couldn't see him, then unpinned the top photo. He would have to scrub his hands, but it was worth it. "So that's where you are," he murmured to the woman, quickly scanning the paragraph or two of text that went with the image. He slipped both clippings into his pocket and was back by the doorway by the time the seller had emerged from his search, triumphantly waving the part.

He returned the smile with one of his own. Genuine, indeed. Just what he needed to complete the restoration of his classic motor cycle. A couple of weeks of evenings, and he'd be ready for a road trip. And—he patted the pocket that held the stolen pictures—he knew just where he wanted to go.

Two

The girls were taking turns on Abbie's totter board, turning physiotherapy into a game that had them in fits of laughter. It was a circle of plywood with a hemisphere of solid wood fixed at its center, and the person standing on the flat upper surface had to recover her balance when given a light shove by the other. Because Abbie's brain injury had left her unable to recognize the sensation of falling before she hit the ground, her brain needed to be retrained, and the totter board was designed as a safe way to learn what off-balance felt like.

"Abbie, be gentle," Claudia warned, as Abbie knocked her friend off the center of the board so that Polly Becker had to put out a foot to save herself. The totter board dipped on that side, touching the ground, and Polly overcorrected the other way, which ended with her having to jump right off the board, catching her balance by holding on to Abbie.

"My turn," Abbie crowed.

Polly, without being asked, offered both hands for Abbie to hold while she took up position on the board, her legs spread, her knees bent.

"They're having fun," Carly observed. The two mothers were leaning on the bench between the small kitchenette and the flat's living room.

"I try to get her to do about ten minutes a day," Claudia said, "but they've been at it for half-an-hour. I should borrow your daughter every day."

"You can, if it will help. Abbie has come a long way, hasn't she?"

Since Abbie and Claudia had moved to Fairburn in time for the start of the school year, she meant. "Riding has been good for her," Claudia noted. Perhaps Abbie had just turned a corner ten months ago after eighteen months of physio, occupational, psychological, and speech therapy. But RDA was a big factor, Claudia believed.

"You should have seen her today!" Carly marveled. "She and Rosie went over the trot poles. You would have been so proud!"

Claudia suppressed a small stab of envy that her friend had seen the achievement and she had missed it. "That's wonderful." Letting Abbie go to RDA with Carly, who volunteered as a helper twice a week, had been hard but right. Abbie had refused to go anywhere without Claudia for months after she was released from Starship, the specialist children's hospital. In recent months, Claudia's counsellor had suggested that Claudia had needed that clinginess as much as Abbie, and that it was time to let go, just a little.

"Abbie, it is time to feed Edward," she said. Another sign of progress. The rabbit they'd bought at the A&P Show in October was Abbie's responsibility. She fed the animal and cleaned his hutch, with Claudia only stepping in to lift anything too heavy for the child.

"Wanna help?" Abbie said to her friend, and the two ran outside, Claudia — as always — holding her breath at the lurch from side to side, each fast step a corrected fall, that was Abbie's run. "Every time Rosie trots, I expect Abbie to fall off," she confessed. Rosie was one of the patient mounts RDA used to provide hippotherapy. Abbie's riding was an ungainly bounce, and it seemed a miracle to Claudia that she ended back in the saddle after each flight into the air on one side of the horse or the other.

"Even more motivation to find your center than on the totter board," Carly observed. "Rosie's just a pony, but still, she's twelve hands. A long way to fall for a little 'un."

Which is what the people running each side of the horse were for, but they hadn't needed to catch Abbie in months, and she'd graduated to a single helper.

"More coffee?" Claudia waved the plunger pot vaguely in the direction of the electric kettle, but Carly shook her head. "I should go rescue poor Trent. He has a book thingy on tonight, and so I'm up for feeding the munchkins and getting them off to bed. I'll just give Polly a few minutes with your giant rabbit, and then we'll be off."

Another stab of envy, this one sharper. Carly and Trent restored Claudia's much dented faith that good marriages were possible, and that the world held men who didn't have to dominate and control their women and children. Not for her, though. Better to be alone than to trust her own judgement again, and be wrong. Again.

"Not another book launch?" she asked.

"Not this time. He got number seven off to the editor, though, so we're starting to plan for May. No, this is a book club over the hill in town. They've been reading the series, and invited him to come and answer questions. He's very nervous!"

"He'll be great." Trent Becker had been writing the first in his detective series more than eight years ago when the three of them had been the youngest people at ante-natal classes. Claudia, back from the United States with no ties except to her grandmother, had been grateful for the way they cheerfully welcomed her into their lives. She'd moved away when her grandmother died, but had met Carly within a week of her return ten months ago, and the three had quickly fallen into their old friendship.

"Of course he will." Carly was Trent's first reader, his sounding board, and his cheerleader. And he returned the support, fitting his writing around stay-at-home parenting for Polly and her two little sisters so that Carly could finish her Masters in environmental studies and work part time as environmental health officer for the local council.

"Anyway, he'll be panicking if I'm not home soon. Polly! Say goodbye to Abbie. Time for us to go."

The girls came obediently inside, Polly clutching Edward, who dangled phlegmatically from her arms and made no objection to being transferred to Abbie when Carly urged her to hurry up and get her shoes on.

Carly, now that she'd decided to leave, hovered impatiently as Polly sat on the doorstep tying her laces. "What's this?" she said, and bent to pick something up—a white envelope that had been slipped under the rubber welcome mat.

"Must have been hand delivered," she commented, handing it to Claudia. "Come on, Pol. Bye, Abbie. Bye, Claudia. See you tomorrow."

Claudia responded, and closed the door as her friend chivvied Polly into the car. She didn't take her eyes off her name on the envelope, written using purple in neat block capitals.

"Whad is i'?" Abbie demanded, her sentence short and blurred and all on one note. After two years of voice therapy and physio, she could manage some of the small muscle movements to stop and start her breath for 'p', 't' and 'k' sounds, but not by the end of the day, when she was tired.

"Let's see." Claudia turned the envelope over. Nothing there. She broke the seal and pulled out the single slip of paper, some instinct warning her to keep her face from reacting. "Just someone selling something," she said, putting the envelope and its pernicious contents up onto the shelf with the cookery books. "Let me get dinner on, sweetheart, and then I'll hear your spelling. Do you have any other homework?"

The evening routines distracted the child, but Claudia's mind circled back and back to the words that had been hand delivered to her doorstep.

"I KNOW WHERE YOU ARE."

Ethan watched from the street as the other woman and girl left, and Claudia and her daughter went inside and closed the door. After eight years, he'd finally found her.

No name on the electoral roll, no name in the white pages. When he'd been free to travel again, she'd disappeared without a trace, and it was only by the merest chance he'd come across a photo of her and Abbie and been able to trace her to Fairburn.

He'd looked there before, arriving just a few weeks after her grandmother's funeral, and she had already left town. No one would talk to a stranger about where she might have gone, if they even knew.

This time, he'd taken a job at the local garage, figuring she would come in for something: to fill her car up, to buy milk or a Lotto ticket, to get her wheels realigned. Something. Sooner or later.

And his gamble had paid off today, when he'd been asked to check a non-blinking indicator light. And there it was on the job sheet, in his boss's clear block capitals. Claudia's address, at last.

So he'd walked this way home. She was as far across Fairburn as she could be from her grandmother's house, and living in what he thought of as a granny flat—a small stand-alone dwelling on the back of someone else's section. The room he was renting in a boarding house was only two blocks away. They were practically neighbors.

He looked longingly at the closed door. The glimpse he'd had of Claudia and little Abbie had left him eager for more. He toyed briefly with the idea of knocking on the door. Would she slam it in his face? He deserved that and more for the pain he'd put her through, but he wasn't that person any more. He hoped for the chance to prove it to her, and to pay some of the debt he owed for the hurt he'd caused.

Approaching her now was too much of a risk.

He couldn't loiter here any longer, but it was hard to walk away.

"Patience," he told himself. In his racing days, they used to call him the hare, but he'd be tortoise slow if it would win him this race. He'd had lots of practice waiting, and he could do some more. But soon—very soon—he and Claudia were going to have their long overdue accounting.

Three

laudia began the run up to Christmas on the first of December, when she put up the Jesse Tree, a painted tree branch, fastened to a stand, that Grandma had made the year after Abbie was born. Grandma had made the felt ornaments, too, one for each day until Christmas. Each ornament had a story from the Bible, for the Jesse Tree was an old traditional way of tracking the salvation story from the creation of the universe to the birth of Jesus.

"But I don't believe what you believe," Claudia had explained, her father's rigid form of Christianity having put her off religion of all kinds. But Grandma said the stories were part of her cultural heritage, and she—and Abbie too, as she grew older—could enjoy them without putting any more weight on them than on tales of King Arthur and his Round Table or Maui fishing up the North Island of New Zealand.

When Grandma died and Claudia moved to the city, she'd packed the branch and the ornaments away, but they'd come out again to decorate Abbie's hospital room after the accident. Claudia had whiled away the days and nights spent waiting for Abbie to recover consciousness by looking up the story to go with the ornament of the day, telling it in simpler words to the child lying still and white in the clean bed, writing it down, and illustrating the page. The pages, now bound, still recalled to her mind the long hours in the hospital, and the joy when, a few days before Christmas, a nurse had interrupted the story of Gabriel's visit to Mary to take Abbie's pulse, and Abbie had wrenched her hand away and demanded that the story continue.

The Jesse Tree had been part of their Christmas last year, too, as part of keeping things normal for Abbie while Claudia worried about what her former lover might do, now the police had been convinced he was not responsible for what happened to Abbie. He was not stupid enough to attack either of them while he was under investigation, but now he was free to carry out his threats.

But as the year drew to an end, Abbie finished the intensive courses of physio, occupational, speech and psychotherapy prescribed by the hospital. Claudia was free to go anywhere she wished. So the day after Christmas, she loaded everything they owned into the back of her old station wagon, and they drove south, meandering through the country, stopping when they felt like it, until they reached Fairburn.

It had been a refuge when she'd flown into New Zealand, pregnant with Abbie, fleeing an angry boyfriend and a controlling father. It became a refuge again. They were welcomed back into the community, and not just by those who remembered them from the three years they lived here with Grandma.

Carly had found them this little studio, on the back of the property belonging to her parents, who were warmly welcoming. It was very private, hidden behind hedges and overlooked only by the main house — currently unoccupied, since Carly's parents were on an extended overseas holiday.

Claudia wished they were home. Since the note three days ago, she had been acutely conscious of how isolated the building was. There had been nothing more, though. It must have been someone's idea of a joke.

She shook off her sense of impending disaster, repeating one of the sayings taught to her by the counsellor she'd seen while Abbie was recovering. "Some positive saying."

"Abbie," she called. "I have the tree up. Are you ready for your story?"

Tonight, the story was just about the tree and its name. Abbie listened intently to the explanation. A tree would grow from the root of Jesse. "Jessie," Abbie commented. "Jessie is at my riding. Differen' Jessie. Not Jesus's granddad." She began laying out the decorations from the shoebox that held them. "Which one comes next, Mummy?"

Claudia was picking through looking for the star that would top the tree and symbolize creation when a flicker of light caught her eye, and she leapt up to rush to the window.

"Edward!" The rabbit hutch stood in the corner of the paved patio, in its own little caged enclosure.

Abbie pressed her nose up against the glass. "It's burning," she observed. Flames licked all the way along the bottom and shot from the interior.

Claudia unlocked the sliding door and hauled it open. "Stay here," she commanded. Should she phone the fire brigade? But it would be quarter of an hour, at least, before the volunteers made their way to the station and got the fire engine moving. Meanwhile, she needed to stop the fire from catching the hedge alight. And poor Edward! It was an inferno in there. Could he possibly have survived?

She was unrolling the hose as she thought, and turning on the tap to spray water on the hedge.

"Abbie," she called out, "I need you to phone emergency. Speak your best words. Tell them we have a fire outside, and we need the fire service. Tell them our address. Do you remember our address?"

"Dwelve... Twelve B Sbendworth... K... resen... T."

"That's it, sweetie. Twelve B Spendworth Crescent, Fairburn. The number is one-one-one. Can you manage?" Claudia whipped a quick look to see Abbie's nod, then turned her attention back to the hedge, catching a smoldering twig in a full stream of water.

Abbie must have managed, because in a few moments the siren that summoned the fire brigade volunteers to the fire station sounded in the distance. She held her own against the fire but couldn't take her attention off the hedge long enough to chase it back to its origin in the hutch, so the shrill warble of a fire engine came with great relief, and soon large men in yellow gear filled her patio.

With their arrival, she retreated to the doorway where Abbie stood watching, hugging Edward in both arms. Claudia fought back tears of relief, and rubbed the rabbit's ears. "Edward. You're alright," she said.

Abbie buried her nose in the rabbit's fur, her eyes defensive.

"Abbie, did you smuggle Edward into your bed again?" Claudia asked, too relieved to try to sound stern.

Abbie nodded, and what was Claudia to say now? For if the child had followed the rules, she'd be mourning the death of her pet. Claudia compromised on a frown and a hug, and together they watched the fire fighters swiftly and efficiently bring the blaze under control. The fire chief asked quite a few questions, few of which Claudia could answer. She had not seen the fire start; had no idea what had caused it.

"It makes no sense," he said. "Look, Ms. Westerson. How about you get the little lady off to bed. I'll just take another look outside while you do that."

Abbie was drooping, slipping almost to sleep then jerking awake so as not to miss anything. She made only a token objection to the exciting evening coming to an end. Soon, she'd been to the bathroom and tucked into bed, her rabbit in a large cardboard box in the corner. Claudia figured she'd be asleep before Claudia closed the door.

The fire chief was waiting, standing by the door, his eyes roaming around the pictures of Abbie that decorated the walls.

"What did you want to say that you didn't want Abbie to hear?" Claudia asked, but she already had an inkling. What else could it be? A fire that made no sense, starting on a concrete patio well away from any source of flame?

"Ms. Westerson, I'm going to have to report this to the police," the fire chief said. "I think the fire was deliberately set."

The police officer who called the next morning meant to be reassuring. "Some kid thought it would be funny, Ms. Westerson, until the fire got away on him."

"Call me Claudia," she begged, and he invited her to use his first name, Marcus.

"We're neighbors, after all," he pointed out.

She fought the temptation to accept to be quiet and good, to allow Marcus to brush her off, and told him about the note. He was very quiet as he handled it carefully, putting on disposable gloves before taking it off her, and asking her for a plastic bag to put it into when he was finished.

"This puts a different complexion on it," he acknowledged. "Do you know of anyone who means you harm?"

Claudia's fears choked her, but she fought them back and gave him as coherent an account as she could. If Marcus thought she was lying or hysterical, he had the courtesy not to indicate that belief in any way, remaining courteous and kind.

"It was that photo," she said once she was finished. "The one at the A&P show. One of them has seen that photo and come after us."

"Talking of photos, do you have pictures of any of these men?"

Claudia thought about it. "Not of Jack. They were all digital, and I lost my files when my hard drive crashed. I have some prints of Ethan and my father." She found them in the keepsakes box with her medals and awards—a tightly stuffed album with photos, newspaper clippings, and certificates.

Marcus leafed through the album. "You were quite the gymnast," he commented. "My little girl Pearl is in your class, but I didn't realize her teacher was a champion."

"Pearl is a sweetie," Claudia told the proud father, and they talked for a few minutes about gymnastics while he continued to look through the pictures. In the end, he took several of her father smiling while Claudia accepted a winner's ribbon and a couple of Ethan, including her favorite. He was also on a winner's podium, looking straight at the camera with a slight smile playing at the corners of his mouth. It had broken back into the broad grin he'd worn since the last ten minutes of the race, when he'd decided his lead made him invincible. His coach's loudly expressed view that his swollen head could have lost him the race had dimmed the smile, but the medal brought it back. He was National Junior Cycling Champion, and on top of the world.

"That was nearly ten years ago," Claudia warned Marcus. It all came apart shortly after that. She had a few more photos of Ethan, and none of that dreadful time between discovering she was pregnant with Abbie and reaching out desperately to the New Zealand grandmother she'd never met. The next photos in the album showed her, Grandma, and newborn Abbie.

"No more men," she'd told Grandma.

"You're young yet," Grandma had said. "You might change your mind. But not till you are comfortable in your own skin, Claudia. That father of yours taught you to be good and obedient, and that's a bad attitude to take into a relationship. Until you feel you have a right to be yourself, don't take the risk. It isn't worth it."

But then Grandma died, Claudia was alone, and Jack seemed kind. What a fool she had been.

She walked Marcus out to his car, and was accepting his assurances that the police would be keeping an eye out to make sure she was safe when she saw his eyes change, hardening and narrowing as he looked at something over his shoulder.

"Your tires are flat, Claudia," he told her.

They were, too. All four of them. "Not slashed," Marcus reported. "I think they've just let the air out. What a nuisance! Do you need me to call the garage for you?"

Claudia shook her head. "I'll do it in my lunch hour. I'm due at the school in ten minutes, and it looks like I'll be walking."

Four

Jack Quinton nursed his bike the short distance to the garage. He shouldn't have taken it out so early in the restoration process, but the engine had been running sweetly, he thought, and the rest of the work was cosmetic; he'd not been able to resist. He shook his head, irritated with himself. A man should stick to his plan.

When he'd phoned, he'd insisted on talking to the mechanic, and been pleasantly surprised. He'd not expected to find a Triumph expert in such a small town, but this fellow Stone seemed to know what he was talking about.

The man's name and the American accent had sent Jack's temper on a slow burn, but it must be a coincidence. This fellow couldn't be Claudia's first lover, the one who had fathered Abbie and then driven Claudia away.

He'd soon be able to check. The dark curls would be a giveaway, and Ethan wasn't that common a name.

When he arrived, though, Stone wasn't available. "I'll pass on a message," the old fellow in the office said, "or you can wait, if you like. He's just gone to do a pickup. Won't be long."

Jack wheeled the bike into the indicated place in the workshop and had a look around while he waited. The man liked everything in order, apparently. Tools neatly racked, work bench clear except for the piece currently being repaired, parts in labelled boxes, everything as clean as a vehicle mechanic's workshop ever gets.

"Hi," said a voice from the doorway. A man pushed another motorcycle, setting it in the bay next to Jack's.

"Stone?" Jack asked, but he didn't think so. The newcomer was dressed all wrong for a mechanic—an open-necked shirt, neat chinos, and leather sandals.

"He's out, they tell me." The newcomer held out a hand. "Rhys Phillips. I've just brought my bike over for a tune."

"Jake." He nodded towards his own bike. "Misfires at 3000 revs. Stone suggested several things it could be. Is he any good?"

Phillips shrugged. "Ben thinks so, but Stone's new here. I've never met him. What about you? New to Fairburn or just passing through?"

This was what Jack didn't like about small towns. Everyone knew everyone else, and nobody's business was private. He smiled, putting as much warmth into it as he could. "I'm on holiday," he explained. "I was passing through but this thing with the bike…" He spread his hands and shrugged.

"Here's hoping Stone can fix you up, though there are worse places to be stuck than Fairburn. I grew up here, so I'm prejudiced, but we have some beautiful bush walks, two excellent boutique museums, and some great cafes and shops. Worth staying around for a few days even when you get the Triumph back on the road."

Jack nodded, cheerfully. "I've nowhere in particular I have to be. I might just do that."

A tow-truck with a trailer pulled into the forecourt just outside the workshop's open doorway, and Phillips frowned. "That looks like Claudia's car. Wonder what's wrong? That poor girl doesn't need more trouble."

He was talking to himself, but Jack answered him. "Someone you know? Wonder what's wrong with it." Most of his attention was on the driver, who was backing the trailer up to the entrance. Black curls.

"A teacher aide at my school," Phillips explained. "Nice

woman. She had a fire at her place last night, and now this, whatever this is."

The truck driver had the trailer where he wanted it and had stopped to pat a large fluffy cat—a nondescript black— that had emerged from under the workbench and hurried to greet him. Phillips went outside to talk to the man and, after a moment, Jack followed.

"I'm Rhys Phillips from the school," the teacher was explaining. "Ms. Westerson works for me, and I'm sorry to see she's having car trouble."

Stone gave Phillips a nod. "Ethan Stone. Someone let the air out of all four tires. I went over to fill them up again, but they're all punctured. Bad luck, especially after the fire last night." He caressed the cat's ears and told it, "Back to sleep, Boss. I've got work to do."

If Stone and Claudia were back together, her employer didn't know it. "Poor lady," Jack commented.

"This is your next customer," Phillips said, helpfully. "Name of Jake. Has a Triumph needs a bit of work."

Stone looked up from whatever he was doing with the ramps, and inclined his head. "Must be the day for them. Yours, Mr. Phillips', and I've got mine in today, as well."

"Was anybody hurt?" Jack asked. "In the fire?" He was looking at Stone, but both men started to answer, Phillips waving to indicate Stone should go first.

"No idea. Ben told me about it when he sent me over to get the car. I haven't met the lady—she was out."

"She's at work," Phillips explained. "The fire was outside, and she and her little girl are fine." He chuckled. "The rabbit would have been in trouble, since it was his hutch that took most of the damage, but Abbie had smuggled him into bed with her."

"That's good, then." Jack shared a smile with the other men. So Stone didn't know Claudia, eh? And Phillips showed too much interest in her for Jack's comfort. Were they dating? Jack would need to ask around. In a small town, someone would know if the head teacher was humping one of his teacher aides.

He nodded towards the car. "What can I do to help?"

"I think we've got this. I'm just going to put Ms. Westerson's Corona into the workshop so Ben can have the truck, then we can take a look at what you need. Shouldn't take long."

Jack stood back, grateful for the time to compose himself. It was him alright. Ethan Stone. The man Claudia never forgot. Here in Fairburn. Did Claudia know? Is this why she had moved back to Fairburn; to be with Stone. And what was Jack going to do about it?

It took more than a minute to winch the car down, unhitch the trailer, and park the truck across the forecourt. "You don't mind if I go first, do you?" Phillips asked as Stone picked a rag from a box of clean ones by the workbench and wiped his hands. "Lunch hour is nearly over, and I need to get back to school. Won't take a moment."

Jack managed a friendly wave. "Go for it," he said.

He had a more immediate concern than Stone's intentions. Could the man be trusted with the Triumph? He'd been a cyclist when Claudia met him, an Olympic hopeful. Washed up and in a downward spiral by the time she fled. Jack knew the man had followed Claudia to New Zealand, and he knew about the fight that had landed one man in a wheelchair and another in prison. When had Stone had time to become a motor mechanic — and a bike specialist at that?

Stone said goodbye to Phillips and crossed immediately to Jack's bike, squatting down to take a close look. "You're restoring her yourself?" he asked.

Jack put a defensive hand on the bike's seat, conscious of all the work still to do. "A bit of a project," he offered.

With a caressing finger, Stone lovingly traced the handlebars, inspecting the set-up, each instrument and every wire meticulously placed. "Nice work. Yours?"

It shouldn't matter what this scum thought, but Jack couldn't resist the rush of pride. "It was. Took three tries to get it right."

Stone raised his eyebrows and gave an impressed nod. "Most people don't take the trouble. I don't know if I could have done a better job myself, and I've been at it for five years now, including my apprenticeship. Cars as well, but the bikes are what I get up for in the morning. Are you a mechanic?"

Jack shook his head. "IT. Hardware, but it's a different scale. You said you had a Triumph yourself?"

Stone nodded to a tarpaulin in the corner. "Over there. I'm working on it a bit at a time in the evenings. A later model than yours, but still a nice slice of history. Do you want to see?"

He stood back proudly when he revealed the machine: a sleek gleaming beast with all the glamour Jack envisaged for his own.

"She's beautiful." Jack couldn't keep the envy from his voice, but Stone didn't remark on it.

"Yes, she is. Yours will be as good. Maybe better, since she's a '62. Let's start her up and have a listen." He drew the tarpaulin back over his bike, and turned his attention back to Jack's.

Jack found himself explaining his decision to drive the bike on his holiday, but Stone was soothing. "It could be timing, plug gap, a faulty solder, a couple of other things. You couldn't have foreseen problems when you set out. I'll take a look, and it should be easy to fix, if I'm right about the cause."

He made a few notes on the job sheet, and read out the address of the Bed and Breakfast place and Jack's mobile number to check they were correct. "We'll soon have her humming again, Mr." — he read the name off the job sheet — "Quill. Do you need a lift somewhere?"

But Jack turned down the offer. "I'll walk, thanks. It's not far, and I'll take a look at the shops. Might have a coffee. And Phillips said the museums were worth a look. Have you seen them?"

"Not yet. I'm new in town and haven't looked around much yet," Stone explained.

"And what brought you to Fairburn?" Jack asked, keeping his tone casual, his posture relaxed.

Stone shrugged. "I read about the job, time for a change, you know." Clearly feeling this was not enough, he added, "I'm New Zealand born, but my family moved away when I was a baby, and since I came back, I haven't seen much of the real countryside. One town is much like another."

He was lying. He was here for Claudia. He must be. That guy Phillips, too. But now that Jack was here, it would all be okay. He and Claudia would be together again, the way it was meant to be.

Five

Claudia moved among the children, correcting a posture here, a movement there. For little ones, the lessons were about fun and accomplishment, but it was not too soon to begin training them in ways to improve their balance, jump higher, and roll more effectively. Few, if any, would take the hard road to gymnastics at international or even national level. But suppleness and balance were useful no matter what they did later.

"You're very good with them," Rhys Phillips observed, when her route took her past the watching parents.

"They're a delight," Claudia said. She taught the beginners' class twice a week in the school hall, having gratefully handed back the older children when the regular gymnastics teacher returned from parental leave.

The last exercise of the day was a noisy round of animals, she calling out the animal her pupils were to move like, and the children throwing themselves with enthusiasm, while slithering, galloping, leaping, hopping, all the time making their approximation of the sound.

Five minutes of that wore off any surplus energy still left after the discipline of the main session, and sent them away buzzing with enthusiasm for next week's session.

"Don't forget," she said, when she had them all back on the mat, the parents hovering ready to collect them, "Practice your forward rolls. Heads…?"

"Tucked in!" they roared back, and she dismissed them.

The parents who had volunteered to put the equipment away got busy while she answered a question about the last session of the year and referred the questioner to the parent in charge of organizing the Christmas party. By the time she had put her notes in her carry-all, Rhys was waiting.

"Thank you for offering to take me home," she said. "I'd hoped to have the car back, but the garage phoned to say the mechanic was fixing a couple of problems. Ben said no charge; just something to make me feel better after the fire. Wasn't that nice? Where's Phoebe?"

"My mum picked her up," he said. "We're having tea there tonight. I'm going to drop you off and follow them over."

"You didn't have to do that. I could have walked," she protested, but Rhys insisted it was not a problem.

"I saw your car at lunch time when I dropped off my motor bike," he said, as she climbed into his comfortable people mover and clipped her safety belt. "The new mechanic seems to know his stuff. Are you going to be okay for tomorrow? You've got RDA, haven't you?"

He was a kind man, Claudia thought, as she assured him she expected her car back in plenty of time to get Abbie to after-school riding.

They pulled up in front of her house, the hedge from the outside showing no sign of the drama of the night before. "Thank you. Have a lovely dinner."

"Have you got someone there?" Rhys asked. "With Abbie?"

"No, she's over with Carly. She and Edward will be home later."

"Then I'm walking you in." Rhys got out of the car, and came around to join her on the footpath. "Do the police have any idea who did it? Both things, I mean, because it beggars belief that the fire and the tires weren't the same person."

Claudia shook her head as she led the way through the gate. On this side, the hedge was blistered and scorched for most of the length of the small fenced yard, and the sad ruin of the rabbit hutch still sat in the middle of a black charred patch of ground. Tomorrow wasn't a work day, and her first job after she'd dropped Abbie to school would be to break the remains down and get rid of them. And how she'd afford a new hutch, she had no idea.

Rhys waited while she unlocked the door, and followed her inside. "I'll just have a quick look at the windows," he told her.

"The police said they are keeping an eye on me," Claudia assured him, but he insisted on doing his own check anyway, Abbie's small box of a bedroom, the bathroom, the everything-else room with the kitchen, sitting area, and Claudia's drop-down bed, currently folded up into the wall.

He was such a kind man, and Claudia felt safe with him, since he was a widower who had, purportedly, adored his wife. She was just thinking that when he took both of her hands and looked down at her, his expression concerned, his face warm.

"I don't like to leave you on your own here."

Should she pull her hands away? Would he get angry if she did? Her heart raced, her sense of safety evaporating as if it had never been.

"I am fine, truly."

"You wouldn't consider coming to stay at my place for a few days? We have a spare room, and Abbie could share with Rhonda. You have to know I care about you, Claudia."

Claudia, greatly daring, pulled her fingers free and wiped them on her sides. "I… that's very nice of you, Rhys. But… Thank you, but I'd… Abbie and I will be fine, truly."

She managed to keep her voice calm though turning out a coherent sentence was beyond her. He didn't seem to notice her anxiety; just put up a hand to gently tuck a stray lock of hair behind her ear. "If you're sure. Well, I'd better get on my way. Dinner with my mother." He looked back from her doorway to where Claudia still stood in the middle of the room.

"She thinks I should marry again, and I'm starting to see the attraction. Lock the door, Claudia."

Marry? Dear Lord. And to think she had thought him safe!

All the way through heating leftovers for her solo dinner, eating and doing the few dishes, and setting out the star for tonight's Jessie tree story, she fretted about what she might have done to indicate to Rhys she might be interested. Men! She would never understand them.

Rhys had spooked Claudia enough that she kept startling awake all night whenever an extra strong gust of wind rattled a window or a car passed close outside. Once it was light, she found a solid branch of wood in her landlord's woodpile and propped it by the kitchen door, where Abbie remarked on it when she came yawning from her bedroom.

"I might need it later," Claudia said vaguely. "Cereal, sweetie? Or toast and an egg?"

Abbie opted for cereal, and went off obediently to wash her hands. "I miss Edward," she mourned, as she climbed up into her chair and picked up her spoon.

Edward had stayed behind at Carly's, an invited guest in the hutch occupied by Bigwig, another A&P purchase. Claudia sent up a brief prayer that both baby rabbits were male, as claimed by the seller, though everyone who'd bought a rabbit had been told the same thing.

Abbie must also have been thinking of the rabbit Bigwig, because she asked, "Why do the Be'gers' animals 'ave such silly names, Mummy?" The Beckers' cat was called Macavity and their dog was Baskerville. Even Carly's beloved horses had not escaped her husband's affection for fictional characters. Epona and Mister Ed roamed the field next to the poultry house, sharing it with Henny Penny and Mrs. McClucken.

"Not silly," Claudia corrected, absently, as she poured herself a coffee. "They are names from books. You'll be able to read about them one day, Abbie."

"Mr. Be'ger wrides books."

"Writes books," Claudia said, and Abbie grinned.

"Yes, he does."

"Cheeky sausage. Go and do your teeth, darling. Mr. Becker will be here soon to take you to school."

"Can I pud oud the thing for the Jesse Dree? I know which one; the abble."

"The apple, yes. Once you are ready to leave: teeth brushed, shoes on, bag packed."

Abbie hurried to good purpose, and had time to search through the box to find the felt ornament where a golden apple dangled from an improbably tiny tree that provided an inadequate hiding place for a snake with a sly expression.

She held it up against the tree.

"I'm nod pudding id on, Mummy," she assured Claudia. "Jus' drying id by the branch."

A knock at the door sent her hurrying to the window, her progress across the room a controlled fall that tugged at Claudia's heart. "It's Mr. Be'ger," she reported, and a few moments later Claudia waved her goodbye from the gate and made her way back inside, locking the door carefully behind her.

A quick run around to tidy, and Claudia was ready to settle down and sew. On the two days that Abbie was at school without her, Claudia had been working on the child's Christmas present: a Wonder Woman costume. It was nearly done, and Claudia might finish today. It would then go up in the cupboard with the other wrapped presents until closer to Christmas.

The knock on the door startled her out of a reverie in which she had saved enough to buy a house here in Fairburn and was putting into practice all the ideas she'd picked up from hours of home renovation shows.

"Just a minute," she called, as she unfastened the lock. She set one hand hovering over her improvised club, opened the door, and nearly slammed it shut again.

Six

"Wait!" That plea, in the voice that still had the power to make her shiver, had her hesitate, one hand ready to slam the door the rest of the way; the other taking a good grasp of the branch.

She glared at Ethan Stone, who stood on her doorstep looking altogether hotter than any man had a right to. The black curls he'd bequeathed his daughter, brown eyes — calm and friendly now, but she knew them in all their moods. The tight jeans did nothing to disguise his cyclist thighs, but in other ways he was different — a firmer jaw changing the lean adolescent face into that of a devastatingly handsome man, broad shoulders and a muscular chest filling out the t-shirt with the logo of the local garage.

"I've returned your car," he said. "It's outside. I've put in a new oil filter and changed the oil. Also balanced the wheels and cleaned the spark plugs. You have new wiper blades, too."

"I can't afford that."

The mulish set of that new jaw was very familiar. "No charge. I did it on my own time."

She thought of pointing out the cost of materials, but changed tack. "How do I know you didn't puncture my tires just for a chance to talk to me."

He spread both hands as if to show they were empty. It wasn't his hands that had hurt her. "I didn't. Didn't burn your rabbit's hutch either. I didn't come here to frighten you, Claudia."

Claudia glared. "Then why did you."

"To apologise." His dark eyes held hers. As far as she could tell, he was sincere, but his sincerity had never been the problem.

"To see if there was anything I could do to help," he continued. "I let you down, and I've been sorry for it ever since." He took a deep breath and then chewed at his upper lip while he waited for her answer.

The softening of her heart made her response terser than she intended. "It took you a while to say so, then." She gripped her makeshift club harder, in case he lost his temper.

Instead, he hung his head. "I was too angry at first. Then in prison—you knew I went to prison, right?" He waited for her nod, then continued, "In prison, I had time to think. At first, I thought you were better off without me. You had your grandma, and I was bad news."

He was. She'd been right to leave him when she did, whatever her father said. "Abbie and I are fine on our own, Ethan." Claudia was shaking, but determined. Now he'd push her out of the way, crashing open the door, never caring about the effects until his temper subsided. This time, she wasn't going to let it happen. She wasn't going to give in, and she wasn't going to run away. Let Ethan leave, and if he tried anything, she'd call the police.

But he surprised her again. "You were always stronger than you believed. I'm glad you know that now. Look, I have a good job and savings. You deserve whatever I can give you. Abbie deserves it."

She shook her head. "I don't want presents from you." Gifts came with strings attached. She'd learned that lesson at her father's knee, and again when she lived with Jack. To be fair, Ethan had never acted that way, but she wasn't about to start trusting him after all that had happened.

"Not presents, Ethan insisted. "Your rights. It was my job to protect you and I hurt you. I wasn't there when I should have been. I owe you both."

Claudia hardened her heart to the apparent change in his. "I don't want anything from you, Ethan. Just go away. Leave me and Abbie alone."

Ethan sighed. "Won't you at least let me tell you what happened to me? Please, Claudia? Ten minutes?"

"Five." She couldn't bear more than that. Already, she was close to believing him, and she couldn't risk it—couldn't risk Abbie like that.

"May I come in?"

She was slightly reassured that he asked, but the answer had to be— "No. You can talk from there."

Ethan pressed his lips together and looked down, and she followed his eyes to watch his booted foot pushing a bit of scorched wood off the path. Was he going to explode? As silently as she could, she began to close the door.

"I'll stay here!" Ethan said, looking up. "Please, Claudia. Don't shut the door." He stayed where he was, not moving towards her, his hands stretched open at his sides. "You're frightened of me. I'm so sorry." He shook his head, sadly. "Look, let me tell you what happened to me. Then I'll go away and you can think about it. I never wanted to hurt you. Please believe me."

"I suppose you think it was my fault." That was what Jack used to say. 'You made me do it. I never wanted to hurt you.' But Ethan was shaking his head, his face blanching. "No! None of it was your fault. It was me. You were the best thing that ever happened to me and I messed it up because I wouldn't get help when I needed it."

Claudia nodded. "The concussions." During Abbie's long rehabilitation she had learned a lot about traumatic brain injury, and had worked out why the sweet, kind boy she'd fallen in love with had turned into a demanding violent monster after several brutal crashes from his bike.

Ethan was nodding. "Yes. And in the end… You know I finished up incarcerated? For a violent assault?"

"Your mother wrote and told me. She blamed me for abandoning you." That had hurt more than it should have, mainly because Claudia feared Mrs. Stone was right.

"She was wrong. You were right to leave me. It might have been you I nearly killed, Claudia. Or killed. It was touch and go. I have this nightmare where…" Ethan shook his head quickly, as if to shed painful thoughts like dogs shed water.

"Anyway. There was a guy who came and gave a talk in prison. I'd been in there about eighteen months, I guess, angry all the time. People left me alone; even the big bruisers. I didn't care if I lived or died. Then this guy—he'd been in prison himself, and the way he talked—he was just like me. But then he started reading to fill in the time. And signed up for a course at university, because it would get him credit with the Parole Board. He was in for murder—killed a man who made advances—and he had a lot of time. Finished a doctorate in the end. He saved himself, and then he worked out what he had done to replace the anger with peace, and now he goes into prisons and tells people about it."

"So you decided to be like him." She couldn't bear much more of this. He was demolishing the walls around her heart she'd built to protect herself and her child.

"I decided to learn," Ethan told her, "but I'm not a scholar, Claudia, you know that. I've always been good with my hands, though. They had carpentry classes, and small-engine maintenance, and I signed up for those. Got myself onto a course for motor mechanics. And I asked to talk to the shrink, the psychiatrist, to see if I could figure out where the anger came from, or at least how to deal with it."

Claudia nodded. "He got you the help you needed."

Ethan screwed up his nose. "Not really. The prison system is massively underfunded. But when he found out I'd taken a few hard whacks, what he told me got me reading. There's some really good therapy—I guess you know. The article I saw said Abbie was in an accident. What happened, Claudia? And how is she?"

At her daughter's name, Claudia reared back, all her fears rushing in to replace the sympathy she'd felt a moment ago. "Leave Abbie alone. Ethan. I mean it. If anything happens to her, I'll make sure you go back inside and stay there."

"Whoa, lady! I would never hurt either of you!" He softened his voice again, holding out a hand as if begging. "I just want the chance to get to know you again; to get to know my daughter."

She couldn't hear him. She wouldn't. "Not your daughter. You weren't there, Ethan. You didn't even want her in the first place." Her voice began to climb. "Get out. Get off my property, and get out of Fairburn. I don't want you near us." The last was a panicked shriek.

"Okay, okay." Ethan's voice was low and calm, and despite herself she began to respond to the soothing sound, her racing heart beginning to slow. "Here. Here are your keys." He tossed them onto the doorstep, and she swept them backwards with her foot.

Ethan continued, "I can't just leave, Claudia. Ben is counting on me. But I'll give in my notice. I don't have any rights. I know that, and I never wanted to frighten you. I'll give Ben my notice. Will that be okay?"

She nodded, unable to speak past the conflicting desires to scream at him again and to respond to the gentleness in his tone, and let him past her walls. He nodded back. "You look after yourself. I'll…" A helpless wave of the hand. "Goodbye, Claudia."

Seven

What had happened to frighten her so? Surely not him. Ethan had never actually hit her, though he'd come close, and he'd shoved her a couple of times and made her fall. He expected caution, perhaps even a little nervousness. But her reaction—it would not be too much to call it terror— was beyond anything he'd imagined.

She'd gone back to her father after she left him, but her father had thrown her out, as he told Ethan when Ethan went to find her; to apologize; to beg her to return. And then he'd heard from a friend that she'd gone to her mother's mother in New Zealand. His birthplace, though he'd not lived there since he was a small boy. Mr. Westerson wouldn't give him an address or even the grandmother's name; threatened him with a gun and told him to get out.

It had taken him months to save the fare, but he'd made it to New Zealand at last. And got into the fight that changed the direction of his life before he'd even left Auckland, where his plane had landed.

Was it Westerson? He had been a brutal coach, though more with words than physically. Still, Westerson had left her with bruises more than once before Ethan persuaded her to come away with him.

Or had there been someone else since; someone who had treated her badly?

Ethan hoped not, for her sake, but if she hadn't been abused by her father or another lover, then her terror was all for him, and that thought was unbearable.

Eight

On the first Saturday in December, Fairburn celebrated the season with a Christmas Parade and a Festival.

Claudia took an excited Abbie to the assembly area for the floats. The school's was an ambitious construction on the back of the local road gang's longest truck (the owner was on the school board). 'Holiday festivals around the world' proclaimed the painted canvas skirt nailed to the truck bed so it hid the wheels.

Every organization and enterprise in the town turned out for the event, which was designed to catch the weekend visitors for whom the Martonvale Valley was a playground. The park sprouted market stalls and amusements. The school, early childhood center, local churches, and multifarious clubs had been building floats for weeks, and Claudia and Abbie had to weave between them to find where Abbie should be. Carla was waiting, toddler strapped to her back, and one hand holding tight to the five-year-old.

The school's theme was traditions from around the world, and most parents had drawn on their own cultural heritage for inspiration, so in a country of immigrants from the northern hemisphere there were lots of midwinter characters in much lighter versions of their traditional winter robes. They were all in costume, Carla as Mother Frost, and the children as snow crystals, the costumes made in light sparkly materials that wouldn't smother them in the summer heat.

"Three kings?" Claudia guessed, as the children of the Italian baker marched up to the float, crowns on heads and presents in hand.

"I reckon," Carly agreed. "Did you see the Tan family? I love the traditional Chinese robes!"

Claudia named the Chinese winter solstice festival. "Dongzhi. Lucy Tan did a lovely presentation on it at school last week." The families had been taking it in turn to teach the rest of the school about their own traditions. When it was the Westersons turn, Claudia had spoken about the Jesse Tree, and today Abbie was costumed as a shepherd boy from ancient Israel, complete with cardboard lyre and a shepherd's crook borrowed from the agricultural museum.

"Sophie Lafao looks comfortable," Carly commented, as the Samoan mother led her children over. She and her daughters were resplendent in palatasi, the traditional Samoan two-piece of top and skirt, printed with island designs, and her sons wore lavalavas. All were crowned and wreathed with flowers.

"Cooler than this beard," said Rhys Phillips, who was dressed as a Druid. He interrupted himself to stop an incipient fight. "No, Jamie Muller. No beating people with your switch." Jamie's mother, rolling her eyes in exasperation, hurried up to retrieve her son and his sack of coal.

"You bedder go, Mummy," Abbie said.

"Are you sure you'll be okay?" Claudia asked, not sure whether she was addressing the question to Carla or Abbie.

Abbie rolled her eyes and Carla nodded. "Fine, Claudia. Go and do your thing with the gymnasts."

"I'll help," Rhys agreed, cheerfully, and went back to directing his students into their places.

Claudia found her class easily enough. The six of them, dressed as fairies in pink tulle and glittery wings, were already assembled on the truck bed. The older classes — also in costume — would walk either side. Or, rather, dance, skip, run, cartwheel, and otherwise entertain the crowds. Her father would have had a fit if she'd suggested such a public display in such an uncontrolled environment.

She clambered up to join the children on the truck, her own Mrs. Claus costume making climbing difficult, and took several photos of the children on her phone, to share with their parents. What little treasures they were. Twenty minutes until the start, according to her phone. She started a game of "I spy…" to keep them entertained and amused, and was surprised at how quickly the time flew. They would be one of the last floats to leave the assembly area, but once the parade began to move past them, the children were happily entertained by studying each float and waving to friends and relatives, so Claudia could relax and enjoy herself.

Ethan waited for the school float in the street behind the supermarket. The parade would be spread out the full length of the Main Street by the time its leaders reached the end of the route. The school float was three or four back from the front, and the one where Claudia ruled over her own little flock of fairies was nearly at the end.

His planning was rewarded far beyond his expectations when the woman watching over Abbie had to rush one of her own children off to the public toilets when the poor little mite whimpered, "I don't feel so good'.

"Polly, stay with Abbie," she commanded.

Ethan waited for her to disappear through the crowds, and then approached the truck, just in time to see Polly help Abbie down to the ground and ran to tug on the hand of the distracted head teacher, who was doing his best to control children whose mothers had not yet appeared to collect them.

Ethan was about to take his chances to speak to Abbie when he heard Polly say, "We will wait under the tree and see the other floats, and we won't move until Mummy gets back."

Perfect. He stepped backwards a couple of steps, and then circled swiftly around a few groups of people until he reached the tree, leaning against it as if he had been there for ages, watching the two girls from the corner of his eye as they approached.

She was beautiful, her elfin face framed in a cloud of dark curls, her bright eyes sparkling as she and her friend pointed things out to one another and waved to people they knew. Abbie. Abigail, he supposed, though the article hadn't said so. But surely Claudia had named her for the grandma he'd never met; the one who had lived here in Fairburn.

"You could ride one of the ponies next year," Polly said, as the local pony club, their horses decked out as fancifully as the riders, clip-clopped across the paved parking lot and took refuge under the trees.

Abbie screwed up her face in thought. "Maybe…" she allowed. "Mummy worries."

Quite right, too. He didn't know the child, and already he'd lay himself down on hot coals so she could cross them without burning her feet. She was his daughter, even if he had blown off all right to the relationship before she was even born.

"Which is your favorite?" Polly asked. "Mine is the white unicorn."

"Begasus." Abbie paused and took a deep breath, then blew out the letter 'P' with some force, pausing afterwards. "P. — egasus."

Polly searched the resting ponies, and Ethan did, too. No winged horse. Abbie giggled, and Polly's eyes lit with understanding. "That's what you would do? Pegasus? Would the pony mind the wings?"

Something light, Ethan thought, and a firm harness so the wings didn't flap to frighten Abbie's mount or the other ponies. A few ideas raced across his mind. He'd always enjoyed tinkering with his hands, making a vision come to life in metal, wood and fabric. After he had screwed everything up and flushed his life down the toilet, it had been his only solace. And, in the end, his redemption.

"You couldn't make them too big," he mused. "But if you kept them to around four feet, say, you'd still have a decent wingspan. Polycarbonate for the framework and struts, and parachute silk to cover. We could make it work, I reckon."

Abbie and Polly were staring, Abbie's face suddenly bland. Where did an eight-year-old learn to hide her feelings like that?

"I beg your pardon," Ethan said, keeping his voice to the calm hum that had worked with Boss, his rescue cat when he'd brought her home, a frightened and abused kitten. "I could not help but overhear, and then I started thinking out loud." He spread his hands to show they were empty. Harmless, he thought. *I am harmless.* "I make things, you see."

"I am not allowed to talk to people my mummy doesn't know," Polly told him, sternly. "Abbie isn't, either."

"Your mummy and Abbie's are quite right," Ethan agreed. "I am nice, but some people are bad."

Abbie's grin flashed again. "Bad man say tha'," she argued, and he returned the grin, his heart turning over in his chest. A car accident, the article had said, and she was improving all the time. What a gallant little warrior she was, and how Claudia must have suffered.

He should have been here for them; should have been their wall against the world and not yet another danger from which to flee.

"Girls?" Here came the friend, frowning at him as she hurried up with her toddler on her hip. "Girls, who is this you are talking to?"

"My apologies, ma'am." Ethan bowed. "I interrupted the girls' conversation, and this young lady was just explaining she could not talk to me." The sound of his heart thundered in his temples as he took the next step. "Ethan Stone. I'm the new mechanic at Peterson's." There. Would she recognize the name? Had Claudia spoken of him?

Apparently not, because she simply gave him a distracted nod. "Carly Becker. Come on, girls. Abbie, your mum will be here any minute. Let's go meet her. Nice to meet you, Ethan."

She hurried the children away, casting a look back at him when Polly told her, "Mummy, Mr. Stone says he could make a Pegasus costume for a pony."

"Could he, darling? Oh look! Here comes the gym club's float."

Time to go. Claudia had told him to stay away from Abbie, and she wasn't likely to understand his burning need to speak to the child, just once.

He took a few steps to put the tree between him and the road, then threaded his way through the crowds to head home. Would Carly mention the man under the tree to her friend? And if so, would she name him? Ethan didn't know whether to hope she wouldn't, or that she would. Perhaps, if Claudia saw he'd spoken to Abbie without any harm coming of it, she might begin to trust him a little?

Nine

As the second week of December passed without further nasty surprises, Claudia began to relax. At the school, the Christmas festivities and the coming summer holiday dominated every classroom, and the end-of-year paperwork harried the teachers. Claudia took her last gymnastics class of the year, and all the girls received a certificate and a personalized drink bottle. She was touched by the gifts she was given in return—soaps, jeweled bookmarks, a potted plant, bars of fancy chocolate.

RDA was not closing for the year until the middle of the third week, but what Claudia would do over the summer, she was not sure. The riding had done Abbie the world of good.

When Carly mentioned she was boarding two of the RDA horses, Claudia raised the topic with the RDA convener while Abbie was riding on Thursday afternoon.

"Carly tells me that Beauty and Podge are staying at her place while RDA is closed for the summer,' she said, naming the ponies.

The convener was watching the circling horses, each with a child atop and a volunteer helper alongside, ready to catch the unsteady and control the unwary, but at her comment he turned to look at her. "Yes, sure. Carly thought you might want Abbie to keep riding over the summer, and she's willing to supervise so we won't get slammed by the health and safety people."

It was as simple as that. "Thank you so much. We'll follow all the rules, I promise."

"I know you can be trusted, and it'll be good for the ponies to keep working. A bit of light exercise, each day, if you can manage it, will be good for them and good for Abbie, too."

One of the other volunteers, currently not needed out in the field, nudged the convener. "That car is there again," she said.

Claudia peered up at the parking lot on the hill above the RDA grounds. A black pick-up truck, a light blue hatchback, and a white sedan. "Which one?" she wondered.

"The white," the convener told her, not taking his eyes off the vehicle. "It has been parked in the car park up on the hill every time we've had RDA for the past week, and look. That flash. I reckon someone up there is using binoculars."

As the three of them watched, the flash disappeared, and moments later the car backed away, turned, and left the lot.

"Did anyone get the number?" the convener asked, but without much hope. Sure enough, all he got was a couple of headshakes. The slope had concealed the base of the car.

The convener shook his head. "I'll talk to the police. Someone watching kids through binoculars? Not good."

Abbie shook off the sense of dread that descended. Whoever it was, it had nothing to do with her. How could it?

She had second thoughts on Saturday. She and Abbie got separated for a few moments in the crowds at the weekend market in the parking lot behind the bakery, and when Claudia found her daughter again, Abbie was white, shaking, and near tears. Under emotional stress, her speech became less intelligible, and it took a while for Claudia to understand her scare was more than just losing sight of her mother.

"I saw jag," she kept repeating, until Claudia made the connection. "Jack?" she asked, and the crying child nodded, vigorously, adding "Jag wanna gill me."

Only Claudia's own suspicions allowed her to decipher that. So Abbie believed 'Jack wants to kill me'? Did she remember the accident, then? She had never said; had always clammed up when anyone asked questions.

"Jack can't reach you, darling. Mummy will keep you safe," she promised, hoping it was true.

Later that day over at Carly's, where Abbie was occupied playing with Polly and her sisters, Claudia told Carly and Trent about the incident.

"He did try," she explained. "The police didn't believe me, but I know. He told me that if I left him he would kill Abbie. After the accident, he said he was just trying to help; that he picked her up at school that day hoping to use it as an excuse to talk to me. He made out I was hysterical, and I was. I was. Abbie was in critical care, and they didn't expect her to live. They said her seat belt failed, but it was a near new car. Why should it fail?"

Carly was indignant. "So they didn't do anything?"

"To be fair, it was his word against mine. No evidence." Claudia had been so angry with the police, but at the same time had understood why they wouldn't listen to her. "He was charming and reasonable. Respectable, too, with his own business building specialist computers. The police officer who interviewed me pointed out he'd been injured in the crash, too; that it had been a wet afternoon and the corner was known for problems at speed. He admitted speeding, you see."

"But you believe he crashed on purpose, to kill Abbie." Trent sounded doubtful.

"See?" Claudia pushed her spoon around her cup, watching the swirl of the coffee rather than meet the derision she expected in Trent's eyes. "You know me, and you've only heard my point of view, and you don't believe me. Why should the police?"

"They might now," Trent suggested. "After all, someone set that fire and let your tires down."

Claudia nodded. "And someone wrote the note that got

slipped under my doormat. I can believe it of Jack. You don't believe me, Trent, but it would be just like him."

Trent threw up a hand in protest. "I didn't say I didn't believe you. You knew the man, and you're no fool, Claudia Westerson."

"That's right," Carly agreed. "If you lived with him, you knew him better than anyone."

"He was fine as long as I gave him all my attention and no other man looked at me."

"Controlling and obsessive." Carly grimaced.

Claudia sighed. "Just like my father."

"Wait a minute," Carly said. "What about the man at the parade?"

"What man?" Claudia suppressed an urge to run out into the backyard, where she could hear the girls' voices raised in laughing play. Abbie was not in danger here on the Becker's property.

"After the parade, actually," Carly explained. "I took Audra to the toilet. Rhys said he'd keep an eye on Polly and Abbie, and he did, but he let them go watch the floats come in. When I got back, they were talking to a man. I'm sorry, Claudia. I meant to tell you, but they weren't upset or anything. Apparently, they were talking about the pony club costumes. He said he could build Pegasus wings. Might that have been this Jack?"

Trent disagreed. "Not if she collapses in tears at the sight of him," he argued. "She was relaxed with this character, from what you say."

Claudia had a fair idea who it was. "What did he look like?" she asked.

Carly confirmed her suspicion. "Tall, fit, dark curly hair. Like one of those Italian-American movie stars. Matthew Daddario or Frank De Julio."

"Same hair and eyes as Abbie, in fact." Claudia sighed. "That would have been Ethan, her biological father. I told him to leave her alone, but Ethan never did take any notice of what anyone else wanted."

"Her father is in Fairburn?" Carly asked, so Claudia explained that Ethan had taken a job at the local garage. "I guess he must have seen that damned photo. He came around to my house. To apologize, he said."

"To apologize?" Trent surged to his feet and turned in the direction of the garage on the far side of Fairburn, somehow managing to broaden his shoulders as his hands formed fists at his sides. "Was he violent to you as well, Claudia?"

"No!" Except that wasn't true, and her impulse to protect Ethan might put Abbie in danger. "He wasn't violent at all. This time. I told him he couldn't come in, and he stayed outside. He went after he'd said his piece. He said he would put in his notice at his job and leave Fairburn."

Trent subsided back into his chair. "He's done that. Ben was complaining about it at Men's Shed." The local handyman's group. Or handyperson's rather, since they accepted anyone who wanted to gather in their little converted garage to use the tools and talk about wood and metal working.

"Wait." The frown returned. "This time, Claudia?"

She spread her fingers, examining one hand while thinking about how to answer. The index finger bent at the second knuckle, reminding her of Jack's methods of making her compliant.

"In the beginning, Ethan was sweet and kind, and even later, he was usually gentle and loving. He was a cyclist, a national youth champion and just beginning on the international circuit. Road, mainly, though he did a bit of track. He had several bad falls. Repeated concussions. They changed him, and he wouldn't accept it, wouldn't take help."

She rubbed the knuckle of her healed finger. "He couldn't hold back his temper. Not like Jack. Jack was like my father. He might hit out in a rage, but far more often he'd smile as if he wasn't angry then plot and plan to make me pay. My father never hit me, but I stopped asking for pets, because I couldn't bear to see them hurt or killed. Jack didn't need to worry about impairing my performance as a gymnast, so…"

"Abbie!" Carly accompanied her shocked outcry with a comforting squeeze of the hand she placed over Claudia's.

"I left Jack. Not early enough, but I did leave. I went to stay with a friend on the far side of town, and the following week he picked Abbie up from school."

Trent's face was grim. "And crashed the car."

"It was never like that with Ethan," Claudia hurried to explain.

"Did Ethan hit you?" Trent's growl was low and dangerous.

"Not me." Never her, but she was afraid the whole time that one day he would forget himself and go too far. "The wall. The side of the old car that was all we could afford. Nothing intentional or planned, but his anger would blow up out of nowhere, and the violence — perhaps I could have helped him if I'd been older and wiser, but back then I just froze. When I knew I was pregnant with Abbie, I left. I didn't want her having the childhood I had."

"Good for you," Carly said, squeezing her hand again, while Trent thought about what she had said. "Would he set light to a rabbit hutch?"

Claudia shook her head then thought again. "It doesn't seem like the Ethan I knew, but he was 18 when we parted. He's been in prison. He's done therapy — or so he says. Has he changed? And if he has, is he better or worse?"

Trent nodded slowly. "Has he tried anything since he talked to you? Other than talking to Abbie?"

"No. Not that I know of. There was the note, then the fire, then the tires. Then Ethan brought the car back and I told him to stay away from Abbie." Which he didn't. What else might he have done? "Someone has been watching the RDA kids. From the parking lot on the hill. With binoculars. And now Abbie says she has seen Jack."

Trent nodded again. "I'll ask around town; see if anyone has heard of a Jack. What's his surname?"

"Quinton. He's a computer engineer. Hardware, not software or systems."

"Jack Quinton. A computer guy. Got it."

Ten

Monday was Ethan's day off, and he took his motorcycle out for a run to help him manage the burning desire to hang around Claudia's place, in the hopes of glimpsing her or his daughter. If he headed out to the coast, he'd spend most of the day unable to offend Claudia again.

Boss was up for a ride. Like all cats, she was territorial, sticking to the place she loved best. Unlike most, her territory comprised the Triumph and Ethan. Had ever since Ethan had rescued her and her brother, two scrawny kittens tossed into a deep drain and left to die. Ethan took them home inside his jacket and stayed up all night feeding them the goat's milk preparation he'd found on the Internet. The brother didn't make it. Boss got her name from the preemptory demands she was making when Ethan returned inside after removing the frail body of the dead kitten.

Boss thrived on frequent feeds, graduating from an eye dropper to a baby's bottle and then to tinned kitten food and biscuits. She lived in Ethan's pocket, or around Ethan's shoulders, or in the pannier bags of the Triumph as Ethan moved from job to job, getting experience but never finding a place he wanted to settle. Two years on, Boss was a magnificent beast; at least, Ethan thought so. Tucked inside Ethan's jacket as they cruised the highway out to Valentine Bay, she mostly slept, but poked her nose out from time to time, her eyes shut and her hair and whiskers streaming back in the wind.

Valentine Bay was popular with tourists and valley residents alike, but on a weekday the little village was nearly deserted. Monday was the day most of the shops closed after a busy weekend, but Ethan found a cafe where he could buy a takeaway coffee and a croissant, plus a salmon sandwich for Boss. They carried on through the village to the small harbor and left the bike in the parking lot between the docks for the fishing boats and the marina beyond.

Ethan exchanged his helmet for a cloth cap to keep the sun from his head and, with Boss trotting at his heels, one watchful eye on the paper bag containing the salmon sandwich, wandered out onto the breakwater between the two harbors to eat his lunch.

Ben had not been pleased with his resignation. In the end, Ethan had told him about Claudia and Abbie. Not names or details, but just that he had an ex-lover and a child that he'd lost contact with, and he'd come to Fairburn hoping to become reacquainted, and to help if they would let him. "She has told me to go away, Ben, and I figure if that's the only thing she'll take from me, I owe it to her. I said I couldn't leave you in the lurch, but I promised I'd put in my resignation."

"Humph." Ben thought about that for a while. "Okay. But not four weeks notice. Not over Christmas and I'm not going to get anyone during the summer holidays. You know that. Shall we say twelve weeks?" His eyes twinkled, and Ethan smiled back. *Yes*. Maybe, given time, Claudia would have a change of heart, and even if she didn't, Ben's support was heart-warming.

Boss licked the bread clean of salmon and wandered off to inspect a few rocks, leaping back with a hiss when a wave had the temerity to splash her. Ethan fed the remains of the sandwich and a few flakes of croissants to some cheeky seagulls, who easily dodged Boss's attempts to get to know them better.

"Okay, Boss," Ethan said when the last crumbs were gone, "How about we go look at some boats?" He wandered the marina, keeping half an eye on Boss to make sure the cat didn't find trouble as she hunted in and out of every interesting box or smelly pile of net they passed, frequently taking a detour along a handy deck, occasionally rushing ahead so she could leap out on Ethan's feet and dig her claws in by way of a friendly hello.

Half way along the third set of docks, he caught sight of a man he recognized. Ethan crouched to pat his cat, fortunately turning up in time to be an excuse. "Quill. Let's avoid him, Boss, shall we?" Half-turned, in sunglasses and a cap, and with his head down, he'd likely go unobserved. To Quill, he was just the lackey mechanic, the one the man had abused roundly yesterday when he'd phoned to find the necessary part for his bike had still not arrived.

So it proved. Quill didn't glance Ethan's way as he passed, deep in conversation about renting a boat from his companion. "I'll want it provisioned and fitted out for a decent voyage," he was saying. "I'm thinking I might go up to the Bay of Islands."

"It'll do that easy," the other man — the boat's owner — assured Quill, and was adding, "Come over to the harbor master's office and we'll finish the paper…" before the two of them passed out of hearing range.

So Quill was planning a sea voyage? Ethan shrugged. Nothing to do with him. "Come on, Boss," he said, scooping his fur friend up and draping him across his shoulders in another of Boss's favorite positions, "Let's go for a ride."

The route to and from the coast led through Barnsley, the main town in the valley, and when Ethan passed a sports store on the way back, he succumbed to the impulse to buy Abbie a Christmas gift. Maybe Claudia would refuse it. He let the thought go. He couldn't do anything about Claudia's actions. He could only control his own.

The riding helmets were in one corner, half masked by a display cabinet full of topographical maps. He searched through them, wondering how to get the child's head measurement, while idly listening to a conversation from the other side of the cabinet.

He recognized the voice — that guy Jake Quill again, turning up like a bad penny and berating some poor shop assistant. "… better than the binoculars you sold me a week ago."

"These tramping boots are the best on the market," the salesman protested. "Waterproof, breathable, with ankle support and a cushioned sole. You won't find better, even in the city. New Zealand-made, too. It's our best seller for trampers and hunters."

He continued extolling the virtues until Quill cut him short. "They'll do. I guess I'm going to need a sleeping bag. Show me what you've got."

The camping equipment would work well enough on a boat, Ethan supposed, but what did the man need tramping boots for?

"They're on the mezzanine, sir," the assistant said.

"In a minute, then. I'll need maps. I'm going into the regional park, and I want something that shows the huts and the tracks to them."

Ethan's curiosity was fully aroused, and he continued to listen while the assistant extolled the virtues of various tracks.

"I want something away from the fire breaks and the road access," Jake insisted, and the assistant tossed out one idea after another until Jake was finally satisfied. "Okay," he said. "I'll take this one and this one. Now for the bags."

Peculiar, but Ethan figured it was nothing to do with him. He turned back to the display of riding helmets, carefully reading all of the specifications. Abbie would have the best he could give her — at least she would if he could get the right size. He supposed the child could always exchange it if he guessed wrong, but he had hated that as a child — a brand new present, and then the wait for the shops to be open so he could actually use it.

In the end, he left without making a purchase. At least asking for permission to give Abbie a present would give him another excuse to talk to Claudia.

The motorcycle part arrived with a courier just before lunch on Tuesday. Ethan, who had already fielded two 'hurry up' calls from the owner, made finishing the Bonneville the first job after lunch, then sent Jake a text to let him know. The man arrived, checked the repair out, paid the account and took off.

"Not very charming, is he?" Ben commented. "Not so much as a thank you."

Ethan shrugged. Not his problem. "Takes all sorts."

"Speaking of which, how's your car?"

Ethan continued tidying the work bench. Work was much more efficient if everything was put away in the right place. "I don't have a car."

"A white sedan." Ben was watching him with an odd look on his face, as if waiting for him to put a foot out of place.

"Nope." Ethan picked up a clean rag and began dusting the bench. "Just the bike. What's this about, Ben?"

"Someone in a white sedan has been parked up on the hill watching the RDA kids through binoculars." Before Ethan could respond, Ben added, "I told them it couldn't be you because you were here at work."

Ethan voiced the question, though he already knew the answer. "Who thought it was me?"

"Friends of Claudia's."

As he thought. "Ah. She thinks it was me."

"No, apparently. She thinks it isn't like you."

That was something. "It wasn't," he grumbled. *But who was it? And why?*

"Didn't think so." Ben gave an expansive wave of the hand. "Besides, you were here all day every day from Tuesday through to Sunday, and that's what I told them."

Ethan's short laugh was unamused. "And still you asked

if I had a white sedan. No, don't apologize, Ben. I'm glad people are keeping an eye on Claudia and Abbie. She's lucky to be here and to have you guys."

Claudia had her seatbelt off before Carly pulled to a complete stop, and the door open before her friend turned off the car. "I'll go on ahead," Claudia tossed back over her shoulder as she hurried through the gate and into the school grounds.

They were only twenty minutes late. Other parents still stood in gossiping clumps. Other people's children waited, climbing on the jungle gym or hop scotching across the painted squares on the sealed court or playing games on their phones.

"She'll be fine," Carly panted, having caught up. "Polly is with her, and Rhys will keep an eye on them both." Sure enough, the two girls were seated together on a bench in the sun outside the head teacher's office, where Ryan could watch them as he worked.

Rhys, his cell phone to his ear, rapped on the inside of his window and held up a finger while mouthing 'one moment'.

"I am so sorry," Claudia began when he came outside, but Rhys waved a hand in dismissal. "You couldn't help your car breaking down, and Abbie is fine, as you see. Abbie and Polly, would you go get your bags from my office?"

Claudia made to go with Abbie, but Rhys put out a hand to stop her.

"I don't want to alarm you, Claudia, but when you phoned to say you'd broken down and you were waiting for Carly to come and get you, I went out to bring Abbie and Polly back in here where I could keep an eye on them. They were fine. Still inside the gate, as they should have been. But as I came up to them, a white sedan car that was outside on the bus stop started up and pulled away. It's probably nothing, but given the other incidents, I thought you should know."

"Stone, come out from under there."

Ethan slid out from under Claudia's car, which Ben had towed in from ten miles out of town, to face two scowling men. Rhys Phillips he knew. The school head teacher, very protective of Claudia. He didn't have a name for the other man, but he'd seen him with Claudia's friend, the one he'd spoken to at the parade.

"Can I help you, gentlemen?" Years in prison had made him an expert at conflict avoidance. Hands in view. Voice mild. Body relaxed with no sign he was ready to run.

A little of the tension drained away, but Phillips' words were still an accusation. "You can tell us where to find your friend with the white sedan."

"I don't have a…" His brain caught up with the meaning behind their presence here. "Claudia! What's happened? Are they alright?"

"So you do know something." That was the other man.

Ethan hoped they were going to tell him what he needed to know soon, because he didn't know how long he could remain civil when his fear was spiking. "Ben told me some scum-sucker in a white sedan has been watching the kids at RDA. Are they okay? Claudia and Abbie?"

Phillips sneered. "Whatever you had planned didn't work, if that's what you want to know."

They were okay. Thank God.

The unnamed man added, "Good try. Fixing her car so it would break down then sending your friend to fetch Abbie. But Rhys here foiled your plot, and we're here to make sure you get out of town."

Stay calm, Ethan. These guys are on Claudia's side. "Look, I had nothing to do with it, and if Abbie and Claudia are in danger, I'm not going anywhere. You think the car was deliberately sabotaged?" In another minute, he'd have worked that out himself. How else would the oil lines have developed a leak in the brief time since he'd thoroughly checked the vehicle?

"You tell us, Mr. Mechanic." They were still hostile. He had to convince them. Someone out there was a threat to all Ethan held dear, and those who wanted to protect Claudia and Abbie couldn't afford to waste energy fighting each other.

"It fits. Look." He pointed to the oil dripping onto the concrete under the car. "Hole in the oil feed line. And I put a new one in not two weeks ago. Someone wanted the car to stop and didn't much care when."

Unnamed man turned to Phillips. "Do you believe him?"

"Not even a little bit," Phillips answered. "What's he doing hanging around Fairburn? Claudia doesn't want him and he doesn't know little Abbie."

"I know she's my daughter," Ethan said. "I know Claudia was the best thing that ever happened to me, and I messed up bad when I drove her away. I know I'd lay down my life for either of them."

"Easy to say." Phillips sneered, unconvinced, but unnamed man considered Ethan from under lowered brows. Before he could speak, his phone rang, a fragment that sounded classical, cut off when he swiped his thumb across the screen. "Trent Becker."

What the caller said shocked him. "What! Are the others alright? Have you rung the police? Okay, we're heading home now."

He slid the phone back into his pocket and met Ethan's eyes. "Abbie's been taken. White sedan guy scooped her right off the pony in our own frigging front field! Carly's hysterical and Claudia's worse. The police are on their way and you're coming with us, Stone."

Ethan grabbed his jacket and led the way towards the car the men had arrived in. "You better believe I am. That's my daughter you're talking about."

They drove a short distance, silent and tense, and turned in through the gates of a smallholding a couple of miles out of town just as the rain that had been threatening all afternoon began; a sudden deluge. They ran through the downpour into the house where Claudia was waiting.

She grabbed his arm as he came into the room. "Ethan! Ethan, tell me where she is! I'll do anything! Just give her back!"

Ethan put a hand over hers. "Claudia, it wasn't me. I haven't done this. But I'll find her for you. I swear to you I will bring her back or die trying."

"Mr. Stone?" The man didn't need a uniform for Ethan to identify him as a police officer. Him, and the other man standing silent at Claudia's shoulder. The stance and the watchful eyes told their own tale. "Marcus Freeman, New Zealand Police. I need you to answer some questions."

"Don't waste time with me, man," Ethan begged. "Go find this damned car. It wasn't me, I tell you. Ask them!"

Freeman wasn't deterred. "Do you know a man by the name of Jack Quinton?"

Ethan took a deep breath. The fastest way to get help for Abbie was to convince them he had done nothing. He had to stay calm. He had to answer the questions. "No. I don't think so."

"This man?" Freeman held out a photo, and Ethan had begun to shake his head before he took a proper look, and then another.

"That's Jake Quill," he stated. "Phillips, take a look at this. That's Jake, the guy with the Triumph, right?" Phillips took the photo and nodded, as Ethan turned back to Freeman. "You think he has something to do with this?"

Claudia's voice shook as she answered the question. "It's Jack, Ethan. He was my… We had history."

Freeman gave her a compassionate glance before resuming the questions. "Where did you see him, Mr. Stone?"

"Here. In Fairburn. He brought his motorcycle in for servicing. I also saw him in Valentine Bay and in Barnsley earlier in the week. Damn it to hell! Look, on Monday, I saw him in Valentine Bay hiring a sea-going motor boat, and on the way back in Barnsley, he came into the sports shop while I was there and bought a sleeping bag, some tramping boots, and some maps to the regional park."

"Where in the park?"

"You'd have to ask the shop. I didn't... I was just there looking at riding helmets." Ethan caught Claudia's eyes, his own pleading. "I thought Claudia might let me buy one for Abbie for Christmas. I stayed in the corner, out of sight. We'd had a bit of trouble, and I didn't want trouble."

"What sort of trouble?" Freeman asked, his eyebrows raised.

"He objected to the time it was taking to get in the part to fix his motorcycle. It was my day off, and I didn't want to hear him going on about it again. I didn't have an idea... Look, can you guys get on the radio to someone out in Valentine Bay to watch for him? If he's taking Abbie that way, he'll not be there for another half hour yet."

Freeman frowned. "We know our job, Mr. Stone."

Claudia moved closer to Ethan, and he put an arm around her. Through his worry for their daughter, it felt good to have her close, to be facing the world with her at his side again, but her next words chilled him to the bone. "If Jack has taken her, we must find her quickly. He has already tried to kill her once."

"We don't know that the kidnapper is Jack Quinton," Freeman explained. "We will act, Claudia, but we don't want to go off in all directions without a plan.

At that moment, Claudia's phone dinged. She pulled it out and looked at it.

"Check that," Freeman ordered. "It might be our kidnapper."

Claudia slid her index finger across the phone and held it to her ear. "Jack! Jack, what have you done with Abbie?"

"Hit the microphone button," Ethan whispered, and Claudia did in time for them to hear, "Mummy, save me."

Claudia clutched Ethan's hand. "Abbie, are you alright? Jack, please let me talk to her. Please, please."

They could all hear the answer. "Shut up, Claudia. I'm talking, and you and Abbie are doing as you're told. You can make sure your little brat stays safe, but you have to do exactly as I tell you. Do you hear me? Do you understand?"

Claudia was nodding "Yes. Yes. Anything."

"Be waiting outside the Cherry Tree on the main highway in forty minutes. Got that? Forty minutes. Who's there with you?"

Claudia looked around at them all. Ethan, Freeman and the other police officer with him. Her friends. "Carly and Trent. I'm at their house."

"Just them?" said the voice from the other end of the call. "Don't lie to me, Claudia. You know I can tell when you lie."

Ethan squeezed Claudia's hand, trying to lend her his strength. She squeezed back as she answered. "Just Carly and Trent. And their children."

"Okay." The voice sounded smug. "Don't call the police. Just be waiting. Alone. One of your friends can drop you off but they had better be gone by the time I get there, or else. You and I are going to take a little trip."

"And you'll let Abbie go?" Claudia asked.

"Abbie will be fine. As long as you follow instructions."

Click. He had ended the call. Claudia turned to Ethan, her eyes huge and swimming in a face drained of color, and his arms had wrapped around her before he'd considered whether his comfort would be welcome. Her own arms hugging him as if he was the one solid rock in a stormy world reassured him, and he dropped a kiss on her hair.

"We'll get her back, Claudia," he vowed.

"He's crazy." Phillips was shaking his head. "You can't go with him, Claudia."

"She might not have to." Ethan fixed the police officer with a glare. "Now will you get hold of the sports shop? If we can find out what maps he bought—look, I'm guessing that the boat is for his escape, and the hut is to stash Abbie, and maybe Claudia, too. Somewhere in the regional park. No road access; he was specific about that. But he has a damned good bike. He'll have left the car somewhere and taken Abbie the rest of the way by bike."

"Or he's dropped Abbie somewhere else, and plans to take Claudia to the hut," Phillips argued. "Or the hut has nothing to do with it."

"No. The hut matters. Hiring a deep-sea boat and a hut makes no sense unless they're both part of his plan." Becker was frowning, and Ethan could almost see the wheels turning in the man's head. "I know the guy who owns the shop. I'll call him. Marcus, you talk to the police station in Valentine Bay and make sure that boat can't leave. Rhys, get hold of Pete from the tramping club, would you, and ask him to bring his topographical maps over? Of the park?"

Ethan nodded. "The hut he's using has to be reachable by motor bike and within three-quarters of an hour of Fairburn. Closer, probably, but let's be certain."

In moments, they were all busy talking on the phone, while Ethan stood there, a useless fifth wheel. No. Not quite useless. Not while he could hold Claudia, his arm around her shoulders, lending her some of his strength. "We'll find her," he assured her again. "We'll get her back."

"I caught the owner before he left the shop," Becker said. "These are the maps." He waved a piece of paper with some numbers on it.

Phillips, who had managed to track his tramping club contact down after several calls, grabbed the paper and read the numbers out. "He's coming straight over," he said, as he thumbed off the phone.

The cop also reported on results. "We've got two patrol cars on their way to Valentine Bay, and the constable who lives out there heading for the wharf to talk to the harbor master."

"See?" Ethan told Claudia. "Your friends will find her. She'll be fine."

"And so will Claudia," Becker announced. He raised his voice to be heard in the adjoining room, where his wife was trying to keep her children from panicking while hiding her own fear. "Carly, love, get me the box of bugs, will you?" To the others, he explained, "Listening devices. I've been collecting different kinds and testing them out."

They were tiny things that needed to be handled with tweezers. As Becker fitted one into a pocket formed by undoing a couple of stitches on the hem of Claudia's wristband, he commented on his selection. "This one is top of the line for its price. It'll be in *Speed of Darkness*. My villain is using them to bug the detective."

"Won't he be able to detect it?" Claudia asked, with barely a quaver in her voice.

"He might," Becker acknowledged. "Unlikely, though. It's pretty sophisticated. Spread spectrum. He'd have to have the right equipment and the training to use it."

Claudia shook her head. "I doubt that he'll look. He thinks I'm stupid. He thinks everyone except him is stupid. He might search me, but he probably won't think of looking inside the wristband. After all, how would I get hold of a sophisticated listening device?"

Ethan was still holding Claudia, his arm around her shoulders. "I don't want you going alone." He turned to the police officers. "Can we get Abbie while he's coming for Claudia? A helicopter?"

Marcus Freeman shook his head, regretfully. "We can't get a helicopter up in this weather. And it's getting worse."

Carly answered the doorbell, and ushered in a man in an oilskin with a satchel full of maps, who was introduced as Pete.

They gathered around the dining table as Pete spread out the two maps that matched the ones Jack Quinton had purchased.

"No way he's got a car up there," Pete warned. "Look, you've got a hill climb here, and another here. Steps, not a track. And the width between trees, here? Not a chance. Not on the swing bridge up here, either. In this weather, I wouldn't want to do it even on foot, and from what you say he hasn't had time to do the hike, let alone get back again. Which he must have, because there's no cell phone coverage in that part of the hills."

Ethan wasn't prepared to believe the maps had nothing to do with Quinton's plotting. Maybe he just felt the need to do something, but surely… "How about on a bike? Quinton has a damned good motorcycle."

Pete stuck out his lips as he thought, then nodded. "People have done it on a bike," he acknowledged. "Be dangerous in this weather, though."

"Quinton made it. And out again."

"If we're right," Freeman pointed out. "If we're wrong, whoever checks out the huts is on a wild goose chase. And a dangerous one."

"Does anyone have any better ideas?" Becker asked, looking around with one eyebrow raised.

Freeman pursed his lips. "We've got a call out for anyone who might have seen the white sedan or the motorcycle."

"How long will it take till you find her that way? And meanwhile she's…" *Calm. Stay calm.* Ethan took a deep breath. "Look, if she's at the boat, or if he's planning to bring her there, you guys'll stop him and save her and Claudia. But if she isn't…"

Claudia's interruption silenced him, and the others who were about to speak. "Then he is in charge, just as he prefers. I won't do anything to risk Abbie. You have to go after her, Ethan. If she's up in the hills…"

"My bike'll get me there, Claudia," Ethan assured her.

Phillips shook his head. "It's a roadster. Great bike, but a dirt bike'd be better."

"It'll have to do," Ethan replied. "We don't have time to find a dirt bike. Can someone drop me back at the garage to collect her?"

"I have two dirt bikes," Phillips told him. "Both of us going will be safer than one, and we'll have a better chance of getting there on the off-roads."

After a moment's thought, Ethan nodded, before turning back to Claudia. "If she's where we think, I can have her in half an hour, or a bit more. I don't like to think of you with that maniac. Can you talk him into waiting? Claim a delay?"

Claudia shook her head. "I'm not prepared to risk it. Trent will drop me off, and listen to what happens, and Carly will relay messages. And the police will be close. Trust them, Ethan. They'll make sure I'm not taken." She stretched up and he bent his neck to accept the kiss on his cheek. "Go and find our daughter. Bring her back to me."

"If I don't find her, the police will. We'll bring her home, Claudia. Just stay safe yourself, okay?"

Claudia had forgotten Ethan's calm. Before a race, he'd retreat somewhere deep within and come back intensely focused; all fear, excitement, anger, joy — all emotions walled off to allow his brain and his body to concentrate on the task. With one or two deep breaths, he had done it again, and the sight allowed her to take her own first deep breath since she saw Abbie taken.

In moments, he and Rhys were gone, out into the pouring rain. Now it was her turn. "Time to go," she told Trent.

"Wait!" Carly rushed off to her room and came back a few minutes later with a heavy-duty rain jacket and pants. "My bike riding gear. In case he's back on the Triumph. It'll keep you dryish."

Claudia insisted that Trent stop a hundred yards away from Cherry Tree Park, planted beside the main highway as a place to contemplate losses in war. "Stay in the car until he arrives," Trent suggested. "It's a deluge out there."

"I'll be fine. I want you gone before he gets here." Claudia would obey Jack. For now.

Trent agreed, and as she trudged along the muddy side of the road, he did a u turn and sped away back towards Fairburn.

Jack kept her waiting, of course. Anything to leave her edgy and defenseless. But Carly's coat kept her dry, reminding her that her friends hadn't abandoned her, however she might have felt as she watched Trent's taillights disappearing into the rain.

Ethan. She held on to the memory of his calm. The repeated concussions had stolen that focus and left a roiling anger in its place. Through her fear for her daughter, her worry for herself, she noted that he had his balance back, and put the thought away to consider later. If there was a later.

Two white sedans passed without slowing down. Then a motor bike, but not a Triumph. Finally, Jack arrived, his bike pulling off the road and stopping a few inches from her feet. She thought so.

Jack had pushed up his goggles and was examining her. "Good. That jacket'll work. There's a cycle helmet in the side panier. Put it on."

"Where's Abbie?" she asked

Jack's grin was smug. "Safe. I've stashed her away. If you do exactly as you are told, I'll let you phone your friends and tell them where to find her."

When he was in this mood, it was safe to try to bargain. "Tell me now, and I'll come with you and do everything you tell me."

"No way." Safe, but not productive, and a glint in his eyes warned her not to push too far. "Get the helmet on, Claudia, and get on the bike. Oh. And give me your phone, first."

She tried one more time. "How do I know she's even alive? You've already tried to kill her once. If you've left her out in this rain…"

"For Pete's sake. Will you stop driveling on about that fricking brat? I left her alive, and she'll stay that way if you just come with me. Stupid woman." His eyes narrowed and his voice dropped in the menacing growl she dreaded. "You're mine. When we have time, I'll remind you of that."

A truck passed, spraying them with water, and a second or two later, a pickup with a dual cab. Marcus's private vehicle; the one he'd been driving today. The driver didn't look their way, and Jack wasn't watching.

He'd decided to give her a bit more information. "Okay. I stashed her in a hut up in the regional park. She's locked in, but she's got food and water. She'll be okay for a few days, and by then you and I will be well away. Now. Get on the bike. Be good, and I'll tell you which hut and let you phone your friends. But you had better obey my every word, bitch, or your daughter may not survive. Not many hikers out in this weather. Give me your phone."

In less than a minute, her phone was in the bushes, and they were on their way north towards Barnsley.

Ethan's phone vibrated against his chest, and he pulled off the road to take the call. "Ethan?" It was Claudia's friend Carly. "Ethan, you were right about the hut. Jack has just told Claudia. Not which one, just that she is up in the regional park."

"Is Claudia okay?" he asked.

"Yes. She's doing what she's told. Ethan, hurry."

Ethan passed on the news to Rhys in a few terse words, and they pulled back onto the narrow, unsealed road that led up into the hills, arriving a few minutes later at a shingled parking lot, currently empty, which marked the end of the road. A white fence comprised of short posts with a single plank a couple of feet off the ground blocked the way into the regional park. A gap in the fence allowed hikers to enter, with another short fence beyond the gap leaving a narrow path to the left and the right. The notice on the short fence pictured a horse, a dog, a motorcycle, and a bicycle, all with red crosses over them.

"What now?" The gap was too small to allow even the small dirt bikes to wiggle through.

"Check to see if there's a loose board," Ethan said, propping his bike on the stand and heading off along the fence to try each board with his hands. Rhys followed his lead, checking the fence in the other direction.

"The only loose board I could find was along there where the manuka scrub grows hard up to the fence," Rhys reported a few minutes later. "We can't get through there."

Ethan followed him over to the board and wrestled it off its remaining nail. It was a bit narrow, but stained rather than painted with a good gripping surface even in this rain. "We'll jump. Have you done any jumping?"

"A bit." Quite a bit from the almost smile he caught on Rhys's face.

With Rhys's help, Ethan soon had the board lined up with the path beyond the entrance, the remaining nails helping to anchor the upper end on the top rail of the inner fence. "Right. Line up straight on the board. Gun it. You'll need some speed to drive you the distance after your tires leave the ground." Rhys probably knew all this, but Ethan wasn't taking any chances. "Once you're airborne, look at the spot you plan to land, not at the ramp. Once you're in the air, look beyond, up the path. Don't brake. Let the slope of the path slow you down."

Rhys sailed over easily, and braked thirty or forty yards up the track. Ethan followed, passing him without stopping, keeping the speed up so his wheels didn't slide on the muddy track.

Jack didn't stop in Barnsley, but turned towards the coast. So Ethan was right again. As quietly as she could, though Jack wouldn't hear anything less than a shout over the noise of the engine and the wind and rain, Claudia said "The road to the coast." If Jack heard, he didn't care, and whoever was listening now knew which road they had taken. She tucked her chin into the coat, keeping as much out of the wind behind Jack as she could. Through the arms he'd insisted she wrap around him, she could feel his tension. Could his words be trusted? Was Ethan even now speeding towards their daughter?

She had a sudden image of Ethan's bike slipping in the mud and tipping him over a cliff or into a tree or a rock. "Please, God, let him be careful." But Abbie. Her little girl was up in the hills, locked in a tramper's hut, frightened and alone. "Please, God, let him be quick."

The route proved to be clearer than they expected. Another bike had been there earlier in the day and left plenty of signs of its passage—deep ruts here, a spray of dirt across a rockface there, broken swathes of muddied undergrowth somewhere else. Ethan grinned as he leapt the evidence of a particularly nasty wipe-out on a rocky outcrop that was slick with mud. Coming out, not going in, so after the bastard had abandoned Abbie. Not bad enough, evidently, to keep Quinton from picking his bike up and carrying on, but at the very least he had some nasty bruises.

Behind him, the school teacher was managing well for a hobbyist; more cautiously than Ethan, but that wasn't a bad thing in these conditions. His fans from the old days wouldn't believe it of him. He used to throw himself at every obstacle, and the only speed that counted was flat out. But a combination of hare and tortoise was what Abbie needed now.

The trail led down a slope towards a stream that would be fordable in ordinary conditions, but that now raged in an ungovernable torrent. A flat rock around halfway down offered a launching point, and Ethan took it, judging his speed and angle just right to drop onto the track on the other side of the gully, gunning the engine to lift him out of the way before Rhys followed.

Rhys's landing wasn't as smooth, but he crashed into undergrowth which at least broke his fall. He was on his feet before Ethan could ride back to check, testing that the bike was unharmed, waving Ethan on as he remounted.

Over the next ridge and down the other side, and repeat. The track led into a stand of regrowth rimu, the trunks nearly half a yard across and the branches starting well above their heads. Ethan, intent on the marks left by the Triumph, would have worn the full brunt of a rogue low branch if Rhys hadn't shouted, "Look out!" As it was, he ducked too late to prevent the outer twigs and leaves from striking him.

No matter. In moments they were out the other side of the forest and climbing again, this time snaking back and forth across the hill face, always climbing towards one of the higher peaks in the range.

The hut was beyond a gully between this peak and the next. As the zig-zag climb ended and the track straightened out to round the peak, Ethan expected to see the swing bridge that was marked on the map. *Just a few more minutes, Abbie.*

The swing bridge was there. Dangling into the gully from the supports on the other side, just a few twisted remnants of concrete and steel remaining of the supports that had tethered it to this side.

Rhys pulled up beside Ethan where he sat on his bike examining the ruin.

"Now what?"

Eleven

Fifteen minutes out of Barnsley, Jack pulled off into a layby, stopping the bike next to a parked car; a red hatchback.

"We do the next bit in comfort," he told Claudia. He dismounted, gesturing her to do the same, then pressed the button on the door handle. "Your chariot awaits."

"I thought you had a white sedan," Claudia said. "Not a red — what sort of car is it?"

He narrowed his eyes. She felt the blow before she saw it coming — not one of the pinches or twists he'd dealt her so often in the past, but a full-on punch that sent her flying. She sat, dazed, where she had fallen while he ranted at her.

"You have a bug, you bitch. You're telling them where we are."

He dragged her up by one arm, and began patting her down, continuing to berate her until he found the bug under her wristband. He whistled into it and giggled, suddenly cheerful again as he dropped it and ground it under his boot.

"It doesn't matter. I have you for safe passage. But you've missed your chance for your daughter, you bitch. I know where she is and I'm not telling. Better hope this weather lets up so they can find her, 'cause we'll be far away before anyone can get to her. Is she nervous, Claudia? Does she have nightmares? About the accident, maybe?"

Claudia let him manhandle her into the car, and stayed silent, grateful that Trent had a writer's devious mind. The second bug — the one sewn into her tank to the hem of her tee-shirt — would be catching the whole tirade.

Not for the first time, Ethan checked to the network indicator on his phone. Nothing. "Going 'round will take hours. I'm jumping." Fifty yards across, and ten down, with unknown terrain on the other side. But what choice did he have.

Rhys blanched at the thought. "I can't do it, man. I'm sorry."

"You shouldn't even try," Ethan told him. "You've got three daughters to go home to. This is my family; it's my job to do." Give the man a crumb for his ego, and Ethan had one ready. "I need you this side, anyway. I'll get over okay, but it's downhill. There'll be no way back. Wait for me here, and when I know Abbie is safe, I'll come and tell you. You'll need to ride out on your own and let Claudia know. Search and Rescue, too, so they can come and get us. Be careful, Rhys. Take your time. We're counting on you."

Ethan was less confident about the jump than he wanted Rhys to know, but Claudia was depending on him, and so was Abbie, though she didn't know it.

He planned it out carefully. How far back along the track he needed to be to get up the speed he needed to have. With Rhys's help, he cleared possible obstacles. Then the two men shook hands. "Good luck," Rhys said, and Ethan returned the wish, before heading back along the track for his run.

A deep breath and another. A whispered prayer, which surprised him because he would have called himself an unbeliever. But if there was a God, then surely that Being would want to save Abbie?

He was riding today for the highest stakes of his career. He put that thought to one side. The incessant rain. Gone, except as it affected the contact of tires to dirt. Claudia, and the hope in her eyes. Not significant. His fear of another crash, one he was unlikely to survive. Not a helpful thought.

He revved the bike. Took another deep breath. Exhaled all his cares and gunned the engine, racing down the track and straight over the cliff's edge. For a long blissful moment he was weightless, drifting across the gully, his senses on such high alert that the handful of seconds seemed much longer. Then the other side was rushing towards him, much too fast, the lip he needed to reach much too high. He shifted his weight, trying to bring up the front wheel, feeling it jar onto the bank, throwing his whole body forward to drive the bike up onto the track to safety, grateful even when it spun out of control and hurled him into the mud, because what was a spill when he had made the crossing alive?

The bike was okay and so was he. He waved to Rhys and remounted. Now for the hut.

The road to Valentine Bay was suspiciously empty of traffic. What had the police done? Stopped all vehicles from both ends? Jack, full of the plans he'd decided to share with Claudia, didn't seem to notice.

"I've planned it all," he kept saying. "Just you and me, Claudia, like it should have been all along. What a piece of luck having your scumbag ex wander into town. An ex-convict? A mechanic? With a Triumph? The police will have a field day. That's why I used the Triumph for part of our escape. Not mine, of course. That's waiting for us at the boat. I stole one off your boyfriend the teacher."

Their escape by sea-going boat was his main theme, but woven into it, constantly repeated, was a threat and a complaint. "If I can't have you, no one will. If you won't come with me, I don't care if I live or die, but I will make sure you're dead before I kill myself."

Then he would remember that he had her in his power, and begin gloating again. "Everything I've done is for you. You kept putting that brat—his brat—first. You've been a very, very naughty girl, Claudia, and you will need to be punished."

He proceeded to detail the punishments he had in mind, occasionally asking Claudia for a response. She managed a meek 'yes' or 'no' while imagining all sorts of horrible punishments for him. If he succeeded in getting her onto the boat, and she was determined he wouldn't, she would wait for him to sleep and have her revenge, whoever else was aboard, whatever the cost to her. She was never again going to be his victim.

Twelve

few more minutes controlling the bike on slick mud up a narrow track, and Ethan arrived at a small hiker's hut; the usual Department of Conservation wooden building. Four walls with a window and door letting on to the small covered porch that ran the length of the front; a stove pipe at one end, and undoubtedly bunk beds around the other two sides.

He was off the bike and up onto the porch before the motor had cut out. The bolts that shut the door from the outside screeched as he drew them back, first the one at the top and then the one at the bottom.

"Abbie?"

He stepped inside into gloom. "Abbie?" He kept his voice low and friendly. She was nowhere to be seen, but someone had been eating crackers straight from the packet, which had been abandoned on the rumpled nest of a sleeping bag on the floor near the iron pot belly stove. No heat radiated from that end of the room. If Quinton had left Abbie with a fire, it had burned out long since.

"It's Ethan Stone. Remember? We talked at the parade." He stood in the doorway. No point in dripping all over the floor, and stripping off his wet weather gear would have to wait until he'd reported to Rhys. The first order of business when he got back would be to start a fire using the logs piled along the wall outside the door.

"Your mother asked me to come and find you."

Abbie's head appeared from the shadows of one of the upper bunks. Her scowl suggested she didn't trust him an inch. *Good girl*.

"Where's Mummy?"

"She couldn't come," Ethan explained. On an inspiration, he added, "That bastard Jack cut down the bridge, and I had to jump the gully on Mr. Phillips' motor bike."

Abbie giggled. "You said a bad word."

If insulting Jack was all it took to win her trust, he was happy to oblige. "He's a bad man," Ethan insisted, and she nodded vigorously and wriggled closer to the edge of the bed.

"Sweetie, can you be brave just a few minutes more while I let Mr. Phillips know I've found you? Then he can go and tell your mummy. She's very worried about you."

Abbie's eyes welled, but she nodded. "Okay."

"Unless… Do you want to come? I can tuck you inside my jacket to keep you dry."

He held his breath while the dark eyes so like his own examined him thoroughly. At last she nodded. "Okay." She shifted to put her legs over the side, feeling for the ladder, and he restrained the urge to rush to help. Still, he was poised to leap to her rescue, his breathing once more suspended until she'd made her careful way down to the floor.

He unzipped his jacket and squatted down.

"Put your arms around my neck, Abbie, and I'll do up the jacket to keep us both dry and warm."

The child obeyed, but expressed her displeasure with the arrangement once he had her zipped in and was carrying her to the bike.

"I wanna see, Mr. Ethan."

Of course she did. He'd have been the same at that age, and he'd lay odds Claudia was, too. He straddled the bike and loosened the zip enough that she could turn around before he zipped up again, to just under her chin. "All comfie, Abbie?"

"Yep. Go!"

Half way between Barnsley and Valentine Bay, where the road ran straight through Whakatami valley, they were overtaken by a sports utility vehicle, and Claudia had to lower her eyes for fear Jack might glance her way and see her glee. Carly's father's SUV had been locked away while they were overseas, so there was no way Jack could know about it, but for sure Trent at least and probably Carly too were inside and on their way to join in the rescue.

Jack was paying no attention to her, instead complaining bitterly about the lack of guts in the hired vehicle as he pushed his foot further to the floor, trying to catch up with the SUV. The road wound up into the hills again, and the SUV left them far behind, but Jack turned his irritation on another car that came up behind them and made several attempts to pass.

Speeding up on the straights and nudging the center line to deny the car its opportunity cheered Jack up again. "Can't drive for tuppence," he chortled. "You've got to make your opportunities. You can't just hang back and wait for them to be handed to you. Like you and me, Claudia. I took you, and you're mine. It'll be good. You'll see."

Claudia said nothing, and suddenly, as they came through the gap in the hills that led to the coast, he put his foot to the floor, leaning grimly over the wheel. "Say it. Say you know it'll be good or I swear, Claudia, I'm driving straight ahead."

Over the sea wall onto the rocks? No. It was full tide, and they'd be straight into the sea. "It'll be good." She put all the enthusiasm into the words she could fake, and he eased off and turned into the curve.

"That's right. We're good together, you and I. We don't need anyone else. Just you and me, alone."

"And Abbie?" She dared, and then screamed as he jerked the wheel, so they swerved towards the sea wall, once again correcting, this time so much at the last moment that the side of the car scraped along the concrete.

He screeched louder than the tortured metal. "Don't say her name. Don't even think about the little bitch."

Claudia sucked both lips into her mouth, stiff with the effort not to react. As they came in sight the first houses of the little seaside town, he broke the silence. "I'm sorry. I'm sorry I shouted. You make me so angry, Claudia. Haven't I always been good to you? Haven't I given you everything you needed? But still you won't do what I tell you. I can be kind. You know I can. Just be nice to me, Claudia. Love me. Everything will be fine if you love only me."

"Where are we going, Jack?" He'd detailed the plan for their escape, but not their destination.

"Far from here. I'm leaving everything, and it's your fault." He returned to his grievance. "Why did you run away, Claudia? Didn't you know it was for the best?"

He had slowed down as they approached the shopping area that sprawled along the street leading to the port, and she wondered briefly whether she could wrench the door open and leap out.

"I'll come with you," she said. "But first I need you to tell someone how to find my daughter. Do that, and I won't struggle or call out or disobey you in any way."

The car surged forward in a sudden burst of speed, and someone sauntering across the road in front of them had to jump to avoid being knocked down. "I told you not to talk about her." It was a grumble rather than a shriek. He was silent, thinking her offer over, she hoped.

He confirmed it when he asked, "You won't try to get away?"

"I won't." Did she sound sincere? She hoped she sounded sincere.

"You promise?"

"I promise." Did promises made to madmen count? She crossed her fingers in the old childhood habit to turn aside the ill effects of lying.

They were entering the port, driving past the working boats belonging to local fishermen and tour guides and taking the road to the marina and its pleasure craft.

"Okay," Jack conceded. "Once we're on the boat and out at sea, I'll give you the hut… the location, and let you phone your friend. But you promise, right? You'll come with me. You'll be mine again, the way it is meant to be."

"I promise," she repeated, her heart lifting at the slip of his tongue. The hut. Ethan was right. Even now, he might be with Abbie.

She waited obediently in the car until he'd retrieved a bag from the trunk, got out when he told her to, and walked meekly ahead of him in the direction he indicated. Let him think her completely cowed.

Near the end of one of the docks, a sleek ocean-going motor launch was moored. Jack frowned at the man waiting; a burly fellow with too many years of good living on his girth. "Who are you?" Jack demanded.

"Mr. Quill?" The man returned Jack's nod. "Bruce Watson, the harbor master here. Andy asked me to do the boat handover, and I have a few questions. Just regulations."

"I did all the paperwork," Jack argued, "and me and my girlfriend are in a bit of a rush. We want to get out through the heads before dark."

Watson spread his hands. "In this weather? You'd do better to wait for morning, Mr. Quinton."

Claudia controlled her wince and for a second thought Jack hadn't noticed Watson's slip, but two words into his reply, he grabbed Claudia by the shoulder and spun her to face him. "You told them. You told the police."

In one quick movement, he threw his bag onto the boat. As Watson dithered, shifting from one foot to another and biting his lip, Jack tugged Claudia around again, holding her against him with an arm across her chest. She felt something cold touch her throat, and then a sting as it cut before he withdrew it from direct contact with her skin.

"No, man," Watson protested.

Jack waved his knife, so close that the weapon was a blur in her peripheral vision. "Get the boat started."

"Now, mister, you don't want to do that." Watson was backing away, his hands spread in surrender.

Jack returned the knife to her throat and she felt the sting of another shallow cut. "Get the boat started," he repeated.

At her yelp, Watson jumped, and then scurried aboard. Jack propelled Claudia ahead of him as he followed, taking station in the corner of the cockpit where he could watch Watson start the engine.

"Now head her out, nice and steady," he instructed. "If you're lucky, I might let you off at the heads. If you cause trouble, I'll just drop you over the side and let you swim."

Watson slid his eyes sideways, but said nothing.

The police launch was waiting just outside the marina entrance. "Let her go, Mr. Quinton," shouted Marcus from among the knot of men in the bow cockpit.

Except for a glance, Jack ignored him.

Claudia found her courage in thoughts of her child. "At least tell them where to find Abbie, Jack. I beg you." She braced for another cut but instead shrieked at the sharp pain when he gave her hair a vicious tug.

"I'm not telling. You broke your promise. You broke your promise." His own voice had risen to a shriek, and he almost lost hold of her, before his eyes widened with alarm. The police launch was drawing closer. Jack pulled her back into his cruel embrace and the knife pricked her throat again. "Get back! I'll kill her rather than let any of you have her."

Thirteen

With his precious cargo aboard, Ethan took the downward slope at just enough speed to maintain control, stopping a cautious distance from the edge to wave to Rhys, just visible through the rain.

Rhys gave him a thumbs up, and Abbie said something. Ethan bent his head, curling his back to bring his ear closer. "What was that, sweetie?"

"Gan we jump? I want my mummy."

"No, Abbie. I'm sorry, but we can't jump." He explained that he'd been jumping downhill, and even alone, he couldn't make it uphill, especially since the rain had intensified. She turned to examine his face as he spoke, and she didn't argue. On the other side of the gully, Rhys had remounted his bike and started it. He waved and left, disappearing around the side of the hill. Ethan hoped he'd take care. And hurry. The sooner the word got to the police and Claudia that Abbie was safe, the sooner they could arrest Jack.

"Let's go back to the hut and get a fire going." Ethan took it slowly, but in minutes they were back in the relative comfort of the small structure. The stove was empty—no fire; not even any kindling—but the wood pile yielded dry logs, and some of them had dead moss on them which would make good tinder. Abbie helped, trotting in with a load of wood and out to fetch another, and soon they had a fire laid and more logs ready to put on once it was lit.

Next, a search for matches, which Ethan found on a nook in the stone wall of the chimney. Only five in the box. Let's see whether enough remained from his half-remembered scouting days — abandoned when he took up cycling — to get the damned thing lit.

He burned through three matches before the tinder caught, but after that the teepee of kindling was soon ablaze. The smaller logs that he'd propped close enough to heat caught fire. As the teepee collapsed, he used the poker to nudge the side logs closer together.

"That should be okay now." He hoped. If they were here overnight, he'd have to keep waking to feed the fire, but that was okay. He could keep Abbie warm, which was what counted.

"Now, sweetheart, let's see what we've got to eat," he said. "Did Quinton leave you with any food?"

"Tha' bassard Jag jus' lef' graggers." Abbie said the mild swear word with great relish. Ethan would be explaining himself to Claudia when they got out of here, but he wasn't about to correct her now. Especially once he'd looked in the plastic bag Abbie showed him. That bastard Jack had left the child locked in a cold hut with a sleeping back and six packets of supermarket brand water-crackers. Nothing to put on them. Nothing to drink but water from the tap. And no fire.

The shelves above the primitive sink yielded some cans of stew, to which Abbie wrinkled her nose, a plastic jar of dried rice, some dehydrated meals well past their use-by date, and — he was pleased to see — a jar of instant coffee and another of tea bags.

Ethan's Boy Scout skills might be close to zero, but he could rustle up a meal out of these unpromising ingredients. Yes, and follow up with one of the tins of peaches at the back of the shelf. Abbie watched with great interest as he rinsed out a saucepan from the selection under the sink, half filled it with water, and put it on the stovetop to boil.

"Wha' you doing, Mr. Ethan?"

"I'm going to boil some rice. Once the water's boiling, I'll put the rice in." He crouched down before the sink bench, searching along the shelf for a can opener, finding three in the tray full of ill-assorted cutlery and utensils. When he applied them one after the other to the can, none of them worked.

He checked the pot. The water was warm, but not yet hot.

"Are we jus' having rice?" Abbie asked. Although she'd screwed her nose up at the canned stew, she was even less impressed at the thought of plain rice. Ethan grinned at her, and pulled his Swiss Army knife from his pocket. "I have a trick or two yet, Princess Abigail."

Ethan worked the bottle opener device up and down in a seesaw motion, working his way around the lid of the can until it dropped loose into the stew.

"Mummy calls me Brincess Abigail," Abbie observed. "How'ju know my mummy, Mr. Ethan?"

Ethan needed time to think about his answer. What would Claudia want him to say? "I'll just check the water." It was boiling, so he poured a cup of rice into it, then set another pot on the stove to put the can into. He turned away to fetch the can and met Abbie's eyes. He'd thought she looked just like a miniature and female version of him, but all of a sudden he saw her mother in her. Abbie had just the same air of patient watchfulness on the point of exploding into questions.

"I met your mother a long time ago," he admitted. And soon he was telling her about their first meeting, and then added more. Not that they were a couple, but just stories about her performances and how good she was; about seeing her in the crowd when he raced; about places they'd seen together and things they'd done.

His stories took them through the wait for the rice to cook and the stew to warm, and then entertained Abbie as she made her way through the despised stew with every evidence of enjoyment. By now, it was full dark and wetter than ever, but inside the cabin they were warm and dry, and Ethan left the stove door open so they could eat and get ready for bed by the flickering light of the fire.

After he'd helped Abbie wash her face and assured her that God wouldn't mind if she said her prayers from inside the sleeping bag, he lifted her, sleeping bag and all up onto the top bunk where she had asked to sleep.

"Mr. Ethan? Dell me again about going in the Big Wheel?"

He gave the hand she'd slipped confidingly into his a gentle squeeze. Just as well the place had no mirrors. He didn't have to look at his own besotted smile. "One more story, and then you must sleep, precious girl. Tomorrow, we have to be ready for them to rescue us."

"You resgued," Abbie insisted. "Sdory, please."

So he repeated the tale. How they had found themselves in a town that boasted a magnificent fun fair. How they had evaded the plans of their respective teams, and spent the day wandering the fair, sampling all the delights, including the big wheel. This time, he added the most precious memories of all, winning the hammer of strength contest, and presenting her with a teddy bear. She then bested him at target shooting, choosing as her prize a gift for him: a key tab in the shape of a lucky black enamel cat with green eyes.

He fetched it from his pocket to show her. "I have two black cats now," he said, wriggling the tab off the key ring and offering it to her. "Back in Fairburn, my cat Boss is waiting for me. I hope someone remembers to feed her."

Abbie folded her hand around the tab, tucking it under her chin. "Dell abou' Boss," she inveigled.

He shook his head. She was fighting to keep her eyes open. "Sleep time, princess."

She shut her eyes obediently then opened them again. "Am I your brincess?" she wanted to know.

"You sure are, Abbie," he assured her, and she nodded thoughtfully.

He gave her a kiss on the cheek, then climbed down the ladder. "Time for me to go to sleep, too." He was speaking mostly to himself, but Abbie responded, wriggling closer to the side of the bed so he could see her eyes shining at him from the shadowed alcove.

"Mummy has tha' bear, and dold me tha' sdory."

Ethan felt a smile welling from the depths of his heart. Claudia had kept his bear; had carried it across half a world and through several moves, and told their daughter where it had come from. "Go to sleep, little darling," he told her, resisting the urge to repeat the goodnight peck on the cheek.

She yawned hugely, smiled, and snuggled down until only the top of her head was visible, and if he had to guess, he'd bet she was asleep before he'd finished making the bottom bunk as comfortable as he could with pillows from the other bunks and no blankets.

The police boat escorted them towards the harbor entrance, staying fifty yards off their port side. Jack had barely moved since they'd left the dock, except to move the knife far enough from Claudia's throat that he didn't slit it by mistake. He might still slit it on purpose. The threat kept the police at bay and the harbor master at the wheel, heading them towards the open sea.

Claudia kept still, her face turned to the gap in the hills that marked the entrance to the bay, darkening now as the sun set behind her. Without moving her head, she could look sideways when the police boat surged ahead and see Trent watching from the knot of police officers in the cockpit, so she saw when he lifted the phone he held to his ear, spoke briefly, then gave her a huge grin and a thumbs up. She risked turning her head to mouth, "Abbie?" His vigorous nod caught Jack's attention, but it was too late. Claudia had already dropped, lifting both feet so that her full weight pulled through his loose grip before he could tighten it. He dived to grab her again, but as soon as she felt his arms brush past her head, she'd kicked off into a forward roll, turning it into a cartwheel across the deck, landing on the bench that lined the side and diving over the gunwale into the sea. She struck out towards the police boat, not waiting to see whether it was heading towards her, but it must have turned immediately, because she'd swum no more than a score of strokes before the steep side of the boat loomed beside her.

From the top of the ladder, she looked over to Jack's boat. Her nemesis lay over the gunwale, the harbor master standing over him with a boat hook.

Trent was there to help her into the launch, with the words she'd longed to hear. "Ethan has her. She's safe."

The storm blew out in the night. Should they risk taking the long route out? Or should they wait where they were? In the end, Ethan decided to postpone the decision until Abbie had woken and had breakfast—crackers soaked in the juice of tinned peaches, with the peaches on top. They ate sitting on the verandah, Ethan's legs on the ground and Abbie's dangling.

"Listen." Ethan tipped his head on one side, and Abbie copied him, staring intently in the direction of the whap whap whap sound, steadily increasing, of an approaching helicopter. "I see id!" Abbie bounced in excitement and Ethan steadied her bowl before the sweet mess slid out into her lap. Sure enough, the helicopter rose over the trees, which bowed and waved in its wind. Soon, they could see faces within and in moments it was landing before the hut.

Before the rotors had stopped, Claudia was clambering from the machine, and Ethan caught Abbie's bowl as she thrust it sideways and tumbled off the verandah to run to her mother. Ethan had no attention to spare for the others climbing from the helicopter. He'd never seen anything lovelier than the reunion between mother and daughter, until Claudia looked at him over Abbie's head, and Abbie turned her head and disentangled an arm from around her mother's neck to hold out to him. When Claudia nodded and stood, lifting Abbie in her arms, he dared to approach.

"Are you alright?" he asked.

"Thanks to you," she said, putting her free arm around him as he put his about them both. His women. Or, rather, he was their man: to serve, to protect, to adore as much as they would allow.

Claudia hugged him, "You saved her, Ethan."

"Proud to do it," he said.

"Of gourse," Abbie pronounced, matter-of-factly. "He's my daddy. I'll ged my jacked." She wriggled, so that Claudia had to put her down and ran off into the hut.

"You told her?" Claudia took two steps back, glaring.

One of the people from the helicopter interrupted. "Claudia? Sir? Shall we get on our way?" Claudia made to pass Ethan, and he said, hastily, "It isn't what you think. Give me a chance to explain?"

Abbie emerged from the hut, tugging on her jacket, and Claudia crouched to do up the buttons, then paused. One finger traced the black enamel cat he'd pinned to Abbie's collar, and she looked up at him with a smile.

"You kept it."

It was going to be alright. Ethan let out the breath he had been holding. "And you kept the bear, and told Abbie that her daddy had won it for you. I swear I wasn't going to say anything, Claudia. But she wanted to know how I knew her mummy, and once I started telling her about stuff we did together… The day we went to the fair was a very special day for me."

"Me, too." Claudia straightened and took one of Abbie's hands and Abbie offered the other to Ethan. Together, they lifted her into the helicopter then followed and they were soon airborne. It was too noisy to talk. Too public, too, with the pilot and two other Search and Rescue guys.

But when the helicopter landed on the sports field across the road from Abbie's house and they were walking towards her friends, Abbie running ahead with an ungainly wobble, Ethan dared to ask the question he'd been holding back. "Look, I'm not going to presume. You told me I don't have any rights and I know that. But Claudia, may I stay in Fairburn? Get to know you again? Get to know Abbie?"

The little minx heard and turned. "Of gourse," she said. "I wished for my daddy on the wishing dree. Of gourse you sday."

Claudia and Ethan stopped short, watching the child run to greet Polly.

"So there you have it." Claudia raised an eyebrow, a small smile curving her lips. "Of course you must stay."

"Only if you are okay with it." It would break Ethan's heart to leave, but Abbie had only known him for a few hours. She'd forget him quickly enough.

Claudia's smile warmed his heart. "I'm okay with it. More than okay. I'd like you to stay."

Epilogue

Claudia followed Ethan from Abbie's room, closing the door behind her and looking around her small living room with a happy sigh. It looked beautiful, all decorated for Christmas. The Jesse Tree still took pride of place, complete now, the last story told and the last ornament — showing a mother and baby — fastened to the topmost branch.

Ethan had a hand in almost all the rest, turning up every day for the past fortnight with another item to add to the festive display. The tree in the corner and most of its decorations. The LED lights that festooned the curtain rails and turned the room into a fairy grotto if they stayed up late enough for night to fall. A nativity scene that he and Abbie had set up under the tree, all complete but for the empty crib. The baby was still in its box, waiting for morning.

The tree also featured more presents than the few she'd been able to provide for Abbie. Ethan again, spoiling them both. "Making up for lost time," he called it. He assured her he wasn't overspending and called up his bank accounts on his phone app to prove it, but still she put her foot down. "Honestly, Ethan, you cannot buy her everything she wants. It isn't good for her." So the pile beneath the tree wasn't as big as he'd have liked to make it, but still included the riding helmet he had consulted her on, a new dress from the swankiest children's shop in Barnsley, a Wonder Woman action doll he'd described but not shown her (which meant it would be the deluxe version with all the accessories), and more art supplies than even Abbie would use in the next six months.

Three of the presents were for her from Abbie. One, she knew, had been made at school. Ethan had been instrumental in organizing (and paying for) the other two, having 'borrowed' Abbie for an afternoon of shopping in Barnsley while she spent the time making the Christmas treats her grandmother had taught her.

"Would you like a glass of wine and some Christmas cake?" She was already in the small kitchenette, fetching the cake from the pantry cupboard.

"I'll pour the wine," Ethan offered. In the past weeks, he'd become familiar with where she kept things, and by the time she'd cut two slices of rich fruit cake and added a couple of pieces of shortbread to the plate, he had the two glasses ready, full of a dark red local wine that he said had been recommended by one of the garage's customers.

They sat in peaceful silence, sipping their wine and nibbling on cake, enjoying the peace at day's end. Ethan was the first to speak into the quiet. "Do I really have to drink Santa's milk?" he asked, plaintively. Claudia laughed. He'd argued for beer in the small snack left by the window, since the studio didn't have a chimney. Abbie insisted that Santa could not drink and drive, so milk it was. And cheese with crackers as a healthy snack, and grass for the reindeer.

She set her glass to one side. "Time to fill her stocking." It was hanging from the back of a chair by the window, another legacy from grandma, lovingly quilted. She fetched the box from under her bed, and Ethan brought a few more bags and packages out of the saddle bags he'd hung by his jacket.

He'd overdone it again, and she hadn't the heart to quarrel with him about it. She sipped her wine, laughing at him as he packed and repacked, trying to fit everything in. "We'll take the chair into her room," she suggested at last. "Stack the books on the chair. The game, too, and put the fruit and drink next to them. Everything else should go in then."

In Abbie's room, Boss looked up from her place in

Edward's box. Edward slept on. After an initial difference of opinion, the cat and the rabbit were fast friends, and the cat had doubled her circle of humans-who-may-touch-me to include Abbie. She even tolerated Claudia, when she was in the mood.

Ethan finished arranging the chair so it would be the first thing Abbie saw when she woke, and spoke to Boss. "You and I had better be on our way, girl. We'll be making an early start tomorrow." He cast one longing glance at the child sprawled on the bed, then moved to pick up the cat.

"Stay." Claudia spoke before she thought, then amended the words as hope and desire blossomed in his eyes. "On the couch. It's too early for…" Abbie stirred, and Claudia put a finger to her mouth and gestured for Ethan to follow her.

In the next room, she reaffirmed her invitation. "Stay the night, Ethan, so you're here when Abbie wakes up in the morning."

He examined her face carefully, as if afraid the treat would be snatched away. "I'll shoot home and get some clothes and stuff. Are you sure it's okay? No funny business, I promise."

That was a disappointment. Or it would be if Claudia didn't believe he'd welcome the chance to rescind that last promise. Not that she planned to let him into her bed, but he hadn't even tried to kiss her, and it was time he did. She could see from his eyes, a dozen times a day, that he thought of it.

In the fifteen minutes he was gone, she made up a bed on the couch. It was a bit short, but he'd manage. "That'll be perfect," he said, when he came back in the door. He'd showered and changed, and smelt deliciously of herb-scented soap.

Not quite perfect. But how did she get him to kiss her? Did she just walk up and take charge? And if she did, would he assume she was offering more than she was ready for?

"Ethan…" she began, just as he said, "Claudia…"

She waved for him to go first, and he took a small package

from his pocket. "I didn't mean to give this to you yet, but…" He handed it over; a jewelers' ring box. "There's a chain you can wear it on if you don't want to… or you could wear it on your right hand. It's a gift, Abbie, not a claim. And I'm not asking the question that goes with it. Not yet. Not till you have a chance to know you can trust me. Slow and steady wins the race."

The ring was beautiful; a cluster of tiny diamonds in the shape a love heart, set on an incised gold band. Ethan was still talking — babbling, even, as he did when he was nervous. "If you don't like it, we can change it. I wanted to buy the most expensive one in the shop but I was afraid you wouldn't take it. You will take it, won't you? No strings attached?" His brows drew together over anxious eyes as he used a thumb to wipe away the tear that escaped from one of her eyes.

She had to swallow twice before she could speak, but she smiled and nodded to reassure him while he waited for her answer. "I will wear it," she said, suiting words to action and — after a moment's hesitation — putting it on her right ring finger. Or attempting to. It stuck on the knuckle. "It's a plot," she joked.

"We can have it resized."

She slid it onto the ring finger of the other hand, where it fit perfectly, and held it out to admire it before warning him. "Just for tonight. I'll wear it on the chain when we go out tomorrow."

"You give me hope, Claudia. Is that what you intend?"

She ducked her head, the mingled longing and need in his eyes setting her cheeks aflame as her own body responded to his. Perhaps a kiss would not be a good idea, after all.

"I'm sorry. I've pushed too hard, haven't I?" Ethan sighed, then tried to lighten the mood. "I keep trying to be the tortoise but the hare breaks through." He turned away to hide his expression, running a contemplative finger along one of the branches of the Jesse Tree.

The joke made a nonsense of her doubts. This was the

Ethan she'd fallen in love with, but grown and matured into a better man than she had known enough to want. He wouldn't press her, so she needed to be brave; to reach out for what she wanted.

"Abbie has her Christmas wish, Ethan. But I have a wish, too, and you're the only one who can give it to me."

"Anything," he replied, the words a vow, his back stiffening as if he expected a blow.

"Kiss me, Ethan. I have missed your kisses."

She had one moment to see his face, ablaze with love and joy, and then he was on her, and the kiss was everything she remembered and more. Her last rational thought was that she'd wasted her time making up the bed on the couch. Ethan was home, and so was she.

The End

Meet Jude Knight

Jude Knight wants to transport you to another time, another place, to enjoy adventure and romance, thrill to trials and challenges, uncover secrets and solve mysteries, and delight in a happy ending.

She writes everything from Hallmark to Regency Noir, in different eras and diverse places, short, medium and extra-long. Expect decent men with wounded hearts, women who are stronger than they think, villains you'll want to smack or worse, and all with a leavening of humor.

Christmas Paws

E. Ayers

One

*T*he cold air made Flint zip up his coat and stuff his hands in his pockets. He looked at the old building, trying to make up his mind. It was smack in the middle of downtown Fullerton that seemed more like a restaurant district. The location had several things going for it. The town had become a Mecca for young professionals and for the artsy older folks who liked living there. Everything was nearby, including the courthouse and a fairly large park. With plenty of room upstairs for an apartment, this particular building also had excellent parking and a wide, grassy alleyway beside it.

The town was dog friendly. Almost every merchant, art galley, and restaurant kept a bowl of fresh water by its door for residents that walked their dogs. Flint looked through the front windows of the empty building one last time. He wanted this place. It would be perfect for his next Joe Wags café.

Paisley called to her daughter, and when she didn't get a response, she took the stairs two at a time. Her youngest daughter was in the world of selfies, earbuds, and text messages, completely oblivious to everything around her. Paisley flicked an earbud away from her daughter's ear, leaving it to hang over the teen's shoulder.

The daughter responded with her typical breathy murmur.

"School!" Paisley reminded her.

"I'm ready." Emily's facial expression of total indifference, yet slightly haughty, was the same every morning.

"Then get downstairs." Paisley was beginning to think that she wasn't going to survive two teenaged girls.

In the kitchen, Mia stuffed her mouth with the last bit of her slice of nine-grain bread coated with a layer of all-natural peanut butter and topped with sliced bananas. "O'm weddie," she mumbled, then swallowed. "Did you know that by eating bananas you'll gain the added health benefit of potassium to help to lower your risk of heart disease? You really should eat more of them, Mom."

"If I wanted a banana every morning, I would eat it."

"I'm only telling you for your own benefit. Besides you don't get enough exercise."

I am going to kill my girls. "In the car, now!"

Twenty minutes later, she had both daughters where they needed to be. She pulled into the parking lot of Cup of Joe's. Four mornings a week, she worked at the coffee café, then she went to work as the comptroller for the grocery store. Between the two jobs, she managed to pay the rent, keep the lights on, and buy groceries.

Jayla's car was already at Cup of Joe's. Jayla would probably say something because she wanted Paisley there much earlier. Except Paisley had to cope with her girls, and she couldn't drop Emily off any sooner at school. It was the same every morning that she worked and had been since the day she was hired.

Paisley walked in the back door punched the time clock, put on her apron, and washed her hands. Jayla might have been there, but she hadn't made any coffee. With doors opening in fifteen minutes, Paisley wasted no time.

The night crew hadn't finished cleaning because the tables needed wiping. After setting up the brew stations, she grabbed a cloth, and the spray cleaner to take care of the tables. That's when she noticed why Jayla hadn't done her morning work. Flint Silverlake sat in the back corner going over something with her. Flint owned the place and was known for stopping in unannounced.

Paisley unlocked the front door as Gail and Todd, Cup of Joe's young employees, came through the back door for their morning shift. The drive-thru was already buzzing with a customer. Paisley barked a few orders at Gail and Todd as she pulled on her drive-thru headphones. In less than three minutes, she had the place running smoothly and was smiling at the morning customers.

Jayla walked over to Paisley. "Flint wants to see you."

Paisley swallowed. *What have I done wrong? I can't afford to lose this job.* She put on her friendliest smile, grabbed a fresh cup of joe, and went to the table where Flint sat. She put the cup in front of him. "Morning. Thirsty?"

"Thank you, Paisley." Flint took the proffered coffee. "I needed this."

Paisley's stomach was curling around itself. She sat still and watched him. He was younger than her by quite a few years, but she never failed to notice that he was quite handsome.

"Good to see you again, Paisley."

She nodded and waited for some axe to fall.

"I've noticed that you've been here for several years. Is there any reason why you've never applied for a manager's job?"

"Which reason would you like? I've got two teenage daughters, a deadbeat ex that half the time won't pay his child support, and this is my second job. It takes everything I have to keep the cash flow flowing."

Flint laughed. "Perfect. What if I gave you a way out?"

That life-changing conversation with Flint had taken place almost four months ago. So much had happened, yet it seemed like yesterday.

Paisley looked around at Fullerton's new Joe Wags, the coffee café where man's best friend was always welcomed. Flint Silverlake owned Cup of Joe's and had started a fledgling company called Joe Wags. Same coffee, same everything, except Joe Wags also catered to dogs with a variety of the highest quality, organic, non-GMO, bakery-style canine goodies. Paisley's food handler's license was updated to accommodate dogs, and her staff was ready to go. The job came with a hefty raise, and she got a great apartment over the café for next to nothing.

She'd also managed to put some distance between her and her ex who wanted the girls only because he knew it drove her nuts. Both girls complained bitterly if they had to spend the weekend with their father. He pretty much put them on ignore when he did have them. His food tended to consist of cans of ravioli and the only way they had clean sheets was to wash them before they had to sleep on them. Mia's days of being forced to visit had come to an end. She recently had turned eighteen.

Fullerton wasn't exactly the big city, but Mia managed to get a job waitressing within walking distance of the apartment. Emily had met a few girls her age and was looking forward to school in the fall. Paisley needed this job at Joe Wags, to be her chance at a decent life for her and her girls. But it didn't help when one of her old friends at Cup of Joe's told her that Jayla was fired two days after Paisley left. She couldn't imagine what Jayla could have done to be fired, but it played on Paisley's mind and worried her. She'd put so much into this job. It was as though her life was on the line. Even her apartment was tied to Flint Silverlake.

The grand opening of Joe Wags was a big event. As always during those first few days, the coffee and everything else was sold for a quarter donation to the local shelter. Almost everyone tossed a couple of dollar bills in the jar for their coffee and treats. Dogs of all sorts visited and they too enjoyed a cool drink and a nutritious treat on a hot summer's day.

Flint stopped in and winked at Paisley who was extremely busy. She never saw him again until closing. She'd opened in the morning and she closed that night.

"How did you do?" Flint asked as she walked out the door that he held open for her.

"Very well."

"I knew you would, and this is a great location."

"Yeah." *I don't want to talk. I want to go home. I'm beat.*

"The next couple of days will be crazy, and then it will settle down. I'm not a helicopter, so I won't hover, but if you need me, I'll be here." He opened the door to his vehicle.

She locked the door to Joe Wags. "Nice to know."

She held her hand up in a stationary wave and watched him drive away before she went to her apartment over the coffee café. Spacious and newly renovated, the apartment was beautiful. Even the bedrooms were large. For the first time in years, the girls didn't have to share a room.

When Mia came in from work, she plopped onto her mom's bed. "How was your day?"

"Insanely busy." Paisley put her book down. Her feet still tingled from standing on them the entire time.

"That's nice." Mia had a faraway look in her eyes.

Nice? Are you okay?

"Met this guy tonight."

Ah, that's what this is about.

Paisley listened to her daughter. "Remember, I used to think your dad was very handsome and super wonderful."

"Just because you and Dad wound up divorced doesn't mean every guy is going to be like Dad."

Here we go.

"Anyway, I was hoping to invite him over for dinner one evening."

"If the madness calms down, I should be off Wednesday by three."

"Oh, Mom, that would be perfect, because I'm off on Wednesdays. Can you make that chicken with couscous?"

Paisley nodded. "I can't make any promises. I've got to see how it goes. Check with me when I get off Tuesday."

"Are you happy, Mom?"

"You mean with the job?"

"Yeah."

"This has been a great opportunity for us – for me. Flint Silverlake is a good boss."

"I think it's kinda neat that a dog can come in and sit with its owner."

"It's different. We had a little growling when a big dog decided to sniff a little one." Paisley giggled at the memory. "But the owners handled it. And the dogs left as friends. They do better than most people."

"They also sniff each other's butt as a way of greeting each other. 'Hi, my name is Fluffy. I ate Chicken Tasty Bits. Can you tell? Oh my, you had garbage. How exciting! Was it from a dumpster or the trash can?'"

"You're silly."

Mia kissed her mom. "Night."

"Night. Brush your teeth."

"I already did. They are brushed and flossed. I don't want rotten teeth."

When did you quit being a kid and turn into an adult? How did I miss that?

Joel Selski walked into the house that he shared with his dad. The place was quiet, almost too quiet. That's when he realized that his father was missing along with Cinnabun. The big Irish Setter had plenty of energy. Joel's dad took her running with him every morning, but he often took her again at night for a long walk.

His dad had gotten into exercising when a routine yearly blood test showed that he needed to do something quickly or he was going to be in big trouble in a few years. His cholesterol levels were not where they should be, his blood sugar was slightly elevated, and his blood pressure wasn't as low as it should have been. At forty-six, he decided he was no longer young. He gave up the nightly six-pack of beer, and ditched the cigarettes. He took up running. A year later, all his levels were great and have remained that way.

Plenty of people wondered why Joel's dad hadn't kicked him out. There wasn't some complicated formula behind it. They were both single males, they got along, and there was plenty of house. Joel chuckled at the thoughts. Free washer and dryer, plus a dozen other benefits made living at home very attractive. He didn't pay rent, but his dad did ask that Joel pay half of the utility bills. Living at home was cheap.

Stopping by the Beehive had made the evening interesting. It was a local watering hole that also served what they called healthy foods. That meant there were no french fries on the menu.

The new waitress was adorable. Said she'd been working there for two weeks, but he'd never seen her. Tiny and petite with naturally red hair, she instantly caught his attention. When the evening's meal traffic slowed down in the restaurant, he managed to converse with her. She had the prettiest smile. It took Jillian Brooks and Ken Harding telling Mia that Joel was born and raised in Fullerton before she'd give him her phone number. She was cautious and he liked that quality.

She said when she got off work she went straight home and to bed. She'd be available before four thirty in the afternoon. He worked until four thirty and often until five thirty. He'd have to call her during lunch.

He looked at his phone for a moment. Then he stepped into the kitchen and opened the refrigerator door hoping to find a late night snack. After grabbing a bottle of super greens mixed with a combo of three different fruit juices, he discovered there was celery. And his favorite filler for it was in the drawer with a half dozen other cheeses. He washed several stalks, wrapped them in a paper towel, grabbed the pimiento cream cheese and a butter knife, and placed all of it on the island's bar where he intended to sit. Cinnabun raced into the kitchen. "Hey, girl, where have you been tonight? Daddy take you for a walk?"

"Oh, did we ever. It was so nice this evening that I decided to go for a *long* walk. Besides, I wanted to check out the new coffee café downtown." Joel's dad sat on the bar stool beside his son.

"How was it?"

"Crowded. There weren't any available seats inside. I grabbed a cup of coffee for me and a dog cookie for Cinnabun."

"Coffee any good?"

"Delicious. And Cinnabun liked her treat." He looked through his pile of mail. "Saw your car parked at the Beehive."

"Well, that makes me feel like I'm being spied upon."

"All I said was that I saw your car."

"Met a girl tonight." Joel fixed a stalk of celery and took a bite. "Cute thing." He munched on another bite. "Do you believe in love at first sight?"

"Your mom hit me that way. I saw her at a friend's party. Looked at my buddy, and for some unbelievable reason, I told him I was going to marry her." He reached over, snagged one of his son's celery sticks, and smeared it with the cheese. "My buddy laughed and wished me luck. Apparently, your mom was going with someone else. I had one heck of a time trying to get her to go out."

"Never told me that." Joel watched his father get that faraway look in his eyes. "Why didn't you marry again?"

"I guess in the beginning, I was still in shock… I had you… a baby takes up a lot of time." He grabbed another celery stick and coated it with cheese.

"But I've never seen you date. I've seen you being nice, taking someone out to dinner for whatever reason, but not actually dating."

"I'm too set in my ways now to even think about that. You want me to marry someone and give you a pack of little siblings?" He picked up the last celery stick.

Joel looked at his father. "You know if you were hungry, you could have gotten your own celery."

"No, son. I'm fine. Eating yours was sufficient for me." His father laughed and left the kitchen.

Joel looked at Mia's phone number one more time before he retired for the evening. He was tempted to at least text her, but she was probably already asleep. He knew he wouldn't like his sleep disturbed over a simple text message that could have waited.

Mia walked out of the shower. She loved this place. Her bathroom was small, but she didn't have to share it. She dried off and walked naked through her bedroom. *Freedom!*

Her PJ's were under her pillow. The tank top and boy shorts were plenty on a summer's night. She turned off the small lamp beside her bed. From a single window, the street's light sent a golden glow between the slats of the blinds making a strange pattern on everything it touched.

She pulled on her PJ's and walked to her window. Fullerton had its own vibe, and she liked it. It was a small town, but it had a big city persona. There were three national companies with headquarters on the outskirts of town. That meant plenty of white-collar jobs. There also was a university about twenty minutes from town. Added up, it meant lots of young professionals and soon-to-be ones.

She felt like she was in heaven. She'd already made plenty of friends, good friends that she could bring home. Jillian was one of them. Still in college, she worked at the Beehive most nights.

Mia pulled a chair close to the window and opened her blinds enough to see down Main Street. It was quiet this time of night, as if the town had gone to sleep.

Her mind drifted to Joel. He was handsome in his own way. Tall and slender, he reminded her of a guy who would be teaching science in a high school. She tended to like guys who were a little brawny. Also, he was older. She wasn't certain by how much, but he was definitely older. She figured her mom would have a fit.

Never had she dated anyone older than Bobby. At the time, he was a senior and she was still a junior. She got to go to his senior prom and that was worth some popularity points.

She left her perch by the window and slipped under the bed's covers. She thought about her senior year in high school. That year, she began to feel as though she didn't fit in with her peers. She began to realize how stupid and petty a pack of girls could be.

She wasn't running off to a fancy college. Her mom could barely make ends meet. Paying for college was out of the question. Her mom promised she'd let Mia live rent free if she earned money and went to college on her own income. Now, every penny of her tip money went to her college fund. She had already applied to the local university and had been accepted. She wasn't certain if she could afford two classes, but it was a start. She could take the classes online and not have to worry about transportation. Did she dare to dream of a better life?

Paisley forced her body to vacate the bed. *All I need is another ten minutes.* Her mind pushed her to get into her shower, but her body was refusing to cooperate. Her shoulder blades and her hips must have joined forces as she slept because they were saying no to all movement. The simple act of getting dressed and going to work became an endurance challenge worthy of reality TV.

Flint had warned her that Saturday would be twice as busy as Friday. She couldn't imagine being busier. She set up the brew stations, made certain the ice machine was working, emptied the dishwasher from last night, and checked to be sure everything was prepped and ready to go.

A man waited outside the door with his big dog. She didn't know what kind of dog it was, but she assumed it was a fancy breed because it looked too cute with its reddish coat. She had another three minutes to go on the clock, but she opened the door anyway. "Come on in, coffee is still brewing, but the pooch food is ready as are the doggie drinks."

"I'll get a couple of those dog cookies for her, and I'll take a plain, black coffee as soon as it's ready. Is it still a quarter?"

"Yes, this whole weekend. Every penny we take in goes to the shelter."

The man nodded and dropped a twenty into the jar.

"Thanks, that was very generous."

He chuckled. "I'm a gold medallion supporter. The shelter gets me for a whole lot more than that."

She passed him the dog cookies and then a cup of freshly brewed coffee. "Stick around. We have free Internet."

"We just finished our morning run. Furthermore, it's Saturday. I don't want to go near a computer on the weekend. I get enough of it during the week."

"Wow, I thought everyone was lost without their computer."

"Not me. There might be Internet on my phone, but I don't use it."

She kept waiting on other customers, and continued to converse with him. "Here let me give you another cup."

"Are you doing that to see if I'll drop another twenty in the jar?"

"No. I'm doing it because you already dropped a twenty." She smiled brightly. "Let me guess, you have a wife, two kids, a cat and a dog, and you live in one of those big houses off of Claymont Road."

"You only got one right – the house. I've got a grown son and a furry daughter." He looked at his dog.

"Oh dear, I have one word for your daughter. Wax."

"She goes to the groomer once a month. She can stick with the usual." He sipped his coffee. "Okay, my turn to guess; husband, three kids, your mother-in-law, two cats, and a house that's too small for all of you."

"Not even close. The husband is an ex, and there's a reason for that. His mother is welcome to get on her broom and leave town as long as she doesn't come to Fullerton. I've got two girls, no animals, and for the first time in my life, I've got an apartment that is actually roomy."

"How old are your girls?"

"One just turned eighteen, and the other is four months from being sixteen."

"Ouch. That's a difficult age for them and for their adult."

She turned her back to him long enough to start brewing more coffee.

"I'll let you do your work. See you later."

She turned around to wave, but he was gone. He'd left too soon. She didn't even know his name.

Two

*J*oel Selski, Sr., mostly known as Joe, walked to his house. He had liked flirting with the gal behind the counter. She was nice and had a sense of humor. She also was easy on the eyes. Obviously, she wasn't young, maybe close to him in age. He wondered if she was the kind of person who baked Christmas cookies. *Whatever made me think of Christmas when the temps today are hitting the upper 90's?*

She was cute, petite, and rounded in all the right places. She had hazel eyes with long lashes, and it didn't appear as though she was wearing makeup. Her light brown hair was pulled into a bun. He would have liked to see it down, but he was certain that the health laws made her contain it. Maybe he'd ask her out to dinner sometime. She'd probably enjoy a nice meal.

He thought he was facing a yard that needed mowing, but his son had beaten him to it. The flowerbeds still needed some work. He loved the weekends. That big hammock on the porch was calling to him.

He unlatched Cinnabun's walking leash and put on her collar that worked with the electric fencing. He didn't want that type of fence for her, but his vet had suggested it. He said it kept the dogs safe, and once they learned where the lines were, they didn't cross them. He also said the jolt that the dogs would get if they crossed the line wasn't enough to hurt them. It wasn't much different than a static-electric shock. Cinnabun scampered away and sat under the tree in the back corner of the yard. She'd dug so many holes under the tree, he was afraid she might kill it. He wondered if the earth was a couple of degrees cooler, and that's why she'd make a hole and then lie in it.

He started on the flowerbeds, but he couldn't quit thinking about the woman at the coffee café. *Don't even go there. There's no point in it. Once was enough. There's no reason to chance being burned again.*

He might have sworn off women, but he would certainly enjoy the feel of one again. *It's not worth it.*

Mia stretched and got out of bed. She had plenty of time before work, but she hated getting dressed twice. She stayed in her PJ's, started her laundry, and began cleaning up her room and bathroom. Housework was something that she despised. Her mom had commiserated with her, admitting that it was a most hated chore. Ever since that conversation, Mia decided that she could handle more than her room, and often took care of the general living spaces for her mom. Mia figured that was one thing she could do for her mother, considering her mom worked two jobs and barely had five minutes to herself. Since moving to Fullerton, her mom had only one job, but Mia continued to help.

Mia's phone rang and when she realized it was ringing, she made a dash for it. She picked it up in time to hear the call disconnect. It showed Joel's number. She shrugged and went back to what she was doing. As soon as she finished, she took a quick shower and pulled on her clothes for her job, jeans without holes and a yellow and brown top with the Beehive's logo on the back. The top was cute, but it was quite revealing. She convinced herself that more would show if she wore a bathing suit.

Her phone rang again, and it was her mom. She also realized she had a text message that she had missed. "Hi, Mom."

"Mia, do me a big favor. Please fix me a sandwich and bring it to me before you go to work. I'm dying down here."

"Yeah, Mom, got it."

"Thanks." The connection ended.

Mia heaved a sigh, and then read her text message from Joel. *Aww, that's so sweet.*

She fixed her mom two sandwiches, added a snack-sized bag of chips, and decided to enclose a handful of those giant grapes that tasted so good. She took it to the café on her way to work. The line for coffee extended to the sidewalk. Everyone acted as though she was trying to cut in line and wouldn't allow her inside.

Desperation made her do it. She raised her arms over her head while still holding the lunch bag in the one hand. "Attention, everyone! Please. May I have your attention? That includes you in the blue shirt." She couldn't believe she was doing it, but she was and wasn't about to stop. "In my hand is lunch for my mom who is managing this place. The last time she ate was at four thirty this morning, and it's now after four p.m. That's almost twelve hours. She's hungry! And I have to be at work in another few minutes. I don't have time for people to hassle me. So, let me give my mom her lunch."

She ducked under one man's arm and almost got twisted in a dog's leash. She shoved the bag across the counter. "Give this to Mom."

When she came out, a man walked up to her. "You must be Mia."

"Yes, I am, and it's time for me to go to work. So, if you'll excuse me--"

"I own Joe Wags."

Mia stopped dead. Her mom owed this guy everything. "Pleased to meet you. Mom speaks very highly of you. But really, I don't have time to spare. I must be at work."

"I'll be around, and I'll catch up with you later."

She couldn't tell if that was his way of hitting on her, but she didn't want any part of it if he was. She knew he was married and almost as old as her mom. *Icky!*

Paisley attempted to eat her sandwiches. It was mostly one bite at a time, and the bread was drying out from sitting on the counter in the back room. But in general, the day was going smoothly. Several times, she had to pull the money from the jar, count it, and drop it into the café's safe. The shelter was doing well. She hoped traffic would slow to a more normal pace because this was unreal. Even Flint had said it was one of his busiest grand openings. She kept seeing him around, occasionally getting a cup of coffee as though he was a customer. He could have come through the back door and fixed himself a cup, but he liked standing in line and listening to the other customers.

Flint came in the back door and caught Paisley with a mouthful of chicken salad sandwich. She wondered if he'd heard Mia making her speech.

"Eat. I'll handle it out there." He rolled up his shirtsleeves, washed his hands, and pulled on an apron.

Paisley sat there stunned. She'd never seen him behind a counter except to inspect things or look for something. She watched him through the door's narrow window. He was very efficient. Not that she doubted his ability, but he was interesting to watch. A bit of a showman, and that great big smile seemed to charm most people. Her mind drifted to the man she'd talked to this morning. He was nice and also quite charming. She finished her sandwich, ate the grapes, grabbed a swig of water, and returned to her place behind the counter. "Thanks, Flint. I really appreciate that."

"That's why I'm here. Anyone else need a break?"

"Tim does."

"Thanks." Tim chucked his apron as he disappeared into the back room.

Paisley began to wonder if moving to Fullerton and taking this job was a big mistake. Why would Flint be hanging out? Offering to fill in so that someone could have a break? Did it appear as though she couldn't handle it? *I'm going to come straight out and ask him. If I'm doing something wrong, I want to know about it because I really can't afford to lose this job.*

Mia made it to work with plenty of time to spare. The chef fixed small plates for the wait staff. He wanted them to taste the special so that they could tell the customers. Mia liked this part of her job, tasting new things appealed to her. At five o'clock, she was on the floor of the dining room and getting her assigned tables for the night.

She might have been new but she was given prime areas almost every night. The strangest thing about it was she wasn't allowed to serve any alcohol because of her age. The bartender had to do that. The manager kept putting her in that section. She wasn't complaining because the tips were great.

Joel came in and was seated in her area. She smiled and went to him. "It's darn hot out there today. Icy cold water to cool you off, and then would you like something from the bar?" She flipped his water goblet over and poured a generous amount of slushy cold water. "How's your day been?"

He smiled at her, and his blue-gray eyes seemed to smile, too. Then he pushed a wayward lock of hair off his forehead. "Hardly exciting. I cut the grass, and straightened up the house."

"House?"

"I share my house with my dad."

She looked at him closely and realized he looked older than what she first thought. "You have a house and your dad lives with you?"

He chuckled. "Nah, Dad owns it. I grew up in that house. It's just the two of us. The expenses are shared evenly. Nice place in a good neighborhood, and it's dirt cheap."

"That's okay, I still live at home. I don't pay rent. Everything I make goes to my college education."

"Wow, that's being disciplined."

"Got to. It's the only way I'll be able to go to college."

"Mia, I really would like to take you out. Get to know you and all that."

"I'd like to go but… You're a lot older than I am."

He cocked his head. "How old are you?"

"I just turned eighteen. This is my first real job."

"You're not jailbait so… I'm more than willing to meet your parents first if you would feel better about going out. I can understand. It's got to be scary for a female."

"There's no parents with an *S*, only my mom. How old are you?"

"Twenty-four. Does that bother you?"

She inhaled. "A little."

"Don't let it. I'm not a horny teen who doesn't understand boundaries, and I can afford to take a woman on a nice date."

She smiled and walked away. Another table had been seated. But she couldn't help stealing looks at Joel every chance she had. He appeared to be a nice guy, very conservative, maybe a little too straight-laced. She just wasn't certain she wanted to be dating someone that much older.

When she brought his entrée, she had an extra minute to chat. "I'm not certain if my mom will be off Wednesday evening. But if she is, would you consider having dinner at my house?"

"Really?" He smiled brightly. "I'd love to meet your mom and have a home-cooked meal."

"I'll text you."

Joe changed from his old shirt into a nicer one. It wasn't as though Cinnabun would care what he wore, but when trying to impress a certain woman, he cared. *Maybe my son is right. Maybe I do need to date again. I'm not getting any younger. Who am I kidding? I've been off the market for so long, I have no idea what is considered normal anymore.*

He put the walking collar and leash on Cinnabun and walked out the door. It was a good distance to Joe Wags, and that gave him plenty of time to think. When he reached the coffee café, he'd decided that he'd just ask her out to dinner. There was no reason to get involved with a female. It would just be a nice meal, a simple diversion from the ordinary.

He stepped to the counter and ordered a dog cookie and a cup of coffee. He opened his wallet, and a woman's voice came across the counter.

"Don't you dare put one more dime in there. You've fed that jar enough."

"This is from Cinnabun. She made me come down here because she wanted another treat. She thinks you're really cute, and that I should invite you to dinner."

"That is the worst pick-up line I've ever heard."

"Oh, well, if it's that bad, maybe Cinnabun's human should at least offer to take you to Killen's Dock for dinner in order to make up for such a lousy attempt."

"Killen's Dock? I haven't lived here a month and I know that place is considered the best around, not to mention the most expensive. Are you crazy?"

"Why, would you prefer a bottle of Chianti, and we could do Lady and Tramp's bowl of spaghetti?"

"Ohmigod, are you for real?"

"The last time I looked, I was."

She shook her head and continued to work.

He failed miserably. Maybe that's why he didn't date. He was lousy at the whole female relationship thing. Maybe he'd ask his son what he did wrong. *Aren't sons supposed to ask their fathers for advice? And I'm about to do the opposite.*

Paisley wanted to kick herself for turning that guy down. She still didn't know his name. She knew the dog's name was Cinnabun. *What a weird business.* Not only was she learning the names of the owners and what they liked to order, she was learning the dogs' names and their preferences, too.

The man was terribly nice and always well dressed. The locals seemed to know him as he was often shaking hands with someone. When Annie from the animal shelter came, she hugged him and smiled as though she were greeting her favorite uncle. He certainly didn't come across as a murderer, yet she turned him down. *I could've had a nice meal. Instead, I ignored his invitation.*

About a half hour before closing, Flint walked in. He knocked-down several brewing machines so he could clean them. Then began to clean a few other things. Not a single word was said about the coffee spill from earlier. Nor did he say anything about the broken cookies sitting to one side, yet she was positive that he saw them.

"This is the first time it's slowed today." She sent Tim to wipe the tables.

"I warned you that today would be hectic." Flint picked up the cookie, walked to her, and handed it to her. "Were you that hungry?"

She didn't know if he was joking or not. "It broke, and I've handed little pieces of cookie to the small dogs as a sample."

"Good idea." Then he looked at her very seriously. "Is something wrong? You seem upset."

She pointed to the back room. Once there, she looked at him and said, "I'm trying really hard. I don't want to lose this job."

"Where did that come from? Has someone said anything that would make you feel as though you're not good enough? Or have I done something to make you feel that way?"

"Maybe it's me. But you've been in here a dozen times today. I feel like I'm being held under a microscope. You're watching me as if you're waiting for me to make some awful mistake."

He put both his hands up as if to indicate for her to stop. "If I had any doubt about you taking on this café, I never would have asked you to become the manager. I would not have moved you here. Paisley, you did a better job with this grand opening than I've seen at a Cup of Joe's or at my other Joe Wags. I never once saw you get flustered. You handled everything beautifully. And I'm sorry you went that long without eating. You should have taken a break and had a real lunch."

"But you started working behind the counter."

"My doing that gave you and the crew a little breathing room. I'll do that at any café when they are busy. That doesn't mean you failed some sort of test. I'll give you an A plus-plus for today. Most of the time during grand openings, I'm behind the counter the entire time. And you were worried about a broken cookie?"

"Yes. That's profit."

"I just lost a few thousand dollars today alone in coffee and treats, not to mention the cost of advertising this event, which is never cheap, and you're concerned about a cookie? Product loss is something that happens." He shook his head. "Paisley, give yourself a pat on the back for a job very well done. And don't ever let anyone tell you that you can't do this job. Another thing to keep in mind, if I ever have a problem with something that you've done, I'm going to come to you and talk to you. There are two sides to everything. If I think something is wrong, I'll let you know. Hey, I was teasing about that cookie but…" He got up, went to where the dog treat jars were, and chose a small biscuit. "Okay, cheese and liver flavored, everything here is human grade food." He popped the little treat in his mouth, chewed it, and swallowed it. "It's really not bad tasting. If it was meant for people, it probably would have a little salt in it."

She decided that Flint was a little strange. She'd heard of children tasting their dog's treats, but an adult?

"Paisley, you're great. Promise me that if you need help, you will ask for it, and you can always come to me no matter what it is. You know I run a good company. I just won't tolerate theft or drugs… or well, anything that's illegal."

"Yes. I know. I'm sorry. It's been stressful. I've worked jobs where employees were treated like paper towels, totally disposable."

"I don't do that." He smiled at her.

I hope not because I really want to keep this job.

Three

Tuesday afternoon, Mia checked with her mother about being off on Wednesday and if she could ask Joel to dinner. Her mom said yes and promised she'd make the chicken recipe that called for couscous. Mia hassled her sister until Emily promised to be on her best behavior.

Joel was making a habit of eating at the Beehive. Mia decided that it was a sweet gesture on his part. The more she was around him, the more she liked him. She kept checking the clock. Certain he'd be in at anytime, she tried not to get nervous or be anxious about his being later than normal.

When she looked at the time and saw it was eight thirty-six, she was certain that something was wrong. On her break, she decided to send a text message to him. *What do I say? I'll ask if he still would like to come to dinner. I hope he does. I hope nothing has happened to him. What if it has? What if he doesn't —*

Her phone pinged an incoming text. She opened it, figuring the timing was just lousy. She didn't want to talk to her friends or sis.

> *Sorry I got tied up tonight at work. Text me whenever you can. I'll be awake and looking forward to your text.*

What could she say? Her mind scattered. She wanted to sound happy to hear from him, but not overly anxious. She wasn't even certain that inviting a guy to the house for dinner was even a date.

Okay, I can do this. She typed a simple message.

Working. Will be off tonight at eleven. Missed seeing you.

She decided that sounded as if she was interested, but not as though she was desperately waiting for him to come to the restaurant. *Why didn't he come? Maybe he's decided I'm too young and doesn't want to hurt my feelings.*

At two minutes after eleven, her phone rang, and she answered, "Hi."

"Are you off?" the masculine voice asked.

"Yes." She recognized Joel's voice.

"Oh good. I've never talked to you on the phone. We've only done text messages."

"I know." She smiled.

"I'm really sorry. The one department under me was having a problem tonight. I had to solve it, or I would've had a nightmare on my hands tomorrow morning."

"Oh." She started walking home. "I guess your job is important to the company."

"I'd like to think that, but not really. I deal with people and their databases. There are quite a few people within the company that probably could do what I do."

"Oh. Ah, my mom said that she'll be off, and you are welcome to come for dinner tomorrow."

"Tell her I'm looking forward to it, and I'm definitely looking forward to spending some time with you."

She swallowed. "Um, maybe I should warn you. I'm not certain what my mom will think about the difference in our ages."

"I'm not worried about that. Does the difference bother you?"

Something inside her tightened. "A little. I've never dated anyone that wasn't my age or almost my age."

"I think that we'll find that the difference isn't a problem unless we allow it to be."

"Okay. Just so you understand. I don't jump into bed with a guy because he takes me out."

"Whoa. I'm not asking you for that. I don't believe in casual sex. If I thought you did, I wouldn't be asking you out."

She relaxed a little. "That's good. I wouldn't want you to get the wrong impression."

"I'd like to think that you thought I was better than that."

"Maybe. I'm just not very trusting."

"May I ask why? Did someone… hurt you… or something?"

Her stomach clenched with the memory. *He tried.* "Seems some guys figure that if a woman is nice to them…"

"Mia, I would never hurt you."

"I'm home now." She slipped her key into the lock and opened the door. After closing it behind her, she locked it, and set the security latch.

"What do you mean you're home now? I never heard a car door or--"

"I walk home. It's less than two blocks."

"Where do you live?"

She giggled. "I guess you'll need that information if you are coming to dinner. I'm living in the apartment over Joe Wags. It's 12204. Green door. You can't miss the place."

"Why didn't you tell me that before? I would have walked you home. It's not safe for a lone female to be out late at night."

"I'm fine, not the least bit afraid. Being within walking distance is part of the reason why I like my job. I don't have a car."

"I don't like you walking that late at night, but you do what you must. I'm sorry. I'm not a controlling person, merely concerned about your welfare. I probably should say good night, and I'll see you tomorrow. What time?"

"I guess since you usually come into the Beehive by five that you could be here by five. If you want to come earlier, you can. I won't mind."

❦

Joel thought about spending the evening with Mia and decided that he'd prefer to take her away from her house if she would allow him to do that. She obviously had a trust issue, and he could understand why.

He called the florist and picked up an arrangement of summer flowers. At quarter to five, he parked the car a fair distance from the apartment. Joe Wags traffic had the prime parking spaces. He really didn't mind the walk.

A few minutes later, he was being introduced to Mia's mother and younger sister. Mia's mom was thrilled with the flowers. Mia took his hand, led him to the sofa, and sat beside him for all of three seconds.

"I need to help my mom in the kitchen."

Emily came into the living room, sat across from him, and smiled.

He smiled back. "How do you like living in Fullerton?"

"It's boring. There's nothing to do."

He knew he needed to converse. "Do you play any sports?"

"No."

"Would you like to play a sport? They have tennis lessons on the other side of the park. There's a pool on the far side of town that the city owns. They have swimming lessons and swim teams."

"No."

That didn't work. "Okay. Maybe I should check and see if I can help your mom and sister." *Failure to chat with the younger sister won't earn me any points in the family category.*

Dinner was a question and answer session. But it wasn't nearly as bad as he expected. Mia had given him the impression that her mother was an ogre that would eat him if he gave the wrong answer.

He looked directly at her mother and asked, "May I take Mia out tonight, and if she's in agreement, may I continue to see her?"

"Are you really asking me if you can date my daughter?"

"Yes, ma'am."

"What turnip patch did you fall out of?"

"I'm six years older than your daughter. I do not want to give the impression that I'm going to do something inappropriate because that's not me. I don't look at the age difference as a problem, but I don't know if you do."

"Here's the deal. Don't do anything that she doesn't want. When and if I give a curfew, there's a reason for it. I don't want her drunk. As you know, drinking will make a girl's panties fall off. I have two girls to prove it." The woman shuttered her eyes and looked at him as if he were about to morph into a monster. "If you get her pregnant, I will haunt you for the rest of your life."

He could barely hold back the smirk that threatened to overtake his face. The woman had a very warped sense of humor. He looked her in the eye. "Ah, yes." He rubbed his hands together. "I shall remember that her mother thinks that threats of evil spells will stop me on my quest to ruin her virginal daughter." He stared directly into the mother's eyes and without an ounce of emotion said, "That's okay; I know a good exorcist."

Mia's face had turned white, Emily was wide-eyed, and their mother was trying very hard not to laugh. Now the real battle began when they locked gazes. Mia's mother lost when she could no longer hold her laughter.

Joel looked at the woman with a certain amount of disbelief. "Really, alcohol makes a woman's panties fall off? My dad never told me that one."

The woman looked down her nose. "Happens every time."

"Useful information. I'll remember that." Joel raised his eyebrows.

"Don't you dare. She's under drinking age."

Now he chuckled. "Ready, Mia? I think your mom approves of me enough to allow me to take custody of you."

Mia looked at him. "Over my dead body. No one is taking custody of me. I'm eighteen."

Monday morning, Joe came into Joe Wags for a quick cup of coffee. Paisley was working behind the counter. Traffic was brisk, and quite a few people didn't have dogs with them. They were like him, looking for that cup of java to start their morning. He wanted the coffee, but he also was determined to take Paisley out. It didn't matter to him if it took six months to break down her defenses.

At this point, he wasn't certain if it was ego or pride, maybe both. He couldn't think of a time when he had been turned down for a date. Not that she exactly refused his offer, but she had a way of avoiding him. He had to think of another tactic. *Flowers?*

On his way to work, he stopped at the florist, picked up one of their gift cards, and wrote on it. *Dinner, you choose where and when. I can take you or meet you. Joe 555-1624*

He paid for the florist to send a dozen yellow roses with the card attached. Then he went to work and waited. By five, he hadn't heard a thing. Ten p.m. came and went. The next day, he stopped at the florist and picked up a dozen of their little cards that they used on bouquets. *Just in case.* He had a white rose sent with a card. Fourteen days and a total of two-dozen roses later, he still hadn't heard from her. He added imported chocolate. Nothing. *What can I do?*

He went to the little gift shop in town and bought a pretty card. Inside, he wrote that he was running out of ideas. All he wanted was a chance to take her to dinner. He asked what was so wrong with that. He signed it Joe. And then wondered if she might have been under the impression that it was the owner of Joe Wags. He added a postscript. *I'm Cinnabun's dad.*

Nothing. He figured he'd give up. He'd been at it for over a month with no response, so that left him with one final idea. He took a sticky note from the pad that he kept in a kitchen drawer to use as a grocery list. It was large and handy to stick on the refrigerator or on the pantry wall. This time it wasn't going to be used for food shopping.

Paisley was working the morning when Joe and Cinnabun came in for coffee and a cookie. Joe left a note on her counter. Picking it up, she pocketed it without looking at what it said. She could feel his gaze upon her.

She didn't know what to say to him. She didn't mean to turn her back to him that day, but they were busy - too busy to have a friendly chat with a customer. Afterwards, it was too awkward. She was slightly embarrassed. Plus, she didn't… Her ex came to mind. She'd allowed him to sweep her off her feet and look where she landed. She wasn't good with men.

She admitted that she liked Mia's boyfriend, Joel. He was always very polite and good to Mia. Paisley knew because Mia was rather upfront about her relationship with Joel. The only thing they were doing was some serious kissing. It wasn't unusual for him to ask Emily if she'd like to see a movie with them. He didn't have to do that, but he seemed to understand that there was no extra money for things, and Emily loved going to the movies. And when Emily was preparing for school, he slipped her some money for school supplies. Paisley wasn't certain how much he'd given Emily, but figured it was substantial. Paisley wanted to talk to him about that. He didn't need to be paying for the necessary things for her girls. She could handle it.

She didn't read Joe's note until she'd taken a break for dinner. This time she couldn't ignore what he said. He apologized to her and said he meant no harm. It had become a game. He promised there would be no further attempts to ask her out. He understood the word no. The phone number wasn't included.

No matter how hard she tried, she couldn't hold back her tears. That wasn't what she wanted.

Mia signed up for her two classes. She couldn't believe how expensive they were, and then she wasn't certain she'd be able to afford the books. She never said a word to Joel since he would have probably purchased the books for her. She hated having him pay for everything. She worked as many shifts as the restaurant would give her and was thinking about working a morning job to help with her school expenses. Two classes a semester meant she'd be in school forever. She needed more money for more classes. The U-Pak Center, where people could keep mailboxes and have packages delivered, was hiring for the Christmas holiday. She knew the guy who ran it because he was a customer at the Beehive. She figured that was worth something.

She left the apartment bright and early to apply at U-Pak. She didn't get too far before she ran into Flint Silverlake. She politely smiled. "Hi."

"Mia, got a minute? I'd like to talk to you."

Four

*I*f Flint wasn't her mother's boss, Mia probably would have rolled her eyes and maybe made a derogatory comment. He always smiled and acted as though he was hitting on her, and she didn't like it. "I've got three seconds." *One, two, three; oops, they're up.*

"I understand that you're going to college this semester. What's your major?"

"Haven't declared it, but I'm looking towards a degree in business admin and applied math."

"Nice combo."

She nodded.

"I have a job that I thought maybe you'd consider. It's computer-based so you can work from home. I've been trying to catch you for ages. I think you'd be perfect for this. Your mother seems to think you're a whiz on the computer, and she claims your math skills are excellent."

Job? Yeah! "Sure, I'd be interested in working from home if it isn't cold calling or something like that."

"No. I can't imagine ever resorting to that type of advertising. Let's sit at one of these tables on the patio."

She wandered over and sat.

He opened his phone. "Sorry, but I don't have a computer on me. This is often my internet access." He scrolled and then went to the web. "Here's what I need. It's becoming too time consuming for me, but I need it. Think you can do this and be accurate?"

She looked at his small screen. "It's easy enough."

Flint continued to talk to her. From what he said, it sounded like it would take her only an hour or at the worst, two hours a day. He'd pay her a salary. Money she could count on each week.

Software gave the totals and the averages, but it required human thought to really see what was happening. It wasn't just a rise in the cost of toilet paper; it was paper towels and every other paper product that was used.

"What time do you want this each day?"

"Before noon if possible."

She nodded. "Not a problem."

He tossed out a figure, and she thought maybe she hadn't heard him correctly. "Excuse me, would you repeat that?"

He told her the amount again. "I figured this job would be up your alley from what your mom said about you. And it will save me a ton of time that I don't have."

He stared hard at her.

"Five days a week?" Mia furrowed her brow.

"Yes."

"What if I'm sick or I need a day off? Does this come with vacation time?"

"You'll get my salaried employee package—holidays, personal days, the whole thing."

Now she knew why her mom felt indebted to him. The 'whole thing' was almost too good to be true.

"If you need time to think this over, take it. I've been doing without for months." He withdrew a business card from his wallet with his name and contact number on it. On the back, he wrote the URL for the salaried employee package. "This is my personal information. Don't be afraid to call me if you have any questions."

She took the card and pocketed it. "Thanks. I'll let you know."

She didn't want to go back to the apartment, and if she took this job, she wouldn't need the U-Pak job, but if she took both... *I can't think!*

She found herself walking to the lake in the middle of the

park. It was quiet there. She crossed her legs and lowered her body to the grass. She had plenty to think about. Pulling out her phone, she texted Joel.

Paisley decided that this autumn was better than any she'd known. Not only did the trees look spectacular this year, but also both girls seem to radiate happiness. Mia and Emily both worked part-time at U-Pak. It was Emily's first job, and her sister had paved the way for her. Emily worked three days a week after school. Her grades, for the first time ever, were almost perfect, putting her on the principal's list. Mia was taking her college classes, working for Flint, working four mornings a week at U-Pak, and four nights a week at the Beehive. Mia was breezing through her classes and swore that she'd be able to take more classes next semester because of her income.

Joe Wags had settled into a routine. Paisley had good help. Flint often would be part of the hiring process. He was skilled at recognizing the oddest things about people. He always amazed her - claimed it was in the body language. Certain traits, habits, and experiences showed if someone paid attention.

Joe and Cinnabun often came for a drink and a treat. Paisley and Joe would smile at one another and be polite. He had become just another customer. She tried not to think about him too much. Still, she felt guilty and wanted to apologize, but too much time had passed.

One morning the tension built in her. The need to put a stop to her guilt was too great. She grabbed a dog treat bag and picked up a marker.

I'm sorry. There's no other way to say it. I didn't mean to hurt your feelings. Then with the flowers and other gifts, I no longer thought I deserved any of your

> *attention, and I didn't know how to respond. I never*
> *had a guy send me flowers. It was a bit overwhelming.*
> *I think you are handsome and very nice. I wish that*
> *none of it ever happened. I'm really sorry.*

By the time she had finished writing, she had covered the front, the back, and around the edge of the bag.

She put a pumpkin treat in the bag and waited for Joe to come with Cinnabun. She had Joe's coffee ready the moment he walked through the door. After handing the two items to him, she tried to give him her best smile. "Compliments of the house."

He nodded. "Thanks." He started to walk away and then turned to Paisley. "Cinnabun said that I forgot to tell you that she thanks you, too."

Paisley knew she was blushing. Her pale skin gave away every darn emotion. "You're welcome, Cinnabun."

Cinnabun turned and tugged on her leash in an attempt to go back to the counter. Paisley came around to the dog with a few of the standard training treats in her hand. "You just know where the treats are kept, don't you?" She petted the floppy-eared animal, giving her a treat. "You be a good girl for your daddy."

She reached out to Joe with the remaining treats, and he captured her hand. Opening her hand, she let the tidbits fall into his. "I have to go back to work."

"I understand." He let go of her.

Something about his touch left her feeling alone, as though she'd been torn from him. She stood as though frozen in place, looking at him. Her teeth slipped over her lower lip. Those green-brown eyes of his never blinked. She could feel her mouth starting to open, and she slammed it closed, sucking in her lips. That was not a path she wanted to travel. She forced herself to break their locked gaze. Then she scurried behind the counter, figuring she was safer there. She expected him to leave, but he stood there watching her. Finally, he smiled and walked out the door.

She took a break, and when she returned there was a single, long-stemmed, yellow rose on the counter. She picked it up and took it to the back room. Sniffing the delicate scent as if to memorize it, she placed the rose in a jar of water and returned to her job. A little part of her wanted to squeal with happiness, and the rest of her was screaming for her to turn and run.

Flint stopped in that morning and told Paisley to close on Thanksgiving. Then he texted Mia telling her to take that Friday off, too.

He looked around and grabbed a cup of coffee.

"Is that your way of being certain that the coffee is always fresh? Do you ever get tired of drinking so much?" Paisley grinned as she said it.

"Never. And your coffee is always fresh. I do have a question for you."

Paisley swallowed and sat at a table. "What's up?"

"Are you doing anything different - something that you find works well and brings in customers?"

"Sorta. I figured it doesn't cost much so I keep training treats and other goodies by the registers. People know that their dogs can sample whatever is there."

Flint turned in his seat and then walked to the jars on the counter.

She followed and whispered, "Stand back and watch."

Aileen brought in her Foxhound. The dog anxiously waited in line. Then he stood on his hind legs with his front paws on the counter. "Here, Major. Here's your little treat. I would like a hazelnut caramel coffee and-- Stop it, Major. You got your treat. Oh dear, do you still have the pumpkin cookies for the dogs?"

Tim smiled as he waited on them. "Does Major want the large-sized cookie?"

"Give him two of the medium ones and a large minty breath chew."

The dog's tail was wagging so hard, it could have been considered a weapon.

"And you always have the jar out there?" Flint asked.

Paisley grimaced. "Sometimes it's a plate with samples of whatever is new or an old favorite. I had the pumpkin cookies for a week, and then I went to the mint chews. This week I have the new Bitty Betty Beef training treats. I announce which treat on the sandwich board by the front door."

"Keep it up." He looked at her. "How do the customers like Bitty Betty Beef?"

"Well, I've not had a single complaint from one of the dogs, and I've never had an owner make any comments."

Flint went to the jar and grabbed a few treats.

Aileen smiled politely at him.

Flint, the perpetual showman, kept that sweet smile on his face and turned on his charm. "They are new treats. Seems your dog likes them. Have you tried them?"

The look Aileen gave him was priceless.

"Really, everything I sell is one hundred percent human grade food. Taste!" He handed her a sample and put a few in his mouth.

Paisley looked at Aileen and reached into the jar. "It's true. It's all top quality."

Paisley popped a little treat in her mouth and immediately spit it out. "Oh, that was disgusting."

Flint swallowed. "On second thought, don't try the Bitty Betty Beef. I promise, you will not like it."

Flint looked at Major. "What did you think? Do you need another to be sure before you comment?"

Flint reached into the jar, grabbed a few Bitty Betty Beef treats, and fed them to the dog. "I do believe, Major approves."

Aileen looked at Flint. "He'd eat road kill if I let him."

Flint put on his best smile. "In that case, I'm sure he'd love a whole container of Bitty Betty Beef."

Paisley vanished into the back room and dissolved into laughter that made tears run down her cheeks. *Oh, Flint, I can't believe you did that. I can't believe I put one in my mouth. I wish I had my toothbrush.* Her laughter rose to the surface again. *Maybe I'll grab one of the mint chews to whiten my teeth and freshen my breath while removing any tartar. Won't my dentist be thrilled?*

Joe realized that he didn't have much in the way of plans for Halloween or even Thanksgiving. He decided he'd better buy some candy.

On the way to the store, he stopped into the town's gift shop, figuring he'd buy something for his front door that looked like Halloween. He wound up spending more than he had planned, but he also bought the cutest fall basket that was meant to hold candy. In the grocery store, he stood in the candy aisle and debated. In past years, he didn't get too many children. There was something at the clubhouse for the neighborhood kids, but he didn't want to disappoint those who did come. He picked up a bag with an assortment of small candy bars. Then he spotted the name of his son's favorite chocolate bar and bought a bag of those.

As he was about to leave the aisle, he spotted the top names of chocolatiers and their chocolate bars in exotic flavors. He chose one of each flavor figuring that there wasn't a woman alive who didn't like chocolate. His secretary seemed to constantly snack on chocolate instead of eating lunch.

Once at home, he hung the decoration he'd bought for the door and dropped the small candy bars into a large crystal bowl near the front door. He hoped Joel wouldn't eat every piece before Halloween came and went. He put the expensive chocolate bars in the basket he'd bought and added a couple of handfuls of the smaller assorted bars. All he had to do was take it to Paisley. He figured that maybe this time she'd say yes, especially if he made it easy for her to do that.

Happy All Hallows Eve,

I'm hoping you might consider starting over and joining me for a cup of coffee on Sunday about 7A.M. I know this great little place called Joe Wags. That means Cinnabun can also join us, so we will be properly chaperoned.

If you'd like to go elsewhere, prefer a different time, or if your answer is still no, you can text 555-1624. Otherwise, I'll be there.

Joe

He figured he'd give her the note on Friday along with the basket.

He thought about Thanksgiving. His parents were dining with his sister and her family. The thought of a turkey with oyster stuffing made his mouth water. It just wasn't practical for him and his son. Several restaurants offered a Thanksgiving meal, but he'd tried those over the years. It wasn't the same as a home-cooked dinner. He debated about getting a turkey breast and trying to do that instead of a whole turkey.

Joel came through the back door. "Hey, Dad. Oh, candy."

"Don't eat what's in the bowl by the front door. And don't touch this basket."

"Why do I get the feeling that you are pursuing a female?"

"Maybe."

"Okay, be that way." Joel reached into the bag filled with his favorite candy bars. He removed the wrapper on the sticky caramel with a chocolate coating and put it in his mouth. "Ghoode stoof."

"Don't talk with your mouth full. I did try to teach you manners." Joe emptied what was left of the candy into a large glass canister. He picked up his note and read it again. *That's got to work. I really hope she's worth it.*

He locked up, and as he passed the front door, he reached into the bowl and took a handful of candies. *I'll eat only these.*

"Hey, Mom." Mia called, as she closed the door behind her and went to her mom's bedroom. "Joel's offered to take Emily and me to the movies on Saturday. We want to go to the matinee that starts at eleven fifteen. If we see both movies, we won't get home until after three, maybe closer to four. Since I'm not working that night, Joel and I plan on going out after we drop Emily home."

Her mom nodded in agreement. "How is everything between you and Joel?"

"Great. We've got a lot in common. I grew up with almost no father, and he grew up without a mother. We want to stick together until the very end of our lives."

"Are you serious, as in marriage?"

"We've talked marriage. I've got my education ahead of me. There are pros and cons of marriage when it comes to financial aid. That could seriously impact our situation."

"Meaning?"

"It might be better if we live together instead of getting married. Right now living at home makes it a moot point."

"I don't want you to do anything rash. I know how much you want your education."

Mia smiled at her mom. "He finished his master's this past spring. You would not believe the money he makes. Living at home allows him to invest a huge chunk for his retirement."

"The amount of money a man makes is not a reason to marry him."

"I agree, Mom. I said that because that's the difference an education makes. I want that super job with lots of pay and benefits."

"Make certain that you are marrying for all the right reasons. You don't want to make a mistake."

"Mom, marrying Dad didn't work for either one of you. You both screwed up, but for different reasons. You paid the most because you had us."

"I wanted my babies."

"I'm glad you fought for us. Joel and I aren't going to repeat our parents' mistakes. Guess we'll be making our own as we go along."

"Life isn't fair."

"I know that." Mia looked around her mother's room. The furniture was mismatched, and the bed squeaked. Mia knew she wanted so much more.

Her mom toyed with the hem on her sheet. "Would you care if I went out once in a while with a guy?"

"Mom, I'd be thrilled for you. You need some happiness in your life. Somebody to take you to the movies - maybe dinner occasionally. Do you have someone in mind? Is it the guy who sent all the flowers?"

"Yes. But maybe it's too soon. I think he's handsome, and he often flirts with me. I don't know much about him... very little... hardly anything."

"Well, you won't get to know him unless you go out with him. Have coffee together, you're right there. Go to the Beehive for dinner. It's casual. You don't have to worry about fancy clothes in there."

"That's a good idea."

Mia went to her room and sent a text message to Joel. He responded immediately. Mia smiled. She was so glad that her mom liked Joel, too.

She sat on her bed and thought about the concept of marriage. Joel wanted to marry her, and said it didn't matter to him if he had to pay for her education. He didn't want to wait forever. When she was in his arms, she didn't want to wait either.

She got up and chose her clothes for the morning. With Halloween coming up, U-Pak and the Beehive expected the employees to dress for Halloween. Some of her co-workers had fancy costumes. She didn't. She thought maybe she'd stop at the thrift shop on her way home from U-Pak to see if she could find something to wear. Maybe if she found a man's shirt in green, she could cinch it at her waist with a brown belt. Her dark green yoga pants would be perfect with it. Then she could pretend she looked like an elf.

Joel looked in his closet at the lilac and burgundy pixie costume he'd bought online for Mia. It came with tights, shoe covers, wings, and a set of pointed ears. He hoped it was going to fit. The neckline was low cut and that made him chuckle. He didn't mind a bit of skin, especially when the skin was covering a set of soft swells.

Then he checked in the small box that was in his top drawer. Four carats in a solitaire setting, he wanted spectacular. It was spectacular.

Now he had to decide when to give it to her. He wanted romantic. *Maybe alone might be better than with a crowd watching.* And some gals didn't like being asked on holidays. That eliminated several days and places, but it wasn't helping him to decide on when and where.

He closed the box and put it in his drawer. He didn't want to wait forever, but if that's what it took, he would. The first time he saw her, he knew that she was the one for him. He was aware of what others might think because she was still young, but he knew in a few years no one would even notice the difference in their ages.

Stuffing the costume in a gift bag and adding tissue paper made gift-wrapping easy. He'd take it with him to the Beehive. *If only giving her the diamond ring would be as easy.* He was obsessing, and he knew it. The last thing he wanted to hear was her saying no, and he wasn't sure that she would say yes.

Five

The first of November, Joe sat on the patio of Joe Wags. It was chilly, but his heavy overcoat kept him warm. Paisley wasn't working. She almost never worked on a Sunday, and he figured that might be a good thing.

He waited, and finally Paisley came to him, smiled, and stepped inside the café only to return holding two hot coffees.

"Maybe we should take a little walk," Paisley offered.

He smiled, stood, and nodded his agreement. Cinnabun walked beside him. He steered Paisley to the lake in the park. They sat in the gazebo at the end of the wooden pier. The layer of morning mist that covered the lake added to the beauty of the tranquil spot.

"Now what?" Paisley asked.

"Is this where we're supposed to chat and maybe tell our deep secrets to each other? I have no clue because I've not dated since I dated my son's mother, and that didn't work out."

Paisley smiled. "I know the feeling."

"When did you split?"

"He… Well, I discovered that he was cheating, and I tossed him out. I had a two-month old and a two-year-old toddler. That started the custody battle. I've got at least two more years of his nonsense, and then he can't do anything else. By then my youngest will be eighteen. I haven't dated either. No time for it, and I'll be honest, I don't trust men very much. I've seen too many marriages break up."

"You are pretty jaded. My wife walked out on our son and me. He wasn't quite a month old. I never heard from her again until our son was eight. She called and wanted to see him. I wouldn't let her near the house. She met us at a restaurant, had a cup of coffee, and left. I doubt she said more than three words to her son. She committed suicide about a week later."

"Oh, that's a… a little hard to take. Does he know?"

"I told him when he was an adult. I figured a child didn't need to know those details. He didn't even know who the woman was that he met. I never said, 'This is your mother.' She was merely the incubator. I had work, I had a child, and I didn't have time for a woman."

"Oh, now I wonder how we've both wound up sharing a Sunday morning cup of coffee."

"I figured maybe I should… " He looked away. He didn't want to say it. "I needed to try again."

Paisley tilted her head. "Why me?"

"Something about you. You seem very natural. There's an old computer expression, WYSIWYG. What-You-See-Is-What-You-Get. I think you're a WISIWYG."

She laughed. "Am I that transparent?"

"Probably not, but I like what I see."

"Sure. I come with stretch marks, and my youthful good looks fled the first chance they had. My face has decided it wants to hang out under my chin and the twins are racing for my waistline. My legs now have the north-south interstates clearly marked. And my arms are no longer long enough to read the newspaper."

Joe couldn't help himself; he began to laugh. "You're funny. But there's something you need to understand. I'm not looking for a Barbie doll. I don't want to hold onto silicone or whatever they are using today. I think with time comes the things that make us unique. I like what I see."

"That's not going to get you into my bed."

"I didn't ask for that."

"It's what all men want."

"And women don't?"

"Not like men."

"Okay, I'll admit that I'd love to have a woman in my bed. And that thought scares the hell out of me."

"Why do you think women read romances? All the men are gorgeous and totally wonderful. There's nothing like a book boyfriend. It's the great pretend." She put her hands to her heart. "Swoon!"

He pulled Paisley to her feet. "Maybe we should go real slow. Do you remember kissing?"

"Sort of."

"Well, we can start there." He leaned down and gently touched his lips to hers for a moment. "That wasn't so bad. Want to try a little more?"

She nodded.

This time he deepened his kiss, and she went with it. He touched his tongue to her lips, and she welcomed him. He broke the kiss. Then he looked into her eyes. He could see sadness, desire, and the need to trust. He softly kissed her. "Let me take you to breakfast."

She nodded.

He captured her hand in his, and they walked hand-in-hand to Cockledoo's, a great 24-hour breakfast restaurant. Cinnabun sat outside and waited for them. When Paisley and he were finished, Joe walked her back to Joe Wags, bought a treat for Cinnabun, made arrangements to take Paisley to dinner on Wednesday, and said goodbye.

He wasn't certain about the morning, but kissing her was worth it. He really couldn't remember the last time he kissed a woman with any meaning. *It's been much too long.*

Wednesday afternoon he met Paisley and took her to dinner at the Beehive. Between the two of them, they managed to drink a bottle of wine with their meal. They talked about living, being a single parent, having a dog, and working. Not exactly stimulating and exciting, but it was the kind of conversation that takes place when two people are comfortable with each other. Then after dinner, he walked Paisley back to Joe Wags.

"Are you certain you can get home from here?"

Paisley laughed. "I live on this block."

"Oh." He stood holding her hand and not wanting to let her go. "I guess I should say goodnight."

She nodded. "I have to go to work in the morning and so do you."

He leaned towards her, and she met him. Her hands slid around his shoulders, and her fingers slipped through his hair. He kissed her. It was warm and full of desire. He pulled her tighter to him, and she didn't resist. They stood in the neon glow of the Joe Wags logo, wrapped in each other's arms. He wasn't sure if this was actually going slow, but he knew how he felt. For the first time in years, he wanted a woman in his bed.

Friday night, Joel walked Mia home from work at the Beehive. When they reached the apartment, Mia invited him to come up. Joel followed her up the stairs and then into her bedroom.

"Are you certain I'm allowed here?"

"Why not? We're adults, and whatever we could do here, we could do elsewhere. So what difference does it make?"

"It's your bedroom, and that's not how people view it."

Mia rolled her eyes, then plopped across her bed. "I don't want to say goodbye tonight. I hate doing that. I want you here with me."

"Bad idea if you want to keep our relationship the way it's been."

She wrinkled her nose and patted her bed.

He crawled next to her.

"We can talk. I'm not asking for more." Mia turned to him and watched to see how he reacted to her statement.

He wove his fingers with hers. She found it to be an intimate sensation. Something that would be done only with someone she loved. Using a very serious tone, she asked, "What do you see in your future?"

He sighed. "You as my wife. I'd like to see a child or two, a dog, a house, a vacation on the sand where the water is clear and warm. What do you want?"

"A cat. I'd like a cat in that picture. I especially like the vacation idea. And I'd like a really cute bikini - something with lots of strings."

"Something to make it twice as difficult for me to remove?"

"That might be fun."

"Mia, if we marry, you won't have to work. That will be totally optional. I make enough to support us and a family."

"Nice to know, but I want to work. I don't want to be stuck at home all day every day. And I want my own bank account."

"That's fine." He rolled over on his back. "I don't know what went wrong with my parents. I know my mother had a serious problem with depression that went unrecognized. It was suggested that postpartum depression might have been a factor in her downward spiral." He put his hands behind his head. "I've got friends who are already on their second marriage. Maybe I'm too idealistic."

"I don't think so. I think we both want the same things, except my college is messing up the timeline."

He rolled on his side facing her. "Don't ever say that. College means the world to you. It's your private path to individual freedom. It's knowing that no matter what, you can take care of yourself. I think that's noble. No one is saying you must do this at this time."

"Do you worry that in a few years that I might change my mind about being married?"

He leaned up on his elbow and planted a little kiss on her lips. "We never can predict the future, but if the lines of communication stay open, I can't imagine that happening."

"I can't imagine loving anyone but you." She grinned at him. "You are the first guy I've ever dated that honestly respected my values. The first guy who didn't try to… I love that about you."

"Aw, Mia, go to sleep."

"Do you think Mom will be upset if you spend the night?"

He slipped out of bed and opened the bedroom door. "We have nothing to hide."

She smiled. "I'd like to have you in my bed for as long as I live."

"That sounds a little like a marriage proposal." He stared into her eyes.

"Is that a terrible thing?"

Paisley noticed her oldest daughter's bedroom door was open. That wasn't like her. Paisley walked to the door and then realized why. Mia and Joel were stretched across Mia's bed fully dressed. *How did I raise such a good kid, and how did she find such a great guy?*

She thought back to when she was Mia's age. She was already working at a fast-food place. Her mom and dad only once mentioned college. It was for rich kids, and she'd better know her place. Something her mother said gave the impression that her mom would've liked to see Paisley get her degree. But that didn't happen.

Then Paisley found herself pregnant and married her boyfriend. It was the beginning of the end for her. Until by a series of odd events, she'd wound up here in Fullerton managing Joe Wags. She'd also met a really great guy. Maybe she'd invite him to Thanksgiving dinner. For the first time in a long time, she could afford a turkey and all the fixings. She assumed Mia would invite Joel, and if she invited Joe, that would make five for dinner. She'd ask Mia about it.

Paisley thought about inviting her parents. They usually went to her brother's house, but she could extend the invitation. Then she thought about sleeping arrangements. She didn't think it was fair to ask one of her girls to give up a bedroom and crash with her sister. *No, I won't do it.*

The following morning, she picked up her phone and texted Joe. *Thanksgiving dinner at my house?*

He responded almost instantly. *I'd love to have dinner at your house.*

"Mia, just the person I want to ask."

Mia turned to her mom with that cornered animal look in her eyes.

"Would you like to invite Joel for Thanksgiving dinner?"

"Oh, I think he'd love it, but I almost hate… You know he lives with his dad, and I think they tend to do holidays together. Could we ask his dad, too?"

"Why not? Another place setting is fine. There's more than enough food at Thanksgiving. But I have asked Joe to dinner."

"That gives the men someone to talk to, right?" Mia smiled. "I think it will be a great Thanksgiving. And you'll get to know Joel's dad. By the way, Joel is a junior."

"Well, that will be an easy name to remember. And I think you're right about the guys. Isn't there a big college football game that day?"

Paisley would be setting a table for six. That appealed to her. She wanted to make it special, not just because it was Thanksgiving, but she'd be sharing it with Joe.

Joe came in from his evening walk with Cinnabun. He found his son sitting at the kitchen bar eating a bowlful of popcorn.

"Hey, Dad. I have an invitation for Thanksgiving dinner with Mia. Her family wants you to come for dinner. They are anxious to meet you."

"Oh darn. I have an invitation for dinner. I accepted it this morning." Joe grabbed a handful popcorn.

"Let me guess, it's from that woman you're seeing?"

"What do you know about that?" He tossed a couple of fat kernels into his mouth.

"Oh Dad. You are so obvious. Clearly you've been meeting someone, and then you come home with that smile on your face."

His father blew out a breath and grabbed another handful of popcorn. "And why didn't you come home the other night?"

"Because I spent it with Mia."

"Son, you've done that several times lately. You're flirting with danger."

"I know, and we've discussed it. We keep the bedroom door open."

"And her mother knows?" Joe grabbed another handful from his son's bowl.

Joel chuckled, "She found out. And she seems fine with it. She says we are adults and capable of making our own mistakes."

"Don't screw up." He picked through what was left for the fattest pieces.

"I won't. I love her too much."

"Please tell Mia's family I said thank you, but I already have an invitation. I'd love to do it another time. Besides, I'm anxious to meet Mia. I think you need to make more popcorn."

"You'll like her and her family. I really think you'll like her mom." He looked down at the bowl in front of him. "Dad, did you have to eat my snack?"

"No, but it tasted good." He pointed his finger at his son. "I don't need you to play matchmaker. I'm doing fine on my own."

❧

Paisley was disappointed that she wouldn't be meeting Joel's father. But maybe it was a good thing. It probably would be awkward for his dad if she had a guy there.

"Emily, grab that pie from the oven. It should be done."

"Okay." Emily placed the pie on the cooling rack. "Do you want the pumpkin to go in the oven?"

"Yes, both of them."

"How many pies are you making?"

"Seven. I wanted to be certain I have everyone's favorite."

"There's a gazillion calories here. I'm probably gaining weight just by smelling them."

"No, you are not! You are a nice, normal, healthy weight. Stop worrying about such things. You wear off what goes into your mouth just by all the walking you do each day. You eat right, and your metabolism is fine. It's perfectly okay to indulge occasionally."

"Mom, all I said was that I... Never mind, you don't understand."

"Emily, you are over sensitive. Is Kevin coming?"

"Yes, but his parents are making him eat dinner at their house first."

"That's okay. Boys eat. I think my brother ate his weight in food every day."

"Is that why he has a beer gut now?"

"No, that's from him overeating now. And if he doesn't stop it, he'll have a heart attack before he's fifty."

"You've kept your shape."

"Thanks, but not really. I gained a little weight after each of you and never quite went back to what I once was."

"Kevin says all the guys think you're hot for being a mother."

"Gee, thanks, I guess. Nice to know that a bunch of teens--"

"I said for being a mother!"

"That's still weird."

Paisley finished baking and cleaned up the kitchen. She felt as though she might explode with pride. To be in this apartment and fixing a special meal for everyone was exciting. She locked up and turned out the lights. Morning would come too soon. And it did.

Paisley prepped the dinner, and then went back and changed into nicer clothes. The turkey was in the oven. The dressing was made, and she'd add that to the oven later. She had all the fixings prepared, and her raw vegetables were cut and on a tray in the refrigerator with three dipping sauces. The sweet potatoes were ready for the oven, and the green beans were ready for the stovetop.

Now it was time to wait. In another hour or so, she'd be introducing Joe to her girls and their boyfriends. Without warning, she felt nervous and a little self-conscious. She wasn't certain what her girls would think of Joe.

He had sent flowers for the occasion. Their bright, fall colors were so pretty. She loved the big mums. Unfortunately there was no room for them on her dining room table, not with all the food. They were relegated to a table by the sofa.

She looked at her dining table. Not all the chairs matched, but Mia had found a tablecloth with an adorable thanksgiving print. Mia also had found instructions on how to decorate chairs with sheets. She bought some fancy ribbon and enough sheets from the thrift store to do it. The holiday table looked elegant.

Time ticked by, and her uneasiness kept rising.

Joel pulled up in front of Joe Wags and got out about the same time as his father did. "Why are you here?"

His father shrugged. "I have a dinner date at 12204 Main Street, the green door."

Joel looked at his dad. "I thought you turned down the invitation from Mia and her family."

"I did. I have my own dinner date." He held up the gift bag containing several bottles of wine.

Joel laughed. "Dad, this is too funny. Come on, I'll introduce you to everyone."

Joe followed his son up the stairs.

When they entered the apartment, Mia looked at Joel surprised. "You brought your dad?"

"Actually, no. He's got his own dinner date."

Mia's mom came around the corner and smiled so brightly. "Joe, you came. I'm so glad you're here. Did my daughter introduce herself and Joel to you?"

Joel tried not to make a sound, but once he looked at his father, he couldn't hold back his laughter. "Seems we already know each other. I'd like to introduce you to my dad, Joel Selski, Senior. He goes by 'Joe'."

Mia's mom stood with a stunned look on her face. Then she began to giggle.

Joe went to Mia's mom and wrapped her in his arms. "I don't think I could be any happier. And my son was telling me how much I'd like you. Think he's right."

Joel was surprised when his father kissed Mia's mom in front of everyone.

Emily came into the room a little late. Mia tried to explain what had happened, and Emily began to laugh. "That's too funny. How did you all not know?"

"Well, no one ever said." Paisley told her daughter.

"Heck, I didn't know who he was dating, and he's my father." Joel chuckled. "And I live with him."

A little while later, Kevin came. After another round of introductions, the turkey was ready.

Joel kept watching his dad. It was great to see him smiling and happy. Joel wasn't certain how serious they were, but he figured his dad had to be because it was totally out of character for his father to be smiling and affectionate with a woman.

Trying not to be obvious, Joel watched Kevin and Emily. He figured Kevin probably wasn't her first boyfriend, but maybe this time it wasn't quite as casual. At least he was polite and well mannered. Emily seemed happy to have him. Joel was pleased to hear that Kevin was a good student and on the principal's list with Emily.

But it was as the day wound down that Joel got his first real glimpse of his father, not as a father but as a man. His dad had helped Mia's mom clean up the kitchen and when they were done, his father took her from the apartment. As the clock ticked, Joel came to the conclusion that he wasn't going to return home. He stayed with Mia.

It was early in the morning when he heard the door to the apartment close. The clock on his phone glowed 5:38 in soft blue numerals. He tucked Mia closer to him and wondered how she could sleep so soundly when his own libido made sleeping almost impossible some nights. He tucked her head under his chin as they lay spooned.

A few minutes later, he slid away from Mia and quietly left her bedroom.

He thought he'd be able to sneak out, but a voice said, "Morning."

He turned and saw Mia's mom.

Six

Fullerton came alive with Christmas lights, garlands, wreaths, jingle bells, and tons of bows. Paisley loved Christmas. Joe had helped her choose a Douglas fir for the living room, and then they decorated it with all the new balls, ornaments, and ribbons that Paisley had bought. When they were done, she stepped away from the tree, leaned against Joe, and admired her creation. It wasn't a child's tree. This one was grownup and elegant.

"I still can't believe that this is my tree." Her voice was barely above a whisper.

"It's beautiful. You've done a lovely job of picking out everything and placing it on the tree."

"You helped."

Cinnabun whimpered.

"What's the matter girl? Want to go out?"

Cinnabun swished her tail across the hardwood floor.

"Well, come on. I'll take you out." Joe picked up his coat. "We'll be back shortly."

"I'll make fresh coffee."

Cinnabun took her clue from Joe and stood.

Joe kissed Paisley. "Hmm, I love your kisses."

She grinned. "Go take care of your daughter."

He opened the door, and Cinnabun scampered down the stairs.

Paisley listened to them leave. Cinnabun sounded like she was dancing on the steps. Paisley went to the kitchen and began to fix dinner. She wasn't sure how many people to expect. She figured if she made too much, it would become lunch for tomorrow.

When she realized that Joe and Cinnabun hadn't returned, she began to worry. About a half hour had passed, then another fifteen slid by. She wasn't certain if she should put on her coat and look for them. She tried to tell herself not to worry. Joe probably walked Cinnabun to the park. Maybe she'd be more comfortable doing her doggie business there. Or maybe something happened. She tried to tell herself that she didn't hear any sirens. *But what if Joe had a heart attack or something, and he's lying on the pavement?*

Joe stepped out of Paisley's apartment and realized that it had started to snow. The weather report called for a dusting, but it was cold and windy. The dusting was already more than an inch. He took Cinnabun to the grassy alleyway. Joe Wags owned it and had made it into a pleasant place to sit with a cup of coffee, and it gave the dogs access to grass. Cinnabun kept tugging on her leash, pulling her owner to the far end of the alley, then behind the café to the dumpster. Cinnabun whined and another dog answered. That's when Joe realized what was happening. He wasn't certain the dog would follow him, and he was concerned about trying to pick up the female dog. "Okay." He used his softest voice. "Will you come with me? You want food? You want a bed?"

The dog responded with a sad sort of tail wag almost as though it was too much effort. Cinnabun nuzzled the other dog.

"Cinnabun, be very good and stay with Daddy." He dropped Cinnabun's leash. He tried to get the other dog to stand. She wouldn't.

He blew out a breath. *Is it too late? Do I dare carry her?*

Unsure, he petted the dog for a moment. Then he reached down and picked her up. The animal must have weighed fifty pounds or more. She looked skinny, but not as though she'd been a stray for a long time. Probably she was once a family pet, and when they realized she was pregnant, they put her out to survive on her own. The cruelty of the situation ripped at his insides.

He hefted the dog. She allowed him to do it, but she let out a small whimper. Cinnabun stayed at his side as he made his way back to Paisley's apartment. Navigating doors seemed impossible, especially the first green door. Then he was facing a long staircase. If he hadn't been proactive about his health, he doubted that he could have done this. Cinnabun stayed at his side. It was as though she knew what was happening. He finally made it into Paisley's apartment. "I need towels, lots of them, and a quiet corner."

"This whole place is hardwood, and the only place I can think to use is the big tub in my bathroom."

"Lead the way."

The tub was huge with a control panel for all the jets and bubblers. Paisley put down towels and somehow Joe managed to put the dog that looked a lot like a golden retriever mixed with something else in the center of the tub. "She needs a drink, and I'm not certain if we should allow her to eat or not, but I think she needs the water."

Paisley vanished and returned with a big bowl that she filled with water from the sink. The dog raised her head enough to lap at the water, but not enough to quench a dog's thirst.

"Shall I call an emergency vet?" Paisley offered.

"That might be a good idea." Joe leaned over the tub and scratched the dog behind her ears.

The vet office was helpful and suggested they watch a few videos on the Internet.

Paisley finished making dinner while he stayed with the pregnant dog.

An hour later, the dog gave birth to the first pup. It was stillborn. The wait was on. About twenty minutes after that, she gave birth to the next one. Cinnabun climbed into the tub and never left the pregnant female.

"When this is over, she might want to eat. I'll run home, if you're comfortable staying alone with her, and bring back some of Cinnabun's food."

"I'll be fine. I'm sure she will be hungry."

"We can't let her have much at first. Little amounts frequently would be better. What about Cinnabun? May she stay here with you and her new friend?"

"Leave her. She seems very much a part of this process."

Joe wasted no time. When he got to the house, he grabbed up extra dog bowls, an extra leash and collar, and anything else he could think of that might be needed. Then he came back to Paisley's.

The dog had given birth again. This time he thought the pup might be a little male. The dog continued to have a pup about every half hour for a couple of hours. When they thought maybe it was over, she had two more. An hour later, she had another. The night ticked away as they sat with the dog.

"Paisley, go to bed. You have to work in the morning."

"I don't want to leave her."

Joe found her pillow and brought her the big quilt from her bed. Paisley put her head on the pillow and went right off to sleep. Joe chuckled to himself, picked up Paisley, and put her on her bed, covering her with the quilt.

All together, the dog had nine puppies, but only five had survived.

Joe gave the mother dog some water and then small amounts of canned food by allowing her to lick it from his finger. By noon, the Golden wanted to go out. When she came in, she ate a partial bowl of dried food and had a little treat. Mommy dog was on her way to recovery. And her puppies knew exactly where to go for their food.

Cinnabun seemed to be much more relaxed and happy. She was willing to go down for her doggie breaks in the alleyway, but she refused to get in the car to go home. She wanted to go back to her friend. Joe gave up and let her stay.

Paisley must have called her boss because he showed up shortly after she came home from work.

Flint smiled as he introduced himself to Joe. "She's lovely. I can't believe someone abandoned her. She might be chipped and have an owner. The only way to find out is to take her to the vet." He picked up a pup. "Oh, so tiny. Don't worry about what to do with the puppies. I'll turn them into service dogs if no one claims the mother."

Joe liked Flint. He treated Paisley like family and never once complained about having dogs in the apartment.

Joe took a few days off from work to stay with the pups. And then he took the mother and the pups to the vet. He dreaded the outcome. Certainly, someone would claim this animal. Cinnabun's heart would break, too, as the dogs had become close buddies.

Joel reached in his drawer for the box that contained the ring he'd bought for Mia. He opened the box and stared at the diamond. Marriage wouldn't stop her from going to college. And *he* certainly would never stop her. *Being married would make it easier on her. If only I could be sure she'd say yes.*

He was going to wait until Christmas, but he decided to do it sooner. *Tonight. I'm asking her tonight.* He pocketed the box and made reservations at Killen's Dock.

Joel called Mia's phone. "Hi. Dinner tonight at Killen's Dock. Do you have a little black dress to wear?"

"Oh, I have something much more exciting."

"Something to look forward to… maybe something very sexy?"

"Ah, sexy, but not overtly. And I have killer heels to go with it."

"Okay, killer heels to go to Killen's Dock. I think I'm going to like this."

"What are you wearing?"

"The man's equivalent of a LBD."

"What's that?"

"My black suit." He could hear her giggling. "I don't wear *killer* heels. My heels are rather masculine."

"I can't wait to see what you are wearing. What color shirt?"

"Well, I wouldn't want to clash with what you are wearing, so shall I do white, black, or gray?"

"Black? You in a black shirt?"

"I've been known to wear black shirts and black tee-shirts. It helps with my bad boy image."

She broke into laughter. "You?"

"Oh, I can be very bad, and I'm very good at it. Does that sound tough enough? Or do I need to buy a bike and a leather jacket to go with it?"

"The leather jacket sounds good. As for the bike… Maybe we should get a pair of matching 21-speed hybrids?" She giggled.

"It's an idea. Where would you like to ride?"

"I love you. But I'm never too certain when you are teasing me or being serious."

"The bikes sound like fun. We could get matching jackets and helmets to go with the bikes."

Mia got her giggles under control. "What time are you picking me up?"

"Five."

"I'll be ready. And I like the idea of having bikes. I haven't had one since I was ten. I used to ride all over the neighborhood."

"Mia?"

"Yes."

"I love you."

At three minutes to five, he pulled up in front of Mia's apartment. He wore his black suit, white shirt, and a black tie that had silver and red swirls. The diamond was in his pocket.

Mia greeted him in a gold dress that shimmered. Her matching heels were ridiculously high, and the leather straps

442 ⁓⁓ *Christmas Wishes on Main Street*

crossed over her ankles twice before buckling. Her hair hung freely down her back, and where it was swept from her face, she wore a rhinestone barrette. She was hot, very hot.

It didn't take long to get to Killen's Dock. The restaurant faced the river and had a large sweeping patio that was delightful in warmer weather. Tonight, the restaurant was decorated for Christmas.

Their table was a booth in a quiet corner. Their waiter was prepared for them. Joel had ordered ahead of time.

He watched Mia's eyes as the different courses were served. The evening progressed like something from a dream. He knew she would love it. She was like that. She'd never ask for it, yet she'd enjoy every minute of it.

"Please tell me there's nothing else, because I can't eat another bite."

Joel smiled. "Only dessert."

"I can't!"

"Oh, you'll manage."

"I can't. It's not going down."

"Then we'll have to get a box for it." He motioned to the waiter. "Box the rest to go. And we'll just have our coffee."

She rolled her eyes at him. "Where am I going to put the coffee?"

"It'll fit, fills in all the little air pockets." He chuckled.

After the coffee was served, he took her hand. "Mia, I love you. I fell in love the moment I saw you. I know you intend to get your degree, and I think that is wonderful. But I'd like you to consider another set of letters to go with your degree. I'd like for you to have your M-R-S." He came to where she was sitting and properly proposed. "I love you."

He held out the box and waited. She didn't answer. She sat staring at the diamond.

"Put it on your finger and say yes. The 'I-do' part can happen whenever you are ready. I'd like that to be soon, but I'll wait for you."

She took the ring and stared at it. "I've never seen such a large stone. Is it real?"

He nodded.

"Movie stars wear rings like this."

He smiled. "It's four carats. Put it on."

She slid the ring into place, and then held out her hand in front of her. "It goes from knuckle to knuckle."

He nodded. "Mia, say yes."

"Oh… I can't imagine ever marrying anyone else."

"Say yes."

"Yes! Yes! Yes!"

The lump that had risen in his throat dissolved. He could breathe again. He stood and then kissed her. She would be his.

"I want a real wedding, except I don't have many people to invite."

"Mia, don't worry about the number of people. Buy your dress; plan your wedding. We'll have enough people to share it, we don't need a big wedding."

She nodded. "I've always wanted the beautiful dress and the big cake."

"Then you shall have it."

"Mom can't afford it."

"You can. Because, I will make certain that you have whatever you need."

"When do you want to get married?" she asked.

"Tonight?"

"No, really when?"

"The sooner the better for me. I'm finding it very difficult to control myself."

Paisley looked up and saw Flint Silverlake in Joe Wags. He seemed to be rearranging furniture. She watched him as she waited on customers. *What on earth is he doing?*

Then he brought in a type of dog fencing and set it up in the empty space he had created. Inside of that, he added a dog bed and some bowls.

"What are you doing?" Paisley asked when she had a moment.

"It will socialize the animals and make it easier on you so that you're not running upstairs every chance you get. She can be the mascot here, and her babies will attract some attention."

"She's not chipped or tattooed."

"That's what Joe told me. She needs a name other than Mom. Let's have our customers name her and the pups."

Paisley wanted to roll her eyes at Flint, but she could see what he was doing.

"We'll name her on Christmas Eve. We'll pull the names from the jars and that will be it." Flint put three jars on the counter with labels. "You might have to manage that naming ceremony yourself because my wife would be very upset if I missed Christmas Eve with my family."

"Okay, I'll pull the names at 2 p.m. What if the name is totally stupid?"

"Manager's discretion."

"Okay."

"That gives us a little more than one week. Think we can do it?"

Paisley smiled. "Of course!"

She watched the jars fill. People brought in their children and let them choose names for the dogs. A lot of people asked about adopting the puppies. Flint had some thoughts on that. The shelter usually screened applicants. There were quite a few dogs that needed adopting at the shelter.

The following day, Paisley discovered that Annie would be coming daily with a few dogs needing homes. Joe Wags was going to showcase several different dogs every day.

Paisley began to wonder if there would be room for her patrons to come for coffee.

Flint kept a close eye on things, and then when the coffee traffic had slowed, he pulled Paisley to one side. "I want to talk to you about something."

Paisley held her breath. Two days before Christmas Eve was not the time for bad news. She poured two cups of coffee and brought them to a table.

Flint smiled. "I have an idea."

Paisley swallowed. That usually meant extra work. "What?"

"I need someone who can keep an eye on things. Someone who can make suggestions to the various cafés - a person I can trust and isn't afraid to make a decision without my approval. I've got quite a few Cup of Joe's and now Joe Wags. It would allow you to work from home and then travel as needed. It'll come with a raise. I think you're that person. You've done a terrific job in this town."

"Thanks. Do I get to think about this or am I supposed to give you an answer now?"

Seven

Mia couldn't wait to show off her ring to her mom and sister.

Emily drooled over it. "Omigod, that is huge. Big diamonds are so expensive." She swiped her phone a few times and showed what diamonds that size cost.

Mia gasped.

"I told you!"

"Oh. I knew it was expensive, but I had no idea it was that much." Mia flopped onto her mom's sofa. "How does anyone get that kind of money?"

"Credit?"

"For that much? Even twenty percent down is a lot."

"Maybe you need to check up on him. Know-who-you-are-marrying sort of thing. Have you even looked to see where he works?"

"No."

"Well, let's go find him. Where does he work? Do you even know that much?"

"Grenfield Technologies."

Emily was back on her phone. "Surprise. They have a website. Let's see what it says." She began to read their mission statement aloud. "Boring."

"Okay, very responsible company. Does it give a listing of email addresses or anything?"

"I'll look under Who Are We." Emily made a face. "That didn't work." Emily tried a few more things. "Oh, I found it. Any chance Joel and Joe work at the same place?"

"No, I don't think so. He said what his father did and where. Hmm…"

"Well then, if this isn't Joel the father, your Joel is listed as vice president of research and development."

"No way, that's got to be his father." Mia started checking on her phone. "Hmm… What if I contacted the company and asked to speak to him? What's the worst that will happen? I might get his dad."

"Think you can tell them apart on the phone?" Emily raised her eyebrows.

"Everyone says they can't tell us apart on the phone."

"Exactly." Emily curled her legs under her. "If you called the company, you could ask if it's junior or senior. That kind of thing usually goes on ID badges."

"Okay, I'll try it. Wait! I need an excuse. Give me your phone, and that way I can say that you accidentally picked up my phone so I'm using yours, and I don't have anyone's phone number."

"That'll work." Emily passed her phone to Mia.

Mia called the company number. She went into an automated voicemail list. Then she heard press 0 for the operator. "Hello. Maybe you can help me, is Joel Selski a senior or a junior?"

"Junior."

"Wonderful! Will you please put this call through to him?" She waited for Joel to answer. Instead, it was a woman's voice.

"R & D, how may I help you?"

"Is Joel available?"

"You mean *Mister* Selski?"

"Yeah."

"He isn't available at the moment. Is there something I can do for you?"

Mia made a face at her sister. "No. This is his fiancée."

"I'm so sorry, Miss. Mr. Selski is in a meeting and probably won't be out until sometime this afternoon. May I have your name and phone number?"

"Mia."

"And your last name, Mia?"

"Just say Mia. He knows my name." She rolled her eyes at her sister.

"And your phone number?"

"He has it. Tell him my sister and I traded phones by accident. I'll call him later." Mia shook her head and disconnected the call. "That was terrible. But that's him, vice president of research and development."

"He's young for that. Wonder how he got that job. Somebody must be a friend of Daddy's." Emily got that haughty look that she had perfected.

"Maybe. Let's check up on Joe."

"Give me back my phone." Emily took her phone and began another search. "Dead end. What do we know about him?"

"He's got a big house nearby. That's about it. Mom doesn't say much."

"I know. Think it's the golf course neighborhood off Claymont?"

Mia shrugged.

"Bingo!" Emily held up the phone's screen to her sister, showing a physical map of the neighborhood. "Big enough house?"

"No wonder they said they didn't know who the other was dating. They probably only discover when they are both in the house by sheer accident." Mia sat back and thought for a moment. "I wonder if you're the vice president, do you have to ask to leave early?"

"You think of the weirdest things."

"We've got to find out more on Joe. Don't you think we need to know who Mom is dating?"

Emily shrugged. "There's got to be a way—" She grunted a few times and inhaled sharply.

"What is it? What did you find?"

"I'm not certain, but Joe has an arrest record."

"What!"

"It's in the newspaper."

"What on earth? Joe? That doesn't even seem possible."

"Well, I thought that was why you wanted me to check on him. We don't want Mom marrying a con artist or something." Emily let out a loud sigh.

"Hurry up. This doesn't seem real. I can't believe Joe... of all people. I wish we could do a credit check."

"That's a no-go. Credit companies have that info under lock and key," Emily said.

"I want to know why Joe was arrested. Do you think he had a heroin addiction or something?"

Emily shook her head. "How did I get such an insane sister?" Emily bit her lower lip. "Oh, my."

"What? You're killing me."

"I think I found out why he was arrested." Emily began to read an article from the local newspaper.

"That's it? He was protesting the county's animal control policy of euthanizing dogs and cats after being held for only two weeks?"

She frowned and found the rest of the article. "He and several others spent two nights in the city's jail for interfering with government operations. And it gives the code numbers. The judge lowered it to a misdemeanor and fined everyone." Emily held up her hand. " Wait! There's more. Joe was the one who purchased the land for the no-kill animal shelter."

"That is so altruistic. So very Joe."

Emily took a selfie. "I look terrible. I wish I had your hair color."

"Color it if you don't like it."

Emily let out a breathy sigh. "Do you still want to check on Joe? Because without more information, I can't find anything."

"I guess not. They say the apple doesn't fall far from the tree. If that's true, then Joe's got to be a good guy because my apple didn't come from a lousy tree."

"When are you getting married?"

Joe looked around his house. It was clean and neat. He had someone come once a week to keep it that way. He was certain that Paisley would find everything satisfactory. He thought about the idea that she might want to change a few things. He really didn't care. Maybe things needed to be changed and updated, although Joel never said anything about it.

He picked up his keys and went to the jewelry store. He looked in the glass cases at all the diamonds. There were bracelets, necklaces, and numerous rings. Each piece of jewelry dazzled with fire under the bright lights. He'd seen the beautiful solitaire his son had bought. That gave Joe an indication so that he didn't choose the same thing. He found rings covered in diamonds and pointed to the case when the saleswoman approached him. "I'm looking for a ring. She wears a size four."

The woman behind the counter unlocked a case and showed him a group of rings in Paisley's size.

"I wanted something more for an engagement ring."

"That size tosses you into youth jewelry."

"She's very petite."

"We might have a set in the safe. Let me check." The woman returned the rings to the showcase and disappeared for a moment. An older woman followed the clerk from the back room. "Would something like this be what you are looking to purchase?"

Joe looked at the two rings on a small tray. They were beautiful. The wedding band matched the engagement ring. He lifted it off the velvet. It didn't even fit on the tip of his pinky finger. A price tag dangled from the ring. He looked and inhaled. *Are diamonds that expensive?* "Is this the top of the line for this sort of style?"

The older woman nodded. "The total weight is over twelve carats and they are all natural diamonds."

It took another couple of minutes for the saleswoman to produce the certificate for that ring. He knew he'd found what he wanted. The price was outrageous, but she was worth it. All he needed now was a simple yes.

Christmas Eve arrived and Paisley made a ceremony of pulling names from the jars. The newspaper was there snapping photos. She pulled the pups' names first.

"Our first little girl is… Madeline." Then she reached into the jar again and pulled another. "This one is Goldilocks." She smiled and pulled the third name. "Freckles." She reached into the gated area and lifted the one little girl with brown spots. "This one must be Freckles! What a perfect name for her."

Then she did the two males. The first one was named Bucky, and the last little puppy was named Bailey. Finally, she put her hand into the last jar and swirled all the entry forms around. "Okay, let's see what we're going to call the mother." She opened the form and stared at it. She put it to one side and opened another. It said the same thing. When she pulled the third one, she grinned. "Someone has messed with the entry forms because each one is asking me to marry him."

Joe stepped forward. "The real entry forms are in another jar." He put his hands in his pockets. "I'd love to know your answer."

She looked up at him and smiled. Then she looked at the crowd who had come for the naming ceremony. "Well, what do you think? Should I say yes?"

The crowd cheered.

"I think that means that they agree with me. Yes, I will marry you."

Joe pulled his hands from his pockets. "This is for you."

She took the ring. Smaller stones surrounded five large diamonds. The whole ring was encrusted with diamonds.

Paisley held her breath as Joe put it on her finger. When her lungs began to protest, she remembered to breathe. "It's beautiful."

She wrapped her arms around Joe. "Yes, I will marry you."

"Think you need to get back to pulling a name for the mother dog?"

"May I have the real jar?"

The other jar appeared, and she reached inside and swirled those forms. "And mommy dog will be known as…" She unfolded a form. She looked up and smiled. "Princess."

She held onto the winning entries because those people would receive free coffee for the month of January along with a Joe Wags travel mug and a few other things.

She called Flint to give him the results of the drawing, and she could hear his oldest daughter cheering when he passed the names along to his family.

At four p.m., Paisley closed Joe Wags until December 26. Two families were about to blend into one, at least for the holiday.

Christmas Eve was spent with everyone chatting. Paisley made popcorn. Joe disappeared into the kitchen, and when he returned he handed them each a mug.

"Hot buttered rum."

"Ah, Dad, you might not want to give that to Mia's mom."

"Why?" Joe cocked his head to the side.

Mia fell into giggles as she tried to tell her future father-in-law. "Mom says alcohol makes her panties fall off."

"Really? There's enough for seconds and maybe thirds." Joe chuckled.

"Better not, Dad. That's how she got two daughters."

"Oh, I see, and I'm going to venture a guess that it's still a possibility." Joe looked at Paisley.

Paisley grinned. "Oh, yes. Most definitely. And you'd better keep that in mind, Mia."

Joel laughed. "We're prepared and have been. If anything does fall off, we can handle it."

Joe made a face. "Joel, may I speak to you in the kitchen?"

Joel got up and laughed. "You're not borrowing anything because I don't want it back. Besides there are some things I'd rather not know about my father."

"Son, I wanted to warn you. Don't do anything you might regret. You've made it this far, you can manage to make it to your wedding night."

"Can you?"

"Don't ask your father things like that."

Joel laughed and walked away.

Underneath Paisley's Christmas tree, there were packages galore. None of the women had ever seen so many gifts. Joe and Joel made certain there would be a very merry Christmas.

Christmas morning, Paisley made breakfast for her girls, Joel, and Joe. She couldn't remember when she ever had a Christmas with this much food. She even had a beautiful standing rib roast for dinner and intended to make Yorkshire pudding to go with it.

As soon as the guys arrived, they ate breakfast. Then they went into her living room and began to open presents.

Paisley looked at the one gift from her older daughter. "What is it?"

"Edible body paint." Mia smirked.

"What is that?"

Joe touched her arm. "I'll show you when we're totally alone." He looked at Mia. "Thank you. I know we'll enjoy it."

Mia laughed, and Joel joined in. "T. M. I. There are some things — that's one image I don't want to have of my father."

Mia laughed. "I think it's great. Those two are a little behind on things."

Joel shook his head. "You have no idea."

"Maybe I do."

"Kids, stop it. You'd think that you invented sex." Paisley whined.

Mia looked at her mother and laughed. "Oh, we know better. Have fun."

Never had Mia and Emily ever seen such a Christmas. Joel and Joe were behind most of it, but this year Paisley could actually afford Christmas gifts. Even the dogs received treats. And when Paisley discovered the Belgium waffle maker, she wanted to cry. She'd wanted one forever. It felt as though she was caught in a fairy tale, because it was the first time in her adult life that she had all of her Christmas wishes come true. She relished every moment of the entire day. As the day drew to a close, she snuggled into Joe's arms.

A few days after the holiday, Paisley texted Flint. She had made her decision. She liked being the manager of Joe Wags. And she was willing to share ideas with him. But for the first time in a very long time, she was happy. When it came to her job, she didn't want to change a thing. *Sorry, decision made. I'm turning down your offer. Managing Joe Wags in Fullerton is absolutely the most wonderful, fun job that I've ever had.*

She made another decision and texted Joe. *Spring wedding. First week in May, I have vacation time coming.*

Joe returned the text. *That sounds perfect.*

You don't mind waiting until May?

It's called going slowly.

So wedding date solved. But I'm wondering when I'll get kissed again.

I think it's been a long time since I kissed a woman. Think we could try it when I get off from work?

She laughed and texted him. *We must try kissing again. Being forced to wait almost nine hours between kisses is not very acceptable. I might forget how to do it, and you'll have to teach me all over again.*

Mia bounced into the kitchen with Joel trailing her. "We made our decision. We don't want to wait to get married.

We've decided on the last Saturday in January. But--"

"We'll delay the honeymoon until her spring break." Joel smiled as he put his hands on Mia's shoulders.

"What? How are we going to plan something that quickly?" Paisley was certain that a wedding that quick would be almost impossible.

"Really, Mom, it won't be that difficult. I'm going to ask Chef Carlos at the Beehive to do my cake. He loves to do stuff like that, and the Beehive doesn't have that sort of thing on the menu." She turned to Joel. "And he said that he could call the country club and reserve one of their private areas for our wedding."

"The country club?" Paisley swallowed.

"Well, yes. It's right there where we live. It's two minutes from Dad's house. And we're charter members, which grants us extra privileges, so renting those rooms is not a big deal. I'll have them cater the reception."

Mia had that dreamy far away look in her eyes.

"Okay, kids. I'm writing this down. Cake is Mia's responsibility. Joel, you are venue and the catering?"

Joel grimaced. "When it comes to the food, I don't know. Does one of you want to select the food?"

Mia looked at her mom. "I can do that, but would you like to come with me? That way it gives us a chance to see the place and maybe how everything will be set up." She shrugged. "Really, I can do it by myself, but I thought you'd like to be part of it."

Paisley nodded. "Yes, I'd enjoy that." She looked at Joel. "We also need to discuss living arrangements because it's about to get complicated."

Joel shook his head. "It won't be a problem. Even if we stay at my dad's, it will probably be temporary. I figured I'd take Mia away for a few days. Just to give us some privacy after we're married." Joel walked to the coffee pot and fixed a cup. "We haven't decided if we're going to move in with Dad, or if we would ask you to allow us to stay here. But I was thinking when you move in with my dad, would Flint consider renting to us instead of you? This is a great apartment." He looked at Mia. "And I know she loves it here."

"I can ask." Paisley smiled broadly. "Joe and I decided this morning that the first week in May we are getting married and disappearing for our honeymoon."

"Oh, Mom, I'm so thrilled for you." Mia put her arms around her mother and gave her a kiss.

"I'm assuming that you will move in with Dad." Joel looked at his future mother-in-law and smiled.

"Right. I just don't know when. That still leaves Emily in limbo."

Joel spoke up. "We're willing to have her stay here until she finishes the school year, but she might prefer to live with you and Dad."

"You two figured out this whole thing?" Paisley asked.

Mia nodded. "We just don't know when you are leaving. And don't say that you're trying to set some sort of example for Emily. I can tell you right now that she's not going to buy it."

Paisley rolled her eyes at her older daughter.

Joe stopped by the apartment to move Princess to his house with Cinnabun. "It's not a problem. I'll bring them to Joe Wags in the morning and pick them up in the evening. That way they are never alone."

The puppies were growing by leaps and bounds. When they reached eight weeks, Flint was hoping to take the puppies. Then four days before Mia married Joel, the animal shelter called Mia.

"Hi, this is Annie from the shelter. Someone brought in several kittens last week, and this week they are ready for adoption."

Mia looked at her mom. "Kitten?"

Paisley rolled her eyes. "What's one more around here?"

Two hours later, Mia brought home a very playful, longhaired gray kitten that had instantly bonded with her. Cinnabun and Princess didn't seem to mind the little kitten, but none of the dogs were pleased with the kitten's sharp claws. That sent Mia scrambling to find the little caps that cover the claws.

Thursday morning, the florist called. The Queen Anne's lace that was supposed to be in all the wedding flowers never came in from the supplier. Mia dissolved into tears.

Paisley knew her daughter was stressed because tears over something so inane weren't normal.

Paisley felt sorry for her daughter. "I'll call the florist. We all know that you want beautiful flowers, honey. They are probably as upset as you are. They promised and now they can't get them, but it's not their fault."

Paisley called the florist, and they suggested several alternatives. The flat white mums were what the florist first suggested. Paisley knew that she loved mums, but she wasn't as certain that her daughter shared the same feelings. "What are the other choices?"

She settled on another flower that they recommended.

When Mia walked into the apartment Thursday evening, Paisley prayed that Mia wasn't going to have a problem with her wedding dress. A local seamstress took the hem up several inches and made some other adjustments so that the gown would fit perfectly. Mia tried on the dress while Paisley held her breath. They were out of time for any more alterations.

The dress fit perfectly. Mia called it a mermaid style, but unlike the normal flare at the knees, this one trailed behind her. With its very fitted top, the dress showed off her figure. The tulle veil matched the tulle on the mermaid tail. Paisley stood back and looked at her daughter. "The dress is gorgeous, and you're beautiful."

Mia and Joel were married at the country club with only a few family members and friends in attendance. Chef Carlos baked Mia the most beautiful cake. Three tiers were trimmed with garlands made of icing. It was delicious, and it was obvious that Carlos had gone beyond what was expected.

Mia and Joel held the knife for the longest time. Mia hated to cut into the fabulous work of art. Jillian audibly groaned when the knife pierced the cake. She probably echoed almost every ones sentiments.

Mia and Joel had the perfect little wedding. Shortly after they cut the cake, they quietly slipped away for their mini honeymoon.

Paisley turned to Joe. "What do you think about eloping?"

Joe shrugged. "I'll do whatever you want."

"I had a wedding and a long wedding dress. I don't need another one. And after what I've been through with Mia, I don't want a repeat performance. I'm in favor of the simplest possible wedding."

"Suits me. Anyplace warm and wonderful, maybe an island?"

Paisley tried to decide if he was teasing or serious. "Oh, you are asking the person who has never left this state where she wants to go?"

"Never?" Joe looked as though he didn't believe a word she had said.

Paisley shook her head. "Never left the state. Born and raised in the same town, moving to Fullerton was a big deal. This is the furthest I've been from home."

"I'll be sure to fix that situation. Better apply for your passport."

"Why would--"

"You'll need it if you're married to me. I'm going to make your dreams come true."

"You already have. I can't imagine more."

Joe curled her against his chest and kissed her. "I love you." He chuckled. "If you don't want a big wedding, then why are we waiting until May? Let's go down and get our license this week and get married next Saturday."

"I guess we could. I never thought about doing that."

He grinned. "I'm tired of waiting. We're not kids."

Paisley looked at Joe and smiled. "So am I. Why wait until the weekend? We can just do it."

"No fanfare?"

"You are more than enough for me." She grinned. "Do you think we forgot how to…"

He murmured into her ear. "Just think of the fun we'll have exploring and learning."

His nibbling on her ear set her on fire. She tried to remain composed when Emily approached. Paisley faced her daughter.

"Mom, Jillian and several others are going to The Wall. They're going to do that indoor rock climb."

Paisley nodded.

Emily continued. "I want to go. May I?"

Paisley hesitated.

"I've gone with my son several times. It's loads of fun." Joe looked at Emily. "You need to change into something that isn't going to show more than you want. It's tougher than it looks."

"Does that mean I can?"

Paisley nodded. "Be careful. Come to Joe's house when you're done."

"I will, Mom."

Joe nibbled on the nape of Paisley's neck and then murmured, "I think we need a refresher course, starting tonight."

Paisley grinned. "Tonight?"

Joe tucked Paisley tight to his body. "Oh, yes. It's been a very long time."

The Trouble with Wishes

Carol DeVaney

One

Not that she noticed, but Ellie Newsome's heart picked up a beat… every time the phone rang.

Frankly, the waiting was making her nuts. She was annoyed with herself for nonetheless expecting a call from Luke, the man who had moved quietly inside her heart in so short a time.

Would he ever call? Did he even think of her? Since almost two months had passed and there had been no word from him, it was obvious a call was still up for debate. She'd thought, at the very least, they'd had a reasonable and friendly relationship. Little did she know...

Hesitant from the beginning, after his accident, but she had taken his children and Luke into her home and helped nurse him back to health. Now, he'd determined it was time to resume responsibility for his family. Ellie realized the timing was right and admired his decision, but wondered how he'd fare with the reality of being a recent widower and now the single-handed care giver of his two young children.

Though Luke didn't punch a time clock, even working at home would have its drawbacks. Children and their concerns weren't written down or followed with a checklist. Ellie absolutely saw a housekeeper and a nanny in his future, if he hadn't already hired one or both. She had no doubt Luke could handle most any issue that came up, but he had a huge and time consuming business to run. She wondered if he actually knew how many different hats he'd need to wear? He'd soon find out—if he hadn't already.

The understatement of disappointment was that Luke Conway hadn't called before now, and as her eyes traveled toward the caller I.D. ringing in, the call wasn't from him this time either. Certainly, a couple of months was long enough to get settled into his home. But what did she know?

Her thoughts shifted back to how and why they'd met. Even though she'd welcomed his children into her home and cared for them after his wife had perished at the car accident scene before Thanksgiving last year, she had also cared for Luke while he recovered from his injuries in the same accident. She wanted no thanks, but to hope for a phone call was within reason.

But then why would he call her? He was dealing with the grief process of losing his wife, which was still raw, for him and his children. Danni, almost ten, was old enough to remember her mom, but Brett was only six months old, so the effect on him wouldn't be so traumatic, at least for now. She worried about Danni, because she'd gone through a painful withdrawal after her mother's death. Danni had embraced Ellie and gave the impression that she looked to her for support. Now, without Ellie's interaction, she suspected, Luke was in for more than he anticipated with his strong, but sensitive little girl.

None of the thoughts and dreams inside Ellie's head were Luke's fault, or for that matter, hers. Certainly she hadn't planned to fall for him. Quite the contrary, she'd fought against it when the concern of caring for him day in and day out had grown stronger with each passing moment. It was clearly one of those reactions, in simple terms, that had happened. He hadn't pursued her or given her any reason to believe that, for the two of them, there would be expectations of a romantic connection any time soon, or ever, for that matter. Only once had she noticed a responsive gaze in his eyes. She should have paid more attention to reasoning, instead of letting her heart guide her into a challenge which she had no control.

Luke would need time, and she'd give him all the time he needed and deserved. Even though she was working through a recent unpleasant break-up with her husband, she'd vowed one day to win Luke's heart.

That one wish she wouldn't let go of, no matter the outcome.

Even though the trouble with wishes were... every now and then... they didn't work out and someone always got hurt. Wishes were held in the heart and this was one wish she hadn't planned or expected.

His children held a special place in her heart, but to use the children to win over Luke, would be the worst mistake ever. That wasn't happening. Ever.

Ellie missed his children. She missed Luke. She would work out a strategy somehow to accomplish her wish. If Luke wasn't to be hers, then it wasn't meant to be, and she'd accept the consequences. If she were to lose him, it would break her heart. She wouldn't think of loss though. She had to stay positive, remain on track and bide her time. Whatever the outcome.

The last thing on Ellie's mind, and the last thing she wanted to do was to carry on a conversation, but picked up the phone when she saw whose name had popped up on the display. Grateful for the bond they'd formed, she'd always made time for Gage. Gage Landon had befriended her and helped guide her through the grief after Ellie had miscarried two babies. When Ellie's husband walked out on her two weeks after the second miscarriage, Gage had been there for her then, too.

"Hi. I thought I'd touch base in case you need anything," Gage said, then giggled. "Plus, you know how curious I am. I wanted to see how you're doing."

Ellie laughed at Gage's energy that projected itself across the line. "Hi, yourself... and yes, I do know how you are by now. Thanks, but no. I don't need a thing. I'm good. One exception. If you could bring the snow to an end, that would be a blessing."

Gage was an valuable friend, and she didn't know what she'd have done without her. She'd taken to Ellie from the day she had moved to Apple Lake. Ellie valued Gage as though they'd been friends all her life. She was full of life and had more enthusiasm than anyone she'd ever known... from taking care of her family, to working at the Children's Center with her director husband, Matt. Gage and Matt had married two years ago after discovering each other, and their second chance at love, at the dog park. Ellie didn't know any two people who were as compatible, or who deserved more happiness.

"I'm afraid I can't do anything about the snow. I know I'm being nosey, but have you heard anything from Luke since he moved back home?" Gage asked.

"Nothing. Nada. Not one word. Not even a phone call from Danni. In fact, I expected *her* to call, even if Luke didn't." Ellie sighed and pulled an envelope from a stack of bills, then discarded the piece of junk mail in the wastebasket beneath the desk. She logged onto the computer, then waited while the sluggish internet opted to come up.

"Give them a bit more time. I'm sure Luke has his hands full," Gage said.

"I'm sure Luke has been getting the children settled and Danni in school after the holidays. I can't believe it's 2018... the New Year has already passed and so has Valentine's Day. Where has the time gone?"

"Tell me about it. I can't believe it's almost March. The older we get, the faster the years zoom by," Gage said, then laughed. "So, tell me how you're adjusting since everyone left? Are you lonesome?"

Gage was aware of how close a connection she'd formed with Luke and his children. There was no reason not to be truthful. "To be honest, I miss all of them like crazy. The house is too quiet, and I have way too much time on my hands. So, yes. It's a bit lonesome around the house."

"Let me help you, Ellie. Volunteers at the Children's Center are forever in demand. There's a position for you if you'd like. There are days we're short-staffed due to illness or other concerns, and now is one of those opportunities for someone with your approach toward children. You have considerable abilities to offer our kids. Plus, with you working at the center, we'd have more time to spend together."

"I don't know, Gage. There are a few choices to consider before I could commit."

"I understand. You wouldn't be required to be here every day. We could set up a schedule, or you could choose to be an on call volunteer. What do you say, Ellie? It'll get you out of the house. I worry about you and wouldn't want to see you become depressed."

Ellie pivoted her chair to face the window and gazed out over the second floor deck at the blanket of glistening, white swirls that spread as far as she could see. The unexpected snowstorm had dropped ten more inches of snow across the North Georgia Mountains over the past three days. Now the snow flurries had, at long last, slowed to a gentle downfall, which was a good thing. The snow they'd experienced the past three months was enough to last a lifetime.

"I have no intention of letting myself become depressed. Before the children and Luke came to live with me, I'd decided to place myself back into the work place. It's important that I do something even moreso now. The house is much more isolated now without the never-ending sounds of children underfoot. I miss them. A steady job will fill the long hours and help keep me sane. Still, there are my mom and dad to consider and working part time with you would allow me to take care of them should the need arise." She sighed. "I'll give your offer some thought."

I miss Luke too, but I won't go there. There was nothing to do except wait on time. Time for Luke to grieve. Time for me to hold to the wish in my heart that Luke will one day be mine.

"Good idea, Ellie. Let me know if I can help in any way. My offer stands though. Please give it some thought if the job offers you receive aren't to your liking. We could possibly find a paying position for you at the center. I can certainly give you the hours, paid or volunteer. When you decide, give me a call, and I'll speak with Matt."

"A job offer is kind of you, Gage. You always go the extra mile to help a friend. What on earth would Matt think of you creating a paying position for me?" she teased.

"Matt cares for you as much as I do, Ellie. You know that. I'm certain he'd be happy for me to spend more time at home." She laughed. "You know how there isn't anything he likes better than to come home to the scent of a home cooked meal."

"Yes, I do. I don't know what I'd have done without both of you being there for me when I lost the babies. Not to mention after Ryan walked out on me." A lump formed in her throat at the thought of losing her babies, but she swallowed back the pain and took a deep breath. "I have a great deal to thank you for, Gage."

"Nonsense. That's what friends are for, Ellie. So, let me know when you make up your mind. Either way is good as long as it makes you happy. Things will work out… you'll see."

"I have no idea how you stay so positive. I'm thankful though. Your way of thinking has a way of rubbing off on me."

No matter how long it took, Ellie was going to do something worthwhile with her life. She wasn't exactly sure what that something was right now. Choices would present themselves if given enough time and if she worked hard enough to make her inspirations happen.

"I've had plenty of experience working through problems. I've found it's the only way to get through life's difficulties, and believe me, I've had more than I ever want to count. Oops. Gotta put you on hold a minute, Ellie. Be right back."

Ellie logged onto her bank while she waited for Gage to come back on the line. Sophie had curled inside her bed beside the desk, with her nose tucked under the blanket.

She grinned, bent down and scratched Sophie behind an ear. "Are you cold, Sophie girl?" She got up and reached for another log to add to the fire when Gage connected their call again.

"Okay. I'm back. I'm sorry to cut our conversation short, but Matt has called a meeting and he'd like me to attend."

"Thanks for calling, Gage. Go take care of business and I'll catch you later. Give my best to Matt."

"Yes, I will and… if you should talk to Luke, tell him we'd love to have him and the children over for dinner one evening."

Okay. Miracles do happen.

"You bet. Catch you later."

When Ellie turned back to pay her bills online, she pulled up the joint checking account she shared with Ryan. Because Ryan was a lawyer and claimed he needed ready cash, they'd kept a minimum of twenty thousand dollars in the account. Ryan insisted Ellie transfer funds from her inheritance account. For unknown reasons, warning bells had gone off in her head. She'd not felt secure doing that, so she'd only deposited from her personal account, which she'd insisted be separate, even after they'd married, and he'd do the same from his personal account.

Something was wrong with the bank numbers.

Two

The snow-storm knocked out the phone line and my cell phone was broken in the car accident. I've been extra busy and with so much else going on, I hadn't gotten around to ordering another phone until yesterday. Now that my house phone's working again, I wanted to call to make sure you're okay and don't need anything." The phone went silent momentarily. "Hold on, Ellie. Danni, please come get your brother while I talk to Ellie. What? Yes you may talk with Ellie."

Ellie's heartbeat increased when she heard Danni pleading to speak with her.

"Oh, Ellie. I miss you," Danni said. "When are you coming by to see us? Soon? Say yes. Please, please, please?"

"I miss you too, Sweetheart. When the snow melts down some, I'll check with your dad on a good time to visit. Plus, we've had so much snow this past week, I'm not sure I can get out of the driveway."

"Daddy can clear the snow for you."

"Daddy isn't well enough yet for that, Danni. I'm scheduled with the snowplow service day after tomorrow."

"Okay." Danni didn't say anything for a moment. "Ellie?"

"Yes, Danni?"

"Daddy makes good pancakes," Danni whispered. "Did you know he could do that?"

"No, I wasn't aware he could cook. For him to make pancakes is quite an accomplishment," Ellie said, then laughed. "It isn't necessary to whisper, Sweetheart. I'm sure your dad would be happy to know you like his pancakes."

"He let me add the blueberries. That was fun. I even made a smiley face on one," she said, then giggled.

"I'm sure breakfast was out of the ordinary since he let you help. I'm sure it's fun to cook with Daddy." Ellie said.

"Oh it wasn't breakfast, it was dinner." Danni sighed. "We have pancakes a lot. Daddy doesn't know how to cook a lot of different food like you do."

Uh-oh. It would seem Luke could stand a bit of mentoring.

"Daddy will learn to cook more dishes. He's a smart guy, your dad. Give him time."

Trouble was, Danni would have to take over some of the responsibilities at some point. That was a good and bad thing, especially when it came to her being a young child. She loved to help, so for now a light load might not be too bad, since she liked and had a natural instinct for cooking. She'd miss out on some of her childhood if the load became too heavy. Ellie couldn't see Luke letting that happen though. She hoped. It depended on how much time he had away from the business… and if he'd hire some help around the house.

"Ellie, I miss your cooking. Could you make us some of your beef stew and cornbread and bring it when you visit?"

"Sweetheart, your dad may not appreciate my butting in." She'd love to make dinner for them. But then Luke would have to approve. With anyone else in the community, she'd cook and simply drop off the meal, but Luke… well he may get upset and think she cooked out of pity. Maybe. She wouldn't do anything for him or his family out of pity.

"The other night, Daddy said it sure would be good to have some of your home cooking again."

Ellie's heart's blood thudded inside her chest. "Did he? Really?" Perhaps she *would* drop off a meal and see how well she would be received. He wouldn't refuse a meal if she simply dropped it off. Right now, the snow was a hindrance.

"Yes, he did. Hold on please, Ellie."

Danni must have held her hand over the receiver, because Ellie barely made out the muffled sound of Luke talking to Danni in the background.

"Danni, you know it isn't polite to ask Ellie to bring us dinner. What's gotten into you? Apologize and say goodbye to Ellie, then give me the phone."

"Ellie, I'm sorry I asked you to cook something. Daddy wants to talk to you." She dropped her voice to a whisper again. "Could I call you later?"

"Yes. Of course you may. Call anytime you'd like, Sweetheart." If Danni were older, she would talk her through making stew and cornbread over the phone, but she was still too young to deal with the boiling water and the heat from the oven by herself.

"It would seem my daughter still misses you." He let out a quick breath. "I apologize for her bad manners."

"Luke. I certainly didn't take offense. We were together for quite some time. The two of us bonded, remember?"

"Yes, Danni admires and cares for you quite a lot, but she shouldn't have asked you to make us dinner."

"Come on, Luke. Danni is still a little girl. A little girl who misses her mom. It's only natural that she has someone to support her. To be honest, I'm honored she's comfortable enough with me to hope I'd give her the very thing she really wants and craves. No conflict. Please don't punish her."

"Of course I won't punish her, but I will remind her of appropriate manners. I can manage her discipline, Ellie."

"No doubt about that, Luke, but she knows she can trust me. Trust is one of the first steps to a relationship, whether it be child or adult. Do you really want to break the trust we've formed? Take away any confidence she's come to know me as… as in a safe harbor?"

"Look. More than anything, I appreciate everything you've done for me and my children. You were more than I could ever hope for taking care of them, but my children aren't your responsibility."

Ellie swallowed back the wave of disappointment that smacked her gut. She wondered why Luke was being so distant since they'd had a pleasant relationship during the time they were with her. She chalked up his approach to a hint of stress she clearly recognized in his voice. Even so, his words were no less prickly to hear.

"I'm afraid I need to cut our call short, Ellie. There's a knock at the door."

"Sure. I'll talk with you later. Give the kids a hug and kiss for me."

"Okay. I will." While Ellie waited, he cleared his throat, then continued. "If you don't mind, I'd like to discuss Brett's feeding with you."

Do you actually want my opinion? "Any time, Luke. By the way, Gage asked me to tell you they'd love to have you and the children over for dinner one evening."

"Great. A good hot meal for the kids would be welcomed."

"And yourself?"

"Of course," he said, then chuckled. "You're aware I have a healthy appetite."

Then, why did you refuse my offer of dinner, Luke?

"Excuse me, I need to see who's at the door. May I call you later?" he asked.

"Sure, Luke. I'll be happy to help. Call when you're ready."

Three

Luke's heart sank when he imagined how Ellie must be feeling right about now. He'd probably fallen a peg or two in her opinion of a gentleman. She had been nothing but caring and supportive to him and his children. It wasn't like him to be so impolite, especially to a lady. Now he had amends to make for his bad-mannered phone call, but it wouldn't do to give her the wrong idea of his feelings. In the back of his mind, there lurked a sinking feeling that she cared a bit too much for him. As much as he appreciated her assistance with his children and himself, he was, after all, grieving his deceased wife.

Luke loaded up his tools, turned the lock on the knob, then pulled the door shut to Whispering Pines, cabin number two, at Hidden Creek cabins. He'd spent the morning doing long overdue repairs. He'd replaced a water line in the kitchen and two window panes that had cracked from a fallen limb during the last snowstorm. He glanced up at Tumbling Waters, cabin number one, that faced the falls. His preference of all four cabins.

The falls and Tumbling Waters cabin held a special place and a book-full of memories in his heart. It had been in the Spring... and they'd just graduated high school. They'd sat on a blanket under a clear night sky filled with thousands of twinkling stars, gazing at the falls. The perfect setting to ask the love of his life, Nora, to share his dreams. He'd finally found enough confidence to ask Nora to be his partner, and she'd said yes. Not that he'd ever doubted her answer, but having her confirm she'd wanted to bear his children and grow old with him put into motion plans for expectations of things yet to come.

Luke dragged in a ragged breath and stood for a long time staring up at the fast moving and roaring falls while he remembered that remarkable night ten years ago. The night his life had taken a turn for the better and the future looked brighter than ever with Nora by his side.

Then last year, before Thanksgiving, the car accident had struck like a bolt of lightning. One minute he and Nora were driving to pick up the children while discussing renovations on the existing cabins and adding a few more. The next minute Nora was gone. All because someone had made the decision to drive while intoxicated.

And now… death had taken away their dreams. Life would never be the same. Her children, their children, Danni, ten-years-old, and Brett, almost one now, were all he had left of the one woman he'd loved more than his own life.

Four

"He did what?" Ellie could not believe Ryan would be so inconsiderate, but then she should not have expected he'd be a gentleman. In any way. What did he expect her to do with no income until the end of the month when funds would transfer from her other account? He really didn't care how she lived. He was the scoundrel of the year. No. The century.

The lady from the bank, on the other end of the line, spoke slowly and clearly. "Mr. Newsome closed the account after withdrawing all funds last week."

"Why wasn't I notified?"

"I apologize if this has caused you any inconvenience, Mrs. Newsome. The account was in both your names."

What a fool she'd been to think that Ryan would rest on his morals and do the right thing. She should have seen this coming. He simply wasn't trustworthy and she'd been aware so many issues could go awry, but closing the account wasn't one of her worries. Now, the reality was, she should have drawn out her portion of the monies. But she hadn't.

Ellie had opened a small account, in her own name only, in case her parents needed anything. She didn't want to delve into those funds for her own use. To be honest and above board in her marriage, she'd almost added Ryan to the account… but she'd had a strange premonition that prevented her from doing so. Had Ryan known about the account, he'd probably have tried to acquire those funds, too. She could, and would have lowered the boom on him then.

As it were, her lawyer had quite the job on his hands dealing with lawyer Ryan Newsome.

Her driveway would be cleared tomorrow. She was going to pay Mr. Newsome a visit.

"Ryan, open the door." Ellie rapped on the glass this time." I know you're in there! I can see you!" *You're such a coward, Ryan.*

When he finally opened the door to his office, barely enough to speak, Ellie wedged her foot inside to hold it open. "I'm not going anywhere, Ryan. I can wait you out."

"Move your foot, Ellie. I don't want to hurt you," he said, sarcastically.

"Seriously, Ryan? Like you haven't already?"

"I've never physically hurt you and you know it," he said as he tried to shove her foot from the door.

"There are some things worse than physical pain. I think you've done your share—and then some." Ellie vividly recalled every time he'd switched back and forth from the sweet loving guy she married, to the control freak he'd become. When she thought about it, he'd probably always been that way, though he'd hidden his personality from her until things hadn't gone to his liking. Then is when he'd showed his true colors.

Ryan finally pulled open the door. "You may as well come on in. I see you're up to your old self. Determined and self-centered."

"Your memory doesn't serve you well. If you remember correctly, you always had need of the last word."

"I'll have it this time, too." He crossed his arms and smirked. "Say what you came to tell me, Ellie. I have work to do."

"You know I will be allocated half of what you withdrew from the bank account during the divorce settlement. Right?"

Ryan's eyebrows rose. "I believe that's accurate." He shoved a stack of folders to the middle of his desk, then sat on the edge.

He had always surprised her by making unwise decisions, now more than ever. "Then why did you do something you know will be retracted? You're a lawyer, for heavens sake."

"In the meantime, I have use of the money." He snarled a grin the best he could. "I did nothing illegal. Why I did it is my business, not yours."

"While withdrawing the money may not have been illegal, it certainly was immoral. You haven't changed a bit. It's always about you, isn't it?"

"Is there any other way?" he asked with a sneer.

Ellie wasn't going to waste any more of her breath talking to him right now. "Maybe you'll be more open to admitting the truth the next time we meet."

Ryan sauntered from the desk to stand beside her. "Missing me so much you can't wait to see me again?"

"No. you can tell your stories to the judge." Ellie stepped back and shook her finger in his face. "Get real, Ryan. Coming here today was the last thing I wanted to do. You've turned my life into tragedy for the last time."

"Maybe not. You're a resourceful woman though. You'll find a way to replace the money."

"You're something else." She turned to leave. "No. You know what? My life isn't a tragedy. Your leaving was the best thing you could've done for me. Thank you."

Five

"Apparently you haven't heard the financial bind Ryan has gotten himself into." Gage stated. "You should take time to pay attention to gossip once in a while. The news is all over town."

"Come on, Gage. I don't take to gossip well. You know that."

"Of course I do, hon." Ellie poured Gage a another cup of coffee, then pushed a plate of warm Coconut Macaroons across the table. "Once in a while, gossip is worth listening to though. I think you'll find this cycle quite thought-provoking."

"Fine." Ellie poured a small amount of warmed cream into her cup, then picked up a Macaroon and grinned. "What's the juicy gossip?"

"It would seem your ex's law practice has undergone rather a stretch of misfortune."

Surprised, Ellie glanced over at Gage. "Really? What's going on? I'm sure it's nothing more than a lag in cases. All businesses go through rough times. I wouldn't think his law practice would at some degree be limited. He's lacked cases from time to time, business will pick up sooner or later." Ellie sighed. "He always lands on top."

Gage's phone dinged. She checked the caller, then set the phone aside. "Well, this time may be an exception."

"How so?"

"News of his treatment of you has spread around town like wildfire. People up here don't take kindly to a man who leaves his wife so soon after the loss of a baby. There's such a thing as respect. The people of this town put their trust in such behaviors. He clearly expressed none when he picked up and left you alone during a physical and highly emotional time."

"So, there is more to the loss of cases than a temporary pause in business."

Gage laid her hand over Ellie's and looked her straight in the eye. "I'm not sure you're aware of the town's feeling and respect for you. We're a tight-knit community and don't take to strangers lightly. They have to prove themselves. Ryan has not. He has rubbed people the wrong way from the moment he moved here. He's proven nothing except he will never be one of us."

"Then the town folks are abandoning use of his practice. Is that what you're saying?"

"Yes. The ones who gave him a chance. Since he left you, one by one, people have pulled their cases from his firm. You, on the other hand, have proven yourself trustworthy and earned the community's confidence and respect. Everyone I know has high regard for you," Gage stated.

"I love this town and it's people. They're real. Like family. I feel welcome here."

Gage smiled. "See, that's what I mean. These folks watch everything newcomers do, their actions. Your character hasn't escaped their observation. They may never, most of the time, voice their opinion, but you can tell by their actions. Plain as day."

Ellie stared off into space, then grinned. "I recall Mr. Darcy passed me in the grocery store one day and gave me a 'How Do.' The others certainly have their ways too. A tip of the hat, a casserole, or a call to see how you're doing. I'm blessed by their acceptance."

"Yes you are. Not everyone is assured of approval."

"I'm one of the lucky ones then."

"You certainly are. Our community loves you." Gage

reached for another macaroon and glanced at Ellie. "Not to be nosey, but have you spoken to Luke lately?"

"No. Not since he called wanting to know about Brett's diet. He's having a little trouble with him eating veggies. I gave him a few tips. Hope they worked," Ellie said, then sighed. "I sure do miss Luke and the kids."

"Luke has his hands full. Eventually he'll need help. It's up to him though. He'll know when it's overload time."

Ellie laughed. "That he will. He's awfully stubborn though."

"I agree."

Ellie stood, picked up both of their coffee cups, rinsed them, then placed both in the dishwasher. "Speaking of approval, I secured a small loan this morning from the bank."

"Matt and I would have loaned you the money, Ellie. You only had to ask."

"Thank you, Gage. I'd rather handle the issue myself. But if the bank had turned me down, I'd have considered asking you."

"Anytime, Ellie. You can depend on me."

Ellie hugged Gage, then lingered at the door while she gathered her coat and keys. "I'll walk you out," she said.

"You know, Sunday afternoon, around four, we're having a fish fry. I'd really like for you to join us. It'll do you good to get out of the house."

"Let's hope it doesn't snow again," Ellie said, then laughed. "Thanks for the invitation. I'll visit with my mom for a while and see you around four."

Ellie pulled the door shut and followed Gage down the driveway. "Hey, Ellie. Would it put you out to make your lemon pound cake? Matt is crazy about yours. He says mine isn't a moist enough."

"Of course. I'll be happy to. Anything to keep Matt happy," she said, then laughed.

Luke and the kids may like a cake. Maybe I'll bake two and drop one by their house after the fish fry.

Gage pulled over to the side of the road, turned off the car and dialed Luke.

Since Luke and Ellie were dancing around each other, it was time for her to help get those two sweet people together. Timing wasn't exactly right, but they had plenty of time to see how things would go. Maybe time at a leisurely cook-out would break the ice between them.

There was nothing wrong with her inviting Luke and the kids for a fish fry. Never mind she hadn't told Ellie or Luke the other would be there too. She'd tell Luke to arrive at three instead of four. He could help Matt and she'd play with the kids, while Luke unwound. Then, maybe, just maybe, he wouldn't be upset with her for butting in his life.

Luke was an easy going guy, but she knew this one thing. He kept his personal business… personal.

$\mathscr{S}ix$

$\mathscr{W}$hen can we go swimming, Miss Gage?"

"Swimming? It's still Winter. Not anytime soon, Danni," Gage commented, then laughed. "You'll have to be content with inside activities. As soon as we open the pool, you'll be the first one I call."

Danni giggled. "I know it's too cold now for swimming. Do you promise to call when it's hot enough?"

"Of course. Now scoot along and check with Matt or your dad and see if they need any help. Can you do that for me? Oh… also grab the diaper bag for me."

"I sure can." Danni ran out the door, then rushed back in. "Miss Gage. When is my surprise going to be here?"

Gage glanced at her watch and stifled a sigh. It was 3:45. "Soon, Sweetheart. Soon."

Gage was beginning to have second thoughts. *Maybe I shouldn't have invited the two of them without telling them the other would be coming. Whatever the outcome, what's done is done. I hope we'll still be friends when they realize that I've set them up.*

Ellie pulled in behind a dark gray Crossover. She hadn't realized there would be others at the get-together. She should have realized since it was a fish fry, she wouldn't be the only guest. Gage always loved a crowd.

Ellie grabbed the cake from the cooler, replaced the ice pack, then shut the trunk. She almost dropped the cake when a loud squeal split the air.

"Miss Ellie! Miss Ellie!" she squealed again. "You're here. You're really here. I can't believe you're here."

Danni ran to Ellie and hugged her so tight she almost knocked the cake out of her hands.

"Danni. I can't believe you're here either. Is Miss Gage keeping you and Brett today?"

"No. Miss Gage invited us to the fish fry," she said. "Wasn't that nice of her?"

So. Gage was playing matchmaker, was she? Fate wasn't working out, so she decided to lend a hand.

The curl in Ellie's stomach was so taut, it ran all the way around her belly-button. Whether to be happy or mad at Gage was a toss-up.

"Yes. Miss Gage was generous and invited all of us for the afternoon."

"Come on in and see Brett and Daddy. They'll be so happy to see you."

I'm not so sure ...

Danni grabbed Ellie's hand and squeezed. "I've missed you so much, Miss Ellie."

"I missed you too. Sweetheart."

"May I carry the cake? What kind is it?" Danni asked.

"Lemon pound cake. Matt's favorite." Ellie laughed as she handed Danni the cake. "Here you go. Hold it tight by the handle. It's heavy. Thank you, Sweetheart."

From the corner of an eye, Ellie fixated on Luke's muscular form as he stood in the doorway, his intense gaze on her. A warm sensation filled her. It was wonderful to simply set eyes on him again. He looked great and none the worse for the wear he'd probably gone through the past couple of months. He had slimmed down a pound or two though. She grinned. Probably running after Brett.

With one hand locked inside Ellie's, the other wrapped around the cake carrier's handle, Danni called out. "Daddy, look who's here. Isn't she the best surprise ever?"

Ellie's breath hung in the wintry air as she waited for Luke's response. Why didn't he say something? Why was he being so hesitant. What was that expression on his face?

Since it appeared he'd lost his means to speak, Ellie took the lead. "Hi there, Luke. Terrific to see you here. Pleasant surprise."

He moved down the steps toward Ellie and Danni, a grin on his face.

Ellie breathed a sigh of relief since she'd assumed he'd be upset to find her at the fish fry. Even more surprising was when he'd walked over and slipped an arm around her shoulders.

"I will say it's a delightful surprise. It's good to see you too," he replied, as he gazed into her eyes.

What was that hug all about?

He moved back and offered to take the cake from Danni, but she shook him off.

"Daddy, Miss Gage needs the diaper bag. I forgot it."

"I'll get it," Luke remarked.

When he came back, Ellie pointed to the cake. "I hope you like lemon pound cake, Luke. Gage asked for Matt's favorite."

"Hey. I admit, I like anything you make, Ellie. Anything." He grinned and opened the door for her and Danni. "I miss that I haven't had your good cooking since I moved back home. Some things are irreplaceable."

Ellie stared at him with mixed feelings. How and why he'd changed so much since their last conversation concerning Brett and his diet was beyond her understanding. He'd stuck to the mission at hand and had been all business.

"Doing without home cooked foods eventually takes it's toll. Let me know when you'd like something and if possible, I'll get it to you."

She bit her lip. She shouldn't be so easy. Though having him admit to missing her cooking was quite a change.

"That's a generous offer. I may take you up on a meatloaf or something, Ellie. Thanks."

Dannie had stood quiet, then glanced at Luke, but didn't get his permission before asking. "I'd like some beef stew and cornbread, Miss Ellie. Some of the veggies we can smash for Brett and he can eat the soup with them."

"Aren't you smart to think of Brett? I'm certain beef stew will be at the top of the list."

"Is that Ellie I hear?" Gage called from the other room.

"Yes. Thank you for my surprise, Miss Gage. It's the best ever."

"I'm happy you're pleased. I knew you would be."

"Are you going to talk all day or help me fry up these fish?" Matt called out from the back door.

"Like you need the help. How many times have you fried fish by yourself?" Luke rolled his eyes, then chuckled. "Sorry girls. Need to assist our helpless Matt."

"Please do," Gage commented. "We're starving here."

Seven

$\mathcal{D}$anni, I almost forgot. There's another lemon pound cake for you in the cooler. Walk with me and I'll get it."

Danni grabbed Ellie's hand. "Oh, Miss Ellie. Thank you."

"You're welcome, Sweetheart. I hope all of you enjoy it. Check with your daddy. Maybe you can come over for a weekend. We'll make whatever cake, pie, or cookies you'd prefer."

"Yes. I'd like that very much. Baking with you again will be loads of fun." Danni regarded Ellie with more than enough love to melt her heart. "I'm sorry we have to leave."

Luke seated Brett, then turned to Ellie. "Would you mind if we came over for a few minutes? I'd like to talk to you about something."

This is a switch. What's on your mind, Luke?

"Of course. If it's not too late to get Danni in bed for school tomorrow."

"Thanks for thinking of her, but it's still early. As long as she's in bed by eight, she'll be fine." Luke took a brief peek at Ellie before settling the cake. "I won't take much of your time."

Danni jumped up and down. "Daddy, may I ride with Miss Ellie?"

Luke twisted his head toward Ellie. "Ask her if it's okay."

"Certainly," Ellie answered. "Having you with me will be like old times. Come on and let's get you buckled into a seat."

Danni hopped out of the car and ran to the house as fast as her legs would carry her, grinning all the way. "I'm so happy to be here again."

Ellie caught up with her and unlocked the door. Danni stepped inside and hugged herself while she dashed from room to room. "Your house feels so good, Miss Ellie. It smells like home. I can still smell the cake," she said, and giggled.

Luke walked in then and heard what Danni had said. His face fell in sadness.

Ellie walked to him and reached for Brett. He flung his arms and flew in to her arms.

Luke was too sad at this moment. She hoped to lighten the mood. "If you'll put on a pot of coffee, I'll have time to play with Brett and you can relax a while."

"Sure. I can do that."

"The coffee's in the—"

"I remember. I got you covered," he said, and grinned.

"Danni, run upstairs and choose a book Brett might like. Do you mind?"

"He likes me to read to him, too. Be right back."

Luke came back from the kitchen then and smiled over at Ellie. "Your house does feel good, Ellie. The kids miss you."

What about you, Luke? Do you miss me, too? She wanted to ask, but didn't. She wouldn't.

With a quick glance at Luke, she tested the waters and shared a bit of her heart. "That goes both ways. It's a lonesome house now. Without you and the kids around, it's awfully quiet."

"Ellie…"

"Just sharing a little, Luke. No challenges." She did have a problem though, but now wasn't the time to delve into any of the issues that troubled her. Time was on their side. She had to believe that… and she had to wait it out. Wait for Luke to move through his grieving period.

"It's just…"

"I understand, Luke. Do you mind if I read the kids a story before we talk? Then I can put on a movie for them."

"Fine. I'll pour the coffee. Two creams only, right?"

"You got it." *I think it's sweet you remembered, Luke. That tells me a lot about you.*

Ellie sat in the over-sized chair, tucked Brett under one arm, while he instantly rested his head on her chest. Danni sat at her feet, her chin cupped in her hands, her elbows on Ellie's knee, adoring eyes staring up.

She'd almost finished the story when Brett fell fast asleep in her arms.

"There are a pair of pajamas in the baby bed upstairs, Luke. I hadn't gotten them out of the wash when I packed the kids clothes. If you'll bring in the diaper bag, we can get him ready for bed. That okay with you?"

"Sure. That would be great, if you don't mind. I'll get the bag."

"Miss Ellie, do you have any of my clothes here?" Danni whispered.

"As a matter of fact, yes. I do. No pajamas though. You could wear one of my shirts and pants. You'd need to roll the pants up. Your dad should approve before you shower and change though."

Danni's eyebrows lowered. "Oh. I don't know about that. Daddy hasn't been himself lately. He's too sad."

"We'll see," Ellie replied, and patted her hand. "I'm here for you, Danni. I'm not going anywhere. You must believe your dad will eventually come around. He, and you, are still having a rough time, but trust me, things will get better. He'll be happy again."

That's what she told herself anyway and prayed, for Danni's sake, it was true.

"I hope so," Danni, uttered. "It makes me unhappy to see him sad."

"I know it does, Sweetheart. Trust that he doesn't want you to see him sad. Give him time to adjust."

After Ellie changed and dressed Brett, she carried him upstairs and put him down on the baby bed. He was so tired, he didn't make a move or a sound. He looked like an angel. He had grown so much since she'd last seen him. She kissed his cheek, gently covered him, turned on the night light, then left the door partially open.

Coffee and conversation — with Luke — waited for her downstairs. She was ready.

Halfway down the steps, Ellie overheard part of their conversation. Danni was in the middle of asking her dad if she could shower and change her clothes, too.

"But, Daddy. My book bag is still in the car. Remember I finished my homework at Miss Gage's house? Ellie can take me to school and drop Brett off to you in the morning."

"Danni, honey. You're taking too much for granted and making plans for Ellie. I realize you have your heart set on staying, but we came over here to have a discussion with Ellie and that hasn't happened yet. Now you're asking me to allow you to take advantage of her? I can't let you do that."

Ellie made her way back down the steps and into the den. "Sorry to interrupt, but what harm will it do to let the kids sleep over? I don't mind one bit. As for school, that won't be a problem either. There are a couple of warm outfits upstairs I haven't returned to you yet. Danni can choose from the two." She grinned at Luke, and mouthed, please.

"Ellie, I had no idea this would happen or I wouldn't have suggested we meet tonight." He studied her for a long intense moment, then groaned. "I see I'm in trouble. You two haven't changed a bit. Still ganging up on me, are you?"

Danni and Ellie both eyed each other, then broke out in giggles.

"You don't stand a chance, Daddy."

"I see. Okay. I'll agree if Ellie will have dinner with us tomorrow night. The meal won't compare to anything you come up with, but I'll do my best to prepare something decent."

"Sounds really good, Luke. Can I bring anything?"

"No. Just yourself. I'm good." He grinned.

How could he come up with a meal and take care of Brett at the same time? He may or may not be able to pull that off. "See what you think of this idea. I take Danni to school and pick her up, and have a little fun with Brett tomorrow. Then we can drive over around five tomorrow afternoon."

"If you're sure it won't put you out. I know the kids will enjoy the time with you."

"It'll be a wonderful visit. I still have my authorization card to drop off and pick up Danni at school. There shouldn't be an issue with that."

"Okay. I'll make something easy for dinner. If there's enough light left, I'd like to take you on a walk to the falls, or maybe we'll go before dinner. We'll drive most of the way since it's almost a mile from the house. Bring a heavy coat though with a hood. The moisture from the falls cuts through to the bone."

"Won't it be too cold for Brett in the cold, moist air?" Ellie asked.

"He has proper clothing, but if it's too cold, we'll park at the cabin and watch the falls from there. The cabin is well insulated and has a gas log fireplace with a blower. It takes scarcely any time to heat up."

"You're going to love it up there, Ellie," Danni said. "Sometimes Daddy makes a fire in the pit and we roast wieners and marshmallows." Quiet now, a lone tear ran down Danni's cheek.

"What's wrong, Sweetheart?" Ellie asked.

"Mommy used to read us stories when we finished with the wiener roast." She swiped at the tears that were now running freely down her face.

Luke's mood shifted in an instant, from easy to talk to, to miserable.

Luke drew in a long, deep breath and wrapped his arms around his daughter. "Baby, I'm so sorry. I know you miss Mommy. I understand how painful the memories are. It isn't necessary we go to the falls. Let's forget it."

Danni ran to Ellie and wrapped her arms around her waist and trembled. "No," she cried out a bit too loudly. "I want Ellie to go with us. She belongs there too."

Luke raised his eyes to find Ellie's gaze on his and her arms around Danni. From his expression, he was flabbergasted. "Whatever you'd like to do, honey. I'm okay with your need to have Ellie there. Do you want to talk?"

"No, Daddy." Danni sniffled, hugged her dad, and then Ellie. "I'm going to shower and go to bed now. Is that okay?"

"It's fine, honey." He kissed her goodnight. "I love you. See you tomorrow at dinner, okay?" Luke hugged her again. "If you decide you want to talk, I'm here for you. It doesn't matter what time."

"Yes. Okay, Daddy." She looked up at him with a half-smile and again wiped at the tears. "I can't wait to see what you're going to make. Please. Let's don't have pancakes."

"Promise," Luke said, then chuckled. "I'll go so you can get in bed. School comes early." He nodded at Ellie. "I'll see you tomorrow."

"Goodnight. We'll be fine. Don't worry."

"I won't. If you need me, I'm a phone call away. Don't hesitate."

Ellie nodded. "Go get some rest. You probably need the extra sleep."

Halfway out the door, he spun around. "Ellie?"

"Yes?"

"You're a good woman. Thank you for loving my children." He turned and walked out the door before Ellie had a chance to respond.

Ellie had barely laid her head on the pillow, when a knock on her bedroom door startled her. She wasn't used to having anyone in the house again. "The door is open. Is that you Danni?"

"Yes." The door swung open and Danni stood on the other side.

Ellie slipped from the bed. "Sweetheart. What's wrong? Can't you sleep?"

"No, I can't," she whispered. "May I sleep in your bed tonight, Miss Ellie?"

Eight

Ellie dropped Danni off at school early the next morning. With Brett in tow, she headed to the bank to set up a personal checking account. Another account may not be a good idea. She refused to open an account in her name, considering the way Ryan had drained their joint account. She wanted to talk to her dad. She called him to see if he was comfortable with her depositing the loan money in his checking account, or open him a new checking account and then she could pay her bills from that account. She would also need to double check on her monthly inheritance income until after the divorce. Would she need to freeze the account? Though he legally had no rights, under the law, the income was too much not to temp Ryan try and finagle a way to get at the money. If he did, manage to withdraw any monies, he'd be in big-time trouble. She couldn't imagine any banker allowing the withdrawal without his name on the account though.

Ryan had taken her for all he was going to get. She was done.

Her phone rang. It was Luke. She pulled into a shopping center, parked, and dialed his number back. Something must be up since he planned dinner at his house tonight.

"Hi. Luke. You called?"

"I did. Checking to see how everything went with the kids last night and so far today."

"We're good. No problems."

"Is it possible for you to come over earlier than the time we agreed on tonight?"

"Sure. I have nothing planned." She couldn't put her finger on it, but something wasn't right. "I hope all is well."

"Fine. Everything is fine. I'd like to talk to you, that's all. Maybe late this afternoon we'll have some uninterrupted time." He chuckled. "Maybe."

"I'll be there as soon as Danni is out of school. Is there anything I can bring from the store for you?"

"No thanks. I stocked up earlier this morning."

"Okay, then. See you later."

Ellie stood on the porch looking over the railing. A rush of wind from the falls blew a fine mist over the four of them. "No wonder you love this place. It's awesome. You couldn't have chosen a better section for a cabin. Absolutely breathtaking. I'm surprised it isn't rented out."

"It's normally booked year round. The repairs took longer to get to than I thought they would. Thank goodness they're completed now and ready for lodgers." Luke stared into space, lost in the moment. "It's time I let go of the cabin's memories."

Should she ask what special memories, or keep her questions to herself? "I'm sure more than one has requested this cabin again and again. I know I would."

He peeked in at the kids. Danni was still teaching Brett how to play with the building blocks. They were okay.

"Yes. There are regulars for this cabin as well as the others." Luke led her to the swing, sat down beside her, and gazed into her eyes. "Do you mind if I vent?"

"Of course not. I'm here for you, any time, or any place."

"The grief at losing Nora took its toll on me and the kids. I'm sure you're aware that we've struggled, especially Danni. I'll spare you the details. But when we lost Nora… well… it's hard to explain the pain to anyone. Unless you've been through the process, the grief is beyond belief." He shook his head. "Unbelievable."

"I'm sorrier than you might realize. It's so hard to watch those you care for go through such agony. Especially your children." Ellie pulled the blanket back over her lap where it had slipped down. "Share only what's comfortable for you, Luke. I'm not going to push. I can only imagine how hard it is to identify with such a horrific loss."

Luke stared out over the falls, then drew in a deep breath. He looked down and focused on his wedding ring, which he turned around his finger a couple of times. "This place"—he waved his hand toward the falls—"is where I proposed to Nora. That's the reason it's special to me. I took my wedding vows seriously. So did she. We were all the other ever wanted. For life. Now, I'm at loose ends. Finding a happy medium is as though I'm floating through the clouds. I keep trying to claw my way out of the haze, but there isn't anything to grasp."

"I'm here for you," Ellie repeated. There wasn't anything she could say to lessen his pain. There never is. "Luke that's what friends are for. Lean on those who care for you whenever you feel the need. You don't have to do this alone. Love and accept the love of your family. In that love, there is healing. Healing takes a while though, so don't give up. Forgetting is impossible, but time helps soothe the heartache."

"Thanks for listening, Ellie. I'm sure you're right… it doesn't feel that way yet. To get the thoughts and feeling out of my head and heart helps some. I guess needed someone to express everything to, and you've been so understanding."

"I'm glad you felt at ease to talk to me. I'm pleased you trusted me to share your innermost thoughts, your sadness." She shivered. She wasn't sure if it was from the weather or the conversation. "It's beginning to get a bit colder. Think we should head back and feed the kids?" Ellie asked. Before he answered, she folded the blanket and handed it to Luke.

"Yes." He managed a laugh. "The crock-pot has worked hard today. I hope you like chicken and dumplings. I found the recipe among my mom's stash."

"I'm surprised. That's a big undertaking for a guy who doesn't cook much."

"Correction, woman. For a man who hadn't cooked at all. I'm learning as I go. Cooking really isn't so bad."

Ellie couldn't resist. "I'll remind you of those words a few months down the road."

"If you don't, Danni probably will."

After dinner, Danni cleared the table. Ellie shooed her out of the kitchen. "I'll help Dad. You go enjoy yourself for a while."

"Danni is quick study and a big help in the kitchen," Ellie commented. "She's going to make a wonderful cook."

"Yeah. She's like her mom." Luke handed Ellie the drying towel. "Sorry. You've been a terrific help. Teaching her how to bake and whatever else you two have been up to."

"There isn't any reason for you to apologize. Little girls are blessed to be like their mom. My mom taught me most everything I know about cooking and baking. I took after her and Danni is taking after her mom. It's a natural thing for most little girls." she said, then stacked the plates in the cabinet. "If I help her at all, then that's time well spent."

Luke nodded toward the den. "Danni has Brett captivated in his favorite movie. This may be the best time for our talk."

"Whenever," she replied.

"Food's put away, dishes done, and the coffee is on," Luke said, then chuckled.

"You're a right handy guy to have around," Ellie noted. "Dinner was wonderful. Thanks for having me over."

"I try." He laughed. "Hey, you're more than welcome. Making dinner is the least I can do."

"So, Luke. What's this all about? This conversation you're so anxious to have?"

"I'd planned to call you last week, but several issues cropped up and I didn't get around to it. Couple of issues with Brett.

Mostly his diet. Then there's Danni. I'm not understanding some of her ways lately. She's becoming moody and sullen at times. I thought you may shed some light on what's happening with her. Is it her age, her mom, not being with you? I simply don't know where to begin." He raked his hand through his hair. "So many things to consider."

"I'll be happy to speak with her. Maybe she could spend a couple of afternoons with me at the house. Being around her will give me a better chance to observe her. That way she won't figure out we're on to her change of ways," Ellie whispered. "I believe the issues revolve around everything you mentioned, or part of them."

Luke ran a hand through his black hair again and let out a breath. "Grateful. I'd be grateful for anything you can do. Believe me."

"Danni is a smart little girl. She's way ahead of many other girls her age. I'd hate to see her grow up too fast though."

"So would I."

Ellie patted Luke's hand. "She's going to be okay. Give her time."

"Ellie, I'd like to apologize for being so curt the other week. I suppose it was a male thing." He grinned and grabbed her coffee cup and headed to the fridge for cream.

Ellie held up a hand. "I understand, though your mood did seem a bit off kilter for you." She checked on the kids. They were kicked back and fully into the movie.

"You know life would be so much simpler if we were still children," she said, when Luke slid fresh coffee and a slice of lemon pound cake across the table.

He laughed. "Don't you know it. We could eat all the cake we wanted and never put on an ounce."

"Wouldn't that be great? I gain weight just smelling sweets."

"Yet you bake sweets all the time, such as this amazing cake," he pointed to the cake on the counter. "What's that all about?"

Elle pinched off a bite of cake. "Someone always needs items for bake sales, school functions, birthdays—whatever.

Besides, baking gives me something to do, keeps me busy and I enjoy helping the community."

Luke leaned back in the chair and crossed his legs. "Speaking of helping…"

Uh-oh. Her heart paused at those simple words. "Okay… there's more? I thought you just wanted to ask about Danni."

"After I'd made up my mind to call and apologize to you, my assistant, Laura, hit me with a bombshell yesterday."

"What happened?"

"Laura is leaving in April to prepare for her third baby. She won't be coming back. Her plan is to stay at home with her twin boys and new baby. Plain and simple."

"What do her position duties include?"

His expression said it all.

"Too much actually. The duties grew one by one over the years, but she never complained."

"You don't find many people that faithful," Ellie commented. "How long has she been with you?"

"She's been with us long before my mom and dad passed away. Her parents were friends with my parents, and Laura practically grew up at the inn. She came to work here when she was fifteen. That's sixteen years ago. I have no idea how I'll carry out her duties. She pretty much created her own position, and I'm embarrassed to admit how much she does at the inn."

Ellie lifted her gaze from the cake she was intent on finishing. "Try," she said, as she slid another bite of cake on her fork.

"Okay. I open up. She gets here around nine and leaves about six or after, depending on the season. She manages the thirty-room inn and the four cabins as she would her own home. She has three assistants. Then there are other staff, again depending on the season, of twenty ladies who report to an assigned assistant, and a full time maintenance man. She handles reservations, housekeeping—which is huge—meal planning, inventory, the kitchen and staff… whatever else is involved. You get the picture. Laura also did payroll and the books up until about five years ago when the twins were born.

"I deal with her when there's an issue with the maintenance man or the staff when necessary. I take care of the marketing and keep on top of the accounting firm. Of course there are always concerns or other unseen problems that crops up."

"Wow, Luke. Your business is larger than I imagined. To organize a staff, maintain the inn and cabins, you'll need someone extremely reliable to run your livelihood smoothly and to replace Laura. A super woman, I believe." She giggled. "You know, you'll probably find someone to replace Laura if you lighten up on responsibilities a little. Or maybe a lot."

Luke said nothing, but gave her a deliberate and intent peek over raised eyebrows and his tipped coffee cup.

Ellie sputtered, then coughed until she could breathe normally again. "No. Oh, no, Luke. If I read you correctly, don't even consider asking me what I have the most horrible feeling you're about to suggest."

"I can't think of another person who could handle the position." Luke flashed a grin, then scooped up the last of his cake. "Delicious cake, Ellie. You're the best. Thanks for thinking of us."

"No. No. No. I won't be responsible for helping keep you in business." She took her cup and cake plate to the sink, then faced him. "And don't try to bribe me with compliments. I'm going to say goodbye to the children… then I'm headed home. End of conversation."

Nine

Ellie mumbled and fumed all the way home. *What did I ever see in Luke? I sense he's a user. Simply trying to use me, that's all. He's shown me his true character. I should've known but missed his type completely.*

Back in the house she listened. Nothing. The silence was deafening. She already missed the kids. And Luke.

Her cell phone rang and she glanced over before answering. Luke could be on the line and she wasn't in the mood to argue or listen to him right now. She needn't have been anxious though, it was Gage.

She needed more coffee. She picked up her phone and headed to the kitchen. "Hi, Gage. What's up?"

"Checking to see how you are and how the dinner went."

"Dinner was wonderful. Luke isn't a bad cook. The kids were happy we spent time together. Danni, of course, wanted me to stay. She doesn't understand why I have to leave them. Brett hung onto my legs until Luke had to pull him away. Sad."

"It is sad. That poor baby," Gage commented.

"I loved the visit too. We drove out to the cabins. Oh, those magnificent falls. They are unbelievable. Have you seen them, Gage?"

"Matt proposed to me on the cabin deck overlooking the falls. The cabin is such a romantic place. We need to make a reservation, if there's ever time to leave the center unattended. Since Matt gave up his detective job and bought the Children's Center, we barely see each other anymore."

"Let me know when you'd like to go and I'll fill in for you," Ellie offered. "Give me some lead time though so you can teach me what I'll be doing."

"You'd do that for us?"

"Certainly. I'd do anything for you, Gage." She hesitated then blurted out Luke's offer. "Don't get me wrong, I didn't apply for the position. He sprang it on me tonight."

"I'm proud for you either way, Ellie. You'll definitely stay busy. I'm sure there won't be a dull moment in the day. Oh and please don't feel bad about not taking a position at the Children's Center."

"Gage, I simply can't take the position Luke offered. It doesn't feel right. Plus, I know zero about running an inn. Zilch. You don't just waltz into a position like that and not expect the business not to suffer. I have no idea what he's thinking." She set her coffee cup down on the table, caught Sophie as she jumped on her lap and rubbed her back, while she waited for Gage to answer.

"My heavens, Ellie." Gage giggled. "What's not to feel right about knocking down thousands of dollars a year? You don't realize how a lucrative a business Luke has built that inn into over the years. I'm not sure of the number, but there is still a boatload of prime acreage to develop or sell."

"I'm happy for him, Gage. His problem is, Laura is leaving in April, and he's forced to hire a replacement for her."

"I'm already aware of Laura's leaving. Luke ran that by Matt this morning. Matt mentioned you may be open for employment. I'm afraid I told Matt how Ryan cleaned out your bank account, and he may have mentioned it to Luke. I'm terribly sorry, Ellie."

"I forgive you, but I'd rather keep my personal business to myself. Especially my finances." Ellie had second thoughts of telling Gage how she felt about Luke now, still she did. "I kind of think he's using me. Plus there are the kids and I'd be there for them also, which would be so wonderful, for all of us concerned, yet create issues with the position. So, no.

I don't think Luke was completely honest when he laid out responsibilities."

"Come on, Ellie. Luke isn't like that. I've never known him to use people, certainly not a friend. He's the most honest person, besides Matt, I know. What gave you the idea he's using you?"

"Come on, Gage. Besides someone to help shoulder his responsibilities?"

"Yes."

"How about being there for his children? That should be enough."

"Good heavens, Ellie. The man trusts you, or he definitely wouldn't have mentioned, or offered, you the position."

"I trusted Luke because he was your friend, and you trusted him. I took you at your word. There's been no question of his integrity until today."

"What are you going to do?"

"I won't be used again. What can I do except sever ties with him? But… that will include the kids too, which will break their hearts… and mine."

"Not to mention Luke. Think how that decision will affect you from here on out. Promise me you'll give it time and thought before doing something rash, Ellie."

She had made a quick decision tonight after Luke's sudden offer. "Maybe giving the situation more consideration isn't such a bad idea, Gage. Thanks for listening and your advice."

"Anything for you, Ellie. Remember, there are two sides to every story. I'll talk to you tomorrow. We have a situation at the Center that needs to be discussed tonight. Are you sure you're okay?"

"I'm fine. I'm tough, Gage. A good night's sleep does wonders for shedding light on judgements. I'm sure I'll feel differently in the morning. Night."

"Goodnight, my friend. Remember your promise."

Ten

The night's sleep had done little to alleviate her suspicions, and the way Ellie had considered Luke's proposition. She wouldn't rest until she put to rest the issue between them. There was too much at stake. She drummed her fingers against the water glass, moisture trailing down its side. Luke was to meet with her at the Corner Café on the square for lunch. She'd arrived early and hadn't expected Luke to be there before noon. But there he was, ten minutes early.

Luke nodded to Ellie, then removed his hat and hung it on the back of an empty chair. "Glad I left when I did. There was a wreck on Mulberry Road. Two lane roads are terrible when there's an accident."

"I hope no one was hurt."

"Didn't look like it."

"Good."

They ordered lunch then got down to the business at hand.

"I offered you the position because I have faith in you. First and foremost because I trust you. Also you're a hard worker and have the confidence the job requires to take on such extreme obligations. Please. You must never doubt my reason."

"You talk a good talk, Luke. Did you offer the position to use me?" she whispered.

Luke strained to contain his resentment. He bristled, his face went red, and he clammed up.

When she was in this frame of mind, she couldn't let

well enough alone. She did, after all, set up this meeting to straighten out the issue between them.

"Well, did you? Was that your intention? If so, the decision blew up in your face."

Luke shoved back his tea glass, nearly spilling its contents. "No. No, Ellie, I certainly did not," he snapped. "You've been good to me and my children. Why on earth would I use you?"

"Then, I apologize for the remark, Luke." she murmured. "I suppose the job offer came at the wrong time. I believed you'd plied me with dinner, the visit to the falls and opening your heart to make me feel sorry for you. Then, I'd accept your offer to help you out."

The sorrow written over his face said it all. She wished he'd never invited her to dinner, or they'd gone to the falls... most of all she'd like to wipe away their conversation of the job offer.

But she couldn't.

"How did we ever get to the place that you'd mistrust me so much, Ellie? I thought we were friends. Friends that respected each other." Luke stood motionless beside her at the table, and drew in a deep breath. "By the way, you know how I feel about anyone feeling sorry for me. I don't like it. At all."

Ellie wrapped her arms around her waist and would've wondered the same about why the mistrust, except the memory of the look he'd given her over his coffee cup last night was the moment when she'd realized he had been searching for an employee.

And I was it. His choice. He'd made no bones about it.

Luke snapped up his hat off the chair and the bill, then flipped a tip on the table. "Thanks for the discussion, though we still have this rotten wedge between us. For that, Ellie, I'm more sorry than you know. Since you still have doubts regarding my truthfulness, perhaps we should both give ourselves time to digest the matter. If we don't have trust, then there isn't much left between us."

"I think you've aimed for a solid decision. More time is necessary," Ellie said, though her heart was breaking.

Luke nodded, turned, and without so much as a glance back, strode to the cash register.

How had they gone from close friends to being capable of stirring such irritation in so short a time? She swallowed back a lump in her throat as fat as a baseball.

Luke hesitated after he paid their bill, twisted back toward her, then closed his mouth. He must have had second thoughts, because he walked back to the table. "Are you okay?"

"I'm fine. Just fine," she said. "Don't worry about me."

With a nod, he turned his hat in his hands and walked away.

She missed the old Luke. The one who'd shared his children with her. The one who'd helped make her feel alive again after Ryan had abandoned her. The one she vowed to wait for, no matter how long it took. Now, the way things were coming together, her wish may never be realized.

That was the trouble with wishes. Wishes aren't always fulfilled.

Eleven

Luke grumbled all the way through town. He steered down the graveled road, then over the creek's bridge that led to The Water's Edge Inn.

Under a covering of Sugar Maple trees, trees he'd climbed as a boy, he pulled over and parked. Trees where he and Nora often sneaked away from the office to picnic. This entire property had special memories, from childhood to married life. Memories that flooded his head.

He removed his hat and swatted at the mosquitoes that swarmed around him. He'd forgotten the spray today before he'd gone to lunch with Ellie.

Ellie. Now there was a lady who also attempted to get under his skin. Oh, not attempted; she had gotten under his skin. Maybe not on purpose, still she had. Not much got next to Luke, though when Ellie had accused him of using her, he'd struggled to put the plug on his temper.

Ellie was close to being the most trying female he'd ever run across. The woman had taken what he considered a generous offer and tossed it back in his face.

Since Matt had passed along the information concerning Ellie's financial difficulties, Luke's intentions were to relieve her stress, but that certainly hadn't happened. He'd only succeeded at nurturing her resentment. Besides, he was in dire need of an assistant, and the offer would've benefited both of them. He'd had no conceivable idea she'd receive the offer as offensive. The worst part was she had accused him of using her.

He wasn't as acquainted with Ellie as well as he'd thought. She was definitely a woman of her own, filled with strong, embedded values.

Ellie had been there for him, when he was in desperate need of someone. Someone he trusted to care for his children, and a couple of weeks later, himself. He owed her, but had offered the position out of respect and believing she could handle the job. Not because he owed her. Certainly not out of pity.

Women. He'd never understand them. Why did everything need to be so complicated? Ellie wasn't the only woman he hadn't understood.

Nora had been complicated too, but she would've been proud to know a woman of such integrity had taken her children under her wing, and treated them lovingly, and as one of her own. This, Ellie had done out of the goodness of her heart, and Luke would be forever grateful for her care of his children.

The inn and cabins were his livelihood. Plans for improvement and further development of four new cabins were already on the table. Now, with April's surprise pregnancy and leaving her position to be a stay-at-home mom, concentration was foremost on a new hire to replace her.

Ellie was his first choice. He shouldn't have been so sure she'd accept the position without another thought. He should have known there were always sticks in the spokes… and he'd stumbled upon the biggest obstruction of all. Ellie had said no. There was no one to replace April.

Now, instead of working with a construction crew, he was forced to search for a new manager. Most of the men he knew were already employed, and the women he'd considered were either too young, already working, too busy taking care of their family, or retired.

Last resort. Run a want ad in the paper.

Twelve

"Honey, I've thought about several issues in regards to you opening a bank account in my name." Bob Rand, Ellie's dad, stated. "I'm afraid it will be impossible. There's my social security and other problems, such as if I should have to go into a nursing home. I wouldn't want the services to be misled and think the money is mine. Probably best if we try to figure out another way."

"I understand. I should've thought about your finances. I jumped the gun without thinking it through."

"I wouldn't want to have to prove where the money came from. I don't think it would matter to them anyway, since the account would be in my name, you'd lose the money. Can't have that happening."

"It's okay, Dad. You mustn't concern yourself. I'll come up with something else."

Now what would she do? Ryan would surely locate another bank account in her name and would list it in their divorce. She wasn't about to give him access to any more of her money. He'd confiscated enough. True, his name wouldn't be on the account, but would he be dishonest enough to try to claim it in the divorce settlement? Yes. If there was a way, he would.

Her inheritance had been set up long before they'd married. Was an inheritance before marriage considered a Non-Marital property?

She made a call to her dad's lawyer in Atlanta.

"If you have proof the inheritance was in effect before your marriage, then Ryan can't touch any of the money," the lawyer commented.

"What about the twenty-thousand I had deposited into our joint account?" Ellie asked.

"Now there is a problem if it was transferred from the inheritance. Since you deposited the money into the joint account, the amount became marital property and he has rights to half of it. It will be up to the judge—wait. Where did the money come from? Were you legally separated when Ryan withdrew the money?"

"Yes. Yes, we were legally separated. The money came from my personal savings account I had before the marriage."

"Then, I'm not a divorce lawyer, but I believe he'll be liable to pay you half of what he withdrew from the account at the final divorce decree. Make certain your lawyer is aware the money came from your personal account, not the inheritance account. That's very important. And that legal separation was in place at the time of withdrawal."

"So, if I should open a checking account in my name only, and from my inheritance only, Ryan can't touch any of the money?"

"I believe that's correct. I suggest you contact your lawyer for further advice."

Two weeks went by. From the resumes she'd left during interviews, Ellie received offers from two investment companies as management positions and one for an office position in a construction company. Neither interested her now. She'd rather work with Gage at The Children's Center than push paper.

Now she could rely on her inheritance as her only income, until after the divorce. The amount was enough… if there weren't any surprises. There was no way on this earth she was going to work, then be required to hand over half her income to her soor. to be ex-husband. Her lawyer hadn't advised her this would or could happen, and she hadn't asked, but she wasn't taking any chances. The divorce was supposed to be final in two months. She'd get by.

She'd seen Luke's ad for a manager in the paper for the last three weeks. She assumed the ad hadn't drawn many takers, or the applicants hadn't worked out.

Had she taken what Luke had asked of her — to take the position at the inn — wrong? She was beginning to have second thoughts.

Time was running out for training a new employee, since Laura would be gone in a few weeks. Luke was about to be in trouble running the inn with no one to rely on. Laura may agree to stay on several weeks past what she'd planned on, if Luke had someone in place to take over.

It was either volunteer with Gage, or work for Luke. If she could get past the feeling that he'd tried to use her, the position was the one her heart was set on. Not necessarily the position itself, but that she'd be close to the kids. Plus she didn't want to be one of the reasons the children might suffer if Luke should need to close the inn. The kids missed her and she missed them terribly.

But, until after the divorce, there could be no monies passed between her and a job. Could she tempt Luke with an employee, free of charge, until after her divorce? Would he go for that solution? All she could do was test the waters. It never hurt to ask, did it?

Managing the inn wouldn't be such a stretch if she gave Laura enough time for training. Would it? Could she be around Luke daily and not resent him? Would he still want her to work for him knowing how she felt about him? After giving the position considerable thought, she could absolutely do the job.

After weighing her options, she took a long, deep breath. She picked up the phone, rang Luke, and hoped she wasn't making the second biggest mistake of her life.

The first mistake, having married the controlling man, Ryan Newsome.

Thirteen

"Are you serious? Really serious?" Luke said, after he listened to Ellie explain her reasons and requests for choosing Laura's position.

"Only if you accept my request for no monies to be exchanged until after my divorce. Then yes. Yes, I'm serious."

She heard Luke chuckle over the phone. "Of course. I accept you with absolutely no reservations. I'm happy you've decided to work with me. And that you've forgiven me."

Honest. She had to be completely honest with him. "You know… I didn't actually say I'd forgiven you. I do however take partial blame for our misunderstanding. I may have jumped to the wrong conclusion. I'm willing to admit I was put out by your sudden offer."

"I definitely didn't mean to give you the wrong impression. I'm sorry I went about the offer the way I did. Laura had only told me of her decision that day. I suppose I was in a state of alarm. Can you at least forgive me of taking you by surprise?"

She took him at his word and believed his apology. "Certainly, Luke. We can work on other issues once I'm situated in the position."

"Great. You've made me a happy man, Ellie."

"Now. When would you like to begin?" She heard his cell phone ring.

"Is tomorrow too soon?"

"Fine. I'll be there at nine."

"That works. Thanks bunches, Ellie. I need to take this call, it's Danni."

"Of course. See you in the morning."

Ellie prayed she'd made the right decision. Only time would tell.

The next morning Ellie arrived at 8:45 and Laura pulled in beside her, then rolled down her window. "I hope you're ready for a demanding training session," Laura said, then grinned at Ellie.

Ellie smiled back, grabbed her purse, then closed her car door. "You bet. I'm a quick study. You dish it out and I'll knock it back."

"Let's roll," she said. "Luke won't be here until around ten. He had to go to Danni's school. She's having problems with math. Of course this is purely speculation, but she may need a tutor."

"Danni's a bright child. She'll catch on soon. Has she had the issue long? I don't remember her having issues when she was with me."

Laura picked up her step and drew closer beside Ellie. With a frown, she glanced at Ellie. "To be honest, she's struggled with math ever since her mom passed away. Once they moved back home anyway. She sure does miss her mom."

"I know. The loss is extremely difficult for all of them. Definitely raises the bar for Luke. He has his hands full, and now this. They'll work it out," Ellie replied.

"They will." Laura unlocked the office and invited Ellie in. "By the way I've called a meeting at lunch, so you and the employees can meet each other. We don't have a bad one in the bunch, except Thomas. He's okay, and a good worker, but does get lazy sometimes."

Ellie giggled. "I'll remember Thomas."

"Okay. Let's get started. Most everything we do is by computer, but this filing cabinet is strictly a back-up for employees. Luke keeps a folder at home in case of a power failure or any other crisis that may occur. So, it's important the files are current—computer and file cabinet."

"Got it."

"You may want to keep a copy at home for yourself. I do," Laura mentioned.

At noon they both stretched then headed to the dining room.

"As luck would have it, we have no lunch diners today, except Wylie Wyndom. He chooses to have lunch in his room though. He's a regular each year about this same time and has a standing reservation. We normally block this month out for his room." She laughed. "Yes, he requests the same room each time."

"That name sounds familiar," Ellie said.

"As well it should. His Mystery books are all over the place. Big-time author. We're fortunate he stays with us. He does a reading his last night here in the dining room. Usually there is standing room only. A generous man, every year he gifts the employees with his latest book."

"Wow. That is generous."

"The employees are good to him, too. After twelve years of coming here, he's like family."

Laura tapped on the microphone. "Everyone. Please feel free to check out the buffet Mr. Conway has graciously provided. We'll get started after lunch, but first allow me to introduce Ellie Newsome, the lady who will take over my position. As you all know, I'm leaving to spend time with my family, as you also know is growing." She grinned as everyone clapped and cheered. "Enjoy your lunch, then we'll mingle."

When they arrived back at the office, Luke was at his desk, his head bent over a set of plans for proposed new cabins.

He glanced up and smiled as they chatted about business.

"Afternoon, ladies. It's nice to see both of you in good spirits. Everything going okay?"

"Sure. We've made a lot of progress this morning," Laura said while she rubbed at her tummy.

Ellie said, "How did the meeting with Danni's counselor go?"

Luke put the cabin plans aside, leaned back in his chair, his hands clasped behind his head. "Danni is ten now. Quite a difficult age. Too, with the trauma she's experienced the last few months, the strain is getting to her. I'm not certain, but I think something else is going on with her, I just don't know what yet. We'll get to the bottom of her troubles though. The main issue at the moment is math. She's simply not getting some of the problems."

"Would a tutor help?" Ellie asked.

"Of course. I think it would," Luke replied. "I don't know if she'd be open to that though. Maybe. We'll see."

Ellie had enough on her plate with Laura's training, but Danni was in trouble. She would support her in anyway she could. "If I can help, you've only to ask."

"Thanks, Ellie. I may take you up on the offer. Training and tutoring may be overload for you. I wouldn't want to be the reason you pack up and run away," he chuckled.

Ellie reached for the folder Laura held out to her. "I always have time for Danni, or Brett." She stared at Luke. "You'll find I'm not one to give up so easily."

"Yes. I know." He gazed into her eyes, then quickly looked away. "A fine quality, too."

Luke rolled up the cabin plans and stood. "I'm meeting with a contractor at the upper creek bed in thirty minutes. Let's see if we can get these new cabins in progress. If you need me, text."

Fourteen

*E*llie pulled the folder list of repair companies the inn used from the cabinet, then made a call.

She promptly called the worker back on her cell. "Someone will be here in less than fifteen minutes, depending on traffic. Use everything you can to catch the water. We don't need a leak running downstairs. I'm sending maintenance with extra supplies to room fifteen, is that correct?"

"Yes," Mona from housekeeping replied. "Tell them to hurry."

Her first morning on the job without Laura. Wouldn't you know the day would start with a bang? The phone was ringing off the hook, her personal assistant was on break, and two of the housekeeping ladies hadn't shown up. She wanted to run upstairs and lend a hand, but leaving the reservation desk unattended wouldn't do. What a day.

With the leak being taken care of, she had a moment to breathe. When her cell phone jingled, she checked the incoming number. It was the nursing home.

"Your mom took a fall. We sent her to the hospital to be on the safe side. She's okay. A little shook up, but none the worse for the fall," the nurse stated. "She's having lunch now. We'll put her down for an afternoon nap after she finishes."

"Are you sure I don't need to come over now?"

"No. We have to call when a patient falls or any other issue comes up."

"Fine. I'll be there around dinner this evening. I'd ask to speak with her, but she gets confused on the phone." Ellie sighed. "I try to make contact with her, but the poor thing doesn't know me. She's barely aware I'm even there."

"She's fine. Don't worry," the nurse said.

Ellie's heart broke all over again as she pictured her mom sitting all alone in her nursing home room. Even now, when she visited, her mom never recognized her. That was too, too hard—to watch the woman who'd once been so full of life, fall into a haze.

Ellie sat in a chair and wrote a Mom memory from her heart.

Graying Embers.

Dim eyes stare through fields of sundrawn wheat as I stand before my mother, a stranger on common ground.

In the darkest corners of her mind, demons dance one final dance, forcing kisses of death and turning her dusk to midnight.

Folding the new red robe, I reach to smooth the sheets, sit in her rocker, and press the afghan close to my chest, engulfed in her scent.

"Sadie died today," Mom said. "She's lucky, you know."

I feel her fear and wish I could bridge the gap. She doesn't try to mask the loneliness; it simply is. I caress her thinskinned hands then lean forward and plant a kiss in her snowy hair. Trembling fingers close over mine as she slips me the letter.

"I wonder if I have children. Maybe so, I don't know. A pretty woman visits, saying she's my daughter."

Hurt candles spill hot tears down my cheeks to moisten the letter. I have no answers, only visions of days behind me as I read on, and wonder if I can do more.

She appears sad. It seems important, so I hug her and tell her I remember her daughter. Her vacant eyes meet mine.

"The forgetfulness, the fear, the uncertainty of reality scares me. Distorted images of children skipping through a thick fog haunt me, adding to my struggle."

Though long past the age of consent, I don't understand her sickness, nor how to deal with it. However, God has been merciful. She is safe in a bed of burning charcoal.

Tears rolled down Ellie's cheeks. Her throat closed. Her heart hurt.

"Ellie. Are you there? Are you okay?"

Luke and Danni stood before her, their concern vividly noticeable.

She wiped at her eyes. What kind of person would allow themselves to go into a stupor while at work?

"I'm so sorry, Luke. I was thinking of my mom."

"I'm sorry. Has something happened? Is she okay"

Ellie accepted Luke's handkerchief and dabbed at the leftover moisture. "She fell earlier today. They took her to the ER for a check-up. She's fine, except a little shook up. She'll forget about it soon, if not already. I despise Alzheimer's. It's such an unfair disease to strike anyone."

"It is. My dad had Alzheimer's. Broke our hearts watching him go downhill."

"Are you going to visit your mom soon?" Danni asked.

Ellie took her by both hands and squeezed gently. "Yes. When we close up the office in a while, I'll visit her."

"Does she know who you are now? I remember the last time she didn't."

"No, Sweetheart. Her memory hasn't gotten any better."

"May I go with you? We could take her some chocolate. She still likes it, doesn't she?"

Ellie smiled and hugged Danni. "If your dad says it's okay, then yes. Yes. you may go with me."

"Well, Daddy? Is it okay? I'll do my homework before we go."

Luke pulled Danni to him and gave her a big hug. "You're a loving child, Danni. I'm so proud of you. Yes you may visit Ellie's mom."

"Thank you, Daddy." She stretched upward and kissed Luke. "I'm going to the TV room to do my homework."

"Fine," Luke replied. "No TV until you've finished everything. Okay?"

"Yes, Daddy."

Danni bounced off in the direction of the TV room and disappeared down the hall.

"Do you have any idea how lucky you are? How bright and loving Danni is?"

Luke grinned and walked toward the office. "Of course, I do. She's always been a sensitive child."

Ellie followed close behind Luke, her mind on her mom. "How's Brett doing? Is he eating any better now?"

"Thanks to you and your suggestions, he is."

"Wonderful."

When they reached the office, Luke stood his plans in a corner, then put on a pot of coffee. "A crew will be here tomorrow to begin grading for the new cabins. We should, with any luck, have four new rental cabins before fall."

"Excellent. I know how important it was to get them underway." She realized if she hadn't taken over for Laura, Luke would be in a bind now. "I'm glad I changed my mind and took this position. I hope we're able to work out our differences."

"I thought we were making progress." He glanced sideways at her while he held the coffee pot above the cups. "Is there another issue, or something you'd like to discuss?"

"No. I simply wanted you to know how I felt." She popped the cream into the microwave to warm. "You've been extremely gracious to me. I have no problems."

"If you do find reason to question me, feel free. I'm not an ogre."

Fifteen

That got a laugh from Ellie. "Thanks. I believe you're a good man, Luke. Despite our disagreements."

"I appreciate you saying so," he said, and handed her a cup of coffee. "Come sit with me and let's have a chat. I'd like to run something by you."

"Sure." She checked her watch. "Danni should be about finished with her homework. It'll be late, so I'll take her for dinner before I bring her home. Unless you'd like to join us."

"Sounds good. I haven't been to dinner in weeks. Thanks for asking. Do you feel like Chinese tonight?"

"As long as Danni likes it, I'm good," she commented.

"Thanks for thinking of her. She loves it. Okay. Chinese it is. I can pick you two up at the nursing home, if you'd like."

"Great. I'll give you a call when we're about ready to leave." Ellie stared at the stack of work yet to be completed. She'd need to come in early tomorrow to catch up. "Now, what is it you'd like to discuss?" she asked.

Luke leaned back in the chair and clasped his hands behind his head. "You have a lot on your plate. I realize that. But... what would you say to adding one more project to your list of things to do?"

"Such as?"

"The cabins. I'll need someone to plan color schemes, order appliances, furniture, and oversee the operation."

"What? Luke. It's already mid-June." She pointed to her desk. "As you can see, work is piling up here. That would be a big job to take over and complete in three months. Even if you think the cabins will be ready for furnishings by the end of September or the first of October."

"Look. I'm sorry. I shouldn't have even brought it up. I thought you'd be perfect for the job. Definitely there is more money involved. Really good pay. I wouldn't ask you to do it without extra compensation."

"Money has nothing to do with it. Time. Time is the culprit. Running down there every time there would be a problem. There wouldn't be enough time to manage the inn properly," she said, with a bit of anxiety.

Luke sat forward and laughed. "Oh, no. Construction is my responsibility."

"So, now you think I couldn't oversee the construction?" she asked, then grinned.

"That isn't it at all, Ellie. You are more than capable of doing anything you set your mind to. I believe that one hundred percent. Don't think I haven't noticed how you jumped into this job, head first and haven't stopped since. The inn is running smoothly and the employees are happy working for you."

"I'm delighted with the way the employees accepted me. The outcome could've gone either way… and conditions could change at any given moment, Luke. You now that. As far as the cabin structures go, cross your fingers the construction crew has no issues and the weather doesn't hinder."

"I don't expect everything will go without some sort of issue. It never does. Something always crops up." He glanced up at her. "Anytime the job gets too hectic, don't hesitate to let me know. I can always hire you another assistant."

"Thanks, Luke. I'm okay. At least for now."

They sat in silence, both lost in their own thoughts.

"Tell you what, Luke. You give me an estimate sheet on expenditures and how you'd like the cabins to look inside. I'm assuming they'll have a rustic flare. That's fine, I can do rustic. But how much you want to spend is an issue. We'll want to use the stores here in Apple Lake, when we can, to keep the owners happy. After all, they support us too. But I may need to have certain items shipped from Atlanta to cut costs."

"You're serious?" Luke stared at her, a smile spreading over his face. "You're actually considering taking on the job?"

"I hadn't intended to take on more responsibility, but yes. I can handle the job. It'll keep me busy instead of staring at four walls at home. Actually, I think it'll be a lot of fun decorating the cabins. Oh, another thing. If you'd like carpet or hardwood. Carpet would be warmer, but wooden floors will last longer. Less cleaning too. I'm thinking out loud here, but do the other cabins have Internet service? That's a huge plus, especially these days when most everyone needs to keep in touch with family, friends and work."

"All but cabin four has Internet. Too far up the mountain for connection."

"You know you can contact your provider to see if they'll erect a tower. I believe they'll even pay for the use of your land," Ellie offered. "If that doesn't work, call another provider."

Luke snapped his fingers. "Why didn't I think of that? Excellent suggestion. I'll get right on that tomorrow morning."

"Why wait? Make the call now," Ellie suggested.

"Right. No reason to put it off until tomorrow." Luke eyed the stack of work on Ellie's desk. "How is it that pile is so sizeable when you don't believe in putting off tasks? Are you certain you don't need at least some temporary help?"

"Some of this paperwork are resumes from this week. The rest are updated forms I requested from the employees. I agree it would be nice to have someone type the information into the computer, but the information is confidential. So... I'll get it done. By the way, if you need any of the information just ask or log on yourself. You should have the password in your files. Everything is backed up daily, stored online and in the safe. I changed the password when Laura left. Not that she isn't trustworthy, but it was a security matter. You can't be too careful."

"Excellent," Luke commented.

"Speaking of work, if there's nothing else you'd like to discuss, I'd like to enter some of this before I leave to visit Mom."

"Certainly. Don't forget we're having dinner tonight."

How could I forget? "Either Danni or I will call and let you know when we're ready to leave."

Was it her imagination, or was Luke warming to her?

Sixteen

*V*iola Rand, Ellie's mom, sat facing the window in a slow moving rocker. Her favorite blanket spread over her lap, and in her arms she cuddled a baby doll close to her chest.

The rocker stilled when Ellie and Danni came into her view.

Ellie's heart broke all over again. It was all she could do to hold back the tears. She refused to let her mom or Danni see her heartache. Today's visit would be a pleasant one. She hoped.

She reached forward and kissed her mom and hugged her. "Mom, I've brought you a young visitor today. Do you remember this pretty little girl?" *Why did I ask her that? Of course she won't remember.*

Viola didn't say anything for a minute. She observed Danni, then smiled ever so gently. "Are you my little girl?" she asked.

From the confused look on poor Danni's face, she had no idea what to say. Ellie regretted she'd brought her now. Whatever made her agree to subjecting Danni to her mom's confusion?

Danni eyed Ellie, then walked slowly toward Viola. She placed a hand on Viola's and looked at her with a sweet smile. "I'll be your little girl. If you want me to be," she whispered.

Ellie all but lost it right then. Not only was Danni an extraordinary ten-year-old, her understanding was that of a much older person.

Viola moved her hand and covered Danni's. "Where have you been? I've been waiting for you."

Her mom did remember she had a daughter, even if she couldn't recognize her.

"I came as soon as I could," Danni said, and squatted beside her. "We brought your favorite. Chocolate. Would you like some now?"

Viola laid the baby doll in her lap and clapped her hands. She reached for the candy without a word. She didn't say another word until she'd finished the chocolate bar, which was now covering a small area of her face and had dribbled down to her gown.

While the aid cleaned up her mom, Ellie wrapped her arms around Danni's shoulders. "Sweetheart. You were wonderful with Mom. How did you get so thoughtful?"

A sad expression passed over Danni's face as she stared up at Ellie. "I remembered when we visited the last time. Your mom was confused then, too. You told me agreeing with her would not make her anxious. So I agreed with her." Her eyes grew large. It was evident she had a nervous moment. "What I told your mom wasn't really a lie, was it? Daddy will be upset with me if I lied."

"I think your dad will forgive you. You didn't actually agree with Mom. You said, 'I'll be your little girl. If you want me to be.' So that really wasn't a lie. Sometimes we change our words to be kind to those who don't understand life as it used to be. To keep them calm and sometimes safe." Ellie hoped she'd given her good advice, but still her words had covered the truth. "We'll tell your dad how you reacted to Mom and see how he feels about it."

"Is he going to punish me?"

"I doubt it. We'll see. You mustn't make a habit of switching the truth. Okay?"

"Yes, ma'am."

Voila had fallen into a peaceful sleep with the baby doll on her chest.

Ellie and Danni slipped from the room and called Luke to pick them up for dinner.

Seventeen

While they waited for the check, a tingle hovered around the back of Ellie's neck. She raised a hand to rub away the feeling. When she did, she turned her head in the direction of the crowded restaurant.

In a corner table dining alone, Ryan, sat watching her with a glare fixed on his face. When she caught his eyes on her, he looked away.

His glare had bothered Ellie, but she pushed back the anxious feeling she'd developed. He'd not been happy when during the divorce settlement, he'd claimed he couldn't come up with the money to buy Ellie out. He'd lost the farm. Their lawyers had battled out financial agreements. Ryan had thousands of dollars at the time he'd left, plus the money he'd taken from their joint bank account. Ryan was now all but broke, or so he'd said. He'd also sealed his future as an attorney in Apple Lake.

Ellie knew Ryan better than he thought she did. He had hidden money somewhere, she was absolutely sure, but refused to wait for the divorce while her lawyer searched for it. It wasn't worth it.

She wanted the divorce. She wanted to be completely free of him. Now she was.

So, what was he still doing in Apple Lake? Why did he remain in a town where he'd lost every client?

"Ellie?" Luke called to her. "Are you okay?"

"What?"

"I asked if you're okay. We've tried to get your attention several times."

"Sorry. I'm fine." She reached for her purse, then followed Luke and Danni from the restaurant.

One month later, and with the grounds leveled, Luke was excited that the construction on all four cabins was about to begin. Except the permits hadn't arrived.

The construction company had hired extra men so the job would be finished on time. Their deadline was September the first to allow Ellie ample time for decorating. Now they were already running a week behind.

Luke rubbed a hand down his beard and jammed his phone inside his pants pocket. "That was the construction supervisor. There is a problem. Every permit I've applied for was turned down."

"What? How in the world can all of them be denied?" Ellie asked.

"Who knows? You can bet I'm going to get to the bottom of it."

Luke returned a while later, mad as a hornet. "Ellie could you spare a few minutes?"

"Sure, Luke." She logged off the computer and closed her laptop. "Okay. What's up?" She'd never seen him so upset, even when she'd accused him of using her.

He paced the floor, then stopped to face her. "It appears we aren't finished with Ryan yet. Take a guess at who stopped our progress."

Ellie's blood ran cold and her heart beat so fast she though it was going to jump out of her chest. "Please tell me it wasn't Ryan. He's a complete scoundrel, but this… this would be low even for him."

"The way he went about it is. You bet it is. I finally wheedled the truth out of Charlie down at Municipal Court. He blackmailed Charlie. And Charlie allowed him to do so, instead of refusing to let Ryan back him into a corner."

"That's criminal. Oh. He's in big trouble now." Ellie could tell the wheels were rolling around inside Luke's head. "How could Charlie allow Ryan to get him to do something that demeaning?"

Luke hesitated, raised his eyebrows, then crossed his arms over his chest. "Ryan had the goods on Charlie. It seems *Good Ole Charlie* has, or had, a girlfriend. Ryan caught them one evening two weeks ago coming out of the Pine's Motel."

Ellie's breath caught. "Tell me you're kidding. You are, right?"

"Cross my heart. Charlie told me the story himself." Luke held up his right hand. "You can't repeat what I've told you. Ever."

"I promise. So, what now? Ryan could ruin Charlie. His marriage, and cause him to lose his job."

"I'm sorry to say this, but Charlie brought this on himself. Ryan happened to be in the right place at the right time." Luke shook his head. "He's playing dirty pool to shake down the guy."

A tear rolled down Ellie's cheek. "I'm so sorry this happened," she whispered. "If only I hadn't married Ryan… maybe…" Ellie turned toward the wall, unable to face Luke.

A moment later, he approached her from behind. He cautiously draped an arm around her shoulder. "You can't blame yourself. I don't blame you. Listen. What Ryan does has nothing to do with you. Okay?"

When Luke touched her shoulder, a fresh batch of tears flowed. She couldn't stop them. "I won't take blame for something he did. It's just that I have the feeling that if I wasn't involved with you, he wouldn't have taken the opportunity to have your permits denied. Why else would he do such a thing?"

Luke put a hand on each of her shoulders and turned her to face him. "Ellie, everything is going to be fine. A new group of inspectors will be out tomorrow, and that'll be the end of Ryan and his spiteful ways."

She gazed into his eyes. "Do you believe that? Without the permits you could be looking at a long delay."

"Yes. I don't doubt we'll be ready to get back to business tomorrow. We can easily make up the lost week, by hiring a third crew." Luke hugged her then. "Now. Charlie is going to man-up and tell his wife everything. If she truly loves him, they could work out their problems. Hopefully she's a loving and forgiving wife. If not, they'll go their separate ways. There are their three children and twenty-five years under their belts to consider though."

Ellie could barely breathe with Luke's arms around her. "They have a lot to lose if they can't agree."

"True. Oh. Charlie promised to call the sheriff and tell him all about Ryan. Charlie will suffer the consequences for going along with Ryan, but since it was blackmail, he should get off light. So, Mr. Ryan Newsome will be quite busy for a long, long while. I don't believe he'll bother you, or me, again."

Evidently Luke had forgotten his arms were still around her. She certainly hadn't.

Eighteen

Danni came dashing through the office door about the time Luke had bent down and kissed Ellie's cheek. She stopped in mid-step. "What's going on?"

Luke dropped his arms and backed away, while his face turned every shade of red until it paused at crimson. "Nothing, honey. We were having a conversation."

Danni set her back-pack on the desk and grinned. "Looks like more than talking to me. It's okay, Daddy. I like Miss Ellie, too. No. I love Miss Ellie. So does Brett. I can tell."

Ellie caught her breath, then came around the desk and hugged Danni. She pushed her hair back and kissed her forehead. "I love you, too. And Brett of course. I haven't seen him in a couple of days. I miss our visits."

Danni glanced up at Ellie. "We could bring him for a visit to your house. He loves being there. So do I."

"How can I refuse such love? What do you say this Friday night we make our own pizza? Would you like that?"

"Fun. Definitely fun. But Brett can only eat a small piece of the pizza if we cut it up."

"I know. We'll make him something else." Ellie stole a peek at Luke. "Is that agreeable with you, Luke?"

Luke looked somewhat embarrassed, then cleared his throat. "Sure. You ladies always have the last say anyway." He laughed. "Friday night time together will be great. I'm so ready for homemade pizza."

Danni winked at Ellie. "I'm going to the TV room to do my homework the tutor gave me."

What am I doing? What?

He'd only wanted to console Ellie, but the moment he touched her, it felt right. Comfortable. As it was meant to be. *Is that it? Are Ellie and I meant for each other?*

He pushed back the plans on the cabins and tried to make sense of how he'd gotten to this place so soon. It had been only ten months since Nora had passed away. *How could I forget her so quickly?*

Luke stood and slammed his fist on the wood paneled wall. *What's wrong with me?*

Ellie stuck her head around the door opening. "Luke, is everything okay?"

"Fine, Ellie." He turned his fist around and checked it out. He'd drawn a small amount of blood. "I took my frustrations out on the poor wall. I think I got the worst end of the hit though."

"Let me see." Ellie pulled his hand to her. His knuckles were bleeding. "Two. You've cut two knuckles. I'll go get the First-Aid Kit."

"It's just a scratch. Don't bother."

"Nonsense," she replied. "Don't be so macho. Now isn't the time." She grinned at him and punched him lightly on the shoulder.

"Okay. I should've known I couldn't win an argument with you." He laughed. "Or Danni."

"Yes. She does have her way with you." Ellie smiled up at him. "I think it's sweet."

"I think you're sweet, too, Ellie." *Oh. Now I've messed up.*

She held his hand in hers and drew in a breath. "Thank you, Luke."

"That was a stupid thing to admit. I'm sorry."

"Please don't apologize. I know you think a lot of me. It shows."

"I can't keep anything from you, can I?"

"Not much. You're fairly easy to read."

"I do like you. A lot. Too much. I'm having trouble with those feelings," he admitted.

Ellie placed her hand on his arm and squeezed. "I have to be honest. Whether you realize it or not, I have feelings for you too. Feelings that are hard to deal with, so I know all about that state of mind and holding in feelings. Especially while you're still grieving. Too, you have many responsibilities. The children, the house, this inn and the cabins. Those are a lot to shoulder. Maybe we'll see how it goes with us when you're ready. Okay?"

"Yes. When we're ready."

"Okay. You'll know when the timing is right, Luke. Don't push it. We have all the time in the world."

He did have too much to still deal with. To get his head on straight. Could he ever let Nora go? To think he could ever love another was mind boggling. Was it possible he was falling in love with Ellie? He shook the thought from his head.

Luke watched as she cleaned and bandaged his hand. He got caught up in the softness and scent of her hair. The way it spilled over her shoulders. The way the sunlight shine brought out the blonde streaks.

What he wanted was to gather her in his arms and hold her close, but the guilt whispered, not yet. Not yet.

"There you go." She tided up and walked toward her office. "Those knuckles are going to be sore for few days," she said, as she turned back around. I'll change it again tomorrow and put on fresh antibiotic."

"Thanks. You're the best," he stated.

"Danni has been gone for a while. Think we should check on her?"

"Yes. I'll go since I've kept you so long. I'm sure you have work to finish before the day's out."

Ellie nodded and stepped inside her office. Quiet now, she had time to think over what Luke had discussed and his list of struggles. The worst, living as a widower.

What should have been a happy moment, saddened her to no end. She'd felt his intense stare while she bandaged his hand. He'd fought against his feelings for her and his grief for Nora. Nora may always stand between them. But Ellie understood.

Luke was a man with principles... and those principles he'd stand by no matter what.

He'd said, 'When *we're* ready.'

Those words gave her hope. Hope that her Christmas wish, to win Luke's heart, would come to pass and had potential. For him to realize they were meant for each other.

Maybe new beginnings.

Maybe.

Nineteen

Brett sat on a thick blanket on the hardwood floor. He filled the room with giggles and waved his arms as Sophie, Ellie's dog, snuggled at his feet. Danni handed Brett a treat for Sophie, but he tried to eat it himself.

"No, no, Brett. It's for the doggie." She held out her hand until Brett unwillingly handed the treat to her. She took the treat and fed it to Sophie so Brett would know, hopefully, it wasn't for him. "See, baby?"

He hadn't understood. Brett cried until Luke picked him up and offered him a cookie.

Ellie removed the pizza from the oven while Danni set the table.

"Do we want cheese and hot peppers for the pizza?" she asked.

"Of course," Luke said, and laughed.

"Daddy, some of the kids from my tutor's class are going to the apple farm tomorrow. Could we go?"

"I have papers to finish tomorrow, but I'll go in early in the morning and get it done." He glanced at Ellie. "Would you like to go with us? That is if you don't have plans."

"I'll visit my mom Sunday afternoon, so I'm free tomorrow. I think a trip to the apple farm is what we all need. A day of fun without any problems."

Danni started to say something, but evidently changed her mind. Then she quietly asked, "Ellie, would you teach Daddy how to make cornbread? We never have it unless we come over here."

"If your dad would like to spend the time in the kitchen. Sure." Ellie winked at Luke. "What do you say, big guy? Ready for a bread making lesson?"

"You mean now? Tonight?"

"After dinner. We have time. Danni has no school tomorrow. Besides, making cornbread doesn't take that long." She giggled. "That is if you pay attention."

"Madam. That was an unfair point to make."

"Well? Are you up to the task?"

"I suppose—since my daughter has requested me to do so. I see no reason to make myself look bad at this stage in the game." He raised an eyebrow at Danni. "Eat up, young lady. We've bread to bake."

Danni had an anxious expression when she glimpsed at her dad.

Luke reached over and patted her hand. "All is well. No worries, hon."

She blew out a sigh, then picked up the last bite of her pizza. "Dinner was delicious, Miss Ellie. Thanks for letting me help make the pizza."

"Sure thing, Sweetheart. You'll be a great cook one day," Ellie said, and flashed her a grin.

Danni beamed at her, while Luke eyed her with affection.

Danni stood to clear the table. "Daddy, I hope you don't get mad at me, but I'd like to ask Miss Ellie another favor."

"I won't get mad at you, hon. What is it you'd like to ask Ellie?"

"The first week of school they're having family week." Danni hunched her shoulders. "Tuesday is Mom and daughter's lunch at school."

Ellie passed a quick peek at Luke.

A tear rolled down Danni's cheek. "I know you're not really my mom. But I love you like a mom. Is that okay?"

Ellie's heart slammed against her chest, and it took her a second to catch her breath. "Of course it is, Sweetheart. That's quite an honor, Danni. Thank you so much."

"Well… could you, would you… come to the school and have lunch with me?"

Ellie dried her hands and hugged Danni. "I'd be proud to stand in for your mom and have lunch with you, Sweetheart," she whispered.

Danni burst into tears then.

"Don't be sad, hon. Ellie is going with you. Is there something else wrong?" Luke asked, then wiped Brett's chin and stood him beside his chair.

"Last year, Jeanne kept saying I don't have a mom now. Can I tell her you're my mom?"

"I'll be your second mom, Sweetheart. Many children have second moms, or stand-in moms. It's all about how we feel about each other. So we aren't really telling a story, we just aren't related by blood. No one needs to know any of the details. Okay?" Ellie took her by the shoulders. "Do you understand?"

"I do." She wiped at the tears away, then hugged and kissed Ellie. "I'm proud you're my stand-in mom. Or my second mom. Whichever you prefer."

"Whatever you're comfortable with, Danni." Ellie questioned Luke with a look, then proceeded when he nodded. "As for Jeanne, pay her no attention. I know it makes you sad for her to say hurtful words, but she may have problems you aren't aware of. Most of the time people are unkind to others to cover their own hurt. Did you realize that?"

"No, I didn't."

"Think about this. You continue being nice to her and she'll eventually come around. Who knows? You two might become friends."

"Okay. If you say so… I'll try."

"Everything is going to be fine, Danni. If you have any more problems with Jeanne, remember what I told you. Also, talk to your dad. Or me. I'm always here for you." Ellie glanced at Luke. "Is that acceptable with you?"

"I'm fine with her coming to you as long as you have no issues with it. Please don't feel any obligation at all. Of course you and I should discuss any of her concerns. Clearly you are so good to, and for, my girl." Luke smiled at her. "I trust you with my children. Thank you."

Twenty

Without warning, a flash of lightning split through the orchard. Almost immediately the heavens opened up. Luke dropped the bucket of apples he held and grabbed Brett from Ellie's arms. As Ellie took Danni's hand, they all ran as fast as possible to the nearest building.

When they finally reached a storage shed, several other people were already there. Luke settled Brett on Ellie's lap and accepted a roll of paper towels from a lady.

He dried Dannie's hair, then gave her some towels. "Here, hon. Dry yourself off as well as you can."

While Ellie dried off Brett, Luke pulled back Ellie's hair and dabbed her hair as much as he could.

Danni laughed. "That was fun."

"It is fun to play in the rain, but it wouldn't have been fun if you, or any of us, had gotten struck by lightning," Luke advised her.

"I'm sorry, Daddy. It was fun running in the rain though."

"I cold, Da Da," Brett said.

"We'll get you warmed up as soon as we can, buddy." Luke thought to remove his shirt to warm Brett, but it was still too wet and cool to wrap around him. He rubbed his hand up and down his arms and legs to get the circulation going.

The storm let up after twenty minutes of downpour. There was a light drizzle when the sun broke through, and they were finally able to make it back to the main building. Luke snagged the diaper bag from the car so Ellie could change Brett's clothes before heading home.

It was mid-August and the McIntosh and Honey Crisp apples were in. Ellie had Luke get a peck of each, since they'd lost their handpicked apples during the storm. He paid for them and came back to where Ellie and the kids waited. A hand came around a pallet of apples and patted Brett's head. Luke flinched, jerked the man's hand off his son's head, and looked directly into the face of Ryan Newsome.

Luke seethed. "If you know what's good for you — Do. Not. Ever. Touch. My. Son. Again. Ever. Do you understand?"

"Cute," Ryan said, as he studied Brett.

"What are you doing here?" Luke was so mad, he shook. "You followed us, didn't you?"

"What if I did?" Ryan replied, with a smirk.

"Then that's a matter for the sheriff. You're a lawyer. You should realize what stalking is, right? You really don't want stalking added to the charges already brought against you."

"I believe I'm aware what a stalker is. I have a right to be here... same as you." Ryan picked up a bag of apples and turned toward the check-out counter.

"I'll be watching you, Ryan. Stay clear of my family, or you'll be sorry."

"That sounds like a threat. Are you threatening me, Luke? I'd be careful how I choose my words if I were you." Ryan laughed.

"Yes, that was a threat. Not a bodily threat, but a threat all the same. I'd tread lightly if I were you," Luke spit out.

Ryan twisted around with a sneer. "By the way, are you referring to Ellie as part of your family?"

"I am, but that's none of your business, and Ellie is none of your business. She is out of your life now. Leave her out of this discussion," Luke said. "Leave her alone. She isn't yours to abuse any longer."

Ryan saluted, picked up his purchase, and sauntered out through the double doors.

Twenty-One

The house still smelled of warm apples and cinnamon when Ellie had rolled out of bed. Before she left for work the next morning, she'd stacked the half-dozen pies she'd baked the night before in the freezer. When she couldn't sleep, baking was her go-to… let-everything-go choice. She'd wished she'd asked Luke to buy more apples.

She'd logged onto the computer at six-thirty a.m., and worked harder than she had in a week. Flooring, light fixtures, and appliances were ordered with a shipping date of three weeks away. The cabins were almost complete and ready for decorating.

Evidently Luke wasn't able to sleep either, because he'd arrived a few minutes after she'd put on a pot of coffee. By eight-thirty they'd drained the pot and Luke had made another.

She couldn't get the conversation from yesterday out of her head. While she poured warm cream into her cup and waited for the coffee, she studied the man who had won her heart. "Did you mean it when you told Ryan I was part of your family, Luke?"

Luke took her cup, filled it and grinned. "You bet I did. Do you have a problem with being known as part of our family?"

It's all I've wanted. For a long time. Ellie grinned back at Luke, knowing now wasn't the time for this conversation, but he'd put her mind to rest. He really did care. "Better watch out, Luke. You're coming close to having a stand-in wife."

"You think so?"

"Yes. You fought for me against Ryan yesterday. I'm sure he had no idea you'd go that far, since his mind doesn't function as a gentleman. Your involvement means more than you know. If you didn't care, you could've let it go. You could've simply taken on the issue with Ryan when he touched Brett, then you would've been done with him."

"I cared enough to put Ryan in his place where Brett and you both are concerned. If I have anything to do with it, he won't be treating you badly again. Not ever. You can count on that."

She shouldn't ask, but there was no stopping her when she wanted an explanation. "Are you beginning to have stronger feelings toward me?" *What if he says no?*

Luke gazed into her eyes. "Ellie, I've thought about us a lot the past few weeks. We're good together… in so many ways. We make a great team."

Ellie's heart picked up a beat, but she wished for more than to be part of a team. Her wish was to win his heart. "So what are you saying?"

"What I'm saying is… we can play it by ear and see where our feelings lead us." He took her hand and held it close to his chest. "I'm ready to deal with Nora and my feelings for her. I'll always love her. There isn't any way around that, I wouldn't want to either. Making room for another woman isn't as easy as people might think, but I'm willing to work on it… as long as it's you I'm fighting for."

"Waiting wasn't and still isn't easy for me either, Luke. You're definitely worth the wait."

Twenty-Two

Luke slid the envelope into the out mail tray and leaned back in his chair. "This afternoon we'll have the last of the inspections on the cabins. Will your workers be available to move the furniture in tomorrow?" he asked.

"Yes. Waiting for a word from me. All furniture, including for the decks, wall hangings, linens, and kitchenware, are stowed inside your shed. Danni will enjoy going to my favorite nursery in Atlanta to help choose the deck plants." She shot a glance at him. "That is if you're okay with her going. My dad and Danni got along very well. He'll be happy to see us again. It's been a while since I visited. I plan going down on Friday evening and coming back Sunday."

"Danni can go anywhere with you. You don't need to ask permission. I'd like to know when and where you go though. That way I won't be concerned. I noticed the shed is packed to the top. You did a great job bringing it all together."

Ellie laughed. "We… pulled off the job together. There were times it looked as though we wouldn't make it though. As you said earlier, we are a good team." *Being on your team is well and good, but I want to be more to you than a team member.*

"That we are. We did it. It's the end of September, and by mid-October, we'll begin taking reservations. I've advertised all over the place. The Internet, magazines, flyers out in every spot that would let me leave them, and of course, there's always word of mouth. If everything goes as planned, the cabins should stay full until a short slow down during Spring break, then business picks up again. We continue to stay busy all year round though. If we had double the cabins, they'd stay full too. Apple Lake is a remarkable tourist town," Luke commented. "Many city visitors come here year after year."

"When I went back over the reservation files, I noticed several names with unchanged yearly arrival dates she'd blocked in. Mandy does an extraordinary job assigning reservations," Ellie said.

About that time, Mandy came into Luke's office. "Hey, Ellie. Mind if I use your computer? I'm not logged on yet and I don't want the customer to wait for a reservation."

"Sure. I'm logged on. I'll be here in Luke's office if you need me for anything."

Mandy gave her a thumbs up before she went inside Ellie's office, checked the reservations, then resumed the phone conversation with the customer.

"Yes, cabin four, at the waterfalls, is available for the upcoming week. Excuse me? Well, yes. You can check in tomorrow, which is Wednesday. Check-out is at ten a.m. next Wednesday. Oh, and linen service will be Friday and Monday, at ten both mornings. Enjoy your stay with us, Mr. Newsome." Mandy took his information, thanked him, then shut down the reservation page.

Mandy came back through Luke's office. "Thanks, Ellie. Cabin four is rented for this coming week, starting tomorrow."

Ellie turned toward Mandy. "An unusual time of the week to check in, isn't it?"

"It is. But as luck would have it, it's empty now and we had a cancellation until the following Friday. Everything's good."

"Super," Luke said, and shrugged at Ellie.

"I checked with Gage and she's available to watch Brett for you this weekend. She's also going to keep Sophie for me." Ellie punched numbers into the Excel sheet without looking up.

"What would I do without you, Ellie? You're always on top of everything. How do you do it?"

"I simply do the next thing, Luke. But, if you don't leave me to finish this work, you may find out how I do it." She glanced up at him and grinned. "You wouldn't be a happy guy taking over all this paperwork."

"You wouldn't dare."

"Then don't put me to the test." She laughed, then shooed him out of her office.

He chuckled, as he turned to leave. "I'm going, I'm going."

"Wait, Luke. You know, you should seriously take time to learn how to do everything here. What if I'm not here one day? Take Laura for intance. She made the decision to leave. If I hadn't taken over her position when I did, I expect you'd have been in some hot water."

Luke stood frozen in his tracks. "Do you anticipate plans of leaving?"

Ellie gazed up at him and bit her lip. "Not at the moment." She sighed. "I have no plans any time soon."

"So, what does that statement mean? Any time soon?"

"Just that. I'm sorry I brought the subject up. Let's forget it," Ellie replied, then turned away.

He walked over to her and stood close enough for her to feel his breath on her cheek. "I can't forget it, Ellie. Without you here now, this place doesn't, and won't, mean much. You're part of the kids, the inn, and the cabins."

She made eye contact and held it. "Anything else, Luke?"

"Oh, boy. Here we go." Luke shuffled his feet and ran a hand through his hair. "Okay. I confess. You're a huge part of me now. I can't get you out of my head half the time."

"Why don't you ever say anything?" she asked.

"To be honest, the thoughts I have of you… they scare me. New beginnings—with you is scary. Without you—would be unbearable."

Ellie rolled her eyes and heaved a sigh. "I've never had someone tell me I'm scary to be with. Knowing I scare you is a bit hard to digest. That's not what I want."

All of a sudden Luke cupped her chin with a palm, then wrapped his arms around her and kissed her in a way she'd never been kissed. Before she had a chance to respond, he dropped his arms and walked away.

In disbelief, she watched him leave with her mouth hanging open. He'd taken her by surprise. Probably himself too.

He turned back, his hand on the doorframe. "By the way, and for your verification, all inspections are completed. You can call your crew to start moving the furniture and appliances in the morning."

Bright and early Wednesday morning a crew of six men per cabin pulled up beside the shed to begin loading furniture into the cabins.

Ellie had spent a couple of hours last night on the phone with Gage. She'd caught her up on how things were going between Luke and herself.

"You may be getting your wish, Ellie," Gage commented, then giggled.

"I believe you may be right, Gage."

Am I ready for Luke and his transformation? Have I pushed him into a decision too soon?

The last thing she wanted was to goad him into a sudden decision. Learning to live without Nora and loving again had to be on his terms. His terms only.

She'd tossed and turned most of the night after Luke's confession and his kiss. She'd dragged herself out of bed and had arrived at the office by 6:30.

Luke had a meeting this morning, so they had time to process what had occurred between them yesterday. Ellie needed time alone and was glad Luke wasn't around right now.

By noon, all the bedrooms were set-up in the cabins and the appliances were unboxed, set in the kitchen, and ready to connect.

The famished men filed into the dining room for lunch. A hot meal was the least she could do for the guys who had worked tirelessly all morning.

She'd had the cook prepare fried chicken, mashed potatoes, biscuits and a table of assorted salad makings. "Please enjoy your meal. You've certainly earned it. Don't miss the dessert table. It's fabulous."

"Thank you, ma'am. We sure do appreciate this wonderful meal," the supervisor said. "We'll finish up here this evening."

"It's our pleasure. Thank you for setting everything up today," Ellie replied. "Oh. I have other boxes in the shed. They're all labeled for which cabin they go into. If you would have your workers place them in the cabins, I'll gladly pay you extra."

The supervisor tipped his hat. "We'll get that done for you, ma'am. Happy to help. After the great lunch you served my men, there will be no charge."

When Luke hadn't called or returned by five that same afternoon, Ellie became concerned.

Twenty-Three

Luke finally showed up at 5:30. Ellie breathed a sigh of relief.

"Where have you been?" Ellie asked, her voice full of concern. "Sorry Luke. You don't owe me any explanation, but I was getting pretty anxious. It isn't like you to not at least call if you'll be late."

"I apologize if I worried you. The meeting ran over, then we drove this side of Murphy to meet with the other two owners. Cross your fingers that they all agree to lease the stable and be one-hundred percent in charge of their horses here. The meeting was positive today. If so, we'll have a stable to build and riding trails to sketch out. I've already gotten the stable approval from the county, but the trails will take some time to map out."

"I realize you must be careful and set up safe trails, but why are they taking so long to map out?" she asked.

"As you know, my plans are to build other cabins on the property. Once the trails are set, I'd rather not have to relocate them. Of course, we could, but the horses may get confused with unfamiliar trails," Luke stated.

"So, other cabins are still in the works?"

"We're shooting to add four more next fall. I've had surveyors in the past, but now I'll need a firm report, since deciding to add the riding stables. I don't want to deal with taking care of horses, that's why I'm working hard at a contract with this group."

"Then why bring in the horses in the first place?" Ellie questioned.

"There's a small riding stables toward Murphy. Other than that one, none are available. The stable will be a huge draw for the inn and cabins. We've had inquiries over the years for horses, more so the past couple of years. I think it's time to make the addition. Twelve stalls should be enough, if not, we'll allow room for expansion."

"You look tired, Luke. Have you had dinner?"

"No. We had an early lunch, so I'm ravenous," he said.

Luke was the hardest working man she'd ever known, besides her dad. She wanted to do something nice for him.

"Tell you what. I put a roast in the crock pot early this morning. I'll bring the kids home with me and finish dinner, while you go home and shower. That'll give you some private time, which you rarely have. How does that sound?"

"Thank you, Elli. You're a woman after my own heart." He stepped closer, put his hands on either side of her face and kissed her gently. "I'll see you within the hour."

Inwardly, Ellie smiled. *You have no idea how much I'm after your heart. That's my wish for the both of us.*

"Brett can have mashed potatoes and green beans. If you'll help me, we'll roast asparagus and red potatoes for us."

"Yes. Asparagus is one of my favorite veggies," she said, then giggled. "Daddy even likes it."

"Good thing. Because that's what is on the menu for tonight. Grab the asparagus from the fridge, rinse it off and wrap it in a couple of paper towels. I'll scrub the potatoes."

"Why are you going to scrub them?"

"Because they've been in the dirt," she told her, then smiled at her innocence.

Her eyes grew large and she had a frown on her face. "Are you going to use soap?"

It was all Ellie could do to control her laughter. "No, baby." Ellie held up a vegetable brush. "With this brush. Just give them a good scrub under clear water so we won't eat the dirt."

"Okay. I understand now. Silly me."

"You aren't silly at all. You haven't roasted potatoes before, right?"

"Right. When is my daddy getting here?"

"Probably about thirty minutes, so we need to get the potatoes in the oven. How about you set the table, then play with Brett until your daddy gets here?"

"Sure." She rolled the asparagus in paper towels, then yawned. "I'm getting tired. Too bad tomorrow isn't Saturday. No school. I can't wait to see your dad this weekend, Miss Ellie."

Twenty-Four

Thursday morning was busy. Ellie and Luke hadn't had much private time to talk. Luke's attitude toward her had changed drastically. He'd dealt with such grief since last Thanksgiving, she had begun to wonder if he'd ever learn to live with the loss of his wife.

She could only hope he wasn't stepping out of his safety net and believing he was ready to love again. Hope for him to have actually come to grips with the grief was on her mind.

By ten that morning, Ellie had pulled up housekeeping work orders for the day and Friday, then sent a text the head housekeeper, Anna. She was in Ellie's office in less than fifteen minutes.

"Anna as you know we have four new cabins. They're ready for your crew. Everything they need is in each cabin. Take Thomas and another from maintenance, or whoever you prefer, and have them install the blinds. Since they're wooden, we decided against curtains."

"When would you like us to start on the cabins?" Anna asked.

"Today, if possible. If you have need of extra help, you have a list of workers that have been through security. Call however many you think is necessary in for today, tomorrow, or both."

"We'll get the cabins in shipshape before you know it. I'll text when we're finished."

"Thank you, Anna. I knew I could depend on you."

Ellie reached to shut down the program, when she noticed a name. Her heart gave way to a lurch. The name was Newsome. Cabin four, for the week. To be certain it was her ex, she checked out his information.

After she spoke to Mandy to watch after Danni when she got in from school, she put in a call to Luke.

"Ryan is on your property. He rented cabin four Tuesday afternoon. Mandy set him up from Wednesday to Wednesday."

"What? Are you sure?"

"As sure as I can be. All his credentials checked out." Ellie's hand shook as she moved the phone from her left hand to the right. "What do you think he's up to?"

"Who knows? Whatever it is, it doesn't sound good."

"I'm leaving now. Since his cell won't work up there, it wouldn't do any good to try and call," Ellie said.

"Ellie. You aren't going up there by yourself. I don't feel good about this. I'll make a call to the sheriff to meet us there, just to be on the safe side. Wait for me. I'll be there in ten minutes. Do not leave without me," Luke instructed her.

"Okay. I'll wait for you. Please hurry." While she waited, she shut down her computer and straightened her desk. She was too nervous to stay still.

When they arrived at the cabin, the sheriff and a deputy were waiting for them. Ryan's car was parked under a tree on the gravel driveway. The trunk lid was partially open.

Luke jumped from the car. Ellie didn't wait for him to open her door; she was right behind him.

"Anything happening, sheriff?" Luke asked.

"I'm surprised he hasn't already come to the door to see what's going on," the sheriff said.

"Be careful, sheriff. We've had words. Many of them. Hard to tell what he may be up to."

The sheriff said something to the deputy, he went to the police car's trunk, retrieved a megaphone, then handed it to the sheriff.

"Ryan Newsome. This is the sheriff. We'd like to talk to you. Please come outside."

After a few minutes went by, the sheriff tried again. "Make yourself visible, Mr. Newsome."

They waited.

"I don't think he's in there. If he is, he certainly isn't coming out," the deputy said.

Both the sheriff and deputy drew their guns and motioned for Luke and Ellie to go behind the patrol car.

"Mr. Newsome. We're coming in." They carefully walked up on the porch, stood to either side of the door, then knocked. They received no answer.

The sheriff tried the door knob. The creaky door swung halfway open.

Twenty-Five

"Mr. Newsome, are you in there?" the sheriff called out. They still received no answer.

"I'm coming in, Mr. Newsome. If you have a weapon, put it down." He motioned for the deputy to follow him. He kicked the door the rest of the way open, his gun aimed for cover.

He saw nothing, heard nothing. The cabin was too warm and there was a faint hideous odor in the cabin. Both he and the deputy held their noses and walked inside.

"This isn't looking good, sheriff."

The sheriff nodded. "Agreed." The cabin was small, so it didn't take long for a thorough search.

"In here, sheriff," the deputy called out.

On the bed, fully clothed... lay Ryan Newsome. Dead as could be.

They put their guns away and went to the door, then indicated to Luke and Ellie, they should come onto the porch.

"We found Mr. Newsome. It's not good. If you're the least bit squeamish, remain outside," the sheriff commented. "I'd rather neither of you went inside though."

"No way. I'll stay out here," Ellie whispered. "I'm not really squeamish, but seeing Ryan like that... well, I don't care to."

"If you need someone to identify him besides you two, I'll go," Luke answered.

"Yes. Thank you, Luke. Don't touch anything though. You know, crime scene and all."

"Crime scene? How can that be?"

"Just procedure. That's all," the sheriff offered.

"Ryan wasn't a very nice person, but he didn't deserve to die this way," Ellie remarked. "What do you think happened?"

The sheriff pulled on his belt and withdrew a pad and pen from his jacket pocket. He glanced at both of them. He bent down and checked the fireplace flue. It was closed. "Yep. Just as I thought."

"We'll know more once we get the coroner's report, but it looks to me as though it could be carbon monoxide poisoning."

Luke used his handkerchief, turned off the gas to the fireplace, then tapped the notice on the mantle. "You see we put up notices to open the flue when the fireplace is used." He slapped his hat against his leg. "Ryan didn't need to die. If only he'd heeded the fireplace warning."

"Trouble is… some people don't bother reading warnings," the sheriff replied.

Luke nodded in agreement. "Evidently not. It's in all move-in packets also. We'll make sure ourselves that everyone is aware. Not that we don't, but it needs restating."

The deputy had taken the megaphone back to the police car and noticed Ryan's trunk still open a bit. He used a rubber glove to raise the trunk. His eyes popped open. In two large boxes were sticks of dynamite. He backed away and turned toward the cabin to bring the sheriff back to Ryan's car.

"Well, well. What do we have here? You could blow up an entire small town with this much explosives. It seems Mr. Newsome had some grievances against you, Luke."

"As I told you, sheriff, we've had issues. Mainly over his treatment of Ellie. I never thought he'd go to this extreme though. Ever."

"I'm aware of the problems he and Ellie experienced. Like Ellie said, he wasn't a very nice man." He crossed himself. "God rest his soul."

"You two can get on back to town. We'll handle everything from here on out. If you would, call my office when you reach an area the phones work. Tell Jerry what's going on here and have them send the appropriate people up here as soon as possible. It's going to be dark soon and I'd like to finish up before then. If we are able to."

"Let me know when we can come in to clean up and air the place out. Okay?" Luke requested.

The sheriff tipped his hat. "Will do."

Twenty-Six

Luke walked Ellie to his SUV, his arm around her shoulder. "Are you okay, hon?"

"I'm fine. A little shook up though. It's hard to believe he's really gone. I'm glad the sheriff didn't want us to go into the bedroom. Not a pleasant sight, I'm sure."

They rode in silence for a while, each with their own reflections. Luke checked his phone. "I have bars." He phoned the sheriff's office and relayed the information to Jerry. "Jerry, the sheriff said ASAP. You have the address."

Ellie keyed in Mandy's number at the inn. "I'm not going to go into anything right now, but don't make any reservations for cabin four until further notice. Please call Anna and have her cancel housekeeping for cabin four also until further notice. Tell her I'll get back to her when they can resume cleaning. Is Danni doing okay? Good. Homework always keeps her busy. We'll be there in about twenty minutes."

"You know, Luke. I should have seen this coming sooner," Ellie pointed out.

"Please. How could you possibly have known what Ryan was going to do?" He gave her an incredulous look.

"Oh, I don't mean what he did today, or whenever it was. I mean how he'd changed since he left me. He was already having illusions of children that weren't even there. I don't mean to speak ill of the dead, but when he didn't get his way, he'd sulk like a child. Actually he was worse than a child. Most children aren't bitter. He was a very bitter man."

"He certainly had his issues."

"I have no idea if he even has family. He never introduced me to any or mentioned them."

Luke pulled into the parking lot at the inn. "Let's pick up Danni and Brett, then go for some Chinese or whatever you feel like tonight. This is a non-cooking night for you."

Ellie leaned over and kissed Luke on the cheek. "Thank you for being here for me. You're a good man."

"I've waited a long time to hear those words, hon." He opened her door and linked their arms.

Ellie looked around. "Luke. What will the employees say?"

"Do you think I care what anyone says? We care for each other—we shouldn't worry what people say, or don't say." He laughed. "People are going to talk no matter what. So, I say, give them something to talk about."

"Luke, you're so bad."

"Hey you just told me I was a good man. Make up your mind. Which is it?"

She took the steps two at a time, then waited for Luke to open the inn's door. "I'll think on that one and let you know after dinner. Don't be so impatient."

"I know, I know. Patience is a virtue," he noted. "I'm learning the hard way."

"How else could you learn patience? It's through trial and error and hard times."

Twenty-Seven

Christmas had rolled around again. It was a week before and Ellie had most of the children's gifts wrapped and under the tree at her house.

"We baked cookies all last week," Danni said.

Ellie high-fived her. "Yes, how well I know. My freezer is running over. Thank goodness we have your class party and the party at the inn for the employees and their families. Those two events will swallow up most all the goodies."

"When are we going to decorate the tree at the inn?" Danni asked. "It's huge. Are you sure we have enough decorations? Do we need to buy more?"

Ellie grinned at her excitement. "Decorations are one of the things we aren't short of. As for decorating the tree, that's tonight. Did you forget?"

Danni came up behind her and tickled her, then giggled. "No. I was making sure you hadn't forgotten."

"Oh, you." Ellie dried her hands, then chased her around the kitchen.

"Whoa. What's happening here?" Luke chuckled and caught Danni up in his arms and swung her around. "You'd think the house was filled with boys with all this rough-housing going on." He let out a deep breath. "You're getting so big, Danni. I won't be able to swing you around much longer."

Danni pooched out her lips and gave her daddy a sad face. "Then you'll still have Brett to play with. He giggles when you swing him."

"Yes, baby. I will and he does. But you'll never get too big for a hug." He sniffed the air. "Is there nothing in the crockpot today?"

Danni and Ellie looked at each other and laughed. "Daddy, you forgot."

"What did I forget?"

"The party at the inn. Yum. We're having some awesome food tonight."

Luke snapped his fingers and rolled his eyes. "So that's what I smelled all day." He winked at Ellie. "Hey! Why don't we skip the party and run out for a burger?"

"No way," Danni replied with a frown. "I wouldn't miss this party for anything. Santa's going to be there with gifts for the kids. Brett, Miss Ellie, and I helped the kids write to Santa so they will get a gift they really want. Santa was at the Children's Center last night. Did you know that?"

"I did. I'm positive they enjoyed every minute of the party," Luke responded.

There were a hundred and fifty employees, plus the children at the party. Once everyone had arrived and gathered around the tree, they had a countdown and Danni waited for a signal from Ellie.

"Now, Miss Ellie?"

Ellie held up her hand, then gave her a thumbs up.

Danni, switched on the tree lights and the entire room burst into twinkling light. Luke took his seat at the piano and played while the group sang Christmas carols.

Ellie took a seat next to Luke and started playing *Silent Night* with him. They looked at each other and laughed.

After the singing was over, everyone filed into the dining room for the buffet.

"Good evening, everyone. I'd like to take this opportunity to thank all of you for attending tonight. My heart is full. I want you to know I think I have the best workers in the world. Bar none. Thank you from the bottom of my heart for the faithfulness you've shown me and my family. I think of all of us as one big family. I realize you're eager to experience this special meal the ladies have spent all day preparing. I know I am. After dinner, we have a special guest. Don't leave early or you'll miss out. Thank you, my friends. And now, without further ado, please enjoy the meal to it's fullest. Dinner is served."

Matt and Gage joined Luke, Ellie, and the kids at their table. "We made it. I wasn't sure if we could," Gage began. I have to tell you the music was outstanding… and the singing… wow. You have a great bunch of singers, Luke."

"We do and they get better every year." Luke replied.

"I didn't know you played, Luke. You've never mentioned it," Ellie pointed out.

"I have a piano, but I put it in storage after I came home from your house. Nora played also. I couldn't bear to pass by the piano everyday. There were too many memories."

"Maybe you'll consider bringing it back to the house now. Who knows? Danni may want to take lessons," Ellie suggested.

Luke gave her a lingering look. "I'll think about it. I suppose it's time to get back to normal."

"Daddy. I would like to learn the piano. You and Mom both play. Plus now we've heard Ellie, too."

Matt chuckled under his breath. "I can see it now. All three of you fighting over the piano."

Luke had tensed up a bit, but Matt brought back a lighter mood with his laughter.

Danni picked up her plate. "I'm going for dessert. Anyone want to join me?"

Luke stood and rubbed his tummy. "I sure hope they made pecan pie. Lots of them."

Twenty-Eight

Christmas Eve was a special time for all of Luke's family. They were spending the holiday with Ellie again. She glanced around at the two beautiful children, and Luke. The memories from last year's Christmas came bursting forth inside Ellie's head, and she all but cried.

Ellie handed Danni a cup of hot chocolate and Luke a cup of coffee, then sat beside him. "Can you believe an entire year has passed since we met?"

He smiled at her, put an arm around her shoulder and hugged her tight. "Time has been good to us though. We've worked through some rough times, and we've enjoyed many good times. A lot has happened in the past year. Good and bad."

Ellie laid her head on his chest and breathed in his manliness. "You smell so good."

Luke stared down at Ellie, with a somber gaze. He put his chin on top of her head, then leaned and inhaled. "And… you smell like a bouquet of roses."

Ellie was caught off guard. "Thank you," she said. She was nervous, and it came out in her trembling voice.

Luke reached down and raised her chin with a thumb. "I've never seen you shy or nervous. Is anything going on?"

"No. I'm surprised that we've made so much progress in our relationship. I'm wondering where we'll be in a few months or next Christmas. Thinking to myself, that's all."

Danni watched the both of them while she was deep in thought. "Are we going to open a gift this year, like we did last year?"

"Sure, Sweetheart. You'll have to tear Brett away from his book. That task may not go so well. Let him bring his book with him. We don't want to make him cry. Christmas isn't about sadness. It's all about love."

"I agree, Ellie." He looked as though he had something important on his mind, but hesitated and said nothing.

"I love you Ellie," Danni blurted out. "I wish we could live here forever."

"You'll always be welcome here, sweetheart. You know that. Don't you?"

"Yes. But I wish we never had to leave."

Luke jumped up and began searching for a present for each of them.

"Daddy, finding the presents is my job. Do you mind if I hand out the gifts?"

He put the presents back under the tree and stepped aside. "You go right ahead, Danni. I've forgotten the tradition. Sorry, hon."

"When everyone has a gift we can open them," she remarked.

Brett opened a soft plastic firetruck that had flashing lights and sound. He clapped his hands and forgot all about his book while he examined the firetruck.

"Now you, Daddy. It's your turn."

Luke took the gift in his hands and removed the wrapping. Danni had framed a photo of him, Brett, Danni, and Ellie. "It's a beautiful gift, hon. Thank you so much."

"Do you love it, Daddy?"

"It's for your desk at the office."

"Nothing else would have pleased me more, hon. It's the best gift ever."

"Miss Ellie, you can open yours now."

Ellie hoped against hope Danni had given her the same photo. She opened her gift slowly. When she saw the same photo Danni had given to Luke, she burst into tears.

"Oh, Miss Ellie. I didn't mean to make you cry. I'm sorry." A tear ran down Danni's cheek.

Ellie quickly went to Danni and hugged her. "Sweetheart, I'm not sad. These are happy tears. This photo will be a treasure for the rest of my days."

Danni wiped the tear away and hugged her back. "Thank goodness you aren't sad. I'm happy you love our picture together."

"I certainly do. More than anything else."

"May I open mine now?"

Luke stood and went to Danni. "Yes you may, but only if you'll let me swap gifts with you."

She looked confused. "Okay, Daddy. If you really want me to."

"I do. I'll be right back."

When Luke came back he had a large box with a huge red ribbon on it. "Go ahead. Open it. All you need to do is remove the lid."

She squealed so loud Brett puckered up ready to cry. Luke picked up Brett and held him close.

"Oh, my goodness. It's a puppy. I have a puppy." Danni buried her face in the sweet puppy and cried. "Don't worry. These are happy tears, like Miss Ellie's tears were."

"She's a toy poodle. Isn't she a beauty?" Ellie asked. "What do you want to name her?"

"I'm thinking of Ginger, but I'll have to wait to name her. Let's see how she acts. Maybe tomorrow she'll get a name."

"Ginger is a splendid name."

"Ellie I have one more gift for you." He reached inside his pants pocket and pulled out a small velvet box, then handed it to her.

Inside the box was a beautiful sterling silver heart locket. Inside the locket was a photo of Danni and Brett smiling up at her.

"Oh, my." Ellie burst into tears again. "Luke, thank you. I'm happy you know how much your children mean to me."

"You mean just as much to my children as they do to you. Thank you for loving my children."

She threw her arms around him and kissed him. She didn't mind that Danni would see her kiss her dad. She hoped this kiss would be the first of a lifetime for the two of them.

"You not only have the locket heart, but you have my heart, Ellie. I couldn't have asked for a more special woman to come into my children's and my life."

"Oh, Luke. There's no way possible you could ever imagine how much I've wished for you to offer me your heart."

"My Christmas wish is complete."

In My Dreams

Jill James

This book is dedicated to all the armed services members who give up Christmas, and birthdays, Mother's Day, and Father's Day, and all the other holidays in between, to keep us safe.
Thank you.

One

"I wish I was home in Lake Willowbee," Jessie Ortega whispered as drops of sweat trickled into her eyes, burning as she tried to blink them away.

Her head whipped around at the rustle of foliage on her flank. A quick glance at the camo-clad soldier had her held breath whooshing out in a shuddered sigh. The stern look from Captain Collins had her pressing her lips tightly together.

What had started as a simple humanitarian effort to a small African village had her squad hunkered down in the middle of the jungle outside a nameless town in Timerlaqua. Through the verdant vines and enormous tree trunks, she spotted the guerrillas invading the unarmed village. At her count, they were outnumbered two to one. More if the villagers were on the side of the guerrillas, instead of her squad bringing aid to the flood-ravaged area.

She blinked again as the sweat continued to fall into her eyes. How could it be almost December? In her mind, she envisioned falling snow and hot chocolate in front of a roaring fire. A vision half a world away and impossible to reach.

I wish I could be home for Christmas. Last year hadn't been her turn for leave to go home. She'd spent last Christmas in Bolivia after a landslide buried thousands of people. She hadn't been home in two years.

The ardent thoughts had barely processed through her brain when the village exploded to violent life in a hail of gunfire and grenade explosions. Her ears rung as clumps of dirt flew into the air and rained down on hard, baked ground. Over the hum in her ears, the screams of women and children reverberated from the short distance away.

At the captain's signal, they rushed forward to the edge of the village. They spread out in their practiced movements. She ran without hesitation, without thought, her training kicking in easily after four years in the army. A cloud of dust and smoke filled the once-peaceful town square. The ground was littered with chunks of stone. Groans of pain replaced the music and laughter of moments before.

A child's cry sounded from the dusty cloud. The captain sent half of their squadron to the right, toward the growing distant gunfire fading into the jungle. With the pointing of a finger, he directed her and Johnson toward the groans and the crying child.

Jessie looked up as Catherine came to her side. With their medical skills they were often paired together. With her dark Latina looks against Catherine's blonde hair and blue eyes, the pair was nicknamed Moonlight and Sunlight from the second day in boot camp.

With her hometown of Sacramento practically spitting distance from Jessie's Lake Willowbee, they were almost neighbors and bonded from the beginning in their love of California and real Mexican food.

Jessie hunkered in a crouch, her weapon in her hands as Cat moved until they were back to back. Syncing their steps, they duck-walked toward the corner of the building growing visible in the dissipating smoke.

She peeked around the corner and spotted the small child kneeling over a prone female body. The little girl yelled in her native tongue and pulled on the woman's arm. In any language, the message was too clear. *Please, get up.*

Tears mixed with the sweat running down Jessie's face. The holes in the woman's chest made it clear the woman was never getting up again. She turned and whispered to Cat.

"The child is twenty, twenty-five feet ahead. No visible hostiles. No other movement."

They hugged the wall until they were straight across from the child. The little girl looked up, streaks of tears mixing with dust and dirt on her ebony face. Fear widened her eyes at their weapons until Jessie pointed to the US flag on her uniform. The little one nodded and ran to their side. She grabbed Cat's hand.

"Mama. Help mama."

Knowing it was fruitless, Jessie duckwalked toward the fallen woman. She placed her fingers on the woman's neck and left them there longer than needed. She turned to the little girl.

"I'm sorry. Mama is gone."

The child collapsed to the ground and her body shook as she screamed. The screams disappeared in the cacophony of sound as gunfire filled the town square again. Her head whipped around as the roar of gunshots grew louder and the eruptions of dirt and shattered stone marched toward them.

Jessie leapt across the space, wrapping Catherine and the child in her arms. She followed them to the ground, covering them with her body. Heat exploded as the rounds continued across the dirt and up her leg. Fire stitched a line from her calf to her thigh.

Another scream filled the air until she realized it was coming from her own throat. Gray mist hovered around the edge of her vision as her friend pushed out from under her and whipped her weapon in front of them. A burst of gunfire and a cry silenced let them know the rounds had found their target.

The only sound remaining was the echo of the gunfire and her heavy panting. Jessie found herself drifting as Cat tied a tourniquet around her thigh and dug into their backpacks for medical supplies. She wanted to tell her friend to not bother, but the words tumbled in her brain, scrambled in twisted circles, and made no sense.

"Tell Juan."

"Tell him what?" Cat whispered as her hands worked on Jessie.

Jessie saw the squad surrounding her. Their downtrodden looks said it all. She wasn't going to make it.

She grabbed onto Catherine's hand.

"Tell Juan Montoya, I'll be home for Christmas." *If only in my dreams.*

Two

$\mathcal{J}$uan Montoya stepped lightly down the stairs to the hallway outside the kitchen. Since they were small, it had been a race for him and his younger sister, Lucia, to see who made it to the kitchen first. The silence from beyond the doorway signaled he may have won for once.

He stepped through with a smile on his face. One glance at the tears streaking Lucia's face and his heart plummeted to his stomach. The last time he'd seen his sister like that had been the night their parents died in a car crash.

Rushing to the table, he went down on one knee and grabbed her hands.

"Is it Diego or Luis?"

When she shook her head, Juan breathed again, unaware he'd been holding it. His mind raced to the only members of the family not here in Lake Willowbee.

"Not Miguel, or Joy?"

Her head shook again as she stared into his eyes. "Our big brother and niece are fine. I'm so sorry, Juan."

She handed him the local newspaper. Folded to an inside page, Jessie Ortega's bright, shining face shone out at him. The enormous smile on her face, wearing her army uniform. The black words below the photograph blurred as tears filled his eyes.

Jessie Ortega, US Army, listed as MIA in Timerlaqua
in West Africa while on humanitarian mission with unit.

Ortega joined the army after high school graduation from Lake Willowbee High School. Our thoughts and prayers are with her family at this time.

The paper crumpled in his clenched fist as his legs gave out and he collapsed to the floor, his head falling to his sister's lap. Her murmured words failed to penetrate his anguished mind. So much was bottled up inside him. Every memory of his childhood included Jessie. She'd been by his side for every victorious event and for every adventure gone wrong. She'd been his best friend since they were five years old on the first day of kindergarten. They'd done everything together until she joined the army and he refused to follow.

Lucia's words leaked through as her fingers ran over his hair. "Juan, you have to go to the Ortega Law Offices. Her parents will know more than the paper."

He raised his head, picked himself up, and moved to a chair beside his sister. Turning away, he wiped his tears from his face. She smiled at him when he turned back to face her.

"One of these days, my macho brothers will realize tears aren't weakness. They are the strength to show your feelings."

He reached out and pulled gently on her long braid. "When did you get so wise, Lucia?"

She yanked her hair out of his hand. "Don't call me that. I'm not little anything. I'm a grown-up with the rest of you."

Juan shook his head. "Doesn't matter if we are all gray-haired and limping along. You will always be our baby sister."

An ink-black brow matching her hair rose as she glared at him, crossing her arms. "I'm your only sister and I'm telling you to go see Mr. and Mrs. Ortega."

"Okay. Okay, I'm out of here. I'll call you as soon as I hear anything."

He snatched an apple out of the fruit bowl as he watched Lucia take the crumpled paper and smooth it on the table. She crossed herself and bowed her head. Juan left her to her prayers. Perhaps God would listen to his sister, because he sure as heck didn't listen to him.

Hadn't since he was a little boy and begged Him to return his mom and dad as he sat beside Jessie, her arms wrapped around him, kissing his tear-stained cheeks. She'd run across a snow-covered town as soon as she heard.

A multitude of random thoughts rushed through his head as he drove across town to the law offices of Jessie's parents. A quick talk with their secretary let him know the Ortega's were at their house this morning.

He cursed himself silently as he trudged back to his car, the arctic wind cutting through his watchman's cap and heavy sheepskin coat. Snow hadn't come to Lake Willowbee yet, but the chill of winter had, nonetheless.

"Of course, they are home, *stupido*," he muttered as the car's heater fought the cold creeping into the vehicle from the short time it had been off. They wouldn't be at work waiting for word on their daughter. The warmth filled the vehicle by the time he arrived at the Ortega's lakeside home.

He swung into the driveway behind a nondescript black car. Sitting there, the heat failed to penetrate to his skin. A chill filled him, and a shiver went up his spine. He'd thought the sadness he'd felt when Jessie left for boot camp, angry with him, was the worst he could feel. Losing his best friend. Juan had been wrong. This was a thousand times worse. A world without Jessie Ortega in it should stop turning. The sun should stop shining. Anything but the nothingness filling his soul.

He buttoned up his coat and got out of the car. A few steps confirmed his worse nightmare. U.S. Army was stenciled on the black car's door. A cross in white set beneath the lettering. A visit from an army chaplain was never a good sign.

Moving as if his legs were stone, Juan stumbled up the stairs and knocked on the door. Footsteps sounded from within and in seconds he had his arms full of a crying Mrs. Ortega. Roger Ortega appeared and took Rita from his arms.

"Come in, Juan. The chaplain was just about to tell us about Jessie's condition."

Condition? Dead wasn't a condition, was it? Dead was dead. Hope flooded his body, heat reaching his fingers and toes.

Roger sat down beside his wife on the couch and optimism flared in the man's eyes. Juan moved to the living room and the chaplain shook his hand.

"This is Juan. Jessie's best friend. He is like family," Roger said, patting his wife's hand.

The chaplain nodded to him and turned his attention to Jessie's parents. "Mr. and Mrs. Ortega, I want to reassure you. Jessie is not dead and not missing in action. Communications were nonexistent in the jungle, but she has been brought to the West African capital and will fly out to the base in Germany for surgery."

"Surgery?" Rita cried out. "What happened to my Jessie?"

"The report I received said she took more than a few shots to her leg. She is stabilized for now. That's why they feel they can move her."

Roger sat up straight and looked the chaplain in the eye. "Be straight with us. Is she going to lose her leg?"

The chaplain fiddled with his cap, but still met Ortega's eyes. "They're not sure. There was a lot of damage. But we must take comfort in Jessie's survival. And in her homecoming."

Juan swallowed past the lump in his throat. Jessie loved physical exertion. She'd been up in trees, down in the lake, and all over the foothills with the Montoya boys. She'd been one of them, up for any adventures. Losing her leg would kill Jessie.

"This is all your fault," Rita Ortega screamed.

Juan looked up, ready to defend the chaplain and by extension, the Army. But, Rita glared at him, red patches painted her cheeks, her dark eyes cutting through him.

Roger tried to hold her back, but the woman leapt off the couch and was in front of him before he could breathe. Her finger poked into his chest.

"You should have asked her to marry you. Then she would have stayed here. This wouldn't have happened."

He stood as still as a statue as Roger walked over and pulled his wife away. The same questions filled the man's eyes as filled Juan's mind.

Marry her? Jessie was his best friend. The thought of marriage had never crossed his mind.

Three

Juan stumbled into the Montoya kitchen to find Lucia dressed for the day and making breakfast. He wasn't sure how he'd driven across town. The whole trip was a blur after Mrs. Ortega's outburst.

He didn't love Jessie, did he? Well, of course he loved her. As a friend. His best friend. He'd never thought of her in any other way. She certainly hadn't treated him like someone she would be in love with, who she would marry. Someone she would give up her dreams of being in the Army for.

"Juan."

His sister's repeated calling of his name finally penetrated the fog clouding his mind. He looked up at her hesitant smile and questioning look.

He didn't want to get her hopes up. She loved Jessie too. "The chaplain was at the Ortega's house. He said Jessie is alive, but she's been shot in her leg. Badly."

"Your face is white. There must be more." Lucia swallowed audibly. "Is she going to lose her leg?"

"They don't know," he admitted, tossing his cap on a barstool and hanging his coat from it. He fell into the adjacent seat at the counter.

Lucia piled food on a plate and placed it in front of him. Absentmindedly, he ate, unaware of what he was putting in his mouth and tasting none of it.

Juan dropped his fork to the half-empty plate with a clatter. "Mrs. Ortega said the strangest thing. She asked why I didn't ask Jessie to marry me. She said if I had asked, Jessie wouldn't have joined the army and got shot."

His sister smiled at him. "I don't know about that. Jessie really wanted to go, to serve our country. I always wondered why you didn't propose before she left."

He was dumbfounded. No words would come. Why did everyone think he wanted to marry his best friend?

"I'm not in love with Jessie Ortega, that's why."

She crossed her arms and stared at him, sending him a look bringing their mother instantly to mind. "Juan Ramon Montoya. Everyone in this town knew you and Jessie were in love. Except for you and Jessie."

She struggled up from the dark. The antiseptic scent flooded her nostrils and sat cloying in her throat. Someone held Jessie's hand, their fingers stroking over her skin. Panic filled her brain as memories flooded back. The last thing she remembered was the doctor saying her leg couldn't be saved.

Tears choked her as she lay helpless, unable to stop them.

"Jessie, can you hear me?" Cat's voice murmured by her ear.

Please let my leg be there. The words filled her head but didn't pass her lips.

"Wake up, please," her friend begged. "I need to hear your voice, Moonlight."

As if they were glued together, Jessie fought to open her eyelids. She winced as the light flooded her vision, a white light haloing Catherine's golden hair.

"An angel," Jessie whispered, her dry throat cracking.

Cat laughed and cried at the same time as she squeezed Jessie's hand tighter. "Not an angel, thanks to you."

"My leg," Jessie whispered.

Her friend's smile fell. "I'm so sorry, Jessie."

She sighed. She'd known even while struggling to consciousness. It felt gone. She couldn't feel a thing.

"It's not as bad as it looks," Cat added. "The doctor says you got a fifty-fifty chance it works again."

"I want to see," she demanded, struggling to pull herself up in the bed.

"Just a second," Cat cried, as she dropped Jessie's hand and pushed the button to raise the head of the bed. "I can't go any further than that. It'll move your legs."

Jessie breathed deeply and glanced down her body. Her right leg was twice the size of the left, surrounded with gauze wrappings and a metal cage with rods piercing her leg. Where there should be pain, there was nothing. If she hadn't seen it with her own eyes, she would have believed it was gone.

"I can't feel it," she whimpered. "I can't feel it at all."

Cat leaned in closer. "They got some excellent drugs here. Believe me, when you start therapy, you'll feel it."

Her gaze shot to Cat. "The little girl?"

"She was fine when we left the village. The Red Cross came in and found her grandmother."

"And you?"

Cat blushed and looked away. "I'm fine. Not a scratch. I'm so sorry."

Jessie reached for her hand and squeezed it. "Don't apologize for that. I'm so glad you are okay."

She glanced at her leg. "Or this would be for nothing."

Cat changed the subject quickly. "Your parents were notified. They should be here anytime."

She grimaced. "Great. I'll get a lecture from my mother about how she knew this would happen, and my father will just look hurt that he didn't protect his little girl."

Her friend smiled, lighting up her whole face. "That's what parents do. I can't wait until I get home and my mom and dad spoil me rotten for surviving the army."

"You are going home?"

"Yep. Enlistment was over by the time we got here to the hospital. I'm going back to Sacramento and nurse sick children without warlords trying to blow my head off."

She settled back into her pillow with a sigh. Jessie had known Cat was only doing her term, but she hadn't realized it was so close to done. Cat had always wanted to do her time and move on and Jessie had wanted the army to be her career.

"Be careful what you wish for, Cat," she muttered.

"What?" Cat leaned closer.

"Never mind," Jessie said, turning her head away.

She was out of wishes. Look where the last one had gotten her. She would be home for Christmas.

She would be home forever.

Four

Seven days.

Seven days since the Ortega's left for Germany and Jessie. Day after day, not one word of her condition. Juan was going crazy with the pictures in his head. Working at the Lake Willowbee Rehab Center with wounded vets painted too clear a vision of what his best friend could be facing. The not knowing was worse than knowing and dealing with it.

In a town where the information you had a cold before your first sneeze made the daily rounds, he couldn't fathom why there was no news from the Ortega's. All too easily, he could imagine that no news was bad news.

His fist thumped the steering wheel as he headed down Main Street and out to the edge of town. A resort town like Lake Willowbee, one relying on tourism dollars didn't really have a 'wrong side of the tracks.' If it did, the frontage road beside the highway would have qualified. The Lakeview Mobile Home Park sat a mile down the road, almost into the next exit on the highway. The irony was not lost on anyone that the park had no view, of the lake or otherwise. To call the run-down, falling-apart trailers sitting on a few weed-infested acres a mobile home park was an upgrade no one believed either.

Juan pulled his car in front of the first trailer and turned it off. He sat there staring at the only decent trailer in the place. Decent being a relative term since weeds sprouted out of every inch of cold-hardened dirt in the space. The building might have been blue, or green, or gray at one time. What was left on the walls defied color-coding.

The only splash of color was the owner's car sitting under the carport. The Candy-Apple-red Mustang was the only brightness on a gray, overcast day.

He shook his head. The car was probably worth more than the trailer it sat beside.

Why was he here?

Grabbing the keys, he shoved them in his pocket and got out of the car. The frigid air took his breath away as an arctic blast shot down the broken asphalt street. He looked up as a curtain twitched in the window and fell back into place. Seconds passed as he blew on his hands and stomped his feet.

Either the man would come out and talk to him, or not, but Carlos was his last hope for information on Jessie and her condition.

Her brother would know what was going on, wouldn't he?

Just as he was ready to leave, the door swung open on the trailer. Juan's mouth gaped open until the cold air hit his lungs. He shut his mouth with a snap. He hadn't seen Carlos in years, but time had not been nice to the man.

At thirty, Carlos was only eight years older than his little sister, Jessie. He looked at least a decade and a half more than that. His thin T-shirt might have been white at one time, but now it matched the weather-beaten color of his home. Stains covered it with substances Juan didn't want to look at too closely. Goosebumps covered Ortega's arms while he seemed to ignore the cold.

One look at his bloodshot eyes told Juan all he needed to know. Carlos was as high as a kite at eight o'clock in the morning. Not for the first time, he wondered how the Ortega's could raise two such different children.

"Little Juan," Carlos slurred his words as he squinted and eyed him. "What cha doing here?"

He sighed. "I was hoping you had heard from your parents. That you knew how Jessie was doing. When they'll be home?"

Carlos stumbled forward and slapped a hand on Juan's shoulder. "You're in luck, Juanito. My perfect baby sister will be home on Monday. With all her parts still attached. So still perfect." He leaned in. "So, still doable, if you ever make up your mind to be a man and do her."

Juan's heart raced as his face heated. How could anyone talk about their sister that way? He would never even think that way about Lucia.

He yanked Carlos's hand off his shoulder and shoved the man away. Ortega stumbled and banged against the side of the trailer. His hand whipped to the back of his waist but came back empty.

"Count yourself lucky, Juanito. No one pushes Carlos Ortega around."

He did count himself lucky. Carlos had left town after he dropped out of high school and found a gang in Sacramento. Either luck or stupidity had kept the man low on the gang crime rungs and out of jail most of the time.

Juan held his hands up. "I'm sorry, man. Just wanted to find out about Jessie."

Carlos punched the side of the trailer. "Well, you did. So, go back to your side of town."

He shook his head as he backed up and got to his car. He slid into the vehicle as Carlos slammed the trailer's door.

Juan shivered as he turned on the car and the heat to full blast.

What if Carlos hadn't just got up? Would he have been carrying a gun then?

"I wish Jessie was here."

He backed the car out of the trailer park and headed back to town. If Jessie had been here, he wouldn't have had to see Carlos at all.

Five

"Come on, Roy. Just a couple more." Juan egged on the paraplegic working the chin-up bar. Not that the man needed him to urge him on at this point. Roy had been coming to the rehab center for months now and could do the most pull-ups in the place.

"What do you mean, a couple more? I've done ten more than usual."

Juan shook his head. He hadn't been tracking and counting. "I'm sorry, Roy. My mind is somewhere else today. I'll do better next time."

The man dropped into his wheelchair and reached for a sweat rag. "No prob, man. Must be a woman got your mind in a fog."

Juan was speechless.

Roy's smile brightened up his sweaty, reddened face. "Go, Juan."

A blush heated his face. "It's not like that. She's just a friend."

If possible, Roy's smile broadened. "Just because they start as friends, don't mean they got to stay that way."

He didn't think his face could get any hotter, but it did. Juan moved to lead Roy to the massage table. Maybe if he got the man face down on the table his comments would stop.

No such luck. Even looking away, Roy still had more to say.

"Of course, friends to lovers is best. Having a lover and a best friend is awesome. One time…"

Juan stopped him right there with a subject he knew would bring the man back to himself—his treatment. His fingers dug into Roy's calf muscles. "You've lost mass here. Have you been doing your exercises?"

"What does it matter?" The man's voice fell, low and quiet. "They'll just keep getting soft and thin."

The resignation in the man's voice hit Juan hard. Would Jessie be the same? Would she give up and accept whatever her injury dictated? No way, not Jessie. And not Roy either. Not if he had any say about it.

"Roy, they are making strides every day in treatments for paraplegics. Our machine that works your muscles when you can't. Tomorrow they could come up with something new, like the electronics implanted into legs and letting people walk again. They will only get better and better."

Roy sighed. "I know that, Montoya. Most days I'm fine. But today… "

Juan walked around to the top of the table and pulled a chair and sat down so he was face to face with the man. "I'm not a doctor, but you know you can tell me anything and it stays in this room."

"Amelia left this morning. Said she wasn't coming back. Said I'm not the man she knew. Well, hell. I know that. I didn't ask for this to happen. To come back half the man I was before."

"Stop right there," Juan spoke up, staring him in the eye. "You still have your same mind. Your same heart. You are the same—inside."

"I don't feel the same. I don't feel the same at all."

Juan didn't have an answer to that. The most he'd had was a broken foot one summer. Nothing like Roy had to deal with. He swallowed deeply.

Nothing like Jessie was dealing with either. Would the Jessie who returned be the person he remembered?

"Like I said, Mrs. Ortega, Jessie is able to go home as soon as her paperwork comes through. We can't do anything further here."

The doctor's voice carried into her room from the doorway. Her mother's trembling voice cut in before the man's words finished passing his lips.

"But she can't feel her leg. She should feel it by now, shouldn't she?"

Jessie could picture her mother with her eyes closed. Her fingers rubbing the finish off her rosary beads, tears falling from her large, dark eyes, and her lips quivering. The same look Jessie had seen every time she'd fallen and skinned a knee. A look that drilled into her as if she'd been seconds from death.

A giggle tried to escape her. She bit her lip. Her mother would never understand why it was funny that she had been seconds from death, and she'd finally understood why her mother had worried so much before.

She sighed. So why did she ache to return to her squad? Why did she want to see all of them again? To eat MRE's in the field and soak through her uniform in the jungle heat. To be part of something bigger than herself. To help others. All she had ever wanted was to make a difference in the world.

Tears fell down her face and puddled in her ears. Now, she was the one who would need help. Because no matter how much she tried, she still couldn't feel her leg. No aches. No twinges. No itching to move.

"Mija, I know you are awake," her mother whispered beside her bed. "We can get you home as soon as the Army gets your paperwork processed."

"Hurry up and wait," she mumbled.

"What?"

She opened her eyes and placed a hand over her mother's twitching fingers. "The Army way. Hurry up and wait."

Rita Ortega shook her head. "I don't understand at all. It is taking longer to get you out of the army than it took for you to get into the army. You would think they would be in a hurry to get you out. It isn't like you can stay in."

Her mother bit her lip and tears fell down her cheeks. "I'm so sorry, mija."

She rubbed her mom's hand, her fingers tangling in the rosary beads. "It's okay. Like I said. Hurry up and wait."

Her eyelids fell as fatigue pulled her under. As far as she was concerned, the Army could take forever. It wasn't as if she had anything to go home to.

As she slipped deeper, her mind traveled to Juan Montoya. Her best friend. The only man who let her down.

Six

Juan sighed as he signed his name to another form. Silence reigned over the rehab center. The clients had left an hour ago and the other therapists had left minutes ago. A few had called to invite him to a local bar before they left, but he'd declined, citing a pile of paperwork. A pile quickly depleted as he signed and threw them into the *Out* basket on his desk.

The truth was he just wanted to be alone. Since he'd been to the Ortega's, he couldn't wrap his mind around Mrs. Ortega's comments. Everyone seemed to think he loved Jessie. As more than a friend. As much more.

He shook his head. Every memory of his childhood had Jessie in it. She'd been like a member of their family. Like another sister. He dug deeper. She'd been his friend. Even though she was a girl, she hadn't been Lucia's friend. While his sister was busy with a needle and thread making designer clothes for her dolls, Jessie had been much happier hunting and fishing with the Montoya boys.

A laugh escaped him. He'd been grounded for a whole month the year they took Jessie with them to the hunting cabin and she'd chopped her long hair off, wanting to be one of the boys. It hadn't been funny at the time, he'd been so angry with her for missing all the events in Lake Willowbee that November. Years later, it was one of their favorite memories, especially when her hair had grown back thicker and darker than before.

His breath caught. Opening his desk drawer, he pulled out a photo of him and Jessie. They had their arms around each other's shoulders, wearing their graduation gowns. With Rita Ortega's and his sister's words bombarding his thoughts, he looked at the photograph.

When had Jessie become a woman? How had he missed it? Her curves fit against him perfectly. Her shape was obviously, even with the gown over her dress. Her long, dark hair fell into waves to her waist. Her dark eyes shone, and a bright smile graced her lovely face.

"You moron," he said, his voice echoing in the empty room. "The woman had to get shot for you to realize she might be more than just a friend."

He ripped the drawer open and flung the picture to the back as far as it would go. Slamming it shut, he pushed his chair away from the desk. This was stupid. All the comments had done was taint every memory he had of Jessie.

Yes, she was a beautiful woman, but that didn't mean she was the woman for him.

Yes, they liked each other, but that didn't mean she felt anything more for him than he felt for her.

Why did that thought rip through his heart? He was sure she'd ripped his heart out already. When she'd enlisted in the Army and at the last moment, he refused to sign up.

When she'd told him they were no longer friends, and she never wanted to talk to him again. In four long years, she *had* never spoken to him again. No letters. No calls. No visits when she was home on leave. In a split-second decision, he'd lost his best friend forever.

Staring out the airplane's window, Jessie watched as dark clouds formed and covered the sun. She shivered and tugged the small blanket to her neck. Picturing the frigid rain that would greet them at the airport, she wondered for the thousandth time of the flight how it could be summer on one side of the planet, and deep winter on the other.

Rubbing her cold fingers together, she marveled she'd been sweating in the verdant jungle days ago and wishing to return home. She bit her lip and gazed unseeing out the damp glass.

"Be careful what you wish for," she muttered.

"Did you say something, dear?" Her mother leaned across the aisle, worry in her eyes.

"Just talking to myself."

With relief, Jessie watched as her mom gave her a small smile and turned away to lean on her father's shoulder. Alone with her dark thoughts, she leaned against the window and watched as the bright lights of Sacramento grew until they filled her view. Her friend, Cat, was down there somewhere, happy to be home. Envy gnawed at her.

Her shoulders tensed as they landed with a bump. All too soon, the flight attendant came up the aisle with the hated wheelchair. She sighed as it took all her father's strength to maneuver her into the chair.

Her leg thumped into the side of the airplane's seat hard enough to vibrate through her body. Every part of her body except for the leg she'd hit.

The flight attendant's face turned bright red. "I'm so sorry. Are you okay?"

"It's fine," she said. "I didn't feel a thing."

Her mother winced and rushed to cover her with a blanket. Tears filled her vision as her mom tucked it in around her as if she was an invalid. Biting the inside of her cheek until she drew blood, Jessie looked down at her lap as her dad pushed the chair up the aisle.

"Wait a minute," Jessie pleaded as they reached the end of the tunnel. With an effort, she pulled off her uniform jacket and handed it to her mom.

"Put that in my bag, please, Mama."

"But, mija. It is freezing outside."

"I don't care. I'm not wearing it through the airport. You know the people who clap for heroes are out there. I'm not a hero," she finished on a whisper.

Her mother tried to sputter a reply, but her father placed a hand on her shoulder and squeezed. "Rita, put it in the bag."

He came around to the front of the chair. Peeling off his plaid flannel coat, he wrapped it around Jessie and helped her put it on. His fingers shook as he buttoned it for her.

Her father leaned over, his forehead against hers. His tears fell on her cheeks with her own. "You are a hero, Jessie. Because of you, your friend, and that little girl are alive. I believe that. The army believes that. Someday you will believe that too."

Fresh tears fell at her dad's words. From the time she was a very little girl he'd encouraged her and taught her how to be strong and confident. He always knew what she needed and when she needed it.

His hand cupped her wet cheek. Her lips trembled as she remembered all the times he'd picked her up, dusted off her skinned knees, and sent her back out to play. This time he couldn't make it all better. She knew it and he knew it.

That hurt more than taking bullets in her leg.

Seven

"Maybe we should go in with you?" Her mother's voice trembled from the front seat of the car.

Jessie captured the sigh before it left her throat. She'd spent three days being treated like an invalid. After the first twenty-four hours, it had been too much. Before all of this, she'd always looked forward to leave and going home to her parents and Lake Willowbee. Before, she'd looked forward to being home. Now, she'd trade everything to be back in that jungle halfway around the world.

Before she said something hurtful she couldn't take back, she opened her door and scooted to the edge as her father came around with the wheelchair.

"I'll call you as soon as I'm done," she said, placing her hand on her mom's shoulder. "If I can go halfway around the world, I'm sure I can manage an hour of physical therapy."

Her mother started to talk, but before she could get a word out, her father stared at her mother, who pressed her lips together and turned away.

Whatever husband/wife thing that was, Jessie knew she didn't want to get in the middle of it. She maneuvered into the wheelchair with a plop and pulled her injured leg onto a footrest. Pushing backward with the other foot, she moved and let her father shut the car door.

He moved closer and kissed her on the forehead. "Call us when you're done."

"I will," she whispered.

Staring until the car turned and disappeared down the road, Jessie put her other foot up and gripped the wheels to go into the Lake Willowbee Rehab Center. As she entered door after door with someone holding it open, her mood turned foul. She knew it, but she couldn't stop herself. Her face overheated and sweat poured down her back. Pushing a wheelchair was harder work than it looked like.

By the time she reached the room on her appointment card, she was ready to turn around and go back home. She gulped through the knot in her throat as she wheeled into the room and glanced around.

A haze filled her vision as she fought tears. A man was doing pull-ups on a bar with one arm. The other was gone, ending at the elbow. A woman was at the bench press, her torso strapped to the bench to compensate for the missing balance from her missing legs.

"Ain't seen you around her before," a warm voice spoke at her side as a man wheeled up beside her. "I know pretty much everyone here, since I've been coming for months."

Jessie turned to him. Dark-brown eyes shone in his ebony face. He held out his hand.

"Roy Morris," he said, a giant smile on his face.

"Jessie Ortega," she supplied. "This is my first visit. I just got home."

He glanced down at her gauze-wrapped leg. "All in one piece, I see. That's great to see in this place. Doesn't happen often."

She glimpsed at the thin legs not filling his pants and not matching his arms and torso. "I'm sorry."

"Don't fret about it. I don't. We got to deal with what we get handed in life, don't we?"

"I guess so," she whispered.

Roy reached over and put his hand on hers. "You won't believe me now. But it gets better."

"I hope…" Her voice trailed off.

"You hope what?"

"Never mind. I'm done hoping and wishing. It doesn't solve anything."

He squeezed her hand. "Mostly it's hard work and effort. But hoping and wishing don't hurt."

"Sometimes they do," she whispered back.

"Jessie."

Her head came up at his whisper of her name. Juan stared at a face he knew as well as his own and the face of a stranger at the same time. The girl he'd known was gone. A woman had taken her place. A woman who'd been through an experience no one should have to go through.

"Juan," she spoke, her face going from welcoming to closed in a split second. "I didn't know you would be here."

Beside her, Roy removed his hand, but his big grin remained. "Oh." The single word was all he said as he wheeled away toward the exercise equipment.

His face heated at Roy's knowing look. Turning back, he watched as Jessie tried to move her wheelchair back out the door.

"I can come back another time," she muttered as the wheel hit the doorframe and jerked to a stop.

He walked over and faced her, his hands on the arms of the chair. Her look of fright stunned him, his heart jumping in his chest as her eyes grew wide, and her olive complexion paled.

Juan stepped back, relieved to see color fill her face again. "I'm sorry. I shouldn't have done that."

"It's fine. I'm fine," she stuttered out and looked away. "I just hate being trapped in this chair."

"I understand," he said.

Her head came up and she glared at him. "Don't even try to say you understand, Juan Montoya. You have no idea."

Why had he thought Jessie would be any different from the wounded vets he saw every day? Why had he thought he could treat her differently? He'd seen that look on too many faces from the moment he'd started work here.

"No, I don't understand how you feel. But I deal with this every day. Look around you, Jessie. You aren't the first and unfortunately, you won't be the last. Are you ready to get back into shape, or not, Specialist Ortega?"

He held his breath as Jessie bit her lip and stared around the room. Would she bolt, or would she stay? Juan still knew her well enough to spot the moment she stiffened her spine and took a deep breath to gather herself.

"Since you weren't man enough to join me, let's see if you're tough enough to get my leg working again."

Eight

*J*uan didn't notice anything different about Jessie as he'd helped her up on the table and left her to change into a T-shirt and a comfortable pair of exercise shorts. Knocking on the door, he opened it at her quiet 'come in.'

One glance and his tongue stuck to the roof of his mouth and his brain turned off. He wished he could blame her mother's comments, but Jessie was a beautiful woman. Sure, she'd been a pretty girl when she'd left for the army. Always in shape from sports and an outdoor life, but the woman on the table was lean muscle and curves in all the right places.

"Your hair," she whispered.

"What?"

"Where are all your curls?"

He laughed, some of his embarrassment fading. "Haven't had them in years," he said, running his hand over his short-cropped hair. "Lots easier to do my job with them out of the way."

Was that sadness in her eyes? If it were, it disappeared in a second, replaced by a frown as she stared at her bandaged leg.

He grabbed a pair of scissors and moved to cut off the wrappings. "Let's see what we have here," he murmured.

Jessie put her hand on his. His breath stopped as his heart raced. "I won't hurt you."

She shook her head, dark curls falling into her eyes. "I didn't think you would. I just… "

Comprehension filled his brain at her trailing voice. "You haven't seen your injuries yet. I've gone over the reports from the army doctors. It isn't so bad."

Glaring at him with tear-filled eyes, she tore her gaze away. "I can't feel it."

He stopped with the scissors in midair. "Not at all?"

Her hand fisted and pounded on her thigh. "Nothing. Nothing at all."

Juan grabbed her hand and placed it on the table. "Jessie, nerve endings are tricky. You can be numb one day and tingling the next and moving the week after."

"Or not," she argued.

He smiled at her. "There's the Jessie I remember. If I said the sky was blue, you would argue it was aquamarine."

She rolled her eyes.

"Let's see what we've got," he said. He helped her scoot backward on the table until her leg was flat on its surface. In seconds, he had the bandaging cut and removed from her leg. His gaze swept the length and width of her leg. Other than some paleness, the leg was intact from the front. The small scars from the steel rods would fade over time.

"I'll have you flip over in a moment. Let me check some stuff first."

Walking over to the counter, he grabbed the rubber hammer for checking reflexes. Tapping over her knee and down her calf, he watched as her muscles responded but Jessie showed no emotion or acknowledgment of the test.

He moved down to her foot. "Can you wiggle your toes for me?"

She grunted, the exertion and strain showed on her sweating face. No movement at all.

"See, I told you."

Juan ran the handle of the hammer up the sole of her foot. "Ouch," she cried out. "What did you do?"

He smiled at her. "The nerves are damaged, not destroyed.

It'll take time for the brain to get messages through and for the nerve endings to send the messages back. If there is feeling in the bottom of your feet, it will get to the rest of your leg eventually."

Her arms crossed in front of her chest and a familiar look crossed her face as Jessie glared at him, an eyebrow raised and fire in her eyes.

"You don't know that. You're not a doctor."

He worked to hide that her comment had hurt. He'd wanted to become a medic when they had gone to enlist. Without the help the service would have provided, he'd settled for community college and getting his physical therapist certificate. He wasn't a doctor, but he helped people, nonetheless.

Juan took a deep breath and let it out. "No, I'm not. But I've been doing this for a while and I know what I'm talking about."

Jessie's hands fell to her lap. "Forget I said that. I shouldn't push my crappy mood on other people. Cat would give me 'what for' if she'd heard me."

"Who's Cat?" he asked as he wrote in her report.

"She's my best friend. We were together in Africa when—"

That sling hurt worse than the last. He could still remember a time when he was Jessie's best friend and they'd been inseparable. Until she'd left for boot camp, and he'd stayed in Lake Willowbee.

"Okay," he said, proud his voice didn't crack like an adolescent boy. "Let's see this terrible injury of yours."

He was joking, but he'd seen the pictures. The doctors in Germany had performed nothing short of a miracle. He still couldn't believe they'd saved her leg. If for some reason she didn't have use of it anymore, it was still attached.

Even if Jessie hadn't been his childhood friend, he would have still moved heaven and earth to get her walking again. This was his job, and he liked what he did.

With just a little help, Jessie flipped over on the table and put her head down on her folded arms.

"It's bad, isn't it?" she whispered, her gaze locked on the far wall.

Somehow the injury appeared worse on Jessie's smooth leg. Maybe because he knew her. Maybe because he'd dealt with so many wounded vets and listened as they described how they'd received their injuries.

"It's healing nicely," he mumbled. What he didn't add was it looked like they'd scooped the bullets out with a spoon and then pulled the skin tight to fill in the holes. Spiderwebs of puckered flesh meandered down her thigh and the back of her calf.

He wanted to cry with the image in his head of her pain and agony in the middle of the battle. But the last thing Jessie Ortega needed was his pity. She needed his help. Because, by God, she was going to be walking by Christmas.

Juan closed his eyes for a second and sent his fervent wish out into the universe. His wish had to be heard this time. It had to be.

Nine

*J*uan's silence filled the room as she stared at the stupid puppy poster on the wall. She refused to let any tears fall. She'd done enough crying when the doctor in Germany had shown her the photos of the damage to her leg.

"This is healing nicely," Juan said.

She shook her head as if the words were gibberish in a language she didn't understand.

"At least its in the back. I don't have to look at it." Jessie tried to joke the pain away, but it fell flat as her voice cracked.

As if he chose to ignore her comment, Juan continued doing his job. His voice stayed calm and steady as if he saw messed-up flesh every day. A chill went down her spine. He *did* see messed-up flesh and bodies every day. Maybe that was how he stayed so calm about it all. To him, she was just another patient. Even if to her, this meant everything.

"Okay, I'm going to put my hands on your leg. Let me know right away if anything hurts."

"I wish," she replied. In an instant she wanted the words back. Wishing was for children, not grown-ups who knew wishes and dreams didn't come true.

Jessie closed her eyes as Juan's warm hands settled on her ankle and pressed. She could feel it and she couldn't at the same time. The flesh moved but her senses didn't register it. A slight tickling occurred as his fingers marched up the uninjured parts of her leg. It reminded her of when a foot or hand fell asleep and then when you moved it, the appendage started to tingle and burn.

She could pinpoint the second his hands moved to her injuries. She felt nothing. No tingle. No pressure. Nothing.

"You're not feeling that at all, right?"

"Nope," she said, gulping down a thickness in her throat.

"Okay, we'll work with this."

"What?" She pushed herself up on her elbows and looked at him over her shoulder.

"I want you to not try to massage the injury sites. With the lack of feeling and not seeing what you are doing, you could make it worse."

She hacked out a disbelieving laugh. "I don't see how it could be worse."

Juan moved to her side and helped her flip back over. Jessie sat up and glared at him.

"There's the Jessie I know. The girl who could keep up with the Montoya boys wouldn't let a few bullets stop her."

"Hey. It was more than a few."

He picked up the folder on the nearby table. "It was five. I've read the report."

"Yes, five," she spit out. "How many bullets have you taken, wuss?"

Juan put the folder back on the table. "I'm not going there, Jessie. We all have to make our own choices in life."

She couldn't stop the words from spilling out. "You wanted to be a medic. Maybe a doctor in the future. Yet, here you are. A glorified masseuse."

Waiting for the famous Montoya temper, she stared as his face reddened beneath the rich, brown color and quickly returned to normal. The familiar outburst failed to appear.

"I don't have to dignify my life to you. I'm happy with what I do. Just so you know, I'm saving up to go back to school, to work my way up to doctor someday."

As if she had lost something, she realized Juan was not the sweet boy she'd known. Her childhood friend had grown up while she'd been gone, and she didn't know this man he'd become at all.

"Now, I really am a physical therapist, so, would you like to hear what I think?"

She nodded, wishing yet again that she could take back stupid words she said without thinking.

"Okay," he said, moving in closer. "Scoot to the end of the table and let your legs dangle over."

"Ow." She winced and grabbed her leg. "Something pulled."

"That's what I thought," Juan said. "You haven't been moving your leg enough. The scar tissue is setting and pulling tight."

"It doesn't move. Remember."

"Right. You have to move it with your arms and hands. I'll give you a sheet with exercises to do. I'll give you some exercise bands to use, but you can use a towel if that's all you have handy."

In twenty minutes and a few exercises, she was dripping wet and panting like a dog in a heat wave. Except for the back of her leg, the front and sides tingled and burned like she'd done a seven-mile march with a rucksack of bricks.

Juan pulled up a chair and massaged her leg harder than before, from thigh to toe. "Do it like this after every exercise session when you are at home. Knead deep into the muscle. Don't touch the injury sites, just every inch of skin around them. Get the blood flowing and the nerve endings firing."

Had Juan's hands always been so big and strong? His shoulders so broad? Had she been blind to not notice her best friend was very handsome?

All those thoughts exploded in her head in an instant. Her face heated as her view of Juan flipped from the guy she'd always known to who he was now. When he glanced up at her with those dark, brown eyes she was thankful her face was flushed from the exercise. She would die if he thought she could think of him as anything except her friend.

"When you come for therapy each day, we'll massage the injury sites and make sure you're healing well and not tearing scar tissue. But, you need to use your leg like normal. Get out of the wheelchair. Sit in a regular chair and bend your leg while you're sitting. Get the leg used to being used."

She heaved a sigh. Her thoughts had tumbled like a bad fall down a hillside and Juan just saw her as a patient and hopefully, still a friend.

Of course, he does. What else have you two ever been?

Ten

Juan stood behind the darkened, entry way glass as Mr. Ortega helped Jessie into the car. He almost jumped back when Mrs. Ortega stared right at him. Only knowing she couldn't see him stopped the movement.

As the car pulled away, the first snowflakes of the season fell across the parking lot. The squeak of wheels came from behind him as Roy wheeled up beside him.

"Man, I was hoping to get going before the snow came," he complained as he stared outside.

"It won't stick," Juan said, looking over at Roy. "Not cold enough yet. Give it an hour or two and it'll sputter out."

Roy changed the subject with a big grin on his face. "I saw your girl leave."

"She's not my girl," he protested. "We're just friends."

"If you say so. I saw the look she gave you as she left."

"She didn't give me any look," Juan gritted out between his clenched teeth. "She was just happy to hear her injuries aren't as bad as she thought."

"Whatever you say, bro," Roy said with a laugh as he wheeled around and headed back to the exercise area.

Juan crossed his arms and leaned against the cold glass. The snowflakes whipped in the brisk wind and danced across the darkened parking lot. Staring up at the street lights, the snow was lessening as he watched until just a few flakes fell here and there.

His hand twitched on his bicep at the memory of massaging Jessie's leg. As a physical therapist he shouldn't have felt anything, but Jessie was his friend. A friend he'd known for most of his life. Feeling the twitches in her leg as he'd rubbed, knowing there was still feeling there, had been a thrill.

Breath caught in his chest. He didn't know what he would have done if there had been nothing. How would he have looked Jessie in the eye and said the leg would never work again? He'd had to say that to patients before and it hurt. To tell her that would have killed him.

A white streak shot across the sky above the lake. A falling star. Juan closed his eyes and made a wish.

Please, let Jessie get the use of her leg again.

Opening his eyes, he smiled. A memory flirted across his mind A camping trip with his brothers and Jessie.

Twelve years ago.

"Make a wish," Jessie said as they lay side by side on a blanket on the ground.

"This is stupid. Girls make wishes. Boys get things done."

"Ow," Juan said after she punched him in the arm.

"Anyone can make wishes. All you have to do is believe."

A white streak shot across the sky.

"Close your eyes and make a wish," she whispered, grabbing his hand.

It was stupid, but Juan closed his eyes and made a wish. The same wish he made when Jessie had him blow a dandelion. The same wish he made when he visited Santa or the Easter bunny. The same wish he made every Sunday when he lighted a candle for his mother and father.

Please give me back my parents.

The same wish that never came true.

He brought himself back to the present with a sigh and a weak smile. He might have grown up, but inside he was still that little boy wishing for his parents to be alive and with him.

Steeling his spine, Juan knew this wish would come true. Jessie would heal, and he would help her do it. He'd worked with enough injured vets to know she had enough feeling in the rest of her leg to get better.

Walking back toward his office, Juan stopped as Roy finished his pull-ups. "The snow's stopped for now, but the weatherman said it could get heavy later. You might want to get going."

"Something tells me you aren't leaving anytime soon, my man."

Juan smiled. "Got some paperwork to catch up on, but I'll be out of here way before it starts coming down again."

Hours later, looking out the front door, he wished he had heeded his own words. A shiver went up his spine. A white blanket coated everything. The cars in the lot were mounds of snow and the street was unrecognizable beyond streetlights on each side and the top of the red fire hydrant across the street.

The first snow of the season was the worse. As if drivers forgot from one winter to the next how to drive in the white stuff. The tow trucks and hospitals would be busy tonight.

He could drive in the snow, he did most of the winter. He just didn't like it. Bad weather brought too many memories of his parents and their fatal crash. Buttoning up his coat, he slammed on his watch cap and pushed the door open. Turning back to lock it, he held on to the cap as the wind whipped snow around him and into his eyes.

He hunched down into his sheepskin coat and trudged to his truck. The cold seemed to intensify with each step. Getting into the vehicle, Juan shivered until the heat started to kick in. Maybe the thought of his parents and their accident was too fresh in his mind. He drove white-knuckled until he pulled into the driveway at home.

His fist slammed into the steering wheel. "I really am a wuss."

He couldn't drive in a little snow. He couldn't man up and enlist in the Army. He couldn't tell Jessie he liked her as more than a friend.

"Whoa, where did that come from?"

His mind and his memories had been in overload since the morning he'd seen the report of Jessie's shooting in Africa.

He turned the truck's motor off and tried to turn his errant thoughts off as well. A light shone through the kitchen window. He needed to pull it together or Lucia would read him like a book and he was not ready for any 'told you so's' from his well-meaning sister.

Eleven

"Son of a pup!" she yelled out as Juan moved her leg in a totally unexpected direction.

"I'm going to tell your mom you cussed," he joked.

"That isn't cussing," Jessie huffed out. "In the army I learned words I didn't ever know the meanings for."

She watched as he lowered her leg into a bent position on the edge of the table. Juan looked her in the eye. "Was it hard in the service?"

Jessie bit her lip. "I thought boot camp would be hard. After hanging out with you and your brothers, it was a snap. I made friends there. Good friends. I was doing something. Something special. Helping people."

Not as hard as two weeks of therapy and she was no better than when she started.

Juan's fingers dug into her calf and rubbed. "Anything?"

She started to say nothing, but she stopped herself. Refusing to get her hopes up, she closed her eyes and concentrated. There. A tingle. An itch. Something.

"I'm not sure. Maybe I'm imagining it. I've been doing the exercises you gave me, but I still can't even wiggle my toes."

His warm hands rested on her ankle as he stared up at her. His dark eyes shone, and a smile graced his face.

"Do you remember the first time we skated on the lake? What were we? Eight or nine? We fell so many times Diego and Luis threatened to take our skates away. But by the time the day was done we were not falling anymore and by the end of the winter we raced laps around them. It's like learning to walk all over again, Jessie. Muscle memory. Your mind knows the signals to send and your leg remembers how to move. They just have to reconnect again."

She wanted to believe him. To believe in what he was telling her, but she'd seen too many wounded vets to know it didn't always get all better.

His fingers moved up the back of her calf. A shiver shot through her. For the first time since the shooting, she felt something. Was it just a memory of feeling or an actual feeling?

They'd been twelve years old that summer. Every day, right after breakfast, they met in a field and ran to the treehouse they'd built on the edge of the forest. That day hadn't been any different from any other until Jessie felt a cramp seize her leg and she'd tumbled to the dusty path.

Juan stopped as soon as he'd noticed she wasn't beside him. Running back, he squatted down beside her.

"What's wrong?"

Tears had poured down her face as she rubbed her thigh and grunted through the pain. Without a thought, Juan pushed her hands away and started rubbing. In seconds, the cramp was gone, and she was going to tell him to stop. Except, tingles shot through her that had nothing to do with a cramp and everything to do with Juan's warm hands on her leg. Suddenly, he wasn't a boy who was a friend. He was a boy.

"All better?" he asked as he leaned forward to put a kiss on her cheek as if she were a sister like Lucia.

At the last second, she turned her face and their lips met. A thunderbolt shot through her heart. Her first kiss.

Juan stood up and reached out his hand to her. "Ready to go, or are you going to sit in the dirt all day?"

Jessie came back to the present and shook her head as she felt Juan's hand on her shoulder. He stared at her as if he was waiting for an answer to a question she hadn't heard.

"I asked if things are going well at home. Your mother isn't hovering too much, is she?"

She grimaced. "If she hovered any more, she'd be a helicopter."

"Let her know you have to do for yourself. You won't get better if she does everything for you."

Sighing, she put her hand on her forehead. "I know you're right, but she feels so helpless. It's like she thinks she is to blame for my injuries. I wish I could get away from her for just a little bit."

Juan smiled. "Now, that is one wish I can make come true."

He felt the smile grow on his face. He'd tried to hide his worry from Jessie during the session, but she should have made more progress by now. He was beginning to worry before he thought about Rita Ortega and how she'd been with Jessie all her life. She would never have had the freedom to camp and fish and hunt with his family if not for her father. Roger Ortega seemed to understand Jessie's need for some escape time from her overbearing mother.

"Come to your appointment tomorrow with extra warm clothes and the necessities. I'll take care of the rest."

"Where are we going? How long will I be gone? My mom will freak out."

"It's a surprise. I'll take care of everything. I'll let your father know where we're going and when we'll be back."

She bit her lip and tilted her head as if she was doing some deep thinking. "What about work?"

"Christmas is days away," he reminded her. "We're closed here at the rehab center until after the holidays."

She nodded. "Okay."

He let out the breath he was holding. He didn't realize how much he wanted her to say yes. How much he needed to do something for Jessie. To bring the laughter back into her life.

Twelve

Her heart raced and pounded against her chest. The world was a white wonderland across the horizon. She didn't know if it were the thrill of heading up the mountain or the excitement of escaping her mother's watchful eye, but Jessie was determined to enjoy every minute of the adventure.

She didn't realize how dull her life had been since her homecoming until her father had come to her bedroom last night to let her know he'd talked to Juan and everything was set for her to leave from the rehab center.

Army life had been tough, but each day had been something new. A new skill or a new mission or just meeting new people in some corner of the world she'd never known existed until they'd arrived there.

Growing up in Lake Willowbee, nestled in the Sierra Nevada had been idyllic, but in no way had it prepared her for how large and diverse the rest of the world was. People and cultures and languages and food and drink. Some missions had been fraught with danger. Just look at the last one, but she wouldn't trade what she'd seen and done for anything. Not even her injuries. Her breath caught and hitched in her throat.

"It's okay if I don't walk again," she whispered. "I saved a little girl in Africa."

"Well, duh," Juan replied, shooting her a quick glance and returning his gaze to the snow-covered road ahead.

She laughed. How like Juan to make everything so simple.

He'd always been able to do that. Her whole life he had been by her side as her best friend. She had to be honest with herself. He'd always been her friend. She was the one who'd shut him out when he refused to enlist with her.

Jessie twisted her hands together, picking at her cuticles. She'd disowned him. Not spoken to him in four years and the second she came home and needed him, there he was. Like nothing had changed between them. He'd made four years disappear as if they didn't exist. As if they were the friends they'd always been.

Friends. That's how he saw them. She'd been seeing him as something more and in his mind, they were still just friends. She'd hurt him before; she refused to do it again. Being friends was great. It was wonderful. So, why did the thought of being just friends hurt so much?

"We're here," Juan announced.

Ripping herself away from her distasteful thoughts, Jessie looked up and out the windshield to the snow-covered cabin in the middle of a glistening white field. The crystal-clear blue sky arched overhead, with tree-covered mountains forming a postcard-perfect view.

"You brought me to The Hideout," she said, smiling wildly.

The small cabin deep in the mountains had been Juan's oldest brother's property before he inherited the horse ranch in Sonora from their grandfather. Miguel had put the cabin and land in a trust and all the Montoya's owned a share of it.

"I loved coming here with you guys. It was like surviving the apocalypse at the end of the world. No people. No sounds. Just all of us together. I felt like I was part of your family."

He turned and took her hand. "You are a part of our family, Jessie. You always were and always will be."

She caught herself before she could read more into his words than were there. When he came around and opened her door, she realized her wheelchair wasn't in the truck.

"Let's get you inside and a fire going," he said, scooping her up in his arms as if she weighed nothing.

When had Juan gotten muscles? When she'd left for boot camp, he'd been one-hundred thirty pounds dripping wet with long skinny arms and legs. Sometime in between then and now, Juan Montoya had become a hottie.

Her face flushed and heated. She wished she could bury it in a snowbank to cool off. Looking at Juan as a man, she was sure some woman owned his heart. No way could someone who looked like that not have a swarm of women after him. Was a jealous woman going to come up the mountain to find out what he was doing up here with her? He would have said something wouldn't he? Or was this more of just doing his job and it meant nothing? Her mind whirled in a vortex of thoughts she didn't want to have.

Once the door was open, Juan carried her in and deposited her on the sofa in front of the fireplace. Logs sat in the grate with kindling and more wood beside the enormous stone fireplace.

His back was to her as he worked to start a fire. Muscles moved as he took off his jacket and got to work. Her mouth dried, all thought leaving her head. Now that she'd seen Juan as a man, she couldn't unsee him. Her earlier thoughts of him having a girlfriend sent painful arrows to her heart and her mind.

Being around him at the rehab center had been different. He'd been professional and doing his job. Now, they were all alone, together.

Too many memories filled her head. She'd thought all brothers were like Carlos. Always in trouble. Running away from home. Her parents yelling and slamming doors. It had been easy to escape and be with the Montoya brothers. She used to think they'd only noticed when she came home from the camping trip with her hair cut short because it was one of the times Carlos had run away and he wasn't there to get their attention.

But, Miguel, Diego, and Luis had shown her how brothers were supposed to act. They'd taught her everything she knew about hunting, fishing, and surviving in the wilderness. Boot camp had been a breeze after a lifetime of outdoor living skills with them.

They'd taught her about brotherhood. Each of them was there for the others. For Lucia too. The boys would die for their sister.

She grimaced.

Sometimes she wondered if Carlos remembered he had a sister at all amid his drug-filled, violent life.

The crackle of a roaring fire dragged her from her morbid thoughts. No more useless meandering in her mind. She was going to enjoy this time away from physical therapy, her mother's hovering, and useless wishes that didn't come true.

Juan glanced at her with a smile on his handsome face and all her good intentions flew out the window. She sighed. It was going to be a long couple of days.

Thirteen

*J*uan stood and brushed the wood dust off his hands. "Okay, let me get the rest of our stuff and get us settled."

Jessie's gaze shot to the ladder leading to the loft. "I'll never be able to climb up there and you are not carrying me."

He sat on the coffee table in front of the couch. "I could carry you if I had to."

"But you don't have to," she said, her face reddening under the rich brown color of her skin.

"That's true," he admitted. "I thought we could make you a bed down here on the couch. You'll be in front of the fire to stay warm and won't have to climb… yet."

Her gaze shot back to the ladder and her expression darkened as if she was contemplating climbing the Donner Summit in January.

"Yeah, like never."

He hated the utter doubt in her voice. This was the same girl who'd free-climbed into their treehouse, the rope wrapped around her shoulders, so she could be the first one there.

"Do you remember when I broke my foot? When I had to spend the summer in the house?"

"Of course," she said, a slight smile on her face. "It was such a stupid way to break a bone."

He had to admit that was true. To this day, he didn't know how he'd managed to break his foot from tripping over an untied shoelace. But that wasn't the point he wanted to make with Jessie.

"Who was there for me? Who read me books even though they hated to read? Who spent their summer vacation telling me I would be fine, I would walk again?"

His heart beat faster as a blush raced across her face again. "I did. But that was different. It was just a broken bone."

"It wasn't just a broken bone, Jessie," he reminded her. "It was broken in five places. They didn't know if I would need pins and screws or if I would be able to have feeling in it again at all."

"But it turned out fine."

"Because you told me it would," Juan said, taking her hand in his. "You believed I would get better, so I did. I want to give that to you. I've seen you in therapy. Sometimes I think you're feeling something, but you don't say a word."

She peeked at him from under her eyelashes. "I think I might be feeling something, but I'm not sure. Is it a memory of feeling or really feeling?"

"Let's try something then, okay? I talked to your doctor and he said it's time to try standing."

Her face whitened as she stared up at him. "I can't."

"The Jessie Ortega I know doesn't know the meaning of I can't."

She stared at the floor. "I'm not that Jessie Ortega anymore."

He laughed, and her face came up, a glare in her eyes, her lips tight and whitened.

"You're not the Jessie Ortega who rushed in to help a little girl and her mother amid enemy fire? Who threw herself on top of the little girl and another soldier? Who received a medal for her heroics?"

Jessie stared at him. "How do you know all of that?"

"The Army sent the report of the incident in Africa," he replied. "It included a report from everyone in your unit. From the captain, down to the soldier you saved, Catherine Johnson. That little girl, Malia, sent a thank-you letter with a picture. You're a hero, Jessie."

"I don't feel like a hero," she muttered.

While her mind was occupied, Juan grabbed her under her arms and stood, taking her with him. Breath whooshed out of her as she whipped her arms around his waist. Her good knee locked, and she stood straight in front of him.

They stood eye to eye as perspiration beaded on her forehead and she started to wobble. He locked his arms around her and pulled her in close.

"Don't put pressure on your right leg. Let the left do all the work right now. Just get used to standing again."

"I can't believe you did that, Montoya," she berated him as her breath came in pants and her arms tightened around him.

"I can't believe you hadn't tried standing yet on your own. You were always the first up the hill, into the lake, climbing the highest tree."

"Juan, I can't feel anything in my leg. I couldn't try and fail. I couldn't fall on my face."

"Why the heck not? That's how we learn," he said, lowering into a squat and placing her back on the sofa.

Jessie missed his arms around her the instant he moved back and sat on the coffee table again. She couldn't believe he'd tricked her into standing. She couldn't believe she'd stood.

"I stood," she whispered.

His fingertips came up and wiped tears off her face she didn't know she'd shed. Through the blur of tears, she watched in wonder as Juan moved closer, his face inches from hers.

Was he going to kiss her? Was she going to let him?

She didn't get to find out as Juan jumped back and leapt off the coffee table. "I'll go get our stuff now."

He rushed out the door like a flame from the fire had bit him on the behind. The door slammed with a crash that shook the window glass in the panes.

Her mood swung from exhilaration at standing, even if it was with Juan's arms holding her up, to crushing disbelief she'd thought he would want to kiss you, to denial that she had wanted him to kiss her in the first place.

Leaning back against the couch, she closed her eyes. Life had been so simple when she'd thought of Juan as her best friend and never dreamed of something more. Too bad there wasn't a way to travel back in time. Of course, if there had been, she could have wished to never be shot at all.

"If wishes were ponies, we all could ride," she whispered her grandfather's favorite saying.

Fourteen

"You don't need to carry me," Jessie complained, her lips in a pout. "I thought you said I needed to start using my leg. I saw the crutches you brought. Can't I try them?"

Juan placed her in the rocking chair on the porch, wrapping a blanket around her. His breath plumed in the frigid air as he stood and stepped away. He threw his head back and stared at the night sky.

Snowfall had stopped for the moment and the sky was a midnight-black blanket of stars. The moon sat on the top of the mountains, a bare sliver of light. The wind blew through the pines with a shush of sound, barely louder than the beating of his heart.

"Is your leg cold, Jessie?"

"You mean the right one?"

He nodded, his vision adjusting to the darkness. His mind traveled to the weeks of therapy he'd done for her. Every test showed the blood was running fine in her damaged leg. No cold or dead spots beyond the scar tissue locations. Her skin was showing no purple tinge of dying flesh.

"My toes are freezing, even with two pairs of socks and your heavy boots."

His breath caught. "All of your toes?"

She stared at him, her eyebrow quirked. "Yes, all ten of them. I didn't lose any of them over there, remember?"

He smiled at her. Watching, he spotted the second she realized what she said.

"I can feel my toes. All of them." Her mouth dropped open and happy surprise covered her face. She slapped her hands over her mouth, but laughter exploded and filled the silent world.

Juan pulled her out of the chair, the blanket falling to the porch. He swung around in a circle, her feet flying out. Her laughter joined his.

He stopped. Her winter cap had fallen off as he'd swung her. Inky-black hair tangled over her shoulders and down her arms. Her eyes shone bright with the light from the cabin. Her smile lit up her face.

When they were teenagers, Juan had thought Jessie was cute and he hoped whoever her boyfriend became, he would be worthy of his best friend. His thoughts ricocheted as he stared at the beautiful woman in his arms and his heartbeat pounded in his chest with the knowledge he wanted to kiss her. He wanted to kiss her until they lost their breath and she forgot every other boy or man who had ever kissed her before.

The thought terrified him. A cold sweat broke out on his back and a shiver ran down his spine. He'd lost four years with her. He wasn't going to risk the rest of his life without her friendship if he did something stupid like think she thought of him as more than a friend.

He started to pull back and drop his arms until he remembered she couldn't stand on her own. If he'd had a free hand, he would have smacked it against his forehead. He was supposed to be helping her walk, not trying to kiss her. What was he thinking? She needed a friend. Not a guy who thought his feelings could possibly be returned.

What was that all about?

Jessie pushed her hair out of her face as Juan's smile turned on like a spotlight and died like it had been shot out by a sniper. One moment she'd been sure he was finally going to kiss her and the next he acted as if she were a stranger in his arms.

She'd spent the past four years thinking of Juan as a wuss who was not man enough to join the Army with her. In her mind he was still the boy she remembered from childhood. The man before her might as well be a stranger for all that she knew the person he was now.

Giving his arm a squeeze, she tried to smile as he looked at her. "Can we go in now? My feet really are cold."

He shook his head as if to clear his thoughts and gathered her in his arms. "We'll get you out of these heavy clothes…"

Didn't that comment send her thoughts places it shouldn't?

"We'll get the crutches and see what you can manage." He finished as he placed her on the sofa, piled high with blankets and pillows.

And just like that, he was back to physical therapist mode.

He sat on the coffee table as he'd been doing before. Only this time, he took her foot instead of her hands. Juan gripped the boot and yanked it off. For a split second, she imagined she felt the fleece lining rubbing against her toes.

Peeling off the two pairs of socks, he dropped them to the floor and his hands returned to her foot. She shivered as his cold hands cradled it.

"Your hands are freezing," she muttered.

"You can feel them on your leg?"

"Of course, they're like icicles," she complained.

"What about here?" he asked, his hands moving up to her ankles and her calf beneath her jeans.

"A little. Not as cold now," she told him.

"Wiggle your toes," he said, his gaze on her foot.

She concentrated, her eyes closed. "It hurts, Juan."

"Of course, it does."

She opened her eyes and gazed in wonder. It wasn't very much, but her toes were moving on their own. A gasp escaped her as pain shot up her leg to her thigh.

A small whimper escaped her as the pain grew and the rubbing did nothing for it.

"I think it's seizing," she said with her teeth clenched. The words came out in a stuttered voice.

His hands pushed hers aside. He gripped her thigh, his fingers digging into her leg. A crimson fog filled her vision as the pain grew. She couldn't move. She couldn't breathe.

"Make it stop," she cried out.

Fifteen

He'd never felt so helpless in his life. Juan knew what he needed to do, but would it upset Jessie?

"Jess," he said, cupping her face in his hands. "We have to get your pants off. I have oils for your leg, but I have to get to it. Think of me as a doctor or a nurse, okay?"

"Whatever," she gasped out. "Just do it."

Working together, they got her other boot off and peeled her jeans down her legs. He flung them to the table top.

He couldn't take the time to find her exercise shorts. Trying to turn his mind to therapy mode was next to impossible with Jessie's long legs and skimpy underwear in front of him. With effort, he focused on the task at hand.

Juan grabbed his bag and dug through it for the rubbing oils he'd brought. As soon as he spotted the green one, he yanked it out of the bag and brought it back to the couch.

Jessie's head was thrown back, her jaw clenched. Her teeth ground together in a painful, audible sound.

"Honey, you'll be better soon," he crooned in a soft voice. "I promise."

He filled his hand with the eucalyptus oil, taking a few seconds to let it warm in his palm. Rubbing his hands together, he placed them on her thigh and massaged in the oil.

Her moan of pleasure was almost more than he could handle. He whipped his mind back to the job.

This is my best friend. Only a friend. Maybe if he repeated it enough it would be true. Yeah, right.

Oblivious of his inner conflict, Jessie sighed as he felt the muscles beneath his hands loosen and relax.

Jessie blinked a few times and opened her eyes. "Thank you," she whispered.

"No problem," he said. "Just doing my job."

A hurt look flashed across her face and just as quickly was gone.

Had that been too harsh? He'd only wanted to reassure her nothing unwanted or inappropriate was going to happen.

She looked away. "Can I practice with the crutches now?"

He sighed. "Can we do it in the morning? I'm beat. It's been a long day."

"Sure," she said in a low voice. "No problem."

Her sadness had him wanting to agree. "Maybe a little bit," he said. "Just, driving in the snow always does me in, remember?"

Her hand slapped across her mouth. "I'm so sorry. I totally forgot. Why did we come up here, then?"

He took her hand from her mouth and held it. "I know you needed to get away. This was our favorite place. I wanted to do this for you."

⚉⚎

She would have kicked something if she'd been able to get up and kick something. How could she have forgotten Juan's fear of driving in the snow? She remembered the first winter after his parents' accident and death. They'd trudged through the snow, across town, to get to the movies at the theatre downtown. Juan had refused his big brother's offer of a ride.

When the storm had grown worse, it had taken all of Miguel's strength to get a crying, screaming Juan into the car for the ride home.

"Well, fudge," she said.

Juan laughed. "You must really be upset. That's your worse almost-cuss word."

He patted her hand. "Really, it's okay. I'm not as bad as I used to be. I don't like it, but I can drive if I have to."

She shook her head. "You didn't have to bring me up here."

He moved in closer. "No, I wanted to."

Clearing her throat, she looked away. *If wishes were ponies.*

"I think I'm done in too," she whispered. "I'd like to go to sleep now."

"Do you need to go to the bathroom again?"

"No, I'm fine," she said. A shudder ripped through her. One humiliation a day was enough for her. She would use the crutches by tomorrow, even if she had to fall into the bathroom to get there.

"Okay," Juan said as he stood and looked around the room. "Let me build up the fire before I bring your bag over and go up."

"Thanks."

Her gaze followed him as he completed his tasks and climbed the ladder to the loft. The cabin was small enough to hear him unzip his duffel bag, get changed, and climb into bed. The iron bed squeaked as he tossed and turned for a while, until the only sound from upstairs was a soft snore.

When the silence remained, Jessie maneuvered herself to the coffee table, straightened out the pile of covers, and got into her sleepwear. The scent of eucalyptus lingered on her skin and wafted over her in the warmth from the fire.

Her eyes remained open, staring into the flames. Yellow and orange danced across the logs. Sparks popped and flew behind the screen. Exhaustion filled her, but her eyes refused to close.

She bit her lip and wiggled her toes. The pain in her thigh was muted as her toenails dragged across the wool blanket. She could feel the weave of the fibers as her toes slowly moved back and forth.

Tears filled her eyes and ran down the sides of her face, into her hair. "I wish," she whispered.

She shook her head. No. Medicine, science, and hard work would get her leg back to usable. She wasn't wasting a wish on her leg.

A gentle snore and mumbling filled the cabin. Her breathing slowed, until she and Juan were breathing as one.

In. Together.

Out. Together.

In. Together.

Out. Together.

Her eyelids grew heavy. The colors of the fire blurred and ran together.

I wish Juan could know how I feel.

Sixteen

Thump. Drag.
Thump. Drag.
Thump. Drag.
Turn.
Thump. Drag.

"You can take a break, Jessie. You've been at it for an hour."

She glared at him and her words came out in huffs as she used the crutches to move across the cabin's front room.

"I will not let you carry me to the bathroom again."

"I don't mind."

"I mind," she whispered under her breath, but he caught the words anyway.

Juan sighed and turned back to making lunch. He flipped the grilled cheese sandwiches and gave the tomato soup a stir. Steam wafted up from the pot, the rich tomato scent filling the room.

A loud thump had his head whipping around. Jessie leaned against the wall by the door, her chest heaving, and perspiration flowing down the sides of her face. Knowing she'd refuse his help for the thousandth time, he didn't go to her. Instead, he turned off the stove and spooned soup into bowls and plated the sandwiches.

"Lunch is ready," he said, taking the food to the table.

He bit the inside of his cheek as Jessie thumped and dragged her way to the table. He took the crutches as she fell into the chair.

"You're doing great," Juan complimented her.

"I wish I could lift my foot some. My toes are sore."

She dug into lunch, inhaling it in seconds. The only sound in the room was the scraping of her spoon in the bowl.

"Did you even taste it?" he asked.

"Gotta eat fast in the army," she replied, placing her bowl on the empty plate, pushing them away.

"Are you going to miss it?"

Her eyes watered until she looked away and scrubbed them with the palms of her hands.

When she looked back, Juan saw sadness in her eyes and a slump in her shoulders.

"I'll miss the people and the places. I wanted to make a career of the army. It was my whole life and now I don't know what I'm going to do."

It hurt to see her like this. What do you tell someone who's had all her wishes and dreams taken away?

"Jessie, I know this isn't the life you planned. But you can still go places and help people. The doctor in Germany thought you might get your leg back to seventy percent. People make do with a lot less."

"Juan, I hear what you are saying, up here," she said, pointing to her head. "But inside, in my heart, I can't accept being less than one-hundred percent."

He sighed. The damage to her leg would never let Jessie be one-hundred percent. If all it took was determination, Jessie Ortega would will herself back to optimal fitness. But, damage was damage. He'd seen the back of her knee. It would never be one-hundred percent again.

"No one is one-hundred percent," Juan said, looking her straight in the eye. "Even your super-soldier friends have some flaw, some imperfection. Tell me, if you had been unable to get into the service, what would you have done?"

"I would have gone into nursing. I've always wanted to help people," she said. "But, I can't even do that now."

"Why not?"

"My leg, duh. I can't stumble along with a crutch in an emergency."

"Let's say that's true," Juan said, taking her hand. "Although, I don't believe that. You don't have to be an emergency room nurse. There are dozens of nursing options."

He squeezed her hand. "What if I believe you could end up with eighty or even ninety percent function of your leg with a knee brace?"

Juan stood up, letting go of her hand. "Just think about it. I'll be back in a while. Firewood is getting low. I'll cut some more."

Even with Juan's words, she refused to get her hopes up. As good as he was with his job, and she had to admit he was good at being a physical therapist, he wasn't a doctor. He'd found his niche. She'd thought she'd found hers, but it had been taken away in a split second of gunfire.

As the door shut behind him, Jessie scooted her chair back from the table with her good foot and reached for the crutches. Hoisting herself up was getting easier each time she did it. Looking at the dishes on the table, she wished she could clear them but that seemed beyond her efforts at the moment.

"Okay, goal for tomorrow. Do the dishes," she muttered as she continued her movements back and forth across the room. With only fifteen steps across the wooden expanse, the distance was getting shorter as her steps grew longer and surer.

By the tenth time across the room, Jessie used her thigh muscles to lift her leg and put it down with a thump. A vibration zoomed up her leg. The pain took her breath away but didn't stop her from continuing.

"I'll need lots of massage oil tonight," she said, a smile breaking out.

The thought of Juan's hands on her skin again brought warmth to her face and chest and other parts of her body as well. He may only see her as a friend, but she would enjoy her deeper feelings as long as possible.

Step. *Move her other foot.*

Step. *Move her other foot.*

Time passed as she traversed back and forth to the occasional thump of the ax against the wood outside. Sometimes, the wind would change direction and Juan's whistling would carry into the house.

Out of breath, Jessie made her way to the kitchen table to finish her glass of water. Taking big gulps, her heartbeat raced and thundered in her ears. Over the thump, thump in her ears, she heard her name on the wind. Faint and coming from outside.

"Jess, I need you."

Seventeen

Red. Red everywhere. Juan laid in a sea of red. The ax he'd been using to chop wood was covered in blood as he moaned, holding his hands against his crimson-soaked jeans. As if she'd seen the accident, Jessie pictured the swing and the miss of the ax. Burying the steel head into his leg instead of a log of wood.

That he'd managed to crawl to the steps of the porch was either pure stubbornness or pure stupidity. She'd decide which later. The winter chill on her damp skin matched the chill in her heart.

So much blood. Was this what Cat had seen in the tiny village in Africa? Her mind whirled with regret at not having her med kit here. Without thinking, Jessie dropped her crutches and hop-hobbled to Juan's side. As she fell to the ground at his side, something ripped deep in her leg. Her breath caught, and her heart stopped beating.

She didn't have time for this. Ignoring the white-hot pain in her leg, she ripped off her sweater and pressed it to his thigh. His groaning was the only sound escaping his lips. Applying more pressure, she noted his condition.

The trail of blood petered out as it reached the porch and Juan's prone body. His color was pale, but his eyes were open, and his breathing was steady. If he'd struck an artery, he'd be dead by now.

Her heart raced with the seriousness of their situation. No landline inside the cabin. No service on their cell phones in the mountain valley. She couldn't walk and now, neither could Juan. She wanted to set down and cry. In her head, Drill Instructor Mike yelled at her.

Get going, soldier! No sitting down in my Army! Move it! Move it! Move it!

"I'll be right back," she promised as she crawled to her fallen crutches and pulled herself up. As the pain shot through her thigh and down to her toes, for the first time since her shooting she wished her leg had stayed numb. Fire spread to every inch of it. As if every nerve and synapsis was detonating at once.

She clenched her jaw and hobbled into the cabin. Finding towels in the bathroom, she flung them out the door to the porch. Spotting the cabin's silver toolbox, she flung it open and found the roll of duct tape. As Miguel had told them often enough, duct tape fixed everything.

Jessie rolled it out the door as she grabbed another sweater and pulled it over her chilled body. She grabbed Juan's keys off the counter and hobbled back out to the porch.

Silence greeted her. Her heart stopped until Juan's chest rose and fell in a steady, albeit slow, rhythm. His hands had fallen from the sweater she'd put on his gashed thigh. Blood trickled and dropped to the white snow.

She bit her tongue as she dropped to his side again and agony shot through her leg. Jessie whipped her blood-soaked sweater away and flung it to the yard. Pressing a towel to his slashed jeans, she wrapped the duct tape around his thigh several times, as tightly as she could.

She welcomed his moans as she tore the tape with her teeth. His eyelids fluttered, and his eyes opened.

"Mi angel," he muttered.

Jessie stared at the blood-covered hands in her lap. "Not even close, Montoya."

"We have to get out of here," he whispered.

"I know."

Tears filled her eyes as the wind increased, bringing the evening chill to the air. Twilight came early in the mountains, and the sun sat on the edge of the peaks now. In moments, darkness would fall. She remembered how dark it had been last night with the sliver moon.

"Okay, soldier. You can do this," she berated herself. They were only an hour or so from civilization. It wasn't like being in a jungle in the middle of nowhere.

She scooted over to Juan and got behind him. Using her upper body, she lifted his torso until he was sitting up, leaning back against her.

"I'm going to push. Don't use your hurt leg. Use your arms to pull yourself up. Grab hold of the post to stay standing."

His yell filled the valley in an echo as he followed her instructions. His arms shook as he wrapped them around the porch post.

Jessie moved as quickly as she could. Tucking the truck keys in her pocket, she grabbed the crutches and stood at Juan's side.

"Here's what we're going to do," she told him. "Wrap an arm around my neck."

Once he did that, she leaned the crutch against the post. "You use the crutch on that side. I'll use this one on this side. We can only do this if we work together. We can't fall. We'll never get up again."

"Just like the 3-legged race at Lake Willowbee Days."

His words were slurred, but she still understood him. She huffed out a deep breath as they started moving. "Except this time, I'd like to not fall into the dog doo-doo."

His laugh ended on a groan as they moved through the snow to the truck. Jessie looked up. Darkness was falling fast, and the truck seemed farther away than before. She counted ten steps as they trudged through the snow, one slow step at a time.

Her leg felt as if the muscles were being ripped from the bone, and Juan's weight dragged on the rest of her body. She would laugh at how pathetic they must look, but she didn't have the energy left to waste.

Just when she was ready to call it quits, Juan fell with a thump into the side of the vehicle. His arm was slipping from around her neck. She tightened her grip around his waist. It took some maneuvering, but she managed to get him into the truck's passenger seat.

Her teeth chattered as she flung her crutches into the truck bed and she pulled herself up into the driver's seat. Her sticky fingers fumbled to get the keys out of her pocket and into the ignition. A turn and the motor started. The cold air from the vents slowly turned warm as the heater kicked in.

Tears blurred her vision. She wiped her eyes on the hem of her sweater and turned the headlights on. Brightness filled the driveway in front of her.

"Everything works except for me," she cried out. She pounded her fists on the steering wheel.

"You can do this," a whisper came from the passenger seat.

She grabbed a fistful of her pants leg and moved her right leg to the side. Driving with just her left leg was going to be tricky, but she could do it. Thank goodness for automatic drive.

The drive down the mountain was an hour she would spend the rest of her life trying to forget. Several times they'd hit black ice and she was sure they would spin over a cliff. She had a new appreciation of why Juan hated driving in the snow so much. As the lights of Lake Willowbee appeared around the final corner, she whispered a thank you to the heavens above.

Pulling into the hospital's parking lot, she drove right up to the emergency room door and pressed the horn until people rushed out and surrounded the truck.

"Juan, we made it," she said, laying her hand on his chest.

A chest that didn't move.

Eighteen

"Where's my brother!" A female voice screamed across the waiting room.

Jessie looked up at the sound. Lucia Montoya stood at the nurse's station, her face red, her hands fisted on her hips.

The nurse said something and pointed at Jessie. She took a deep breath as the young woman raced over to her chair. Bracing herself for accusations and blame, her mouth dropped open when Lucia grabbed her in a hug.

"Are you okay? Have you heard anything?"

"I'm fine," Jessie whispered as Lucia moved back and took the chair next to her. Juan's sister took her hands and held them, ignoring the blood still coating them. "My leg hurts some, but I'm fine. They haven't told me anything since they rushed him to the OR."

As if she'd just realized what covered Jessie's hands, Lucia dropped them and rushed to the nurse's desk. Her voice carried across the room.

"That is a wounded vet over there and she has been here for hours, and you haven't even checked her out or helped her clean up."

She bit her lip to hide her inappropriate smile. When Juan's sister got going, it was easier to just do what she said. Jessie, Juan, and Lucia had been small when Mrs. Montoya had died, but her memories of the woman matched who her daughter had become. The Montoya's would have been so proud of what their children had grown up to be.

"Ms. Ortega, I'm so sorry no one has checked you out tonight. There's no excuse."

The nurse from the desk had come over with a wheelchair and Lucia. Her face showed real regret.

"I'm fine, really," she said, frowning at Juan's sister.

"Let the doctor decide that," Lucia replied with a frown of her own.

"You are as stubborn as your brother," she said, pushing herself up and into the wheelchair. She fell into it with a groan and a wince.

"See," Lucia said with an evil grin. "Told you so."

In minutes, the nurse and Lucia had her undressed and on a hospital bed, her bloody clothes in a bag on the chair. Another nurse came in with a smile and a pan of warm water.

"Let's get you cleaned up, shall we?" she chimed with a British accent.

In no time at all, Jessie felt like a new person. She'd been cleaned up, the doctor pronounced her fine, although she would need to see her regular doctor tomorrow, and the desk nurse had returned with the news that Juan was out of surgery and in a room upstairs.

They gave her a set of scrubs to wear and Lucia looped the bag of her clothes on the handle of the wheelchair she pushed to the elevators.

Jessie rubbed her thigh as the elevator doors closed and Lucia pushed the button for the third floor.

"Are you okay?" Lucia's face was set in a frown and worry clouded her dark eyes.

Jessie shrugged. "The doctor said so, but it feels like my leg is being electrocuted constantly. It tingles from my thigh to my toes."

"I would think that is good, right? Juan said it was numb before."

She guessed. She didn't have time to think anymore about it as the elevator dinged and the doors opened into the hustle-bustle of the patient's rooms.

A young nurse at the desk smiled at them and nodded. "Juan is in room C."

"How did she know we were here for Juan?" she added as Lucia pushed her wheelchair down the hall.

"I went to school with Maggie. She had a ginormous crush on Juan. She used to spend the night at my house just to catch a glimpse of him in the morning."

Lucia's words fell like rocks down a landslide into the pit of her stomach. Of course, girls had liked Juan. Who wouldn't? He was handsome and kind and gentle. He was everything any woman would want.

Her useless thoughts flew out of her head the moment she was wheeled into Juan's room. His face was as pale as the covers on his bed. Only the rising and falling of his chest reassured her. Lucia's breath caught in an audible gasp.

The doctor turned at the sound. "Ah, Lucia Montoya. I was sure you would be up here as soon as you were able."

He gazed down at her. "This must be Jessie. I'm Doctor Hernandez."

"How do you know my name?"

The man smiled. "Before we put him under for the surgery on his leg and afterward in recovery, all he could talk about was his angel, Jessie, who saved his life."

A blush heated across her face. She overheated at Lucia's tinkling laugh. Thankfully, the doctor shook hands and left the room.

Lucia's hand trembled as she took Juan's and gave it a squeeze. She leaned down. "Don't you ever scare me like this again," she whispered.

She turned to Jessie. "I'm going down the hall to call my brothers. I'll be back as soon as I can."

Rolling the chair close to the bed, Jessie grabbed his hand and wrapped her fingers around his. She knew Lucia had left her alone with Juan, so she could talk to him in private, but she didn't know what to say.

She was out of wishes.

Each one she'd had had gone terribly wrong.

Nineteen

"Do you remember that time you refused to wish on a falling star?"

She laughed through the unchecked tears rolling down her face. "Do you realize we start most conversations with 'do you remember'?"

Of course, they did. From the first day of kindergarten to when she left for boot camp, every memory of her life had Juan Montoya in it. For every important event in her life, he had been at her side. Just as she'd tried to be at his. Until the day they went to the recruitment office to enlist.

They'd sat at the desk, filling in the paperwork. Juan had dropped the pen and stood up.

"I can't do this," he whispered.

He'd looked into her eyes. "I'm sorry."

She stood as he stumbled to the doorway.

Her breath caught on a hiccup as the tears flowed faster. She tightened her grip on Juan's hand. Bowing her head over their joined hands, she took a deep breath. She closed her eyes.

"Do you remember when I said I hated you and I would forget you?" Her sobs ripped into her chest. "I lied. I never forgot you, Juan. You were my best friend. You were a part of me. From the moment you pushed the bully in the mudpuddle for teasing me until you took me on a family camping trip when they took Carlos away to jail that first time. Every summer of treehouses and skateboards. Every winter of skiing and skating on Lake Willowbee. Every wonderful memory of my childhood has you in it.

"You were my first kiss. I bet you don't remember that, do you?" She leaned down and kissed his hand, her wet tears glistening on the pale flesh. "I want to wish for you to be okay, but my wishes don't work. When I was in Africa, hot and sweaty in the jungle, I wished so hard to be home for Christmas. It took getting my leg shot up to come back to Lake Willowbee. Not what I had wished for at all. I thought I was going to die and all I could think of was you, of being able to tell you good-bye. Then I wished you could feel what I feel and look what happened. You almost chop off your leg and I don't even know if there is damage or you'll be able to walk or anything," she stuttered to a stop, her body shaking with her crying.

A hand touched her hair. She flinched and looked up. Juan's dark eyes stared back at her.

"It was my first kiss too."

Wild, ink-black curls framed a beautiful face. Even with dark circles under her eyes, nothing could dull her radiance as she stared back at him.

His gaze travelled the room until it returned her. She wiped the tears from her cheeks. "You're awake. I should get Lucia."

He grabbed her hand before she could push away in the wheelchair. "Wait," he rasped out through a dry, sore throat. "What did you mean, feel what you feel?"

Her cheeks turned a rose-red. Had he heard every foolish word she'd uttered? "I meant that I've liked you as more than a friend for a long time. That you would have the same feelings for me."

He felt his mouth drop open. Man, he really was slow on the uptake. "I wish…"

Jessie's fingers came to his mouth to stop the words. "No wishing. It doesn't work."

Taking her fingers in his hand, he held them against his chest. "I wish I could say I knew, but I didn't. It took you getting shot for me to realize I couldn't imagine a world without you in it. You are my best friend."

"But..." she whispered, new tears falling down her face.

He reached and wiped the tears away with his fingertips. "But, I love you as so much more, I promise, and you know I always keep my promises."

Christmas music filtered through the hallways as he gazed at her. "What day is it?"

She glanced up at the clock across the room. "It's after midnight, so Christmas Eve."

He smiled at her and heaved a sigh of relief she returned one of her own. "I promised you would walk by Christmas, and I'm pretty sure you not only walked to the truck but practically carried me there as well."

The notes of the song *I'll Be Home for Christmas* came over the sound system. Jessie hummed along until the end. "… in my dreams."

"This isn't a dream or a wish. This is real. I love you, Jessie."

He heard her voice as his eyelids grew heavy and the room dimmed.

"I love you, Juan."

Epilogue

"I can't believe we had to wait for New Year's Day to open presents," Lucia complained as she shook a brightly wrapped gift.

Juan laughed as he sat on the couch with Jessie snuggled up against him. "Didn't someone remind me not so long ago that she was a grown-up?"

Lucia pouted as Jessie laughed along with him. "Do you remember?"

He hugged her tighter. "Don't start with that. We can't let our families know all of our deep, dark secrets."

With everything Juan and Jessie had been through, the Ortega and Montoya families had decided to delay the Christmas celebrations and celebrate together on New Year's Day. Diego and Luis were in the kitchen putting the finishing touches on dinner, Miguel and Joy were due any minute from Sonora, and Roger and Rita Ortega had said they were on their way.

Lucia plopped herself onto the ottoman beside Juan's propped up leg. It was healing nicely, but it hurt if he didn't have it out straight from time to time.

"You can't just tease with 'do you remember,' you know."

Jessie looked back and forth across the room. "Okay, before Joy gets here. One year, Miguel was in charge of being Santa. Juan found out where all the gifts were in the attic. We went up there, opened them all, saw what they were, and wrapped them back up."

Lucia's mouth dropped open and Jessie laughed as he gave her his mock-angry face.

"I guess there is only one way to stop you from telling tales of our nefarious deeds." He reached into his pocket, pulled out a sprig of mistletoe, and held it above Jessie's head.

He leaned in. "Just so you have something to compare to my awkward twelve-year-old fumblings," he whispered as he claimed her lips.

Her breath sighed as his lips warmed against hers. Her hands wrapped around his neck and clasped at the nape. She pulled him closer. Their kiss deepened. As sweet as that pre-adolescent quick peck had been, he would remember this kiss forever. Years from now, when she teased him with 'do you remember that kiss under the mistletoe' there would be no doubt which one it was, or what it meant.

He'd fallen in love with his best friend and she loved him back.

The End

.

www.ingramcontent.com/pod-product-compliance
Lightning Source LLC
Chambersburg PA
CBHW050057120726
47904CB00004B/1123